THIS WAY UP

Happy Reading

Paige Nick .

(franschhoek 2012)

THIS WAY UP

Paige Nick

PENGUIN BOOKS

PENGUIN BOOKS

Published by the Penguin Group
Penguin Books (South Africa) (Pty) Ltd, 24 Sturdee Avenue, Rosebank,
Johannesburg 2196, South Africa
Penguin Group (USA) Inc, 375 Hudson Street, New York, New York 10014,
USA
Penguin Group (Canada), 90 Eglinton Avenue East, Suite 700, Toronto,
Ontario, Canada M4P 2Y3 (a division of Pearson Penguin Canada Inc)
Penguin Books Ltd, 80 Strand, London WC2R 0RL, England
Penguin Ireland, 25 St Stephen's Green, Dublin 2, Ireland (a division of
Penguin Books Ltd)
Penguin Group (Australia), 250 Camberwell Road, Camberwell, Victoria
3124, Australia (a division of Pearson Australia Group Pty Ltd)
Penguin Books India Pvt Ltd, 11 Community Centre, Panchsheel Park,
New Delhi – 110 017, India
Penguin Group (NZ), 67 Apollo Drive, Rosedale, Auckland 0632, New
Zealand (a division of Pearson New Zealand Ltd)

Penguin Books (South Africa) (Pty) Ltd, Registered Offices:
24 Sturdee Avenue, Rosebank, Johannesburg 2196, South Africa

www.penguinbooks.co.za

First published by Penguin Books (South Africa) (Pty) Ltd 2011

ISBN 978-0-14-352755-8

Typeset by Nix Design in Minion
Cover by Adam Hill
Printed and bound by Interpak Books, Pietermaritzburg

FOR BRIONY, STEPHANIE, ASHLEIGH, JANICE AND BARRY

STELLA

They were the perfect couple on a breakfast plate. Stella hated cooked tomato but liked mushrooms, and Max couldn't stand mushrooms but loved cooked tomatoes.

The problem with cooked tomatoes was that they always got so volcanically hot, and Stella had burnt her tongue severely on every occasion she'd ever tried them. She knew they got hot when cooked, it wasn't news to her, but somehow she was never quite cautious enough. It was a life lesson she was destined to never learn. And it was the kind of burn that rendered her tongue numb, scorched and unable to taste anything for days on end.

And as strongly as Stella felt about the evils of cooked tomato, Max felt even more strongly about mushrooms of any description, cooked or raw. He couldn't stand them touching anything on his plate, and he'd once even moaned at her for keeping them in the fridge, they offended him that much.

There was no tangible reason why he shouldn't like them. No childhood incident or scarring episode as far as Stella knew. It was just one of those things.

As long as she'd known him they'd made the trade the second their breakfast plates were placed on the table in front of them. Stella would scoop up the fried tomato, careful not to leave any pips behind, and dump it onto Max's plate. Then she'd spoon up the mushrooms from his plate and deposit them on her own – she wasn't allowed to do it with a knife or fork either, lest, heaven forbid, she pierced a mushroom and its juices contaminated the rest of his breakfast. He was such a baby about it; he didn't even like his cutlery touching them, which is why the rule was that she managed the entire exchange. Sure, they could have simply asked the waitress not to include the offending items on each plate, but the swap had become something of a ritual. And, of course, this way, if all went according to plan, it meant that they each got two portions of the food they liked, and none of the food they didn't. It was a comfortable situation. Just like their marriage.

Stella leant back in her chair with her pencil in her mouth and did the maths. She and Max had been married for exactly six hundred and seventy-two hours. Stella had never consciously planned on counting the hours. It had started out innocently enough: she remembered holding his hand at the wedding reception, looking up lovingly into her new husband's eyes with a goofy smile and commenting that they'd been husband and wife for an hour. And then suddenly it had been five hours. And then they'd been Mr and Mrs de Villiers for twenty-four hours. And now here she was, back from honeymoon, firmly ensconced in the day-to-day routine of real life, and suddenly married to Max for four weeks. Which was six hundred and seventy-two hours in total. Not that anybody was counting.

Their wedding photograph perched on the edge of Stella's desk in a gilt frame, to remind her of the most amazing day of her life. The warm memory of it made her smile whenever she caught a glimpse of it.

Their honeymoon in Mauritius had been wonderful too. She loved Max. The fact that he was a primary school teacher was nice. The fact that he was strong, and clever, and sort of handsome was nice. And he didn't mind if she didn't always shave her legs so much in winter and sometimes in summer as well, that was also nice. Together they'd settled into a very nice married life.

As far as Stella was concerned, Max was a pretty typical South African guy. He loved his biltong, his sport (especially rugby) and his braai. He was an only child and his mother, Eileen, had spoilt him terribly growing up, and now somehow Stella had subconsciously slipped right into Eileen's role. She had no recollection of how it had happened, they'd never actually discussed the running of the household, but she did all the shopping and cooking and cleaning during the week after work. And then they usually went out with friends on a Saturday night and ordered pizzas on Sunday night from Baccini's, a local Italian restaurant at the very top of Kloof Street, six minutes away from their flat. Max always always always had the one with salami, ham and bacon and Stella always always always had the one with spinach, feta and avocado (when it was in season). And so, even after only being married for just six hundred and seventy-two hours, they had managed to settle into a very definite routine.

Max was Stella's first and only boyfriend, ever. They'd met in high school when she was seventeen and they'd been dating ever since. It was comfortable, Stella thought. And nice. Yes, nice and comfortable.

Stella's cellphone rang, pulling her out of her thoughts. Her mobile screen flashed with the word *Lucy*.

'Hey, Luce.'

'Hey, do you want to get lunch at Newport Deli in Mouille Point later?' her sister asked. 'I've got a client presentation at the Waterfront at two, so we could go before. I've been craving one of their Cajun chicken burgers for days now.'

'I can't.' Stella grimaced. 'I have to finish these stupid thank-you cards from the wedding.'

'You haven't done those yet?'

'No. It's so boring!' Stella moaned. 'And the worst thing is that everyone expects some kind of spectacularly clever insight because I am a writer, or beautiful sentimental poetry, or something.'

'No, they don't, Stel. That's all in your head. You're overcomplicating it. Just write "Thanks for the toaster!" or "Shot for the coffee maker!" or "Cheers for the cheese grater!", or whatever, and be done with it,' Lucy said.

'Yeah, I probably should.'

'Of course you should. Hey, are you and Max coming to Mom and Dad tonight for Friday night supper? I'm bringing Jake, I want you all to meet him.'

'So things are still on with you two?' Stella asked, sounding surprised.

'He's amazing,' Lucy gushed. 'You're going to love him, Stel. I know we've only been together for a couple of months, but I really dig him. He's smart and funny, and so hot. And he's incredible in bed! We do it everywhere!'

'Urghhh,' Stella groaned. 'Too much information, Lucy!'

'Don't be such a prude, Stel,' Lucy said. 'So, you and Max will definitely be there tonight, hey?'

'Of course, I wouldn't miss meeting Mr Fantastic for the world!'

'Good, because I've got other big news too, Stel. See you tonight.'

'News! What news?' Stella pounced, but only the dialling tone answered her. Lucy was gone.

Stella hung up and turned her focus back to her desk. She often wondered how she could be so different to Lucy. They may have been identical twins, carbon copies of each other on the outside, but they were so acutely different on the inside that sometimes she couldn't believe there was anything even vaguely similar about them at all.

Stella was six and a half minutes older than Lucy, but you couldn't tell, not even with a magnifying glass – they matched each other line for line, curve for curve, wrinkle for wrinkle. But Stella wasn't just the older one, she had also always been the 'gooder' one. In all their childhood photos they were indistinguishable; every mole, every freckle mirrored. But close friends and family could always tell the difference between them. 'That's Stella on the right,' they would say assuredly. Or, 'The one on the left is definitely Stella. You can tell because she's got her socks pulled all the way up.' And it was true, she always did. Her socks always matched and were always pulled up as high as they could go, practically to her armpits in some pictures. And her hair was always neater than Lucy's. 'You're such a good girl,' Stella's aunts always used to say as they practically squeezed her cheeks right off her face.

Each of the Frankel girls had their traits. Of the five sisters, Daisy was the one who never smiled in photographs, and always cried on aeroplanes (she said her ears hurt), Lucy was the fun, wild one who always had a new and even better looking, more fabulous boyfriend than the one before, and Stella was the one who liked things neat and ordered and planned and just so.

Lucy worked as an account manager at a huge ad agency in Woodstock. And right now Jake was the flavour of the month. Stella was starting to get tired of hearing how funny he was, how amazing he was, how good looking he was and how great he was in bed. She was looking forward to meeting him in the flesh and seeing if he really was all he was cracked up to be.

Stella picked up her pen and reached for a stack of preprinted thank-you cards. She held her pen poised above the perfect glossy paper that she'd personally selected. Then she took a sip of her now cold coffee. Then she got distracted by her watch. Then she did some more maths and figured out that she'd been putting this chore off for almost five hundred and four hours now, ever since they'd returned from their honeymoon. This was the last of the wedding admin. All she needed to do was to stop proscrastinating and thank everyone for the various coffee machines, waffle makers, salt and pepper shakers, sets of glasses, towels, vases and picture frames. That was all. How hard could it be?

Well, in this case, pretty hard, Stella thought. They had somehow ended up sharing their special day with three hundred and fifty of their closest friends and family. It had been a monster affair, which had resulted in three hundred and fifty wedding guests giving them one hundred and seventy-six gifts, which meant one hundred and seventy-six thank-you notes. There were so many presents that they hadn't even opened all of them properly yet. The majority of them still stood stacked in the spare room in her and Max's apartment, like the skyline of a small city. Some with the wrapping only peeled open at a corner, just enough for them to discover what was inside, so they could add it to their list of what people needed to be thanked for.

They hadn't always planned on having such a big wedding. In fact, they'd started out with a guest list of a hundred, but that had soon spiralled to a hundred and fifty, and then if we're inviting Uncle Jordan we can't not invite the Little Cousins, and whatever happened to your great step-uncle's cousin's brother Jason? And the next thing she knew she had one hundred and seventy-six thank yous to hand write. Stella yawned. She was bored by it before she'd even begun.

Shoving the pile of cards to one side, Stella reached instead for the stack of work letters piled up on her desk. She'd get to the thank-you cards later, she thought. Of course they were urgent, yes, but work was work.

Stella picked up a letter from the top of the pile and read through it.

Dear Dr Dee,

I am a twenty-three-year-old male student and my problem is that I'm still a virgin. I've always been very shy and I've never had a girlfriend or even been on a date. I masturbate almost every single day, but desperately want to have real sex with an actual live woman. I have thought about paying a hooker to have sex with me, but I am not really sure I want to do that for my first time, and I'm scared I'll just regret it in the long run. Because shouldn't a first time be special or something? What do you suggest, and do you know of any support groups for people in my situation, i.e. people who want to lose their virginity and be normal?

Virgin

Stella rubbed her face with her hands and sighed loudly. She'd been in this job for just over two years and she still struggled to believe that it was actually what she did for a living. She cringed whenever she thought about it. 'Hello, my name is Stella, and I'm a sex column agony aunty.' She was immensely ashamed of her job. It didn't feel like something that a proper journalist should do. It just didn't feel in any way serious or worthwhile. She wondered at least ten times a day whether she could actually consider herself a proper writer and more often than not came to the depressing conclusion that she probably couldn't. At this stage of her life she certainly felt like a fraud calling herself one.

Two and a half years earlier Stella was fresh out of a journalism course at UCT, ready to hit the ground running, with dreams of changing the world. She was going to write serious articles. She would travel the world, writing about 'issues'. She would make a real difference with her words. But it turned out that while she may have been ready for the world, the world wasn't anywhere near ready for her.

After five months of futile interviews and a short-lived internship on a fishing magazine – *Rods, Reels and Red-bait* – Stella finally accepted that it was a buyer's market and she was going to have to take whatever she could get, in the desperate hope that she could work her way up from the bottom. Which was how she found herself interviewing for and finally accepting the position as the writer on the brand new Dear Dr Dee column at Publisher's World.

At least she had her foot in the door at a real magazine publishing house, in a job that actually paid, she'd reasoned to Max. That was more than a lot of the other graduates from her class had managed. And, she'd thought, one day when she was a famous journalist it would make for a fabulous story for her memoir – how she got started in the business, working her way up from the bottom. And anyway, she was going to get her own column, how bad could it really be?

The answer: bad.

As a nice girl from a nice neighbourhood, who had enjoyed a rather sheltered upbringing, Stella had been completely unprepared for the job. She'd had no idea how many lunatics there actually were out there, and how many of them would be writing to her on a daily basis. However, as weeks turned into months her embarrassment at the nature of her first proper job had turned to fascination, and for a while she'd even kind of enjoyed answering the letters. She'd often call Lucy in the middle of the day to read out some of the more bizarre ones. And they would shriek with laughter. But after two years the work had become tedious and Stella's embarrassment had escalated to the point where she would do just about anything to avoid telling people what she did for a living.

Now, finally, after years of sucking it up, it seemed that there was an end in sight, and that her gamble might just pay off. Right from the beginning Stella had made it clear to her boss that she was desperate to work on the Features Team, that she wanted to be a serious journalist. And now, after two years, two months and nine hours of waiting patiently, a gap had finally opened up on the team. A gap that had Stella's name written all over it. And it wasn't a second too soon, either. Stella had started to worry that no other magazine or newspaper would ever take her seriously as a journalist now that she'd become Dear Dr Dee. In her worst nightmares she pictured herself as an eighty-year-old agony aunty. Bitter, twisted and bored, with a long thin cigarette permanently attached to her downturned bottom lip. A chill ran down her spine whenever she thought about it. It wasn't pretty. She was slowly losing confidence in her ability as a proper journalist. It was time for a change and Stella was looking forward to finally being able to tell everyone that she was a fully fledged features writer at Publisher's World. All she had to do was stick it out for a little bit longer, until they announced that the job was hers.

Stella sighed loudly again and then opened a new page in Microsoft Word and started typing in the letter, word for word. Once it was down she made a start on her response.

Dear Loser, she wrote.

You need to stop masturbating and watching Star Wars *and get yourself out there. A virgin at twenty-three, that's just embarrassing! You should be ashamed of yourself! If you spent half of the time you spend masturbating over pictures in* FHM *getting out there and meeting real girls, then you wouldn't be in the sad situation you're in. Dude, you need to get a move on. Otherwise you're going to wake up in a couple of years and find yourself a blind thirty-year-old virgin with hairy palms.*

Love, Dr Dee

Stella smiled at her work, then deleted what she'd typed and made a start on her real response.

Dear Virgin,

Of course you're normal! It's just peer pressure making you feel like you're not. There are plenty of twenty-three-year-old virgins out there, I promise. It's just that no guy will ever admit to it, because society has made it unacceptable for men to remain virgins past the age of eighteen.

It sounds to me like you may have begun to feel isolated and lonely, but you really don't need to feel that way. You are certainly not alone.

I'm glad you asked about a group. Maybe you should think about joining some kind of cultural society. You say you're a student, so why don't you see if there are any extra-curricular clubs or societies that grab your interest on campus. It's a great way to meet like-minded people and put yourself out there. You never know, you might just meet someone you feel comfortable enough with to build a proper relationship.

In the meantime, masturbation is a great way to relieve sexual tension, temporarily of course, while you enter into your search for a real-life partner to share your feelings and sexuality with.

Good luck,

Love, Dr Dee

Creating the fake responses had become a sort of writing ritual for Stella. A harmless way of venting her frustration at the constant stream of freaks, virgins and masturbators who crossed her desk daily.

She reached over to the pile and pulled out the next letter.

Dear Dr Dee,

I was thinking about getting my nipple pierced, but what will happen if, like, after a couple of years I suddenly decide, for whatever reason, that I don't want to have my nipple pierced any more and I take it out? Will the hole be there forever or will it close up? I also want to know if I will still be able to breastfeed if I have my nipple pierced. And I want to know if getting your nipple pierced is sore, because if it is very sore I don't think I want to do it.

Love,
Unsure

Stella groaned audibly and returned to her Microsoft Word document. First she typed out the original letter and then she began her response.

Dear Unsure,

Look, let me be frank with you here, you just don't seem all that committed to getting your nipple pierced. You also sound like a bit of an idiot. Of course it's going to be sore, dumb-ass! Somebody is going to take a needle and stick it through your nipple! So, while getting a nipple ring might sound cool when you think about it, and it will definitely give you bragging rights amongst your friends, and of course it will give you a neat place to hang your sunglasses when you don't need them, at the end of the day I just don't think you've got the balls.

Love, Dr Dee

Stella leant back, reread her initial response and then deleted it, shaking her head with a smile. Then she reached across her desk for one of her medical textbooks, which were lined up next to her computer and framed wedding photograph, together with her dictionary. Without them she'd be lost. She often referred to them, especially for the more complicated or bizarre questions. Stella also had a file which contained the details of all sorts of specialists and organisations, from local clinical psychologists to depression helplines. She called it her 'crazy file' and she'd managed to build it up nicely over the last two years, constantly updating it to keep it current. As Dr Dee, next to a sharpened pencil and a strong stomach, her crazy file was her most useful asset, containing the numbers of just about anyone she might conceivably need to get in touch with in the course of an ordinary working day.

After spending about an hour between her books and the Internet, researching the subject, Stella began typing up her legitimate response.

Dear Unsure,

I'm so glad you've written in. You've brought up some very valuable points about the long-term risks of nipple piercing, points that I think all people considering the procedure should be aware of.

First things first, I'm sorry to have to tell you this but a nipple piercing is an incredibly painful experience and can take up to a year to heal. It has also been known to cause scarring, and this scarring can affect your ability to breastfeed, because it can block the release of milk from the breast. So if you are thinking of having children any time in the near future you might want to consider the possible consequences. However, while it is a risk, most women who get their nipples pierced can usually breastfeed without any problems.

Finally, you'll be pleased to hear that should you ever decide to take the jewellery out the piercing should heal and close nicely after about six months to a year. Having said this, a piercing anywhere on one's body is a serious business and I would suggest that if you're really interested you should do your homework thoroughly. I would even recommend you discuss it with your doctor before making your final decision.

Good luck if you choose to go through with it.

Love, Dr Dee

Stella sighed. Again. Then she dropped her head into her hands and wondered how much longer she could stomach this. They had to announce her promotion soon, she thought. They couldn't go on without filling the position for much longer, it just wasn't a viable option.

Stella did some sums. She had been a sex column agony aunt now for two years, two months and nine hours. That was eighteen thousand nine hundred and sixty-nine hours in total. She took a deep breath, her time would come, she thought as she reached for the next letter in the pile. She just needed to be patient. She'd waited all this time already, what harm could a few more hours do?

'Did I tell you Lucy's bringing that guy she's been dating to dinner tonight?' Stella said.

'Tonight?' Max asked, changing gears as he turned the car onto De Waal Drive. 'She's never brought anyone to Friday night supper before.'

'Hasn't she?' Stella said, smoothing her skirt down with her hands and picking off some invisible pieces of lint. 'I'm sure she has.'

'Nope, she must really like this guy. It's been two months and they're still together. That must be some kind of record for Lucy. She's never been with anyone that long before.'

'Don't be ridiculous, of course she has,' Stella said indignantly.

'Name one!' Max challenged her. 'Name one guy she's been with longer than two months.'

'Well,' Stella said, scratching her chin thoughtfully. 'What about that guy with the pool-cleaning business? Pool Boy. She was with him for a while.'

'Not longer than two months,' Max said. 'Remember, she dumped him for that commercials director.'

'Ah, Camera Man, I remember him,' Stella said. 'He was an arrogant jerk. I didn't like him.'

'Neither did Lucy, that's why she ditched him for the rugby player.'

'Oh, yes, Ball Boy. That didn't last long either, he went off on rugby tour to Argentina or somewhere and that was the last we ever saw of him.' Stella paused. 'Hey, remember Bendy Boy?'

'Wasn't he a stuntman or something?' Max asked, scrunching up his forehead in thought.

'Yes.' Stella smiled.

'Why did you girls call him Bendy Boy anyway?' Max asked.

'No reason,' Stella said, blushing a little and smiling to herself. 'He didn't last very long either.'

'You see,' Max said, 'that's my point. This guy must be really important if she's still got him around after two months, and she's bringing him home to meet the family.'

'I suppose so,' Stella said, 'but you know Lucy, we shouldn't start planning the wedding quite yet.'

'What's his name?' Max asked.

'Jake.'

'And he has an actual name!' Max said, adding mock surprise to his voice. 'Well, now I'm really looking forward to meeting this guy – they don't normally have real names. He must be something really special.' He paused to check his mirrors before moving out to overtake a truck. 'See, babe,' he continued, reaching a big meaty paw over and squeezing her knee, 'you're lucky you found the man of your dreams so early on. I saved you from having to spend all those years dating stuntmen and film directors and international men of mystery.'

'Mmmmm, I suppose so,' Stella said, turning to look out of the car window and watch the scenery fly by.

Stella's father, Hylton, was seated at the head of the long oak dining table, with Stella's mom, Iris, on his immediate right. Next to Iris was Stella, and then Max. Lucy sat on Hylton's left, and next to her was Jake and then Daisy, who at twenty-three was the second youngest Frankel sister.

Stella looked across the table at Jake and Lucy. Besides touching her constantly, Jake had barely taken his eyes off Lucy for a second since they'd arrived. She felt a small pang of jealousy. He was so good looking he made Stella's breath catch. Looking at him was like looking directly into the sun; it was only a matter of time before you had to look away. Jake was about as tall as Max, at just over six foot, but he was much leaner. He had a strong jaw and perfect soap star good looks, which were only marred by a small dent in his earlobe where a piece of flesh was missing. Which somehow only managed to make him seem even more good looking and mysterious to Stella. She bit her tongue and decided to wait a couple of hours before she asked him about his ear; she didn't want to be rude, but she absolutely had to know how he'd managed to lose a chunk of his earlobe. Jake's brown hair was cropped short against his head and his matching stubble was perfectly unshaven; the grey spikes scattered here and there, giving him an air of accomplishment. Stella turned slightly and glanced at Max. He was a couple of weeks overdue for a haircut. It looked like he hadn't had one since before the wedding. She would have to make him an appointment, she thought, since he was clearly incapable of taking care of it himself.

In contrast to Jake and Lucy, who seemed completely at ease, Daisy seemed fidgety and preoccupied. Stella watched her down the dregs of her Savanna, then jump up to go grab another one from the kitchen. At twenty-three, Daisy was two years younger than Stella and Lucy. She was studying at film school and had dreams of becoming the next great South African director. Her hair was short and matted – much to their mother's horror – though she insisted it wasn't matted, but was rather dreadlocked. She was slightly shorter than the other girls, but she was more muscular than all of them. Stella reckoned it came from lugging around film equipment all day.

'It's just us tonight,' Iris said, passing a platter of roast chicken down the table. 'Please start, before it gets cold.'

'Where's Violet?' Daisy asked, making her way back from the kitchen.

'She's gone over to the dark side,' Lucy replied. 'That's what we call my sister's in-laws,' Lucy explained to Jake. 'They go to Violet's husband's family every second week or so.'

'That's what happens when you get married, you get two families for the price of one,' Stella said, looking at Max. He held his second beer in one hand while he used the other to stuff an entire piece of bread into his mouth. A small smudge of butter had lodged itself in the corner of his mouth and Stella made a show of licking her own lip, trying to get Max to mirror her movements, but he wasn't looking at her, he was focused on buttering another piece of bread.

'So, Jake,' Stella said, giving up on Max. 'Lucy says you used to be a model?'

'That was a helluva long time ago,' he said, laughing, without a hint of vanity. 'These days I spend much more time on the other side of the camera. I'm a commercial photographer now. That's how I met Lucy.' He winked and squeezed Lucy's hand on the table.

Across the table Daisy cleared her throat loudly. 'Guys …' she said, her voice shaking slightly. She cleared her throat again and took a big sip of cider. 'There's something I wanted to …'

'Hey, I almost forgot!' Lucy shrieked, interrupting Daisy as she jumped out of her seat and began tapping at her glass with a spoon. 'I have huge, huge, huge news.'

'What?' Stella asked.

'I found out this morning that I got a promotion at work. They made me an account director!' Lucy belted out, with an enormous grin on her face.

'Wow, Luce, that's fantastic!' Stella shrieked, standing up and going around to Lucy's side of the table to give her twin a hug.

'Darling, we're so proud of you,' Iris said, tears welling in her eyes.

'There's my girl,' Hylton added, raising his glass.

'Shot, Luce,' Daisy said, trying her best to smile.

'I know, I'm so excited,' Lucy said, clapping her hands together. 'And not only is it a massive salary increase, but early next year they're sending me to Buenos Aires, to an agency group conference. There'll be representatives from all the network's agencies from all over the world, and I'm going to be the South African representative! Can you believe it? And I've only been there six months!'

Again the table erupted.

'Stella, weren't you also waiting to hear about a promotion?' Iris asked when the noise had died down.

Stella felt every eye in the room turn on her and she blushed violently. 'Absolutely,' she said as she made her way back to her seat. 'I'm next in line. It's just a matter of time.'

'It's going to be any day now,' Max said, putting his arm around Stella with pride as she sat down.

Stella smiled at Max, lifted her napkin and used it to wipe the butter from the corner of his mouth.

After supper they cleared the table and moved into the lounge for coffee and dessert. Max settled on the couch next to Iris and Hylton, helping himself to an enormous piece of cake while Stella's parents bickered quietly between themselves over something unimportant. Stella craned her neck and caught a glimpse of Daisy through the lounge window, outside the back of the house, by the pool. She was having an intense conversation on her cellphone, pacing up and down the side of the pool as she spoke, gesticulating wildly with her free hand.

Jake sat down in one of the old overstuffed armchairs and Lucy climbed into his lap. Stella watched as Jake whispered something into Lucy's ear and the two of them broke out into giggles. They hadn't stopped whispering and giggling together like children all night, and watching them Stella felt another pang of irritation and jealousy – there were two other empty chairs in the room, why did Lucy have to squash herself into the same chair as Jake? Stella tried to sit down next to Max, but there wasn't enough room for all four of them on the couch, so she perched, balancing uncomfortably, on the arm of the couch.

'I'm just going to show Jake around the house,' Lucy said, climbing out of his lap and pulling him out of the chair.

Jake was wearing a pair of tight-fitting black jeans, a pair of boots and a baby blue V-neck sweater with nothing underneath. Stella admired his sense of style as Lucy led him out of the lounge. She looked across at Max, evaluating his shapeless, worn chinos – the ones with the green Koki stain on the knee, that he'd come home from school with one day and that she'd never been able to get out. 'How come you never wear those Levi's I bought you?' Stella asked him.

Max had to crane his neck awkwardly to look at her, perched above him on the couch arm. 'I don't know,' he said. 'They're not all that comfy. The waistband digs into my stomach. I may have put on a couple of kilos since the wedding.' He patted his stomach proudly. 'Anyway, I told you, I like these pants, the ones with the elastic waist. They have more room for movement, if you know what I mean.' He moved forward to cut himself another piece of cake. 'Hey, shove up a bit, Stel, you're right on top of me,' he complained, nudging her and pointing to one of the three empty armchairs in the lounge.

Stella sighed and got up. She wondered where Lucy and Jake had gone. She wanted more details about Lucy's promotion and the trip. She felt jealous. It wasn't really fair, Stella had been slogging it out as an agony aunty for over two years now, waiting for a spot in editorial to open up, and Lucy had only been at that agency for just over six months, and here she was promoted already. But she shoved the jealousy aside as quickly as it arrived. She loved Lucy and she was proud of her. She was an amazing woman who was great at what she did, she deserved it, and anyway her own turn would come, she just needed to be patient.

Stella left the lounge and went in search of Jake and Lucy. The Frankel family home in Claremont was laid out on one storey. A long passageway ran down the middle of the house – the lounge and formal dining room on the one end, Iris and Hylton's bedroom at the opposite end and all the other rooms laid out along the length of it.

Stella could hear hushed voices and giggling coming from halfway down the passage, so she headed towards them. As she got closer it sounded like the voices were coming from the guest bathroom, which was towards the end of the passage on the right-hand side. Curious, Stella looked up and down the passage to make sure nobody was coming, then she crouched down and put her eye to the keyhole. What she saw made her suck in her breath in shock.

Lucy was sitting, balanced on the edge of the basin in the narrow bathroom, her skirt pulled up above her waist, her legs wide open and both stilettoed feet wedged up high against the opposite bathroom wall. Jake was standing between Lucy's legs, his jeans and boxer shorts crumpled around his ankles.

Stella jumped back from the door, covering her mouth with her hand. She couldn't believe what she'd seen. She couldn't believe Lucy would sneak away after Friday night supper to have sex in the guest bathroom of their parents' house. She was horrified. But she was more than a little curious too. Looking up and down the passage again, to make sure nobody had seen her, she crouched back down and looked through the keyhole.

Stella caught her breath again. The effect of what she was seeing was bizarre. She knew it wasn't her, shoved up against the basin, but it still looked just like her. Lucy had her head thrown back, a look of complete ecstasy spread across her face, both her eyes shut tightly as their bodies rocked together, gaining momentum. Stella wondered if this was what she looked like when she had sex, but she doubted it. She couldn't remember ever feeling that wrapped up in the moment during sex. They both seemed so far away, so focused, so utterly and completely taken with what they were doing.

Lucy groaned deeply, primally, and Jake gently covered her mouth with his hand, to keep her quiet. Stella needed to stop watching, but she couldn't tear herself away. She stared in shocked fascination as Lucy's whole body shook and arched with intensity. For the first time ever, Stella didn't recognise herself in her twin. Lucy's reaction was completely foreign to her – she was certain that she had never experienced anything that had made her feel like that before. She watched in captive awe as Jake grunted out his own powerful orgasm, and then dropped his forehead into Lucy's neck, which was damp and shiny with sweat.

Stella instantly felt deeply embarrassed by her voyeurism. She stood up quickly and adjusted her skirt, smoothing it down. She was undeniably turned on by what she'd seen, but she felt incredibly embarrassed and confused at the same time. She'd never seen anyone else having sex in real life before. What if she'd been caught? Hurrying back into the kitchen she filled the sink with scalding hot soapy water, then she sank her hands into the sink and got to work scrubbing an already clean pot.

As she scrubbed Stella's cheeks flamed red with shame and excitement. In their eight years together, she and Max had never had sex anywhere other than in the bed, in a bedroom. As young adults, dating, they had necked just about everywhere of course, like all kids did – at the movies, in the car, on the couch. But sex had always been reserved for the bedroom. That was where Max liked it, and Stella had never really considered that there were other options. But there was something else too, something bigger that bothered Stella about what she'd just witnessed. She had always glossed over it, telling herself that it wasn't really important, that it didn't really matter, but the fact of the matter was that in all of her twenty-five years Stella had never had an orgasm. Somewhere in the back of her mind she'd always wondered whether she was doing sex right, especially since her experience never quite matched up to what she saw on TV or read about in novels. But she'd always rationalised it away, telling herself that Hollywood probably made a bigger deal out of it than it warranted. A couple of seconds of pleasure couldn't be all that great, could it? The earth didn't really actually move for anyone, did it? She'd always thought that people were probably exaggerating, making a big deal out of nothing. But now, after watching Lucy, she was beginning to wonder what she was missing out on. There was no way that Lucy had faked her orgasm, Stella thought. It was incredibly real and powerful. And if Lucy was experiencing that kind of intense pleasure, why shouldn't she? Stella wondered if it was her own fault. Maybe she was bad in bed, maybe there was something wrong with her? Or maybe it was Max? Either way, she decided, she wanted what Lucy had.

Stella stood in her bathroom at home and got ready for bed. She washed her face and eyed herself in the mirror. She hadn't been able to stop thinking about what she'd seen earlier. In fact, she'd been so preoccupied that she'd barely said a word in the car the whole way home. Not that Max had noticed.

Mixed in with the feelings of shame she felt at being a peeping Tom, Stella realised that she was still also a little turned on. Which was rare for her. She wasn't the kind of girl who felt particularly sexy most of the time. And she never initiated sex with Max. That was just one of the things he did. Like she did the shopping, cooking and cleaning, he did the 'starting'.

But there really was no reason why they shouldn't also be having hot sex, like Jake and Lucy, Stella thought. She could be sexy like Lucy, couldn't she? After all, she was exactly the same as Lucy, wasn't she? Just because she didn't wear short skirts and heels and sexy lingerie all the time, didn't mean that she didn't have sexy somewhere inside her, even if it was quite deeply buried. Padding into the bedroom in her socks and flannel pyjama top Stella opened her underwear drawer, rummaging through it, looking for something even vaguely sexy. She could hear Max in the lounge, shouting at some sport on TV as she rifled through the drawer. There was lots of white and what used to be white, but was now varying shades of beige and grey. Piles of sensible, neatly folded underpants stared back up at her uselessly.

She had to have something sexy, didn't she? Didn't every girl have at least one sexy thing in her underwear drawer? Even usually unsexy girls. Then she spotted it. Right at the back of the drawer she saw a flash of black. It was the corner of a pair of very lacy black panties a girlfriend had given her on her hen night. She'd never worn them before, but right now they were exactly what she needed.

Stella grabbed the corner and pulled, but the panties seemed to be stuck in the back of the drawer. She tugged a little harder, but they still wouldn't give, not until she planted both feet and gave them a really good yank. She heard a small rip as they came free from where they'd been snagged.

Cursing, she held them up to assess the damage. The lace had torn a little in the back, but the front of them was still perfect. She slipped out of the white cotton panties she was wearing and pulled on the lace ones. Then she turned and craned her neck to catch a glimpse of the back of them. Her bum stuck out of the hole a little, but as long as she didn't turn around she'd be fine.

Undoing the top two buttons on her pyjama top, she tied the shirt tails in a knot just above her belly button. Then she dug around in the very back of her shoe closet and pulled out a pair of high black stilettos that Lucy had once given her as a present. She dusted them off using the corner of the bedspread and put them on, wobbling around the bedroom as she tried to get used to them. She had no idea how Lucy wore such high heels. The highest shoes Stella had ever bought were a couple of pairs of sensible, two inch-high pumps.

Stella sashayed into the lounge, doing what she hoped was a sexy walk. Max was on the couch drinking a beer and working his way through a slab of Cadbury's Dairy Milk. He had a small smear of chocolate in the corner of his mouth, and Stella also noticed another dark crumb of chocolate melting into the beige fabric of the couch. She felt a pang of irritation and wondered how it was possible that after all these years of owning exactly the same mouth he still didn't know where it was.

Max looked up and wolf-whistled. 'Wow ...!' he said, eyeing her up and down in surprise.

Brushing her irritation at the chocolate stain aside Stella overplayed the swing of her hips as she approached the couch.

Max looked up at her as she walked towards him, clearly surprised but also obviously pleased. Nervous that he might say something to ruin the moment, Stella leant down and kissed him hard. He tasted of chocolate mixed with beer and was that biltong?

Straddling him as sexily as she could – wobbling a bit in the brief moment that she only had one high-heeled foot on the floor – Stella sank into his lap, pulling Max into another passionate kiss. But as she did so she felt a sudden crunching pain in her knee and the TV went haywire. Loud kwaito burst out of the speakers, tearing through the room. Ears exploding and knee searing with pain, Stella pulled back from Max and covered her ears with her hands. Then she clutched at his shoulder for balance and reached down to pull the remote control out from where she was crushing it under her knee.

'Here, give it to me,' Max shouted, taking the remote control from her and muting the TV. 'You okay?'

But Stella wasn't listening. She'd somehow managed to get the heel of one of the stilettos caught in the piping of the couch and as she twisted around to try unhook it she heard a small tear as the fabric gave. 'Don't move!' she barked, carefully shifting her whole weight onto Max's one leg as she tried to extract her heel from the couch without tearing the material further.

'Ow, you're digging your knee into me,' Max said, rolling her off his lap and onto the couch next to him. He appraised her outfit again. 'Sheesh, babe, it's not even my birthday,' he said, looking worried. 'I haven't missed an anniversary or anything like that, have I?'

'No, Max ... I just thought, you know ... we could try something different tonight,' Stella said, sitting up and trying to compose herself. There had been some setbacks in her hastily concocted plan, but she knew that they could be just as sexy as Lucy and Jake, they just had to put in a little more practice.

'Okay, let's go to the bedroom,' Max said, smiling as he got up and reached for her hand.

Ignoring his hand, Stella took a deep breath. 'Max, I thought maybe we could do it here?' she said, looking up into his eyes. 'You know, something different.'

'What, here on the couch?' Max asked, with surprise in his voice.

'Or in the bathroom?' Stella said, suddenly blushing. 'You know, I mean, anywhere ... We could do it anywhere. It doesn't always have to be on the bed, does it?'

Max looked at her and then he looked at the couch, clearly weighing up the options. 'But this couch is so small, where would we fit?' he asked. 'I'm over six foot, you know. And I have that back thing ...'

The couch was only a two-seater, Stella conceded, but Lucy and Jake had made it work in her parents' minuscule guest bathroom. She was determined to try something different. Leaning forward, Stella grabbed the front of Max's shirt and pulled him down towards her to kiss him again. She was resourceful, she thought, she could make the couch work if she tried hard enough.

Max sat back down next to her, reached up and stroked her hair out of her face lovingly. Then he looked at her with a small grimace. 'Stella, babe ...'

'Yes, honey,' Stella drawled seductively.

'You've got a little booger, just there,' he said, pointing at the side of her nose.

Stella shrieked and covered her nose with her hand. Mortified, she jumped up, still facing Max, and then with both hands covering her nose she backed out of the lounge awkwardly in her wobbly stilettos. So much for sexy, she thought as she bumped into a wall. She wasn't going to turn around now – she didn't want him to see her bum hanging out of her torn lace panties. The humiliation of the booger was already more than she could bear.

'Where are you going, Stella?' Max shouted after her. 'Come back, I don't mind a little booger!'

POPPY

Poppy stood on one side of the highway and stuck her thumb out for cars heading north, while Buck stood on the other side of the highway with his thumb out, trying to stop cars heading south.

'First one to bag us a ride wins!' she shouted at him across the highway.

'Shut up,' Buck yelled back at her, 'you're putting me off my game.'

A truck barrelled towards Buck and he lifted the leg of his jeans as high as he could, displaying a white hairy leg and a biker boot. The truck whooshed past him, honking its horn.

Poppy burst out laughing. 'For fuck's sake, Buck,' she shouted. 'I don't think that's the kind of ride we're looking for.'

'Hey, it's been an hour and a half. At this stage I'll take whatever we can get,' he replied. 'I'd even take my shirt off if I thought it would help.'

'No, please, please,' Poppy shouted, miming strangling herself. 'Whatever you do, don't take your shirt off. That will guarantee we don't get a ride.'

Buck pulled a zap sign at her.

Poppy looked down her side of the highway to where four or five cars were heading towards her. She brushed her pink hair out of her face and adjusted her stance, sticking her thumb out as far as she could and putting on her most innocent, pleading face. All of the cars zipped by, barely even slowing down.

'Who knew Middle Americans would be so stingy,' she shouted as she watched the last of the cars disappear into the distance. She kicked at her backpack, which lay next to her on the side of the highway. 'You'd think they'd never seen a hitch-hiker before!'

'Don't worry,' Buck shouted. 'It'll be worth it when we get there.'

'And where is there, again?' Poppy shouted back.

'I'll tell you when we get there,' he said, pulling a silly face.

Forty minutes later, just as they were giving up hope of ever getting a ride, and contemplating living on the side of an American highway for the rest of their lives, an old brown station wagon trundled down the road on Buck's side, slowing as it passed him and pulling over about a hundred metres further up the highway.

'I got one! I got one!' he shouted. 'C'mon, Poppy, move your pink ass!'

Poppy shrieked and picked up her backpack, slinging it onto her shoulder. Checking to make sure no cars were coming from either direction, she raced across the highway to where Buck was leaning his head into the front passenger window of the car.

Poppy waited patiently while Buck spoke to the driver and passenger. When he finally pulled his head out of the window he was smiling broadly. 'Cool,' he said to Poppy. 'They don't mind giving us a ride to wherever it is they're going.'

'And where's that?' Poppy asked.

Buck shrugged his shoulders. 'I didn't ask,' he said.

'Awesome,' Poppy said, high-fiving him and then bundling herself and her backpack onto the back seat of the car.

STELLA

Stella sat at her desk and prodded at her wedding thank-you notes with the back of her pen as if they were radioactive. So far she'd answered four Dr Dee letters and uploaded a further three to the magazine website. She'd set the rest of the morning aside to write her wedding thank-you cards. It was an uneventful morning that only highlighted the boredom she felt with her job. And the worst part was that Wednesdays were Features Meeting day. Every Wednesday the Features Team, of which she was not a part, met to discuss ideas for the upcoming issues. The conference room was quite close to her cubicled desk, and although she couldn't hear what they were saying, she could hear the excited murmur of voices and the episodic bursts of laughter as the team threw their ideas around. Stella always felt particularly jealous and dissatisfied on a Wednesday morning.

To make matters worse, Stella couldn't stop thinking about what had happened after Friday night supper. She'd had four whole days to think about it now and she'd come to the conclusion that something was very definitely wrong. The fact that she'd never had an orgasm had never really bothered her all that much before. But now, after watching Lucy and Jake, she was starting to feel a little differently about it.

For the umpteenth time Stella reviewed the sexual experiences she'd had in her life so far. It didn't take very long. She'd lost her virginity to Max at a respectable twenty years old, after they'd already been dating for three years, and she'd never slept with anyone else. There was no question in her mind that watching Lucy and Jake in the bathroom after Friday night supper was the most sexually deviant thing she'd ever done. And she still couldn't quite believe she'd done it; it was completely out of character, and the thought of it made her feel embarrassed and dirty all over again.

Yes, Stella sort of enjoyed sex with Max, but she certainly didn't live or die for it. Sex with Max was simply another part of the routine of her life and one of the responsibilities of being in a relationship, like shopping, cleaning, cooking and writing thank-you notes for all your one hundred and seventy-six wedding presents. It was just something she had to do. Not that it was entirely a chore – it could even be kind of nice sometimes, when she was in the right mood – but she'd certainly never experienced anything that had given her the kind of pleasure she had seen on Lucy's face after Friday night supper.

Every now and then, while making love, she had briefly considered asking Max to shift a little to the left or right, or to do something a little differently, or try a more interesting position, but she'd never actually built up the courage to go through with it. They weren't really the kind of people who talked during sex, and over and above that, Max always seemed to be enjoying himself quite a lot and she didn't want to throw him off his stride.

A blonde head with a severe asymmetrical bob popped up over the lilac cubicle wall, catching Stella by surprise and completely severing her chain of thought. Stella's hand jerked out in shock and the pen she was holding scrawled a jagged line onto the blank thank-you card on top of the pile. At last, she'd made a start on the thank yous, Stella just had time to think before Connie, the person behind the bob, started to speak.

'Oh, and this is Stella,' Connie said, appearing around the side of Stella's partition. She was closely followed by a pretty girl in her early twenties who was wearing a brightly coloured floor-length dress that Stella recognised from a big local designer's hot, new range. 'This is Yolanda Mabuza,' Connie said, making the introductions. 'And this is Stella de Villiers.'

Stella shook Yolanda's hand, which was dry and firm, realising too late that hers was damp and clammy.

'Stella is our agony aunty. She writes the Dr Dee column,' Connie continued.

'Oh, cool,' Yolanda said as Stella blushed and cringed. 'Your column is a scream, eh. It's so cute!' Yolanda dragged the word cute out way longer than necessary, adding insult to Stella's injury. 'But what a bunch of freaks, hey?' Yolanda continued, either oblivious or indifferent to Stella's embarrassment and discomfort. 'Seriously, what kind of crazy writes in to a magazine with their deepest, darkest, most embarrassing secrets?'

Stella flushed even redder. 'I actually studied literature and journalism at UCT. I mean, I'm a journalist,' she stuttered. 'I'm just doing this until ... you know ...' she petered off.

'I always wonder if all those letters are for real or if you make some of them up here?' Yolanda said, not really addressing the question to anyone in particular.

'Yolanda is our new features writer,' Connie explained with a cruel kind of glee. 'She's joining the team today.'

Stella's heart sank. 'She's what?' Stella couldn't disguise her horror. 'But ...'

'Right, Yolanda,' Connie said, walking away from Stella's cubicle. 'Let me show you where the bathrooms are ...'

'See you around, Dee,' Yolanda shouted over her shoulder as she followed Connie through the office.

'It's Stella,' Stella mumbled as she sank back into her chair, devastated. She wanted to cry. That was meant to be her job. She'd been waiting for a position in editorial to become available for over two years. She'd watched each of the writers on the Features Team like a hawk, desperate for one of them to fall pregnant, or get a skin-eating virus, or get poached by another magazine. And at last that fat cow Julia had moved up to Joburg to take a position at *True Love*. Stella had applied for Julia's job instantly and she'd just assumed it would be hers. And now here was this Yolanda chick, taking her job and calling her column 'cute' with lots of *us*. Stella couldn't bear it.

Stella chewed her lip and fought back the tears. Then she stood up, took a deep breath and made her way purposefully through the open-plan, studio-style offices, down to the end of the building where Denise had her corner office.

Denise MacDonald was the queen of Publisher's World. She was the editorial director of the company which ran a total of seven of South Africa's top publications. Denise was also the person who had hired Stella two years earlier to run 'Dear Dr Dee', the sex agony column which appeared in one of the stable's weekly publications.

Connie, Denise's secretary and guard dog wasn't manning her desk because she was still out wafting Yolanda around, no doubt introducing her to everyone and showing her where they kept the good coffee. Stella knew if she didn't see Denise now, in the heat of the moment, she would cool down with time, and she wouldn't be able to pluck up this kind of courage again. And anyway, once Connie was back on duty there was no way she would make it into Denise's office without some kind of prearranged appointment. It was now or never. Stella cleared her throat, took a deep breath, pulled her shoulders back, stuck her chest out and – summoning all her courage – tapped a knuckle on the half-open door.

'Denise, do you have a second?' Stella asked, trying to sound assertive as she pushed the door open.

'Sure, Stella, come in,' Denise said, looking up from behind her enormous desk and pointing to one of the chairs in her office with a long, plum-coloured fingernail.

Denise was incredibly thin and of indeterminate age – Stella would have put her anywhere between fifty and seventy. She was always dressed immaculately, and always in white. She had shoulder-length red hair, and smoked long menthol cigarettes. Denise didn't care much for anti-smoking legislation and she was renowned for having one cigarette lit in her ashtray, while she held another between her well-manicured fingers.

'Denise, I was hoping to chat to you about that position on the editorial team, now that Julia's gone,' Stella said, trying to temper the angry shake in her voice.

'I'm afraid it's already been filled,' Denise said, stubbing a cigarette out in the ashtray. 'A girl from Rhodes, Yolanda somethingorother.'

Stella shuddered when she heard that Yolanda had studied at Rhodes. 'Yes, that's what I wanted to talk to you about. I just met her. Didn't you get my application? I thought ... I mean, you always said that I was next in line for a position in editorial.'

Denise studied Stella closely before taking a long, pensive drag on the other, still lit cigarette that was resting in her ashtray. 'Stella, I'm going to be frank with you,' she finally said. 'I'm sure you understand my predicament?'

'Your predicament?' Stella asked, not sure what Denise was talking about.

'The problem is, Stella, that you're doing a stellar job on Dr Dee, and I don't want to mess with a winning formula,' Denise said in her posh Bishop's Court accent.

Stella felt like her head was going to explode. 'Denise,' she said, her jaw clenched tightly, 'when I joined and took on Dr Dee, you said it was just temporary, until something came up in editorial. It's been over two years already!' Stella's voice was becoming increasingly high-pitched and she cleared her throat, trying to remain as calm as possible in spite of her heart racing in her chest. 'Denise, I'm a serious journalist. I studied at UCT! I want to do research and write proper articles. I mean, what about all the pieces I keep sending you? Isn't there a single article in amongst them that you like even just a little bit? What about the cougar piece, or the piece on the women in that cult in Texas? Or that piece about the sex lives of Siamese twins?' Stella could hear the desperate begging whine her voice had taken on, but she couldn't help herself, that was how she felt: desperate.

'Stella, don't get me wrong. I'm not saying you're not a good writer, but you're doing such a great job with Dr Dee. If I promoted you, then who would answer the letters?' Denise drawled. 'You see my problem? You're so good at what you do that you simply give me no choice. And Yolanda is lovely; I think you'll really like her. She was top of her class at Rhodes, you know. I tell you what, the very next gap that opens up in editorial is all yours, all right?'

It was a question, but it was clearly rhetorical. Stella stood bolted to the spot in a haze of cigarette smoke and disappointment as Denise stabbed at her telephone with a plum-tipped talon. 'Connie, get Liesel in here, we need to discuss next month's covers,' she barked, lighting up another cigarette.

'Right away, Denise,' Connie replied through the speakerphone.

Slowly Stella realised that at the end of Denise's last sentence she had become instantly invisible. Her meeting was over, whether she liked it or not.

Back at her desk Stella stared at her wedding photograph and wondered how this had happened to her. Numbly, she thumbed through some of the letters in front of her, and stopped to read one towards the middle of the pile:

Dear Dr Dee,

I get really really sexually aroused by feet. Ones with shoes on and bare ones too. With or without painted nails, I don't mind. Am I a freak, or what?

The Foot Whisperer

Stella covered her face with her hands and rocked in her seat. 'Freak,' she whispered into her hands. She pictured the rest of her life, laid out before her: a hundred more years – eight hundred and seventy-six thousand more hours – spent responding to letters from freaks.

After ten minutes of rocking she picked up her phone and dialled Max.

'Hi, Stel,' he said.

'Hi,' she replied, close to tears.

'What happened?' he asked, hearing immediately in her voice that something was up.

'Max, I have news about work ...' she said, her voice quavering.

'You got it!' Max whooped, his voice suddenly loud and excited. 'You got the promotion! I knew it, I just knew it!'

'No, Max ...' Stella said, trying to stop him. But he was shouting so loudly into the phone that he couldn't hear her. Stella's lip quivered. She didn't know what to say. She was already so upset, and he would be so disappointed for her. She couldn't bear to hear pity in his voice. The thought of him in his elastic-waisted, Koki-stained pants, feeling sorry for her, just tore her apart. She'd been telling him for months now what a shoo-in she was for this promotion, and now the promotion was gone, had disappeared into thin air. And who knew when there would be another spot opening up in editorial. What if she had to wait another two years, or heaven forbid, even longer? And even if she did manage to hold out another two years, doing the awful, depraved Dr Dee thing, there was still no guarantee that good old Denise wouldn't just bring in somebody new next time too.

Stella took a deep breath before she spoke. 'Max, I ...'

'Stella, I knew it! I could hear in your voice that something big had happened! That's awesome!' Max shouted into the phone. 'I told you! You're a brilliant writer! I'm so proud of you, babe. This is great news! You see, all that hard work finally paid off!'

Stella gripped the phone and shook her head, a silent tear rolling down her cheek. She closed her eyes, praying that if Max said it loud enough and she believed it hard enough it would be true. She'd once written an article for Denise about visualisation techniques, about how if you simply visualised something happening in your mind, you could improve the odds of it actually happening in real life by something like forty-eight per cent. There were statistics to prove it and everything. She'd even interviewed one of South Africa's top female pole-vaulters, who had claimed to visualise every jump before she began it. But the article had been a non-starter. Denise had said it wasn't what their readers were interested in. Perhaps Stella hadn't visualised it being published hard enough.

Stella visualised herself as a successful features writer, proud to come to work every day; doing research, writing meaningful articles, changing people's lives. Then she opened her eyes again. But her visualisation hadn't worked. She was still just the agony aunty for a laughably smutty weekly publication.

'Oh, shoot, there's the bell, I'd better go,' Max said as the school bell rang on the other end of the phone. 'We should go out to celebrate tonight, Stella. I know it's a Wednesday, and we always do stir-fry and *CSI* on Wednesdays, but this is big news, we have to celebrate!'

'Wait, Max …' Stella said, trying to stall him so she could get the truth out.

'Oh, you're right, I've got that parent-teacher conference after school,' Max said. 'I almost forgot.'

Stella moved her mouth, trying to form the words that she needed to tell him what had really happened, but the words wouldn't come. 'Max …' she stuttered again.

'Hey, I know, why don't you just meet me in the bar at La Perla afterwards? I'll come straight from school and meet you there, then we can pop some champagne to celebrate.'

'No, wait, Max …' Stella mumbled, swallowing deeply.

'I know it's a little late for a school night, but, Stel, this is huge for you, we have to celebrate. Meet me there at around eight thirty, okay?' Max said. 'I'm so proud of you, babe. Okay, listen, I've got to go, but I'll see you later, all right? Love you, bye.'

Stella could hear that he was already pulling the phone away from his ear as he said goodbye. 'All right,' she said quietly, her voice tapering off into a whisper. She hadn't been able to correct him. The words just hadn't been there. He had been so happy for her that she hadn't had the heart to upset him with the truth.

Stella chewed on her lip and tried to breathe. She'd tell Max tonight that she hadn't actually gotten the promotion, that it wasn't true. She would do it the second he got there, before he ordered the champagne. She would tell him she had lost her mind. She would plead temporary insanity, brought on by the grief of not actually getting the job, especially in the face of Lucy's big promotion. He would understand, he was her nice Max after all, he had to.

Stella sat at the kitchen table and tried to force down some dinner. Their apartment was a small, neat, two-bedroom flat in Vredehoek, just above Cape Town's city centre. Stella found the apartment deathly quiet when Max wasn't home, and doubly so tonight. Max would grab a bite to eat at the parent-teacher's conference – there was never a shortage of overzealous

PTA moms bringing lasagne or a chicken pie or something like that to the meetings, in the hope of improving their child's chances of academic excellence. And as they'd only planned to meet at La Perla at around eight thirty Stella had a couple of hours to kill. She poked at her stir-fry unenthusiastically, nausea rising from the pit of her stomach.

La Perla was one of their favourite restaurants, and they usually ended up there whenever there was something special to celebrate. It had been a five-star feature on the Cape Town restaurant scene since the beginning of time, or at least as long as Stella could remember. The bar adjacent to the restaurant was comfortably chic. It had a large bar counter along the entire back wall and large windows placed across another wall reflected the warmth of the room back into it, making it feel bigger than it was. A series of luxurious leather couches and armchairs covered much of the rest of the bar floor and a humidor full of expensive cigars took pride of place near the door. Stella and Max loved the up-market style of the place, but it was comfortably familiar too.

Half an hour later Stella stood in her underwear, facing her closet, trying to decide what to wear. She wondered what crazy women wore. She'd made a terrible mistake and for once in her life she'd much rather be staying home and eating stir-fry with Max than getting all dolled up to head out for a night on the town. Eventually, after much humming and hawing, she chose a simple, sombre, black wrap-around dress, to match her mood, and a pair of low black pumps. She felt foolish. Max had misunderstood the meaning of her call, and she hadn't corrected him. Essentially she'd lied to him, and now she was going to have to come clean – how embarrassing. He was going to think she was completely mad. She shrugged her shoulders at her reflection, she was just going to have to face the music and get this nightmare over with as quickly as possible.

Stella pulled up outside La Perla just after eight thirty. She walked through the door furiously tugging at her dress, trying to adjust it where it had become twisted during the drive, and trying not to trip over her pashmina, which was trailing along the floor behind her. Looking up, she was surprised to see that the place was packed. The restaurant was always busy, but the bar was never usually this full, not on a work night anyway. Then her eyes went wide as the room erupted, her name roaring through the air as the crowd surged forward. The crowd wasn't a crowd at all; it was every friend Stella and Lucy had in Cape Town.

'Congratulations, Stel, I'm so proud of you …!' Lucy said, appearing out of the crowd and swooping in to give her a bear hug, shrieking excitedly over the noise of the room. 'Why didn't you call and tell me? I knew you'd get it. It was just a matter of time. You earned every inch of that promotion, Stel. And it's such great timing because now we can celebrate our promotions together!'

'I'm sorry, I … I …' Stella stuttered, but the rest of the crowd was all over her and she didn't get a chance to say anything else to Lucy before she was swept away. Jen and Gav, Sam and Sean, Teresa and Stef, Tamara and Paul; everyone was there. She was passed through the crowd by her friends, kissing and hugging everyone as she went and being patted on the back; the room was full of congratulations. She saw Amanda and Gavin, Chryssa and Joe, Karin and Shaun, Kathi and Schalk – everyone was there, waving, shouting, drinking, cheering and chatting. Stella felt completely overwhelmed. Max and Lucy must have set this up, she thought. She wondered how they'd managed to pull it all off at such short notice.

Somewhere a champagne cork popped and seconds later someone thrust a glass of bubbly into her clammy palm. How could this be happening? Stella wondered. How had everything gotten so completely out of control so quickly? She could manage coming clean to Max about her lie, and maybe even to Lucy, but this was a catastrophe. How was she going to explain to a room full of their closest friends that not only was she still an un-promoted agony aunty, but she was now also a massive liar.

Stella started to feel unbearably hot. She stood on her tiptoes and tried to find Max in the crowd. She had to follow her plan and tell him the truth immediately so he could put an end to all of this madness, call it all off and send everybody home. But she couldn't see him anywhere in the sea of people.

'Are you okay?' Lucy asked, grabbing her elbow. 'You look a little pale.'

'No, no, fine,' Stella lied. 'I just got a shock, that's all. This was totally unexpected.'

'I know, isn't it amazing?' Lucy said. 'Max called me after you told him about your promotion this morning. He said I should come meet you guys here tonight for drinks to celebrate both our promotions. But I thought it was the perfect opportunity to have a party, so I got on the phone straight away. You know me – I love a party!'

'Congratulations, Stella,' a voice boomed. For the first time that evening Stella noticed Jake, standing next to Lucy. Still so tall and still so handsome. He was wearing jeans and a close-fitting brown leather jacket, which enhanced, well, just about everything. Jake leaned forward and pecked Stella on her cheek, then flicked his hair out of his eyes boyishly.

Stella felt her tongue go thick in her mouth and a hot blush spread across her cheeks as the memory of watching him and Lucy in the guest bathroom at her parents' house flooded her mind.

'There's so much to celebrate,' Jake said, pulling Lucy towards him and putting his arm around her affectionately. 'It's so cool that you both got promoted at the same time. Although I must say I'll be very sad to see you leave Dr Dee behind. I love your column, I always read it.'

Stella wiped her hands down her dress to try and dry them off, then she pasted a big plastic smile on her face. 'Lucy, come with me,' she whispered, nodding to Jake apologetically as she dragged her twin towards the stairs that led down to the bathroom. 'Where's Max?' she hissed.

'He's here somewhere,' Lucy said, straining to try catch a glimpse of him in amongst the crowd. 'We've got another surprise; he's probably busy with that.'

Oh no! Stella thought, not another surprise, she was barely coping with this one.

Locked safely in the small downstairs bathroom with Lucy, Stella tried to pull herself together. She had to stop this craziness somehow. She had to tell someone. It was all spiralling horribly out of control. She had to confess what she'd done. Otherwise it was going to go on and on and on. She took a deep breath. 'Luce ...'

'I know … Isn't he amazing?' Lucy said, facing the mirror and freshening up her lipstick. 'I still can't get over how hot he is. Sometimes I can't believe that I actually get to be with him.'

Stella turned and stood next to Lucy. With both of them facing into the mirror there were now four of the same person standing in the bathroom. Stella stared at their repeated images and nodded numbly. 'Yeah, Luce, he really is something. But listen …'

'He's definitely my favourite so far, Stel. I think he's a keeper,' Lucy said, interrupting her.

'Oh, Lucy, you always say that about your new boyfriends,' Stella said, trying to blot some of the sweat off her face with a tissue and rescue her make-up. 'Until you get tired of them and move on to the next rock star, or mountaineer, or multimillionaire winemaker, or whatever big fish you manage to hook next.'

'No, Stel, I'm telling you, this one's different. We can't keep our hands off each other. It's like he's determined to have sex with me everywhere on planet earth. We've done it in every room at my place and his, and I mean every single room. We've even done it in bathrooms and in restaurants and once at the movies.'

'I know, I've seen,' Stella said, her cheeks burning for the second time that evening. 'I mean, I'm just saying, I've seen him. I mean, he doesn't take his hands off you for a second.'

'And he's funny too,' Lucy continued. 'Can you believe it: great in bed, hot and funny? It's the trifecta. It's like finding a unicorn. I'm telling you, I've finally hit the jackpot. He might just be the one, Stel.'

Stella felt the all too familiar pang of jealousy. She looked at their reflections in the mirror again. Identical in every way, but somehow Lucy had always managed to be the prettier of the two, by far. Stella eyed her twin, wondering how it was possible. They both had the same thick auburn hair that came down to the middle of their backs. All three of their other sisters and their mom had thin, dead-straight hair, but Stella and Lucy's had always been naturally wavy, just short of curly. They both had big brown eyes, flecked with green, and full lips, which Lucy knew just how to draw into the perfect sexy pout. And both girls had weighed exactly the same their entire lives, to within a kilo or two of each other. So how was it that

Lucy always seemed so much thinner, so much more glamorous?

There was a knock on the bathroom door.

'Stel, Luce, are you two in there?' It was one of their friends, Jen. 'Max told me to come get you. You've got to come up – they're ready with the surprise.'

Stella looked at Lucy with a panicked look on her face. 'Luce, I have to tell you something,' Stella said, taking a deep breath. 'Oh, my goodness, this is a disaster …'

'Come on, you can tell me later,' Lucy said, unlocking the bathroom door and pulling at Stella's arm. 'This is our party, to celebrate our success; we can't spend the whole night locked in the bathroom, what would our fans say?' She grinned. 'And anyway, you've got to see this.'

Up in the bar the crowd had gotten louder and the atmosphere more festive, and Stella heard more corks popping. Suddenly the lights dimmed and Max appeared from the darkness at the back of the restaurant holding a large silver tray. Stella did a double take. Max was carrying one of the biggest cakes she'd ever seen, the surface of it covered with dozens of long, tapered, flickering candles that lit up the room. Each of them was easily double the length of a normal candle.

The crowd cheered and clapped as Max crossed the bar carrying the cake and came to a halt between Stella and Lucy, his eyes shiny with pride and excitement. Stella looked at the cake in horror. What had she done? What was she going to do? How was she going to get out of this now?

Shouts of 'Speech! Speech! Speech!' rang in Stella's ears as Max stepped up onto a big, sturdy-looking coffee table in the centre of the room, still carefully balancing the cake in his arms, before holding it up high so everyone in the bar could see it. Stella covered her mouth with her hand, unable to believe what was happening and powerless to do anything to stop it.

'Stella de Villiers and Lucy Frankel,' Max said as the crowd hushed. 'My beautiful wife and her wonderful twin sister, we all wanted to get together tonight to wish you both congratulations on your promotions. I'm so very, very proud …'

The rest of his words washed over Stella as she looked out at the large group of friends who surrounded them. The world slowed down; Max's voice distorting in her ears. She would have to tell them all now, she thought as Lucy clutched her hand and squeezed it tightly. She had thought she would be able to get away with nipping the lie in the bud and telling Max before things got out of control, but she didn't have that luxury any more. And it seemed that the longer she left it, the worse the damage would be and the harder it would be to unpick the deceit she had sown.

Maybe, she thought as Max droned on somewhere just above her, everyone would see the funny side and just have a piece of cake and a laugh and celebrate Lucy's success. These were people who loved her, she rationalised, and they were all on her side. Of course they would understand. She really didn't want to ruin the celebration, but she also couldn't keep the secret in any longer, it was just so wrong. And surely people would find out eventually anyway, and then it would be even more humiliating.

Taking a deep breath, Stella let go of Lucy's hand and stepped up onto the table next to Max and into the circle of light thrown by the candles on the cake. Looking around at all her amazing friends she felt absolutely terrified, but she knew it would be like ripping off a plaster. It would hurt at first, but then everything would go back to normal, just as soon as she came clean.

Suddenly she felt a drop of water land on her cheek. Reaching up she touched it with a finger, wondering if she was crying. She didn't feel like she was crying. Then there was another drop and another. Confused, Stella looked up towards the ceiling, and that was when the skies opened. Water rained down on her like she was in the middle of a tropical storm as around her people started to scream, taken completely by surprise by the sudden deluge.

Stella looked over at Max, who was still holding the cake with both hands and staring up at the ceiling, obviously completely confounded. It was only then that it dawned on her what had happened. Max had been standing on the coffee table, holding an enormous cake full of candles directly below one of the bar's smoke detectors. The smoke from all the candles must have set off the automatic sprinkler system in the bar and restaurant and now it was raining inside La Perla.

As Stella ran her hands through her now wet hair in shock she heard the people around them shrieking as they grabbed their things and raced for the door, where they bottlenecked in their haste to get out of the bar. Looking back into the restaurant she took in the empty tables and chairs, the abandoned food slowly drowning in water, but somehow it was as if it was all happening in slow motion, as if it wasn't really happening at all. Then she felt Max's hand grabbing hers – he had climbed down, abandoning the cake, and was trying to help her off the coffee table – and she knew that it was really real, her chance to say what she needed to say had gone.

Out on the street groups of excited, drenched people were standing around in clumps on the pavement – pointing at each other's running make-up and ruined hairdos and taking photos of each other with their cellphones to post on Facebook. A South Easter, straight off the ocean, whipped around them and Stella's teeth chattered, partly from the cold, partly from shock and partly from panic.

One by one their bedraggled friends said their goodbyes, congratulating them both one last time before they disappeared off to their cars, hooting with laughter. Stella pasted a fake smile on her face as she and Max and Lucy and Jake thanked everyone for coming and apologised for the downpour. Until finally it was just the four of them left standing, dripping on the pavement outside the restaurant.

Lucy pecked Stella on the cheek with a laugh. 'All right, babe,' she said. 'Play delayed due to rain. But we'll pick this celebration up on the weekend, okay? At least nobody will ever forget the day we got promoted, eh. Your face when it started raining was priceless!'

'Wait ... Lucy, Max, Jake,' Stella said. 'I need to tell you all ... I need to tell you all something ... Well, first I can't begin to tell you how grateful I am that you guys planned this whole thing, and at such short notice. I mean, I just can't believe it, but I have to tell you guys something else ...'

'It was mostly your sister,' Max said. 'She absolutely insisted we needed a party to celebrate. All I really did was pitch up.'

'All right, I'm drowning over here,' Lucy said, laughing and waving off the compliment. 'Let's go, babe,' she said to Jake.

Jake and Max shook hands, Lucy gave Stella a hug, and Stella watched helplessly as they walked up the street towards Jake's car, holding hands.

Stella raised her hand to call them back, but it was too late, they were gone. She dropped her hand down to her side and sighed deeply.

'What's wrong, Stel?' Max asked her, looking into her miserable face. 'Why the long face?'

'Max, I am so, so sorry!' Stella said, dissolving into a pile of tears.

'Don't be silly, babe. There's nothing to be sorry about. It's not your fault. I set off those blimming sprinklers! I suppose I shouldn't have held the cake up so high. And we probably could have done with fewer candles. But you know Lucy, she doesn't just do candles, she does über candles!' He laughed. 'Did you at least get to see the cake before it got waterlogged? She got it from Charly's Bakery; it was a work of art!'

'I can't believe you guys organised all of that,' Stella said. 'You really didn't have to, you know.'

'What are you talking about, babe? Of course we did. It's not every day that you both get promoted. I'm so proud of you, Stel,' he said, squeezing her tightly. 'You've been working towards that promotion for ages, and you really deserve it. Anyway, like I said, Lucy did everything. All I did was rock up, and then set off the sprinklers.'

Stella nodded and then opened her mouth to tell him the truth. Then closed it. Then she opened it again and took a deep breath. 'Max …' she said. 'I …'

He laughed and pushed a damp strand of hair that was stuck to her cheek out of her face. 'Like I said, you really don't need to thank me, Stel. We did it because we love you. Come on, let's go home, we might still make the end of *CSI.*' Max grabbed her by the hand. 'Hey,' he said as he walked her to her car, 'is there any stir-fry left? I'm starving.'

Stella hung her head in shame. She needed to speak up, and soon. They had come in separate cars, so she couldn't tell Max on the drive home, but she would tell him as soon as they got home, she resolved. Or maybe she would wait until after she'd made them both a cup of tea and they were sitting together on the couch, then she would tell him everything.

POPPY

An old man and woman were sitting in the front seats of the station wagon. Poppy figured that they must have been somewhere in their seventies. He was balding and clean shaven with a small neat head, like a pin. In contrast, his wife had an enormous purple hairdo which was so high it brushed the roof of the car, making Poppy think of Marge from *The Simpsons*.

The two old folks both craned around and eyed Poppy and Buck from their positions in the front of the car. Poppy smoothed her hair and planted a sweet, unthreatening smile on her face, attempting to look as respectable as someone with luminous pink hair and a stud in her nose can look to a pair of old folks. 'Hello, Sir, Ma'am,' she said politely. 'Thanks so much for stopping for us; we've been out there waiting for a ride forever. I'm Poppy, and this is Buck.' She slapped Buck lightly on the shoulder. He smiled cheerily and waved.

'I'm George, and this is my wife Chrissy,' the man said, indicating his wife, who also smiled and nodded. 'Where y'all headed?' he asked.

'Wherever you're going will suit us just fine, thank you,' Poppy said.

'Best we get going, George, if we want to make good time,' Chrissy said in a bossy, high-pitched voice.

George nodded and turned to face the road again, easing the station wagon back out onto the highway.

'Sooo, where y'all from,' Chrissy asked, her thick American accent bending its way around the words.

'We're from South Africa,' Poppy said. 'Cape Town, actually.'

'Ooh, we ain't never met no one from Africa before, have we, George?' Chrissy remarked loudly, clapping her hands together, while George shook his head vigorously, easing the car up to a sluggish thirty miles an hour.

'We're from Dickinson, North Dakota, George and me,' she continued. 'That's about nine hours' drive that-a-way, as the crow flies,' she added, pointing in the opposite direction.

'So, where are we headed today, Chrissy?' Buck asked jovially.

'Darwin, Minnesota,' she replied proudly, nodding to herself at the truth of this statement.

'Sounds like as good a place as any,' Buck said, leaning back and closing his eyes, settling in for the ride.

'So are you two boyfriend and girlfriend then?' Chrissy asked, eyeing Poppy's finger, searching for a wedding ring.

'No way!' Poppy said just a little too loudly. 'We're just friends. You know, best friends, travelling together.'

'Oh,' Chrissy said, her voice laden with disappointment, but she still didn't turn away. Instead she continued to stare at the two of them as if they were exhibits in a zoo. Finally, she scrunched her nose up in thought and said, 'You know, I thought all African people were black. Didn't you, George?'

'I sure did,' George said, both hands gripping the steering wheel tightly as the needle on the speedometer nudged a dangerously slow thirty-six miles an hour.

'Nope,' Poppy said, plastering a tolerant smile on her face as an enormous truck sped past outside her window. 'A lot of people in Africa are black, but not everyone is, there are lots of white people too. And anyway, we're from South Africa, which is quite different to Africa itself.'

Poppy wasn't altogether surprised by Chrissy's naivety; it wasn't the first time that they'd encountered Americans who were ignorant about Africa. In fact, she was rather impressed, just about everyone else had confused South Africa with South Australia. At least these two had managed the right continent.

Chrissy nodded, seemingly satisfied with Poppy's brief explanation and smiled politely. 'Oh, I see,' she said. 'Well, George and I have never actually been outside of the U S of A. We did go to New Mexico once, and I have a friend who lives in Canada, but I've never actually been there.'

'Oh, that's interesting,' Poppy said, trying hard to remain polite and look interested. 'New Mexico must have been nice?'

'I don't know so much,' Chrissy said. 'We went down there with some Rotarians. But it wasn't really our cup of tea, hey, George?'

George shook his head.

'Just so many Hispanic people everywhere,' she continued, shaking her head and tutting.

Poppy couldn't think of any response to Chrissy's blatant racism, so she just kept the smile pasted on her face and nodded. Without any kind of real response from Poppy and none seemingly forthcoming from Buck, the conversation petered out and Chrissy shrugged her shoulders. Then she turned around and faced forward, finally settling into her seat.

Relieved that the excruciating small talk had come to an end, Poppy stretched out and made herself comfortable. She knew how lucky they were to have been picked up by a station wagon, even if the owners were racist bigots. One of the rides they'd picked up some days earlier had been a Mini and that had been unbearable. Buck was over six feet tall and their backpacks also took up a lot of room, so the station wagon was quite a luxury.

Poppy and Buck had been attempting to hitch-hike their way around America for the last few months, but it wasn't as easy as they had imagined it would be. It turned out that Middle America wasn't quite ready to pull over in their expensive cars and pick up two perfect strangers, one a freakishly tall ladder and the other with bright pink hair and a stud in her nose.

Poppy was just starting to feel settled, enjoying the endless view of wheat fields racing past her window when something wafted past her nose. She breathed in, sampling it cautiously and then scrunched up her face. The smell was vile. She looked out of the window, to see if they were driving past any factories or abattoirs, but they really were in the middle of nowhere. Cornfields lined either side of the road as far as the eye could see. She looked over at Buck, who was also sniffing the air curiously. Soon the smell passed and Poppy leaned her head up against the closed window again and shut her eyes.

Minutes later the smell flooded the car again. Only this time it was ten times stronger. Rotten egg, mixed in with manure, mixed in with what she could only imagine startled skunk might smell like. It was rank. It was foul. It was downright disgusting. Poppy looked cautiously towards the front of the car, but George and Chrissy didn't seem to have noticed anything. In fact, Chrissy was smiling and swaying her head and humming loudly to the country music that was playing on the radio.

Poppy covered her nose with her hand and looked over at Buck with wide horrified eyes. Did you fart? She mouthed at him in horror.

What? No! Buck mouthed back, his eyes bulging as he covered his face. 'You think I smell like that?' he whispered. Then he pointed subtly to the back of George's seat.

Poppy had to look away, terrified she would burst out in an uncontrollable fit of hysterical laughter if she caught Buck's eye.

Buck rolled his window down and hung his head out of it like a puppy, panting as the car filled with more of George's noxious gases.

Poppy rolled down her window as well, hoping to hell that Darwin, Minnesota wasn't very far away.

STELLA

The morning after the night it rained inside La Perla, Stella sat at her desk, shuffling through a dozen work letters that she urgently needed to get to. She was starting to fall behind schedule, which wasn't like her at all. But she had so much on her mind that she couldn't concentrate. She felt miserable. She hadn't managed to tell Max about what she'd come to think of as The Big Misunderstanding yet. She'd planned to do it in at least a dozen different pauses in their conversation after they'd arrived home from La Perla, but the timing had never been right and when it had been right, she'd chickened out.

Arriving back at their flat the night before they'd first dried off, then Stella had made them tea and opened a box of chocolate digestives. After that they'd settled on the couch and Stella had watched as Max single-handedly worked his way through three quarters of the box of biscuits before falling asleep with crumbs all the way down the front of his shirt. And now it was the following morning and they'd had coffee and breakfast together, and then gotten ready for work together, and she still hadn't come clean. The lie was now almost twenty-four hours old. And the longer she left it the harder it was getting to tell the truth. Inch by inch, Stella was slowly losing her nerve.

Stella poked ambivalently through the letters she needed to get to. She usually liked to keep them neat and organised so that she could meet her strict daily schedule. Not only did she have the weekly column, which was usually two or three letters and her responses, but she also uploaded a handful of letters onto the magazine's website every day. So, each morning, once she'd sifted through all the letters and weeded out the unprintable, the overly bizarre, the smutty and the hoaxes, she would make her selection for the website from the day's mail. Her only rule was that the letters she published needed to cover a variety of topics – she didn't like it if the subject matter overlapped. Once her selections were made, answered and uploaded, Stella would then get to work answering the rest of the letters – it was part of her job to respond to every single letter that crossed her desk, whether she published them or not.

Stella often thought about the kind of people who wrote in to a column like hers. Most of them seemed massively undereducated and Stella felt kind of sorry for them. They clearly had nobody else to turn to, nobody else to ask even the simplest of questions. Things that one would ordinarily rely on a mother or father, sister or brother, or even a school teacher to advise you on. Over the last two years Stella had been horrified at the lack of sexual awareness she had encountered in her fellow South Africans. Many of them didn't seem to know their asses from their elbows, quite literally.

In the beginning Stella had to run the responses she wanted to publish past the overworked features editor, Cath, but after the first couple of months Cath had blown Stella off, saying she already had way too much on her plate to deal with a handful of silly letters. The problem, Stella had concluded early on, was that her column simply couldn't be categorised – it wasn't editorial, politics, fashion or celebrity gossip. Stella was an island with a population of one. So she worked autonomously within the magazine, with free rein over which letters she answered in her column, and what she uploaded to the magazine's website every day.

At first the letters had been slow to trickle in and on some days early on she'd had to create a few of her own as filler, but as the column picked up speed and popularity the pile of letters had grown steadily, and now she struggled to get her responses off to absolutely everyone. The editor was happy because the column was popular, but also because it didn't create any extra work for her, and so Stella was by and large left to her own devices.

And that had been fine when Stella had thought that Dr Dee was a means to an end, and that if she just hung in there she'd be next in line for a job in editorial. But after her conversation with Denise the day before, she now felt like there really was no end in sight; it seemed like she was destined to be Dr Dee forever. Her nightmare had come true. She couldn't leave the magazine – who would hire her? She had no experience of doing anything other than the Dr Dee column. And now she had the added humiliation of having to tell everyone she knew that while Lucy had actually been promoted, she hadn't, and that it had all been a big, fat lie. She wasn't sure what was worse, the fact that she hadn't been promoted, or even come close to being promoted, or the fact that everybody, including her husband, believed that she had. Stella chewed on her lip and shuffled through the letters grudgingly, looking for a handful that she could use for the website.

'Hey, Dee?'

Stella looked up. It was Yolanda, the new features writer, standing at the edge of her cubicle in another even more stylish designer dress.

Stella shuddered. 'It's Stella, actually,' she said. 'The column is called Dr Dee, but my real name is Stella.'

'Oh, sorry,' Yolanda said, covering her mouth with her hand in faux embarrassment. 'Do you know where I can find more paper for the stat machine?'

Stella followed Yolanda to the photostat machine and dug in the cupboard next to it for the spare paper. She held out a ream over to Yolanda.

'You wouldn't be a honey and do it for me, would you?' Yolanda said. 'It's just I've never used this machine before, and I only just had my nails done, and you know … I really don't want to ruin them.'

Stella blushed and tried to curl her unglamorous fingers – which were unpolished and unevenly bitten to the quick – around the ream of paper, to hide them. 'Sure, sure,' she said overenthusiastically, tearing open the ream. 'So what's your first project then?' she asked, trying hard to keep her voice even as she stacked the paper into the machine.

'I'm working on a feature piece on serial divorcees. It's fascinating really. You know, some of these women have had six husbands. It's like a full time job for them. And why not, it seems to pay well enough.'

'Wow, that sounds cool,' Stella said blandly. 'There you go.' She shoved the drawer closed and the machine beeped its appreciation.

'Thanks a mill, Dee,' Yolanda said, holding her hands in front of her as if she was praying and bowing slightly, before turning and getting to work at the stat machine.

This time Stella didn't even bother to correct her. This had to be one of the most unfair weeks of her life, she thought as she returned to her desk. That was her job. She should be the one writing about serial divorcees and photostatting interesting things, not answering letters from freaks. Stella shuffled angrily back through the letters and eventually randomly selected the third one from the top.

Dear Dr Dee,

I have a really strange question to ask. And I have no one to turn to. I asked my pastor, but he simply recommended prayer, and that doesn't seem to be working, so I'm turning to you, my last hope.

Would you be able to tell me why it is that my girlfriend always laughs during intercourse, usually after I ejaculate?

When I ask her why she does it she says it's nothing and that I shouldn't worry about it. Is this normal? Should I be worried? I can't help but take it personally.

No Laughing Matter

Stella typed the letter into her computer and then whipped up her first response.

Dear Weeny Winky,

Your penis is obviously tiny and soft, and you are tickling your partner on the inside with it during sex – that's why she is laughing.

Chin up, mate, it could be worse, she could be crying. Or, even worse, yawning.

Love, Dr Dee

Stella deleted the fake letter immediately. Even the faux response could do nothing to dull the miserable mood that had settled over her after the events of the last few days. She was just totally unequipped to deal with this kind of question. How could she answer questions about sex when she herself had never even had an orgasm?

Moping over to the office kitchen, careful to avoid Yolanda or any of the other editorial staff, Stella poured herself a fresh cup of coffee. She looked into it and then poured the steaming cup down the sink and made herself a cup of herbal tea instead. She hated herself and she needed to change. She needed to drink less coffee, be healthier, eat better, exercise more and lie less. She traipsed back to her desk with her tea and typed up her real response, with her mouth turned down at the corners.

Dear No Laughing Matter,

People are all different, and we really do all express our sexual enjoyment in a whole range of different ways. While I don't believe there is such a thing as 'normal' behaviour, laughter after climax does fall well within the range of different behaviours that people have been known to express during intercourse.

Other expressions commonly include crying, sighing, swearing and even a hearty praising of the Lord. These behaviours are quite natural after-effects of the sexual act. And you may find that it's an entirely involuntary response, and your partner possibly doesn't even realise she's doing it at the time.

That being said, it is important that you feel comfortable with your lover, particularly if you'd like to make this a long-term relationship. So if her reaction causes you concern, I suggest you try talking to her. Perhaps you can come up with a new after-climax response together. It could even be a tool for bonding, which could ultimately bring you that much closer together.

Love, Dr Dee

Satisfied with her response Stella paged through a few other letters. When she came to a query about anal sex she studied it with part horror, part disgust and part fascination.

Dear Dr Dee,

My wife and I have been happily married for almost four years. We recently started discussing the possibility of having anal sex for the first time. It's something we think we might like to try out, just to keep the relationship exciting.

We were wondering if you could advise us on the best way to go about it.

Many thanks,
First Timers

For the hundred squillionth time Stella shuddered and wondered how she'd gotten herself into this situation. On a planet populated by hundreds of millions of people she was the least equipped person for this job. Not only was there the orgasm issue, but she'd also never had anal sex, or a threesome, and she wasn't even the biggest fan of the blow job, although she would indulge Max on special occasions – needless to say he never forgot a birthday or an anniversary. Stella was way out of her depth here. Just about anybody else would be better suited to answering all these icky letters. Someone more experienced. Someone like anyone other than her. She picked up the phone and dialled Lucy.

'Hey, babe,' Lucy said, picking up on the second ring. 'Last night was crazy, hey?'

'Thanks so much again for pulling it all together like that,' Stella said. 'Max said you planned the whole thing, and that cake … It was really something.'

'I know, cool, hey?'

'I'm just sorry about the water and everything …' Stella trailed off.

'Please, don't be, I thought it was awesome! I'm going to go down in history for throwing the world's most insane promotion party for us. People are going to be talking about the day we both got promoted for decades to come,' Lucy said proudly.

Stella gulped. She considered coming clean, but she didn't know where to begin. She couldn't just come out with it, especially not while Lucy was on such a high about the party and her own promotion. Stella couldn't rain on her parade like that. Lucy would be devastated, and not only that but she'd think Stella had done it out of jealousy. She decided it was something she was going to have to do in person, so she could explain the intricacies of what had really happened. 'Luce. Listen, I need to ask you something kind of strange, for work,' she said, quickly changing the subject.

'Okay, go for it,' Lucy said.

'All right … um … have you ever had anal sex?'

'Stella!' Lucy spluttered. 'What the fuck kind of question is that for a Thursday morning before I've even finished my coffee? And you know I work in open plan.'

'I know, I know, it's just that I got this Dr Dee letter about anal sex, from some freak, and I'm trying to answer it. I want to be honest with this guy, but what do I know? So I thought, you know … maybe you had, you know, done it?'

'Actually …' Lucy said.

Stella could hear the smile in Lucy's voice. 'Really?' Stella shrieked back, covering her eyes with her hand. 'You're crazy!'

'It's not that crazy,' Lucy said. 'With the right guy and the right lube, it can be quite nice.'

'Jeez, Luce, you never said anything!'

'Well, it's not the kind of thing you go around blabbing about, is it?' Lucy whispered into the phone.

'What about a ménage à trois?' Stella asked. 'Have you ever had one of those?'

'Well, of course,' Lucy said, 'hasn't everybody? Wait a second, Stel, how come you're still answering letters? What about the promotion to editorial?'

Stella gulped and her face burned. She'd briefly forgotten about her lie. That was the problem with lies. 'Oh, ja, that … yes …' she stuttered, foraging desperately for a decent excuse. 'It hasn't kicked in yet. Um … I have to wait till they find someone to replace me before it comes into effect, you know how it goes?'

'Well, it's not for much longer, just hang in there, Stel,' Lucy said. 'Listen, I've got to run, I've got a status meeting in ten and then lunch with a client.'

'Rough life for some!' Stella said sarcastically.

'Don't hate me just because I've got an expense account,' Lucy said smugly. 'Hey, maybe now that you're a fabulous features writer they'll give you one too. So that you can wine and dine important sources on groundbreaking stories.'

'Maybe,' Stella mumbled unenthusiastically.

'All right, laters, babe,' Lucy said. 'Mwah!'

As soon as Lucy hung up Stella put her head down on her desk and squeezed her eyes as tightly shut as she could. Then she kicked the leg of her desk hard. Why had she done that? What was she thinking? She'd just lied again, and this time to Lucy.

Opening her eyes, Stella looked down at the anal sex letter on her desk. She felt like such a loser. There was still so much she needed to do in her life. She pictured having a conversation about trying anal sex with Max and shook her head. That wouldn't happen in a million years. And as for a ménage à trois – an image of her and Max and Jake together on a bed floated in front of her eyes, making her blush – well, that was out of the question, it was going to be hard enough trying to start a conversation with him about orgasms. Shaking her head to clear her mind of the image, Stella made her way back to the kitchen where she dumped her herbal tea down the drain and filled the biggest mug she could find full to the brim with coffee. To hell with tea, she thought, this day required strong coffee, and lots of it.

Back at her desk Stella sat down and reached for her computer mouse, shaking it to bring her monitor out of its screensaver, which was a picture of her and Max on their wedding day. Opening Internet Explorer she went to Google and typed the words *anal sex* into the search engine. Nervously she looked up over her cubicle to make sure nobody was around; she would be mortified if somebody saw what she was Googling, even though it was obviously research for her column.

The results of her search scrolled down the screen, all forty-eight thousand of them. She leaned in closer to her monitor, deep in nervous concentration, studying her options. Stella clicked on the link fourth from the top, and took a sip of her coffee while she waited for the page to load. The liquid was too hot to drink, so she blew on it and then put the mug back down on her desk. Suddenly a series of graphic pictures popped up on her screen. Stella's eyes almost exploded out of her head. She'd never really looked at porn before and it was shocking and terrifying at the same time. Her face flushed a burning red as she took in the mass of intertwined arms, legs and other body parts in front of her. Revolted and fascinated in equal measure she turned her head sideways to try and figure out the configuration of people, to better understand what it was they were doing.

Suddenly Stella's cellphone beeped loudly, shocking her back into reality, giving her such a fright that she instantly jerked her hand out to grab at her mouse so that she could close the offending web page. But instead of her mouse her hand met her full cup of hot coffee, knocking it over, the boiling liquid splashing right across her desk and up onto her shirt and into her lap. Cursing loudly, Stella leapt up, pulling her blouse away from her skin to stop the boiling liquid from scalding her chest further, while with her other hand she lifted her keyboard up and shook the coffee out of it. 'Darn, darn, darn!' Stella yelped, her chest burning.

Once she'd managed to mop up most of the mess with an entire roll of toilet paper, shut down her computer and balanced her keyboard upside down to drain it off, Stella slumped back into her chair, her soggy blouse sticking to her chest. She shook her head and sighed deeply. Then she reached for her cellphone. It was an SMS from Lucy:

Client just cancelled. Want 2 have lunch w me? Table booked at Bistro in Sea Point. SMS if u can't make it, otherwise c u there at 1:30. L XXX

Stella sighed, well, at least the day wasn't a complete disaster, this was her chance to make things right with Lucy. She could tell her everything face to face, at lunch. It was the perfect opportunity. It was time for Stella de Villiers to tell the truth. It was now or never.

Stella drove down Sea Point Main Road until she saw the gaudy orange sign for Bistro. She'd never been there before, but she knew from what Lucy had said about it recently that it was the funky new spot in town. Stella parked her car and made her way inside.

'Rough day?' the annoyingly good-looking hostess asked as she welcomed Stella into the restaurant, nodding at the large brown coffee stain that covered the front of Stella's blouse.

'Rough week,' Stella replied, pulling her cardigan closed over her stained blouse and standing on tiptoes to try catch a glimpse of Lucy across the crowded restaurant.

'Do you have a reservation?'

'Um, no. Well, yes,' Stella said. 'I'm supposed to meet my sister here. Lucy Frankel. The reservation will be under her name.'

'Ah, yes, Ms Frankel,' the hostess purred. 'She's not here yet, would you like to wait for her at the bar?'

'Sure, yes, that's fine,' Stella said.

Stella followed the petite hostess through the restaurant to a bar area off to the side. Enormous chandeliers hung from the ceiling over roomy velvet booths, and Stella wondered silently how much the decor had cost as the hostess motioned towards an empty bar stool at the far end of an enormous wooden bar.

Stella clambered onto the bar stool as the hostess disappeared back to her position at the door and tried to focus on what she was going to say to Lucy. She checked her phone. It was twenty past one. She was a little early. She had ten minutes to figure out how to confess to her sister. She would have to do it immediately, Stella thought. She couldn't wait. She had waited too long already. It had to be the very first thing out of her mouth, otherwise she knew she would chicken out again.

'Hi, can I get you a drink?' a voice asked from above her.

Stella looked up into the eyes of the barman. Because the floor behind the bar was raised he seemed to loom over her. It was a little intimidating.

'Um ...' Stella said, feeling more than a little clueless. 'What do people usually drink here?'

The barman looked at her like she had two heads, then he turned and swept his arm across the back of the bar, indicating the rows of bottles lined up on display. 'Booze, usually,' he said.

Stella blushed. But maybe, she thought to herself, that was exactly what she needed. Maybe this day, with these problems, didn't need herbal tea or coffee. Maybe it needed alcohol. There was no question that she could do with a little bit of Dutch courage before she faced Lucy. She eyed the wide array of bottles on display behind the barman and realised that she had no idea what she wanted to drink – not being the kind of girl who usually found herself in a bar in the middle of the day during the week. This was a new experience for her. She hardly ever drank. When she and Max went out with friends she might have one or two glasses of champagne or wine. And at a braai she might sip on a shandy or a Savanna, but none of those options felt quite appropriate in this kind of situation.

'What I mean,' she said to the barman, still blushing slightly, 'is what would someone like me usually drink in a place like this, during the day?'

'Wine, maybe?' the barman said, looking at her uncertainly, obviously wondering if this was some kind of test.

'But it's the middle of the day!' Stella said, horrified. 'I don't think I can drink wine in the middle of the day.'

The barman looked at her strangely again and then looked around for some kind of escape or assistance. 'What about a Bacardi and Coke?' he asked. 'Some of the ladies who come in here drink that.'

'Bacardi, isn't that some kind of rum?' Stella asked.

The barman nodded.

'Okay,' Stella said, nodding her head and shrugging her shoulders. 'That sounds nice. Bring me one of those.'

Twenty minutes later Stella was halfway through her second Bacardi and Coke. It was actually quite nice, she thought as she took a long slug of the sweet drink. And what was more, she felt a lot less miserable and a lot more philosophical about her situation now than she had a drink and a half earlier. She had her whole speech planned in her head. All she needed now was for Lucy to hurry up and arrive, so that Stella could get it over with. Stella looked at her watch again, Lucy was ten minutes late. Stella would give her another ten minutes and then she'd try and call her. She was probably just running late, Stella decided. Lucy was always running late.

As soon as she'd confessed to Lucy, and they'd had a spot of lunch and hopefully a laugh over the whole misunderstanding, then she would go to the school where Max worked and come clean to him too. It wouldn't be that hard. He would understand and everything would be fine. Then she'd call each of her friends one by one and fill them in. Or perhaps she might email them instead of calling. Then she wouldn't have to act all cheery on the phone and they wouldn't have to pretend they didn't feel sorry for her. And once she'd done that, the entire debacle would be over and she could carry on with her life. She took another sip of her drink, realising she'd almost finished it. It didn't even taste like alcohol, it tasted like Coke, and it was delicious.

Then something else occurred to Stella. Maybe she could just pretend the promotion had fallen through, that they'd given it to her and then had to take it back. It was a recession after all; these things happened all the time. In fact, she thought, she could tell everyone that she wasn't even too upset about it, that she was just relieved and grateful to still have a job. Everybody knew how hard the industry had been hit. Or maybe she should just resign and tell everyone she'd decided she didn't want to be a journalist after all.

'Shit! Is that you? I haven't seen you in ages!' a voice boomed in Stella's ear, distracting her from her scheming. A man was standing next to her, and as she looked up at him, he leaned down and gave her a big hug.

Stella pulled back from him and studied him intently. He had a head full of dreadlocks, but the funky, cool ones, not the manky, rotten ones that you often saw. He was boyishly good looking in a retro kind of way and he had a bolt through the middle of one eyebrow, which just added to his overall funkiness.

'Hey, it's been like forever!' he said with enthusiasm, touching her gently on the shoulder.

Stella squinted and looked at him a little closer for any clues as to how she might know him. Perhaps he didn't have the dreads back when she knew him and that's why she didn't recognise him. No, she concluded, she definitely didn't know this guy from a bar of soap. He must have her confused with Lucy. It happened to both Stella and Lucy often – in supermarkets, in the traffic, at the gym. Perfect strangers would wave excitedly from a distance or come over to say 'hi', and immediately Stella would know they had the wrong identical twin.

The worst part was telling people that they had the wrong person, particularly the ones who didn't know they were one of a pair of twins. The usual response was generally disbelief and then embarrassment, closely followed by uneasiness and an awkward silence, and then, ultimately, a nervous laugh and an uncomfortable goodbye. Stella didn't think she could stomach it with this good-looking guy. Not today.

'Yeah, it has been absolutely ages, hasn't it?' Stella said, pasting a huge smile on her face and trying her hardest to channel Lucy. 'It's really lekker to see you again. So what have you been up to?'

'Ah, you know,' the dreadlocked guy said, 'a bit of this, a bit of that. Mainly trying to get my music off the ground. Also been doing a bit of graffiti and mural work on the side, you know, just to pay for spliff and rent.'

Stella nodded. He was probably one of Lucy's old friends from advertising college, she thought. 'So you're not doing the advertising thing any more?' she asked, taking a shot in the dark.

'Nah, it was fun while it lasted, but I wanted to do something a little more creative, you know, not be restrained by clients and crap like that. What about you?' he asked.

'Yeah, I'm still in advertising, it's a blast,' Stella said. 'In fact, I just got promoted.' She lifted her glass up in a mock toast and then drained what was left in it.

'Hey, that's fantastic, congratulations. Let me buy you a drink, to celebrate, and we can catch up!' he said, pointing to her empty glass. 'Or are you waiting for someone?'

Stella looked down at her phone. It was ten to two and there was still no sign of Lucy. It would be just like her to be over half an hour late, she thought. 'Sure, why not,' Stella said. It wouldn't hurt to have a bit of company while she waited, she decided. And it would be funny to see the dreadlocked guy's face when Lucy finally showed up. That would teach her not to leave Stella sitting at a bar all on her own. 'I'm just waiting for my sister; she's running late for a change.'

The guy beckoned for the barman while Stella embraced her inner Lucy. She wondered whether Lucy had ever slept with this guy, or if they'd just been friends. Knowing Lucy they'd probably slept together. Stella was repulsed by the thought, but also, simultaneously, kind of jealous.

'You know, you haven't changed a bit,' the guy slurred at her a couple of hours and several drinks later.

'You don't know the half of it,' Stella slurred back. 'All right ... um ... all right ... er ...' Stella trawled through her brain, hunting for his name, before finally realising that she still had absolutely no clue who he was. 'All right, dude,' she eventually managed, holding up her phone and trying to read the time on it by squinting her one eye shut. It was ten to four and Lucy still hadn't shown her face at the restaurant. Stella had tried to call her a couple of times but her phone had gone straight to voicemail. She clearly wasn't coming.

Besides feeling incredibly drunk, Stella also felt mildly irritated. How rude, she thought, but also how typically Lucy. She was always so unreliable. Something urgent had probably come up at work and Lucy must have forgotten about her entirely.

'I think I'd better get going, I can't believe it's almost four,' Stella drawled, slapping her hand down on the bar counter. 'Seriously, it's been awesome catching up.'

Outside on the street Stella shielded her eyes from the harsh sunlight. For some reason she had imagined it would be dark outside, which was ridiculous, considering it was still the middle of the afternoon. The dreadlocked guy followed her outside and watched her fumble around in her handbag, looking for her car keys. Unable to find them she crouched down and turned her handbag upside down onto the pavement. She watched with detached amusement as tampons and lip ice and the rest of the contents of her bag fell onto the ground between her feet. With a giggle she stirred her hand through the pile. 'Aha, gottem,' she said grabbing her keys in triumph.

Dreadlocked guy crouched down next to her, laughing, and helped her pick her things up and shove them back into her bag. Then he watched her stumble over to the nearest car and sway slightly as she tried to get the key in the door. Stella fumbled and dropped her keys with a clatter on the pavement. Bending down she picked them up again, but as she stood up she bumped her head on the car's wing mirror. Rubbing her head, she swayed a little, then laughed as she carried on trying to unlock the door.

'Jesus, Lucy, are you sure you're okay to drive, chick?' dreadlocked guy asked her, swaying slightly himself.

Stella looked up at him and then looked at the key in her hand and then at the car she'd been stabbing it into. 'Dude, this isn't even my car,' she said, bursting into hysterical giggles and slumping down onto the kerb.

'Lucy, I really don't think you should drive,' he said. 'And neither should I, I'm way over the limit. Is there anyone you can call to come and get you?'

'Yes, I think I'm drunker than I thought I was,' Stella slurred, nodding. 'I probably should have had something to eat. I think I'm going to walk to Lucy's flat. It's just a couple of blocks from here.' Stella waved her hand in the general direction of High Level Road.

The guy looked at her strangely. 'You mean your flat, Lucy?'

'Yeah, yeah …' Stella said, stumbling to her feet and brushing off her skirt. 'Her flat, my flat, the flat. Yeah, that's where I'm going – Lucy's flat. No problem. I mean, my flat. It's just up there.' She pointed up the street vaguely. 'It's been amazing seeing you again, um, dreadlocked dude. Really, really fun. We must do it again, okay? But let's not leave it so long next time.'

He kissed her on the cheek and waved at her as she tottered up the street, then he sat down on the pavement, shaking his head with a smile and reached into his pocket for his Rizlas and his cherry-flavoured tobacco.

Stella concentrated hard to try and get her bearings. Lucy lived in an apartment on High Level Road, which was just a couple of blocks up from Bistro. The walk would help sober her up, she thought.

As she walked Stella thought about her afternoon. She couldn't believe that Lucy had stood her up. She wanted to give her a piece of her mind, and, of course, she still had to tell her about the lie. And now she also needed to tell her about bumping into the dreadlocked guy. And maybe she'd also tell her about watching her and Jake have sex too, while she was about it. She would come completely clean about everything, she thought. She was all Dutch couraged up. Lucy would forgive her immediately, she decided – she had stood her up, after all; she owed Stella one. Taking a deep breath she pushed on drunkenly up the road.

POPPY

'But what's it for?' Poppy asked, staring up at it as she twirled the piercing in her nose distractedly.

'How should I know, Pops?' Buck said, shoving the brochure under her nose. 'See, it says here, it's the world's biggest ball of twine.'

'Well, I can see that, dummy, but I still don't understand what it's for.'

'Maybe if you've got a lot of packages to wrap or you want to play with a giant kitten,' Buck said.

Poppy took another step backwards to take it all in. The brochure wasn't lying; it certainly was the biggest ball of string Poppy had ever seen. Fat American tourists bustled around them, shouting loudly at each other in excitement and taking turns posing in front of the enormous ball of twine for photographs. George and Chrissy were in the middle of the excited fray.

Between George's gas and Chrissy's tuneless singing, the car trip, all three hours of it, had been torture. When they'd finally arrived in Darwin, Minnesota, home of The World's Biggest Ball of Twine, Poppy had practically fallen out of the car and kissed the ground. And then, when George and Chrissy had offered them a ride on the next leg of their trip Poppy had shouted 'Hell no!' so loudly that she'd even given herself a fright, having to quickly cover her mouth apologetically as if she wasn't responsible for her sudden case of Tourette's.

Poppy looked at Buck, who was standing next to her, reading the brochure. He finally had his colour back, but the memory of the gagging, nauseous, desperate, pleading, pathetic green look on his face an hour into the three hour drive had been priceless, she would never forget it.

'Whose idea was it to come here again?' Poppy asked.

'It was yours,' Buck shot back. 'If I recall, you said, "Let's both try and hitch-hike in different directions, and we'll go wherever the first car that stops takes us. It will be a fuck-off cool adventure!" Those were your exact words, I think you'll find.'

'Oh!' Poppy said, smiling sheepishly.

'Listen to this,' Buck said, preparing to read out loud to Poppy from the brochure. '"Francis A Johnson was a quiet man who spent his entire life in Meeker County. For reasons that are lost to time, he began rolling a ball of twine in 1950. Francis rolled twine for many hours a day, every day. Eventually, when it got too big to roll manually, he lifted it with a crane to continue proper wrapping. For thirty-nine years, this magnificent sphere evolved at Johnson's farm, before he finally moved it to a circular open-air shed on his front lawn." That's this,' Buck said, indicating the structure in front of them.

'Wow,' Poppy said, 'that's incredibly sad, don't you think? He never left here, never went anywhere other than this place.' She swept her arms to encompass the town, which really was a one-horse affair.

'Dude!' Buck shouted suddenly, smacking the brochure with the back of his hand. 'Check this out, Poppy! The world's largest beaver is in Fergus Falls, Minnesota. We're in Minnesota, aren't we? I wonder how far away Fergus Falls is?'

'Fuck off, Buck, we are not going to look at the world's largest anything, unless it's the world's largest bourbon,' Poppy said, punching her friend in the shoulder. 'Come on, let's get outta Dodge.'

STELLA

Stella had a spare key to Lucy's apartment on her key ring. It was an 'in case of emergencies' key. Lucy had Stella's key on her ring too. They had always been each other's 'in case of emergency' person.

Stella was sloppy drunk for the first time in her life. She was also starving and in need of a nap, so when she rang the buzzer at Lucy's flat and nobody answered, she let herself in. Standing in the entrance to the apartment Stella looked at her watch, squinting to see it in the singular. Then she covered one eye with her hand to try and get the hour hand to stop weaving. From what she could gather it was some time after four. She was pretty sure Lucy would only be home after five, when work ended, that was if she hadn't fallen off the planet completely. She was going to need a pretty good excuse to explain why she'd stood Stella up.

Stella loved Lucy's apartment. It was all high ceilings and wooden floors.

It was the kind of apartment Stella would have liked to have lived in, had she not moved straight out of her parents' house into a small but sensible starter apartment with Max. She walked down the passage from the front door, trailing the fingers of one hand along the wall to keep her balance. If you stood on a stool, looked out the front window and turned you head just so you could see the sea. Stella knew this because it had been the first thing they had done when Lucy moved in – the ad for the apartment had boasted 'sea views' and they had been determined to find them.

Living away from each other had been a challenge for both sisters. Growing up they'd always shared a bedroom. Stella on the right-hand side of the room with her yellow duvet and Lucy on the left-hand side of the bedroom with her pink duvet. So moving in with Max had been a major adjustment for both of them. Stella had only ever spent a handful of nights away from Lucy before she'd moved in with Max, just … how many hours was it now? Stella looked at her watch and squinted again, trying to do the maths, and realising in the process just how drunk she was.

Stella washed her face in Lucy's bathroom sink, but it didn't help, she still felt incredibly drunk. Next she wove her way into the kitchen. She needed some food to soak up some of the alcohol swimming around in her stomach. She was as famished as only an incredibly drunk person can be.

Stella opened the fridge, swaying slightly. She placed one arm along the top of the open door and used the other hand to steady herself on the other side of the open fridge, then she leaned forward, sticking her head right inside, enjoying the cool air on her burning cheeks.

She surveyed her options. There was a jar of mayonnaise and a jar of pickled cucumbers in the door of the fridge. The rest of the contents included a small heel of mouldy cheese, two Tupperwares with indeterminate contents, half a roasted chicken from Woolworths, a six pack of cider, two bottles of sparkling wine, some salad dressing and a six pack of beer. The fridge of an unmarried girl, Stella thought. She reached forward and drunkenly ripped a large piece of white meat off the chicken carcass and shoved it into her mouth.

As she chewed, Stella heard a key slipping into the front door lock. The door handle squeaked and then a voice said: 'Lucy, babe, it's me, you home?'

Stella recognised Jake's voice instantly; Lucy must have given him a key too. Stella froze on the spot, her head still shoved in the fridge, too drunk and too scared to move, her mouth too full to speak. She heard Jake's footsteps get louder as he walked down the passage, coming ever closer and eventually entering the kitchen. She closed her eyes, some warped part of her brain thinking that if her eyes were closed and she didn't see him, perhaps he wouldn't be able to see her either.

Seconds later she felt Jake come up close behind her, his hands on her hips, one on either side. She chewed the enormous chunk of chicken in her mouth and swallowed it practically whole, feeling it clunk its way awkwardly down her throat.

'Hey, anything good to eat?' he asked her, his voice lyrical and sultry. 'Oh, yes, look, I believe there is,' he continued, a smile in his voice as he kissed her neck and ran his hands around her waist, slipping one of them under the front of her coffee-stained blouse and trailing it upwards.

His fingers were warm and soft, and Stella sucked in a breath. She could feel him pressed up closely behind her. Standing up sharply, she tried to speak, but no words came out. Her back was pressing right up against his chest, his one arm wrapped around her waist while his other hand worked its way under the fabric of her bra.

Stella's breath caught in her throat as his fingers brushed her nipple. She couldn't move. She couldn't think. She couldn't breathe. She should stop him. She knew she should say something, but what? She couldn't think of anything suitable for this kind of situation. It had all happened so fast. Just a nanosecond earlier she had been alone in Lucy's kitchen shoving half a chicken into her mouth. She opened her mouth to speak but still nothing came out except a small whimper. She stared into the fridge, focusing on the jar of mayonnaise, then cleared her throat, preparing to speak again. But before she could get a choked word out she felt his lips on her neck again. Goosebumps raged across Stella's skin. The sensation was unbelievable; the heat of his unfamiliar body pressed against hers, mixed with the cool coming from the still open fridge. Stella felt like she was in the middle of a dream that she couldn't wake up from.

Jake was incredibly strong and completely in control. In one smooth move he turned her around so she was facing him and her back was up against the open fridge, covering her mouth with his, kissing her passionately. Stella's eyes were wide open but she noticed that his were tightly closed; she could tell how turned on he was, his face was intent.

Open your eyes, Jake! She wanted to shout, but then she realised, even with his eyes open he would still only see Lucy standing in front of him, instead of who she really was: Stella the fraud. Stella the liar.

Within seconds Jake had run both his hands under her bum. He lifted her up and swung her around effortlessly, as if she weighed nothing. Then he balanced her on the edge of the kitchen table, swiping the wire fruit bowl full of apples and lemons off the counter so they tumbled to the ground. Stella turned her head to the side and watched the green and yellow orbs roll across the wooden kitchen floor in slow motion. 'Jake!' she said urgently, her voice suddenly coming back to her, but only in half a whisper, cracking and shaking.

'Lucy,' he groaned, running his flat hand forcefully up the middle of her chest, pushing her back till she was lying spreadeagled on the table. Lifting one of her legs up onto his shoulder he bent down into her crotch, nuzzling and gently biting her inner thigh before slipping his fingers beneath the elastic of her panties, teasing her. Stella gasped, wondering how something that was so bad could feel so amazing.

'Jake!' she shouted again, her voice rising in pitch, suddenly clear and strong. She needed to sit up, but she couldn't. She knew she needed to rectify the situation which had somehow spiralled out of control.

But Jake must have mistaken her shout in the heat of the moment for amorous encouragement because seconds later the buttons of her stained blouse had magically come undone and she felt his hand pulling her bra aside, his hot mouth on her nipple, which hardened immediately. And the next thing she knew she felt him pushing gently inside her.

As Jake moaned intensely the true realisation of what they were doing suddenly dawned on Stella, and she instantly sobered up. She couldn't do this. This was crazy. She was having sex with her twin sister's hot boyfriend. She was married. This couldn't be happening. 'No, Jake, stop!' she shouted, at last finding the strength and motivation to sit up.

As she bolted upright she collided with Jake, their heads meeting with an incredibly loud *thunk*. He shouted out in agony and pulled out of her, stumbling backwards, grabbing at his forehead.

Stella felt her own forehead and then looked at her fingers to see if she was bleeding. She tasted iron in her mouth and realised that she must have bitten her tongue. As she shook her head again to try and see straight, she saw something in her peripheral vision. Her vision was blurred and the image was hazy, but she knew straight away and with a sudden piercing horror that it was Lucy, standing in the kitchen doorway with her handbag dangling limply in her hand, her mouth gaping.

'Lucy!' Stella whispered, her voice shaking as her vision cleared.

'Stella?' Jake said sounding confused, looking between Stella and Lucy as he rubbed his bruised forehead and got his balance back.

'Jake!' Lucy said, silent tears pouring down her cheeks as she stood glued to the spot in horror, apples and lemons scattered around her feet.

Stella scrambled off the kitchen table, pulling her skirt down and trying to button up her stained blouse. How had this happened? Just a second earlier she had been drunkenly poking around in Lucy's fridge for something to eat, and suddenly it was the end of the world. 'Wait, Lucy, it was an accident!' Stella shouted, stumbling towards her, her bleeding tongue thick in her mouth.

Jake was busy trying to pull up his pants, his face white. 'I thought she was you,' he mumbled as he swung his confused gaze between the two girls.

'He thought I was you!' Stella echoed. 'It was an accident!'

'Get out, Stella!' Lucy said, her voice almost a whisper.

'Lucy, you have to believe me ...' Stella sobbed.

'Get the fuck out of my house!' Lucy said, this time shouting and pointing at the front door.

'No, wait, Lucy ...' Stella tried to touch her arm, but Lucy slapped her away and pushed her backwards as hard as she could with both hands. 'I said, get the fuck out of my house!' she shouted even louder. 'I don't want to talk to you!'

Stella stumbled back and bashed into the wall. Then she turned around, grabbed her bag and ran out of the door, tears streaming down her face and splashing onto the floor at her feet as she ran. She'd never seen Lucy so angry before. The way she'd looked at her with such hatred was terrifying.

POPPY

'Hey, Buck,' Poppy shouted loudly towards the end of the aisle in the Walmart.

Buck was standing with his hands on his hips, his eyes wide with wonder as he examined the row upon row of shotguns neatly displayed up against the wall. 'What, Poppy?' he asked, irritated at being interrupted.

Poppy shifted her feet and turned back to the dozens and dozens of different hair dyes that were stacked floor to ceiling. 'Do you think I'm more a Summer Ash, or more a Strawberry Blonde?'

'I don't even know what you are talking about,' Buck said, picking up a foot-long hunting knife.

'They're hair colours, dummy. Do you think it's true that blondes have more fun?'

'How should I know?' Buck said.

Sometimes he was so annoying, Poppy thought. He was being no help at all. 'Well, I want to change my hair colour, but I can't decide what colour to choose. I mean, it depends where we're going next. Like, if we go to New York City then I should pick a more serious colour, like one of these,' she said, picking up a box in each hand. 'Medium Auburn Brown, or Dark Auburn Copper.' She paused to consider her options. 'But if we're going somewhere a bit more crazy, like San Francisco, or Vegas, or somewhere like that, then I definitely want to go with something a little more fun, like this one.' She picked up another box with a picture of a peroxide blonde on the front of it. 'Or this one,' she said, pointing at a box that had the words *Purple Haze* written underneath a picture of a smiling woman with dark purple hair.

Poppy looked up to gauge Buck's reaction, but he had disappeared. 'Buck!' she shouted.

'What?' he said, reappearing suddenly by her side wearing a huge Mexican sombrero and carrying a giant brightly coloured piñata under his arm. 'Can we get these?' he asked.

'Buck, be serious,' Poppy said. 'I need to know where we're going so I can decide what hair colour to choose.'

'Poppy, I don't even know where we are now, so how am I supposed to know where we're going next? Where do you want to go?'

'I don't know. I think we're somewhere in Kansas right now. But we have to decide where we're going next so I can pick out a hair colour, either East Coast or West Coast?'

'I know,' Buck said. 'Let's flip a coin. Heads we go to the East Coast, tails we go to the West Coast.'

Poppy shrugged her shoulders. 'Okay, sounds good to me,' she said. 'Either way, as soon as we leave we get to say, "We're not in Kansas any more, Dorothy!"' She grinned.

Buck dug around in the front pocket of his Levi's, looking for a coin. 'Hey,' he said, 'what do you think, should I get a shotgun or a revolver?'

Poppy rolled her eyes at him. 'Just toss the coin, Buck! You can keep the piñata, but we are not buying a gun!'

STELLA

Stella stumbled out of Lucy's apartment block and limped, sobbing, back towards the main road where her car was parked. She was a mess. Her tongue was sore where she'd bitten down on it, and some of the buttons on her coffee-stained blouse were missing, so that she had to pull her arms across her chest to hold her top closed. But that was nothing compared to how she felt. She felt raw and exposed; her stomach churning as wave after wave of nausea washed over her at the thought of what she had just done.

Suddenly, as she turned down a small side street, Stella's mouth filled with bitter saliva. She looked around in panic, then raced across the road towards a small semi-detached Victorian cottage. Leaning over the waist-high stone wall she instantly began to vomit into a thick bush of flowering hydrangeas, her body purging the booze from its system. The acid burn of the alcohol coming back up was harsh and did nothing to stop her tears.

She had literally made herself sick.

When she had finished vomiting Stella wiped her mouth with the sleeve of her torn blouse and looked around, hoping desperately that nobody had seen her. Especially the poor, innocent owners of the now violated hydrangea bush. She heaved a big sobbing sigh of relief – the street was quiet, there were no cars and nobody seemed to be around – and quickly pushed herself up off the wall and continued stumbling down the street towards Sea Point Main Road. The sooner she got to her car the better.

As Stella walked she caught sight of a pair of bergies a few houses down the road. They had obviously been rummaging through a big black bin, but when they'd seen Stella vomiting they must have stopped what they were doing and were now frozen where they stood, both elbow-deep in the bin, watching Stella in disgust.

'Sies man!' one bergie said to her as she passed them, wagging a garbage-covered finger at Stella in revulsion.

Stella hung her head low as she quickened her pace. She'd managed to repulse two people who were digging through the garbage for their dinner. One didn't get much lower than that, she thought.

Once she'd made it out of the small side street and reconnected with the main road, Stella walked three or four blocks hugging her handbag in front of her chest. Finally locating her car, parked up a narrow street to one side of Bistro, she fumbled for her keys with shaking hands.

As she drove home she smashed her palm against the steering wheel, fat tears rolling down her cheeks. 'What have you done? What have you done? What have you done?' she repeated to herself over and over as she drove towards the end of High Level Road and the top of town.

'Hey, babe,' Max said as soon as he heard her come through the front door, his voice coming from the lounge.

On the drive home Stella had prayed that he'd had to work late, or that he had been stuck in traffic, but she'd known it was a vain hope. Max was almost always home on time.

Stella stuck her head around the lounge door, covering her front with her handbag to hide her very obvious deceit as well as the coffee and vomit stains.

'What's for supper?' Max asked, looking up briefly from the rugby he was watching on television.

'I'm just going for a shower,' Stella mumbled, and then hurried off down the passage, desperate to get away from him as fast as she could.

In the bedroom Stella slipped off her vomit-stained shoes and pulled off her blouse as quickly as she could. She would have to get rid of all the clothes she had been wearing, she thought, her shoes too. She would have to burn them; she could never wear them again.

In the shower she stood under a stream of achingly hot water and let it pelt at her skin. She scrubbed at her body, so desperate to remove the scarlet letter imprinted on her chest that she used up an entire bar of soap and washed her hair three times.

When the hot water ran cold, Stella climbed out of the shower and wrapped her long, dripping hair in a towel turban. Then she brushed her teeth for at least five minutes, trying to rid her mouth of the sour taste of booze, vomit, Jake and lies.

Finally, mission complete, she put on her fluffy bathrobe and dragged her feet miserably along the floor, down the passage and into the lounge. She hovered in the doorway, watching Max staring intently at the television set, the vein in his neck pulsing, his fist clenched. He seemed completely unaware that she was even there and that she had just gone and changed both their lives forever.

'Max,' she said quietly.

'Yeah,' he replied, not taking his eyes off the television set.

'I don't feel so good; I think I'm going to go to bed early.'

Max turned to look at her, his face showing his concern. 'Why? What's the matter?'

'It's nothing major; I've just got a migraine. I'm going to take a couple of Myprodol and crash.'

'But what about dinner?' he asked, turning down the volume using the remote control. 'It's Thursday. We have chicken on Thursdays.'

'I know and I'm sorry. There are some leftovers in the fridge, or you could order something in if you wanted?' she suggested.

Max looked at her, disappointment written all over his face. 'Oh, okay,' he said. 'Maybe I'll order Chinese.'

'All right then, goodnight,' she said.

In the bedroom Stella took two sleeping pills and got into bed, pulling the covers up over head. As she lay there the events of the day washed over her once again, the memory of Jake inside her and the look on Lucy's shocked, pale face played and rewound and then played again in full colour. She curled up in the foetal position and shuddered in horror, her body racked with sob after silent sob. The sleeping pills couldn't work fast enough.

Stella opened her eyes and rolled over. She watched the numbers flip from 4:56 a.m. to 4:57 a.m. on the digital alarm clock next to her side of the bed as she slowly surfaced. Her mouth was dry and tasted disgusting and her head was pounding. Then she remembered why she was feeling so rotten. Turning over, she peeked at Max, who was snoring peacefully next to her. She hadn't even heard him come to bed and she was grateful that the sleeping pills had totally zonked her out. She was also grateful that she'd vomited up all that booze. Stella shuddered as she imagined how much worse she would be feeling if she hadn't puked. She couldn't believe she'd drunk so much. It wasn't like her at all. But then nothing she'd done in the last forty-eight hours had been anything like her at all. She didn't even recognise herself any more.

Stella slipped out of bed silently and dressed quickly and quietly in the bathroom. She couldn't bear to look at herself in the mirror, she knew that the reflection that looked back at her would be the ugliest, guiltiest thing she'd ever seen.

Stella made herself a cup of strong black coffee but she didn't sit down at the kitchen table with it. Coward that she was, she scribbled a quick note for Max, which she left on the kitchen table, before fleeing to her car with her mug, terrified that if she didn't leave soon, she might have to face him.

Morning Max,

I have an early meeting. Sorry about last night. I'm feeling much better this morning.

  Don't forget we have Friday night supper at Violet's tonight. See you at home after work.

Have a nice day.

X
Stella

Stella sat at her desk chewing on her lip and fidgeting with the wedding ring on her finger, twisting it round and round while staring aimlessly into space. She felt bereft. She'd gone and destroyed her life in one fell swoop. She needed to speak to Lucy. She needed to apologise and explain to her what had happened. She needed to tell her that it was all an accident and a misunderstanding and a matter of mistaken identity. And that she'd been drunk. And that it wasn't her fault. And that she'd never meant for any of it to happen. And that she hadn't known what she was doing. And that she was very very sorry.

  Swallowing hard, Stella took a deep breath, picked up the phone and dialled Lucy's number. It rang and rang and rang and eventually went to voicemail. Stella chickened out at the beep and put the phone down. Then she picked it up and dialled again. This time the call was rejected after the second ring. When Stella tried a third time Lucy's phone was off altogether and wasn't taking messages.

  The pile of ignored, coffee-spattered letters from the previous day lay open on her desk, mocking her quietly, and next to them lay a fresh pile and Stella's still unwritten wedding thank-you cards. Stella picked up her letter opener and slit open the length of an envelope, her fingers shaking. Then she examined her letter opener closely and ran the edge of it across each of her wrists in a slick cutting movement. Once, while researching suicide for a letter she needed to answer, she'd read somewhere that if you wanted to do the job properly you had to slice downwards and not crossways like they did in the movies. Unfortunately, though, even if she did have the courage, her letter opener didn't have a serrated edge and all it did was leave a slim white line on each wrist, which quickly faded, leaving her skin clear and normal again. She tapped the letter opener against her lips as she read:

Dear Dr Dee,

Is it at all possible that my penis is too big to have sex? My girlfriend and I have been together for seven months and we're both virgins. We tried to have sex the other day but we were not successful. My penis just seemed too large to enter her vagina. Is this possible? Or were we maybe just doing it wrong? Like, for example, maybe we were in the wrong position or something. Please help.

Clueless in Cape Town

Stella dropped the letter onto her desk, threw the letter opener on top of it and shrugged her shoulders. 'How the hell should I know?' she said out loud. How on earth was she expected to solve these people's problems if she didn't even have a clue how to solve her own, she wondered. She was a fraud and an adulterer and a liar and a terrible writer.

Stella turned to her computer and drafted a letter of her own, while hopeless, desperate tears rolled down her cheeks.

Dear Dr Dee,

You have to help me, I've gone and screwed up completely. First I lied to my husband of only about eight hundred and forty hours, and my identical twin sister who is also my best friend in the whole wide world. And then, on top of that, I lied to all my friends about getting a promotion that I never actually got. And then I made my twin sister's boyfriend think I was my twin and knowingly had sex with him. And then my twin sister walked in and caught us in the middle of it.

I haven't told my husband about any of this. My sister isn't talking to me. I thought about committing suicide using my letter opener. And to top it all off, it seems I've started talking to myself. I must be going mad.

Help!

Unforgivable Adulterer

Stella reread the letter, wondering how Dr Dee would answer it. Her eyes blurred as they refilled with tears of despair and self-pity. She pushed her chair back from her desk, grabbed her sweater and her bag and left the office, running out of the door and down to her car. She couldn't sit there for another minute.

Fifteen minutes later Stella arrived in Newlands, at Violet's practice. At thirty-six, Violet was the oldest of the Frankel sisters by quite a bit. She was married to Stewart, the stockbroker, and together they had three boys under the age of seven. Violet shared offices with a handful of other doctors of varying specialisations in a small business park in Newlands. Stella ran her finger across the brass plaque on the door as she walked in. It felt cool and important. It said: *Violet Frankel-Sherman, Clinical Psychologist, Suite 6.*

Violet didn't have a traditional kind of office. There was no smiling receptionist sitting behind a big wooden desk taking calls. Instead Violet had a smallish waiting room just outside her office, which she shared with two other doctors, a chiropractor and a chiropodist, whose offices also led directly off it. The waiting room was decorated in the style of old people's lounges and doctors' rooms the world over – badly covered couches and a collection of mismatched, almost-antique, but not-nice-enough-to-be-valuable chairs which were shuffled around an old coffee table, covered in even older magazines.

There was a small light attached to the outside of Violet's office door. It was a similar system to that used by radio stations. If the light was red it meant Violet was busy in a session and was not to be disturbed, and if it was green it meant the next patient was free to enter.

Stella had only visited Violet's office twice before and each time she'd been tempted to toss all the magazines in the bin by the ancient coffee machine and pop to the shops to pick up some fresh ones. How hard could it be for Violet to pick up a new *You* every once in a while? But today she didn't give the magazines a second glance. She didn't give the light a second glance either, even though it was glowing red.

Stella burst through the door without knocking, desperation seeping out of her pores. Violet was sitting in a straight, high-backed armchair. Across from her a man in his fifties was curled up in another mismatched, badly covered armchair, rocking and sucking his thumb, crying like a baby. 'Stella!' Violet shouted, clearly startled. 'What on earth are you doing here? The light is on. I'm in a session!'

Stella couldn't stop herself. 'Vi, I've done something terrible, you have to help me, everything is a complete disaster,' she wailed as her shoulders shook and the tears gushed out of her eyes.

Stella collapsed in a heap on the office couch, grabbing a handful of tissues out of a box balanced on the low coffee table as she did so. But instead of wiping her eyes, she began to shred the tissues into millions of little pieces that floated onto her lap and the floor.

'Stella, I'm right in the middle of a session!' Violet said, gesturing at the man. 'You can't just come barging in here like this!'

The man meanwhile had stopped crying, popped his thumb out of his mouth and was sitting up straight, looking increasingly more uncomfortable with every passing second.

'I'm so sorry for this interruption, Doug,' Violet said, turning her attention back to him. 'This is my sister, Stella.'

'I'm sorry, but, Violet, you have to help me!' Stella howled. 'I mean it! Everything's a complete disaster! First I lied to Max about getting a promotion at work. And I was going to tell him the truth, really I was, but before I got the chance he went and told Lucy, and then they threw a surprise party with all our friends ... And I didn't get a chance to tell them all that it was a lie because it started raining inside La Perla because of the candles. And then, last night, I accidentally made Jake, Lucy's boyfriend, think I was Lucy, and we ended up having sex on Lucy's kitchen table. And then Lucy walked in and caught us, and she totally freaked out, and now she won't take my calls. I'm really scared, Violet! I don't know what's happening to me and I don't know what to do! And I still haven't told Max about any of this! I'm screwed, Violet, screwed! My life is over!' Stella sobbed loudly, her chest heaving as she tried to suck in air.

As Violet stared at Stella open-mouthed, taking it all in, Doug stood up, shaking his head, and grabbed a fresh tissue out of the box in the middle of the table. 'Don't worry, Violet,' he said, handing the tissue to Stella, 'she can have the rest of my session if she wants. It sounds like she needs it more than I do.' Then he sat back down again, perched on the edge of his seat, his eyes now riveted on Stella as he waited to hear the rest of the story.

'Shit, Stella!' Violet said. 'So that's why Lucy isn't coming to dinner tonight. What did you go and do all that for?'

'She's not?' Stella asked through her tears.

'Nope. She called me earlier and said she wouldn't be able to make dinner. She said she had to work late.'

'How did she sound?' Stella sobbed. 'Did she say anything? Was she upset? She won't even take my calls. She's never ever going to talk to me again. What am I going to do?'

Violet stood up and walked over to where Stella was sitting, putting her hand on her back and rubbing it gently for a couple of minutes while Stella gathered her composure and tried to control her breathing. Violet had dead-straight, shoulder-length black hair dotted with thick stray strands of grey. There was a battle being waged on her head, Stella had thought the last time she'd seen her sister, and the grey was winning. Over the last few years Stella had also noticed that Violet had started to dress in a simple, practical, dull-looking style, and that her eyes always seemed to be tired, in the way that only a mother of three boys under the age of seven's eyes can be tired.

As Stella's heaving sobs began to subside, and her breathing slowly returned to normal, Violet put her hand on Stella's elbow, gently lifting her from the chair and guiding her towards the door. 'Sorry, Doug,' Violet said again, over her shoulder. 'I won't be a second. Now, while I'm gone I want you to think about three influential people and two pivotal moments in your life, and we'll discuss it when I return.'

Stella looked back at Doug apologetically. He raised his hand to her in a sort-of wave, and gave her a hopeful chin-up kind of smile.

Outside in the still empty waiting room Violet sat Stella down on one of the couches. 'Now listen here,' she said sternly. 'I know you're having a rough time right now, but you absolutely cannot come barging into my practice whenever your life is falling apart. I have clients! It's not professional.' Violet sat down next to her on the couch and held her hand gently. 'Now, have you told Max any of this at all?' she asked in a professional, businesslike tone.

Stella shook her head and snivelled.

'Okay,' Violet said. 'You need to pull yourself together. Go back to work, clean yourself up and come through to my place later. I'll be home by five and you and I can discuss what you should do then, all right? Just don't do anything rash, okay? We'll figure this thing out. I know it feels disastrous and unmanageable right now, but that's just because you're in a bit of a state. Breathe deeply and try not to think about it too much. We all love you. I love you, Max loves you and Lucy loves you; everything will be okay eventually, all right?'

Stella nodded. Just talking to Violet had made her feel a little better. She was a trained professional, after all, not a pseudo problem-solver like she was. Violet knew what she was doing and Stella knew that she had made the right decision in coming to her. Her big sister would help her sort out the mess her life had become in the last forty-eight hours.

Violet nodded encouragingly and waited for Stella to nod back, to indicate that she knew what Violet now expected of her. 'Stay here as long as you need, but I have to get back to my session, okay?' Violet said gently.

Stella nodded and watched as Violet swooshed off, disappearing back into her office, probably to make Doug cry again.

POPPY

'Vegas, baby, Vegas!' Buck whooped, punching his fist in the air as he bounced up and down on his bed in their hotel room.

Poppy was spread out on her own single bed next to his, staring at the ceiling. 'Just being here feels so cool, like, there's such a buzz. Can you feel it, Buck? Even though, in reality, it's all really just completely tacky,' Poppy said, running her hand over the hideously patterned bedspread.

'I wonder what porn we can get on TV?' Buck said, bouncing onto his back and reaching for the remote.

'For the amount you'll have to pay for that kind of viewing here, you'd be better off heading down to the strip, finding yourself a couple of cheap hookers and making your own porno,' Poppy said, reaching over and pulling open the drawer of the shared bedside table out of curiosity. Nestling inside was a black, plastic-covered Bible with its red silk ribbon peeking out the bottom of its pages.

'Good idea, Poppy! Let's do that,' Buck replied, dropping the remote control back on the bedside table.

'There's some kind of weird irony in this, don't you think?' Poppy said, holding up the Bible to show him. 'Just think, there's one of these in every drawer in every hotel room here, possibly the most sinful place on the planet.'

She stood up on the bed and opened the book to the bookmarked page. Then she cleared her throat and read out the first paragraph that her eyes fell on. 'Timothy, chapter six, verse ten,' she read. 'For the love of money is the root of all evil: which while some coveted after, they have erred from the faith, and pierced themselves through with many sorrows.'

'Amen, sister!' Buck yelled. 'Now, let's go make a porno, or gamble, or something.'

Poppy closed the Bible and examined it. 'Do you think people ever steal the Bible from hotel rooms? They must. And is that considered a sin? It can't be. I mean, it's not like you're stealing it to hurt someone with ... Chances are you're stealing it to read it, and that's what it's for, isn't it? So it can't be a sin. But stealing a Bible is a complete conundrum, don't you think? It's like doing bad to do good. Unless you're stealing it to sell it so you can buy crack, of course.' She sat back down on her bed. 'I suppose the hotel could always bolt them down or chain them up, like they do with the pens at the bank, but that kind of goes against everything the Bible stands for, because then they'd be imagining somebody wants to sin instead of seeing them as innocent like the Bible says. I suppose they don't bolt them down in the end because they want to have faith in the ultimate goodness of people, right?'

'Hey, Poppy,' Buck said, ignoring her sudden detour into the ethics of stealing Bibles from hotel rooms in Las Vegas. 'Do you realise this is the first proper hotel we've stayed in since we started this trip? We don't even have to share a bathroom with other backpackers, or bears, or anything.'

'I know, look, real toilet paper,' Poppy said, jumping off the bed and heading into the bathroom where she stroked the one-ply lovingly against her cheek. She looked at her reflection in the mirror. Her hair was now a deep purple. She'd done the dye job herself, in the toilet at a gas station somewhere on the road between Kansas and Las Vegas, so it was slightly imperfect and some of the pink still showed through in places. She'd also removed her nose ring. New city, new look, she thought, running her hand through her hair.

'Hey, I'm starving,' Buck said. 'What do you say we grab something to eat?'

STELLA

Stella sat balanced on the edge of the bathtub, trying not to get soaked, while Luke, six, and Nathan, four, tried to achieve the opposite. Violet was standing in the doorway of the bathroom, negotiating with her youngest son – Jack, aged three. She was trying to coax him into the bathtub. When it came to negotiating the United Nations had nothing compared to the kinds of challenges Violet faced on a daily basis with the three boys.

'Look, see, Jack, both your brothers are in the bath, and look what fun they're having,' Stella said, trying to sound as enthusiastic as possible.

But her nephew shook his head defiantly and crossed his arms across his chest, his bottom lip jutting out.

'I'll give you some foamy shaving cream to play with?' Violet offered.

The child was naked in three seconds and before Stella could move he'd dive-bombed into the bath beside his brothers, instantly undoing all her efforts at staying dry.

'Shit,' Stella swore, jumping up as she tried to get some of the water off her lap and back in the bath.

'Shit, shit, shit,' Nathan mimicked.

Violet gave Stella a death stare. 'Do you have to swear in front of them, Stella?' she said through gritted teeth. 'It took me a month to get him to stop saying that word Lucy said last time she was here.'

'Fuck, fuck, fuck,' Nathan parroted as the other boys rolled around in the bath, laughing and screaming.

'That's just great!' Violet grumbled, storming out of the bathroom. 'Now look what you've done!'

'What? I didn't say that, it was Lucy!' Stella said, following Violet into one of the boys' bedrooms. She sat down on the edge of a motor car-themed bed while Violet dug around in the cupboard for three different sets of matching pyjamas and three pairs of slippers in three different sizes.

'So, have you thought about what I told you?' Stella asked, chewing on her lip. She sounded about as desperate and pathetic as she felt.

'Stella, I've barely had a chance to go to the toilet today, I must be honest,' Violet said.

'What do you think I should do?' Stella prodded.

'Well, first you need to tell everybody that you didn't get the promotion, Stel. You know that. Communication is the only solution to that problem. It's not like they won't find out in the end anyway, when you're still answering the Dear Dr Dee letters in a month's time and there are no articles in the magazine with your name on them.'

'I know,' Stella winced, 'but Lucy won't even take my calls.'

'You really managed to mess everything up completely, didn't you? Listen, you have to make her talk to you. You'll probably have to go to her if she isn't taking your calls. The two of you will be fine, you've always been fine; you'll get through this together, you're practically one person. You've always shared everything; there's no reason why there shouldn't be the odd guy in there too. She'll come round. Look, it may take some time, and I wouldn't be surprised if she didn't want to talk to you until she cools down a little. You'll have to give her the space she needs to heal, but she'll come around, eventually.'

'And what about Max?' Stella whispered, close to tears again.

Violet pulled an anxious face. 'I think you have to tell him about the job, for obvious reasons, but when it comes to the sex ... Well, in my opinion, sometimes a don't ask, don't tell policy is best for all concerned. That way nobody gets hurt. Especially if, like you say, it was just an accident and you never plan on doing anything like it again.'

'Yes, it was absolutely an accident, Vi, really. So you think it's okay if I don't tell Max?' Stella asked with wide eyes. She had spent just about every second of every minute of the last twelve hours wondering if that was even an option. 'Do you think I could get away with that?'

'Mooooom!' Luke shouted from the bathroom. 'Jack made a poo in the bath again!'

Rolling her eyes Violet stomped out of the bedroom and back into the bathroom.

Stella remained on the edge of the bed for a few minutes more, weighing up her options. A surge of relief washed over her as she formulated her plan. She would carry on trying to get hold of Lucy, so she could tell her about the lie, and apologise for everything, and explain what happened with Jake, and swear it was an accident and that it would never happen again. And she would find the right time to tell Max about the job as soon as possible, but she would never tell Max about what happened with Jake. That was the best solution, she thought. He didn't need to get hurt, and what he didn't know wouldn't hurt him, surely? Telling him about the promotion was going to be hard enough, but telling him about Jake too, that would be impossible.

Once Stella had composed herself, she made her way back to the lounge, feeling relieved and hopeful.

'Stel, how's another beer?' Max said, holding up his beer bottle and shaking it in her general direction as she came through the doorway, not even taking his eye off the TV.

'Good call,' Daisy said, holding out her empty Savanna bottle.

Stella took the two empty bottles and went to the kitchen. Nothing had to change, she thought, he never had to know.

The family sat around the dining room table slurping at their soup. Stella had no appetite but she was trying hard to act normal. She twirled her spoon in her soup, wondering if this was what Friday nights would be like from now on if Lucy continued to refuse to speak to her.

'So where's Lucy tonight, Stella?' Iris asked in a motherly tone, as if reading her mind.

Stella caught Violet's eye and Daisy looked up skittishly.

'She couldn't make it, she said she had to work,' Violet said.

'Oh, yes,' Iris said proudly. 'Well, I guess with the big promotion she must have more responsibility at work.'

'Will someone please pass the bread?' Stewart, Violet's husband, chimed in. 'More wine, Hylton?' he asked Stella's dad, who sat quietly at the head of the table, absorbed in his soup.

'Hey, speaking of promotions ...' Max said, looking up from his soup.

Stella panicked, suddenly realising that he was about to tell them all about her imaginary promotion. Not knowing how else to stop him she kicked him hard on the shin under the table.

'Ow!' Max said, looking at Stella with surprise. 'What the ...'

'Actually, I have kind of big news myself,' Daisy piped up from the other end of the table, standing up with her drink in her hand. 'It's a pity Lucy's not here, I was hoping to catch everyone together, but I can't wait any longer to tell you.'

Stella turned to look at Daisy, doing her best to ignore Max's stare. She couldn't let him tell the rest of her family about her fake promotion, she'd lied to enough people already and the thought of adding her mom and dad to the list filled her with horror. Thank goodness Daisy seemed to have something important to say, she thought, it was the perfect cover.

Daisy cleared her throat nervously and took a big sip of her Savanna. 'Guys,' she said, raising her voice a little in an attempt to get everyone's attention over the clatter of spoons in bowls. 'There's something I've been wanting to tell you all.' She cleared her throat again nervously and took another sip of her drink.

Stella looked at her curiously as slowly everybody stopped eating and focused their attention on the second youngest member of the Frankel family. She thought Daisy sounded nervous and she noticed that she also hadn't touched her soup yet.

'Mom, Dad, everyone …' Daisy continued. 'This is very hard for me to say, and I wanted to tell you all last Friday night, but then Lucy had her promotion announcement … I'm tired of keeping it inside, I don't want to keep secrets from you any more, it's killing me. I love you all, but you need to know who I really am …'

There was a deathly silence. Even Violet's boys sensed the gravity of the situation and stopped what they were doing to stare at their aunt.

'Mom, Dad, everyone,' Daisy said, taking a deep breath. 'I'm a lesbian.'

The entire room took in a synchronised shocked breath.

'What's a lesbian?' Luke asked.

'Lesbian, lesbian, lesbian,' Nathan mimicked as Jack knocked his glass of red grape juice over, the stain spreading instantly across the white tablecloth.

'Mom, what's a lesbian?' Luke asked again as Violet jumped up to try and mop up the spill.

Daisy cleared her throat, 'Luke, a lesbian is a girl who likes to have sex with other girls,' she said authoritatively.

Violet's face went a puce colour.

'What's sex?' Nathan asked.

'Sex, sex, sex,' Jack mimicked.

Stella's dad dropped his spoon into his soup bowl. It clattered, splashing soup onto the already ruined tablecloth.

Max was either choking quietly, or giggling to himself behind his serviette, Stella couldn't tell which. Meanwhile Stella's mother, Iris, seemed to be having some kind of panic attack. 'But that's impossible,' she shrieked, clutching at her neck as if she needed the Heimlich.

'How can that be?' their father asked, throwing his hands in the air.

'Are you sure?' Iris choked.

'Daisy, what's really going on here?' Hylton lamented.

'We've done nothing but the best for you!' Iris cried in a high-pitched voice, slamming her hand down on the table. 'The best schools. Everything you've ever wanted. Why would you do this to us?'

Daisy moved her eyes between her mother and father, a panicked look on her face. 'Mom, Dad, this isn't something I'm "doing to you",' she said. 'It's just who I am … And anyway, I don't know why you're so upset with me.

I'm not the bad one here, you know! Stella had sex with Lucy's boyfriend!'

Once again the room gasped collectively and then dropped into silence.

'No, Stella!' Iris whispered dramatically, breaking the silence and covering her mouth with her hand, turning slowly from Daisy to Stella. 'Is this true?' she asked with horror.

Stella convulsed. 'Daisy!' she shrieked.

'Violet told me!' Daisy whined, pointing at Violet.

'Violet!' Stella yelled. 'I can't believe you told her! Whatever happened to doctor-patient confidentiality?'

'I'm not your doctor and you're not my patient! There's no confidentiality!' Violet shouted back.

Stella was sitting next to Max at the table and she could feel his rigid stare burning into the side of her face. She ignored her parents' angry horror and forced herself to turn her head slowly to face him. His face was bright red and his lip was quivering.

'Is this true, Stella?' he asked quietly.

Stella's eyes filled with tears.

'Is it true?' he asked again, this time a little louder.

Stella nodded slowly. 'But it was nothing,' she said, grabbing hold of his arm. 'I swear, it was a mistake. He thought I was Lucy.'

'And who did you think you were, Stella?' Max shouted, throwing her hand off his arm as if he'd been stung. Then he threw his napkin on the table and stood up sharply, knocking his chair to the ground behind him as he did so. Turning around, his eyes blazing with fury, he stormed out of the dining room, grabbed his keys off the phone table by the door and left, slamming the front door in a powerful rage behind him.

'Stella, how could you?' Iris gasped in horror. 'And to your own sister!'

'Stella!' her father boomed, looking at her with shock in his eyes, shaking his head.

'Mom, Dad, I can explain. It was an accident, it's really not what you think,' Stella said, tears of shame rolling down her cheeks. 'I have to go after Max. But I'll explain everything later, I promise.' Then she turned to glare first at Daisy and then briefly at Violet, before she grabbed her handbag and ran out of the door after Max.

'**M**ax …'

'I don't want to hear it, Stella!' Max said, silencing her, his voice shaking.

After following him out of Violet's house she'd had to chase the car down the driveway before banging on the passenger window to make him let her in. But even though he had opened the door after she had pleaded with him, he hadn't been able to look at her yet. She'd never seen him so angry before. He was obviously right on the edge of losing it.

The indicator ticked loudly inside the car while Max waited for the traffic lights at the Paradise Motors intersection to go green. It was the loudest noise Stella thought she had ever heard.

'Please, let me just …'

'I'm not interested in what you have to say, Stella!' Max shouted, his face red, the vein at his temple pulsing in time with the car's indicator.

The light changed and Max took the turn.

Stella chewed on her lip. 'Max …' she tried again.

Max slammed his foot on the brake suddenly. The car screeched to a halt and Stella grabbed the dashboard as she was flung forward.

'I said, I don't want to hear it,' Max yelled. Then, very deliberately, he turned on the radio and rolled the volume button between his fingers until it was as loud as it could go, so she wouldn't be able to speak to him. This done he placed both hands back on the steering wheel, very deliberately at ten to two, took a deep breath and drove on.

When they eventually arrived home Max pulled into a parking space on the street outside Victory Court, climbed out of the car and stormed into the apartment block, his shoulders hunched. Alone in the passenger seat, Stella took a minute, breathing deeply, trying to decide what to do, and then cautiously she followed him inside.

When she walked into the apartment she stood at the door and silently watched Max stomp out of their bedroom with an armful of clothes, his toothbrush balanced on the top of the pile. He still wouldn't look at her. Instead he strode into the spare room purposefully and slammed the door, making the entire apartment shake. Then Stella heard him lock it from the inside.

Collapsing on the couch Stella hung her head in her hands. What was she going to do? Thanks to Violet and Daisy the cat was out of the bag now and there was nothing she could do to get it back in. It was all out of her control now. She wondered if Max would ever be able to forgive her, if he would ever even be able to talk to her again. How had her life spiralled so quickly from perfect to all-out craziness?

Stella's cellphone rang. She reached into her handbag and saw that it was Violet. She rejected the call and shut off her phone. She didn't want to talk to Violet; she was furious at both her sisters. How could Violet and Daisy do that to her? She felt lost and alone and totally betrayed.

Stella thought about everything that had happened in the last few hours. Daisy was gay. Well, that explained a lot. She ached to discuss it with Lucy, and had things been normal between them she would be on the phone with her right now, doing an autopsy of Daisy's coming out around the Friday night supper table, in front of the candles, heaven forbid. In one way it was just another announcement from Daisy in a long string of announcements that had punctuated their lives. Growing up there had been the vegetarian announcement, the vegan announcement, the raw foodist announcement, and then directly after that the all-out biltong-eating, meat-gorging announcement. She'd also been a peace protester, an animal rights activist and a paintball specialist. There had even been a six month period where she'd been a Rastafarian. Growing up Daisy had tried karate, playing the guitar and women's rugby. For as long as Stella could remember Daisy had skipped from passion to passion, never settling on one long enough for it to actually stick. It had always felt to Stella that life was simply a series of outfits for Daisy, and that she was trying on every single one until she found the perfect fit. But Stella was sure this one would stick, it made sense and Stella and Lucy had long suspected Daisy was gay. Which was fine by them. Ultimately whatever made Daisy happy would make her and Lucy happy. And even though her parents may not feel the same way about it immediately, Stella knew they'd get used to the idea with time. But judging by the looks on their faces, the one idea they'd never get used to was what Stella had done to Lucy. She felt ashamed. How was she going to live with herself? Her parents had never been disappointed in her before. She'd always been the good one, the responsible one, the one who did the right thing, but tonight all that had changed. She would never forget the look of utter horror and complete disappointment on their faces. She'd just undone twenty-five years of good behaviour in one night.

Stella rubbed her eyes, trying to staunch the tears. She couldn't believe her own sister had outed her like that at the Friday night supper table. Daisy outing herself was one thing, but how could she throw Stella under the bus like that? She shook her head. It was a classic Daisy manoeuvre. She'd needed someone to take the focus off her because her parents weren't taking the news well, and were doing their predictable part by freaking out loudly, just like they always did. And Stella had been the perfect diversion. Now, instead of just having to mend things with Lucy, she had to mend them with Lucy and Max. It was a monster task, almost too big for any one human being to consider in a single lifetime.

Stella tossed and turned in their unbearably empty king-size bed all night, and eventually fell asleep around four. When she woke up she found a note on the kitchen table. It was written in bold, careful letters that slanted downwards a little at the end of each line, subtly indicating Max's subconscious feelings of distaste at her behaviour.

Stella,

I think it's best if you packed up your things and left. I can't deal with you right now.

Max must have been up and out of the house incredibly early. Usually on a Saturday morning she'd be the one jumping out of bed early. She would head to the gym, leaving him to sleep in and read the newspaper and walk around the apartment in his boxers. Then he would go back to sleep again till at least late morning or lunchtime when Stella got home with provisions. But today obviously wasn't that kind of Saturday.

He hadn't even signed his name on the note, Stella realised as she looked down at it again. She felt sick to her stomach. How could her marriage be over? She did the maths, counting it out on her fingertips – it was only eight hundred and sixty-four hours old. She hadn't even finished writing the thank-you cards yet. She twisted her wedding band around on her finger anxiously and chewed at her lip.

POPPY

Poppy undid the top button of her jeans and breathed out with relief as she leant back and balanced both arms along the back of the restaurant booth, spreading out her body. 'Wow, that's more than I've ever eaten in one sitting. And I come from a big Jewish family, so that's saying a lot!' she said.

'I told you this six-dollar, all-you-can-eat buffet would be a winner,' Buck said. 'Anyway, that's nothing, I ate way more than you. I had the chowder, shrimp, pasta, a steak with a baked potato, hash browns and at least three different kinds of dessert.' He burped and then blew out in Poppy's face.

'Gross, you freak!' Poppy yelled, punching him on the arm.

They sat in silence for a while, watching people milling around them and trying to let their food settle. The restaurant was located in the lobby of the hotel, neatly lodged off to one side, with the gambling floor across from them and the hotel reception area on the other side of that, which meant that there was a constant stream of traffic coming past them.

Poppy took it all in – the fat American families, the exhausted waitresses and the Elvis impersonators. 'People-watching here can't ever be disappointing,' she said. 'It's like dinner and a show. Better than any TV programme I've ever seen. And the best part is that it's completely free. We can sit here as long as we want, drinking bottomless coffees, and nobody would care.'

The thought shifted her mind to their money situation. They had been careful and had so far managed to cross the country over a couple of months on barely anything. But now their money was starting to dwindle.

'Hey, Buck.'

He had a toothpick dangling out of the corner of his mouth and he was leaning back in their booth, watching a couple of ageing showgirls drinking coffee at a nearby table. 'Yeah,' he said, the toothpick bobbing as he spoke.

'Where to from here?' Poppy asked.

'I dunno,' he said. 'I always wanted to see that fountain with all the different coloured lights. I saw it on TV once. It goes off like every half an hour or something. And there's also that show with the tigers, which would be awesome. And you know that they've got an Eiffel Tower here too? That would be cool to see. Then I don't ever have to go to Paris itself, I can just tick Eiffel Tower off my list right here. Also, I saw a poster over there in the lobby earlier, Weird Al Yankovic is in concert right here at our hotel. We'd be crazy not to see that!'

Poppy rolled her eyes at him. 'No, dummy, I mean after Vegas. What's our next plan? You know, where to from here?'

Buck shrugged his shoulders and swivelled the toothpick over to the other side of his mouth in contemplation.

'How much cash have you got left?' she asked.

Buck dug in his pocket, pulled out his wallet and emptied out a pile of cash onto the table, then he rifled in another pocket and pulled out a handful of coins which he added to the notes. Poppy pulled out her purse and did the same. Then, while Buck made eyes at the exhausted showgirls, Poppy sorted through the pile, picking out the lint, old mints and till slips. 'Three hundred and sixty-seven dollars and fifty-three cents,' she said finally, pointing at the notes and coins now neatly stacked. 'Shit, I thought we had more.'

Buck tore his gaze away from the girls for a second and eyed the pile. 'We could always stick around here and get jobs,' he said. 'I could be a barman and you could be a stripper.' He burst out laughing.

'Har dee fuckin' har har!' Poppy said, rolling her eyes yet again. 'Seriously, Buck, we've got the hotel for another two days, but after that, then what? If we carry on hitching and moving, this cash will probably only last us another couple of weeks at the most. So, what's the plan?'

'The way I see it, we've got a few options here,' Buck said, sitting up straight. He counted his ideas off on his fingers as he listed them, still balancing the toothpick between his lips as he spoke. 'One – we can wait till the money runs out and then go back to Cape Town on our return tickets. Two – we can try and find some kind of job somewhere here in Vegas, which shouldn't be too tough. Or, three – we could take a chance and bet everything but the airport cab fare and take it from there. This is Vegas, baby! Who knows, anything can happen!'

Poppy's eyes shone. When she'd left home to hitch across America with Buck neither of them had ever even left Cape Town before. The furthest she'd gone was Hermanus. She and Buck were best friends, they'd been at school together and when they'd matriculated they'd both been hungry for excitement and adventure, which is how they'd come up with this plan for their gap year. This would be the perfect ending to their trip, Poppy thought, and what a story to tell. If they lost the money it meant they would have to go home, but if they actually won, and if they won big, well then they'd be loaded, and they'd be able to do anything, go anywhere. Their gap year could go on indefinitely. It could become a gap two years. Buck was right, it was Vegas, and anything could happen.

'That's a hectic idea, Buck,' she said, her eyes wide. 'All or nothing, hey?'

'Yeah, Pops. Why not? We've had great luck so far, and we've had an amazing trip. I mean, I don't know about you, but I'm nowhere near ready to go home yet. And with the amount of money we've got left, going home soon is what's going to happen. We only have a couple more weeks at the most. But you never know, if we won big we could go ahead and buy ourselves another couple of weeks or even months. If it's going to happen anywhere it's going to happen right here in Vegas.' Buck stabbed the table with his finger for effect. 'Do you feel lucky, Poppy?' he asked dramatically.

Poppy thought about it for a second. 'I love it!' she said eventually, her eyes lighting up with excitement. 'Go big or go home!'

STELLA

'Can't you stay with one of your sisters rather, Stella?' her mom asked with an exasperated look on her face.

Stella stood on the threshold of the front door at her parents' house, her bags lying strewn around her feet. 'Aren't you even going to let me in?' she asked her mom. 'I can't stay with any of them, you know that. Lucy isn't even talking to me.'

'What about Violet?' Iris asked.

'Well, I'm not talking to Violet right now, Mom!' Stella said with irritation. 'And even if I was talking to her there's no way I can stay there, she's got the boys to deal with.'

'What about Daisy?'

'Jeez, Mom! I can't stay with Daisy, not after what she did to me! I'm not talking to her right now either. And anyway she lives in a student digs.'

Stella's mom tut-tutted and shook her head vigorously, then she stepped back and pulled the door open grudgingly. 'Fine, then, come in. But just so you know, firstly, this is a temporary arrangement, you can't stay here forever, your father and I only just managed to get rid of the lot of you. And, secondly, you need to know that I'm not happy with what you've done to your twin sister, Stella Rose Frankel! What were you thinking?'

'Urgh, Mom!' Stella grumbled. 'Firstly, you have my word that I won't be here forever, and, secondly, can I at least get through the door properly before you start in on me!'

Stella dragged her bags into the house and then traipsed through to the lounge where her dad was sitting in an armchair reading the newspaper. 'Hello, Stella,' he said. 'Is everything all right?'

'No, Hylton,' Stella's mom barked back at him, 'everything is not all right! Your one daughter thinks she's gay, and your other daughter slept with her twin's boyfriend, and now her husband's kicked her out, so she's coming back to live with us!'

'It's just temporary,' Stella broke in, her voice cracking, 'till I get a chance to figure stuff out. I promise I won't get in your way.'

'Why is it that when they do something bad they're suddenly my daughters?' Stella's dad grumbled, folding his newspaper deliberately into his lap.

With the sound of her parents bickering loudly in the background Stella dragged her bags down the passage. Passing the kitchen, she dipped into the first door on her left and deposited her suitcases in a heap on the floor in what had once been her and Lucy's shared bedroom. The room was pretty much the way they'd left it. It consisted of two single beds, one pushed up against the left-hand wall and one pushed up against the right-hand wall, and a wardrobe. The bedspread on Stella's bed was still the same old yellow one from her childhood, and the one on Lucy's bed was the same old pink one. Stella felt desperately nostalgic. She remembered how she had always kept her bed perfectly made, with the yellow duvet tucked neatly in along all the edges, while Lucy had had no problem climbing into an unmade pink bed every night, getting right back in under the crumpled duvet lying just as she had left it that morning. Once, when they were ten, fed up with Lucy's untidy ways, Stella had dug up a tape measure and a roll of duct tape.

She had measured out the room precisely and then stuck a duct-taped line down the middle of the carpet, separating the two sides of the room into the tidy yellow side and the hurricane-afflicted pink side. Then she'd taken her school ruler out of her neatly ordered yellow pencil case and used it like a stick, spearing any of Lucy's items that found themselves on her side of the line and tossing them back over into the pink chaos.

When Iris appeared in the bedroom doorway she found Stella sitting on the edge of her yellow bed, staring into space, surrounded by her memories. Iris sat down next to her on the bed and put her arm around her. 'Don't worry, Stel,' she said, patting Stella's arm. 'It's all just a phase. This too shall pass.'

Stella looked at her mom with sad eyes and hoped she was right. That was a mother's job wasn't it, to always be right?

Stella couldn't find sleep. She'd been looking for it everywhere for hours, tossing and turning, but it was nowhere to be found. She lay on her back and stared at the ceiling. Then she turned onto her left side. Then she sat up and plumped up her pillows. Then she tried lying on her stomach. Sleep was in another country and she obviously wasn't planning on visiting any time soon.

Her parents' house in Grace Road in Claremont was unnervingly quiet. There were no bergies shouting at each other on the street outside. No drunken upstairs neighbours stumbling home at all hours of the night, clomping up and down in heavy boots and then proceeding to argue loudly for an hour and a half (before doing what sounded like either rearranging the furniture or dragging each other's dead bodies across the floor). House-living in the suburbs and apartment-living in the city were two entirely different extremes, Stella decided.

Stella studied her childhood bedside clock radio. It was well after two. She wondered what Max was doing, whether he was finding sleep any easier. Then she wondered what Lucy was doing. Whether Jake was there with her, and whether they'd been able to make up and make love again since The Incident. Stella suspected that was unlikely. It would probably be just too weird for either of them to handle for a while, at least.

Then Stella's mind rolled over first to watching Lucy and Jake having sex in the guest bathroom down the hall, and then to the sex she'd had with Jake. She'd struggled to get just the little bit of it that she'd experienced out of her mind. At random points in her day the memories had come flooding back to her completely unbidden. She wondered if it was just the newness of it that had made it all so exciting, so all consuming, compared to what she usually experienced with Max.

Stella turned back onto her side and pulled her knees up into her chest. There was nobody she could turn to and she felt lost. She knew things always seemed worse in the middle of the night, but she couldn't see the up side of any of this. There didn't seem to be any silver-lined cloud or hidden opportunity in the situation. She would get a glass of milk, she thought. People did that in the movies all the time when they couldn't sleep, maybe it would work for her too. And if that didn't work she had a stash of sleeping pills she would dip into to make the bad night go away.

Stella padded on socked feet down the passageway and into the kitchen. As she stepped onto the cold kitchen tiles a figure caught her eye in the darkness and she jumped back in shock, darting her hand up to her chest and gasping in surprise.

When her eyes eventually adjusted to the dark she saw it was her dad, sitting at the kitchen table. He was wearing his pyjama bottoms but he was naked from the waist up. 'Jesus, Dad,' she whispered. 'You scared the living crap out of me.'

He didn't answer. Instead, as Stella watched in shocked silence, he brought his hand up from beneath the table and moved it towards his face. Between his fingers was the glowing tip of what was clearly a lit cigarette.

'Dad?' Stella said, watching as he puffed on the cigarette. But it was as if she wasn't there at all, as if he couldn't hear her. 'Dad?' she repeated, this time more urgently. 'What the hell are you doing? I didn't know you smoked.'

Still nothing. He continued to gaze right past her. Stella looked over her shoulder to see where he was looking, but the only thing behind her was the microwave, with the time, 3:15 a.m., beating out of it in neon piping.

Stepping forward, Stella waved her hand in front of her dad's face, but he didn't even blink. He just lifted the smoking cigarette up to his mouth and took another deep drag, the red coal moving ever closer to his lips.

Stella sat down across from him at the table, flabbergasted. In her twenty-five years she'd never seen her father smoke. It was the strangest sight, completely foreign to her.

'Dad?' she said again, waving her hand in front of his face one more time. Still he ignored her, unblinking, as if in a trance. Stella dropped her mouth open in astonishment, the only possible thing she could think of was that he must be sleep-smoking. And also sleepwalking – because how else had he got into the kitchen from the bedroom? However bizarre, it was the only thing that made any sense.

Stella dropped her hands back into her lap. Best not to wake him, she thought, she'd read somewhere that it was dangerous to wake a sleepwalker. She wondered if that was true or if it was just an urban legend.

Unsure what to do next, Stella sat with her father for a couple more minutes, watching him intently. She wondered if she should wake her mom. She would know what to do. Just then Hylton finished the cigarette and ground the butt out in an ashtray on the table in front of him. Then he stood up and walked slowly out of the kitchen.

Stella followed him at a safe distance, watching as he walked down the passageway, past her bedroom, past the guest bathroom and towards the master suite at the opposite end of the house, still hardly able to believe what she was seeing. As they reached the bedroom door her dad turned right and disappeared into the en suite bathroom. Stella waited outside the bathroom for him, listening carefully to his movements. She heard the tap running and then being turned off, and then her father reappeared, walking straight past her, not seeing her at all, as if she were a ghost. 'Dad?' she whispered again, but he still didn't hear her.

At the door to her parents' bedroom Stella caught a glimpse of her mother sleeping peacefully on the far side of the bed, her chest rising and falling. She watched her father slip into his side of the bed and roll over. He was snoring loudly in just under a minute.

Shaking her head in disbelief, Stella returned to the kitchen, wondering if she'd dreamt what she'd just seen. Still shaking her head, she turned on the light and examined the ashtray on the kitchen table. It contained some ash and just the one stompie, smoked right down to the filter. Half a pack of cigarettes lay next to it. Camel Lights. Stella was astonished. She picked up the pack and examined it closely, as if to make sure that it was real. She hadn't even known that her parents owned an ashtray, let alone cigarettes and a lighter. Both of them had always been vehemently anti-smoking, and they had always made it quite clear to all the Frankel girls early on that if they were ever caught smoking they would be lynched. How could things have changed so much and so quickly? Stella wondered. She'd only moved out of their house a few years earlier.

Stella opened the fridge and looked into its cool bright glow, thinking about the bizarreness of the situation. Suddenly memories of the moment Jake's arms had snaked around her while she leaned into the fridge at Lucy's house swamped her mind. She shook her head, grabbed the milk and then slammed the fridge door as fast as she could. She was cursed, she thought. As long as she lived she would never again be able to look into an open fridge without thinking of Jake. Jake's hands. Jake's fingers. Jake's body. And her disaster. She felt so guilty she didn't know which way to turn. She wondered if she'd ever sleep a full night again. Sleep, she knew, was reserved for the innocent, while the guilty were forever sentenced to tossing and turning.

Stella drank straight from the carton, making a point of finishing the milk so that she wouldn't have to open the fridge again. Then, tossing the empty carton in the bin, she went to sit back down at the kitchen table, across from where her father had been sitting only minutes earlier. She shook her head and eyed the cigarette butt again, still lying in the centre of the otherwise empty ashtray. Stella wondered if all families were this crazy and if indeed her mother was right and it was really all just a phase?

When Stella eventually woke up it was after ten on Sunday morning. She had finally fallen into some loose version of sleep just before five. She felt exhausted.

Clambering out of bed, Stella assessed the dark bags under her eyes in the mirror on the inside door of the wardrobe. She and Lucy had shared the mirror growing up and Stella had often wondered if the mirror had recognised that they were two different people, or whether it had thought it was just one person who looked at herself twice as much as she should.

Stella joined her mom in the kitchen where Iris was brewing a fresh pot of percolated coffee. 'Morning, darling,' Iris said. 'Sleep well?'

'Not really,' Stella groaned. She ducked her head and looked through the partition that opened up between the kitchen and the dining room. 'Morning, Dad,' she said, catching sight of her father sitting in the lounge reading the newspaper.

'Morning, Stel,' he replied, pulling the top corner of his paper down.

Stella searched his face for any indication that he'd been pulling her leg the night before, but if he had he was doing a very good job of hiding it.

'Mom,' Stella said, lowering her voice and sidling up next to her mother as she poured the coffee out into three cups.

'Yes, dear?'

'The strangest thing happened last night.'

'What's that, love?' Iris asked, looking at her over the top of her glasses.

'Well, I couldn't sleep, so I came to the kitchen in the middle of the night to get a glass of milk, and Dad was sitting right there, at the kitchen table, smoking a cigarette! Can you believe it?' Stella said, feeling silly as she said it. Suddenly the events of the night before seemed like some kind of weird dream.

'Yes, dear, the doctor says there's nothing to worry about, he's fast asleep,' Iris responded, stirring the coffee and returning the milk to the fridge nonchalantly.

'You mean you know about it?' Stella asked, her voice raised in shock.

'Shhhh!' Iris hissed sharply, covering her lips with a stern finger. 'Keep your voice down. I don't want your father to hear. He's only been doing it for a couple of weeks and he doesn't even know he does it. The doctor says it's quite harmless. Apparently it's probably a reaction to stress caused by some kind of shift in his life.'

'But I didn't even know he smoked!' Stella whispered.

'No, he doesn't,' Iris said matter-of-factly. 'Only while he's sleeping.'

Stella shook her head in confusion. 'Mom, are you listening to what you're saying? That's the craziest thing I've ever heard! Where did he even get the cigarettes from? And the ashtray and the lighter?'

'Shush,' Iris scolded her again. 'Your uncle Ivan left a couple of packs here when he was visiting from London at the end of last year. They're in that drawer over there. I'd been meaning to throw them out for ages, but it seemed like such a waste. Your father must have pulled them out. Really, it's nothing serious, Stella. I'm sure it's just a phase.'

'But, Mom, how come you didn't tell any of us about it? Doesn't it bother you? Aren't you worried about him?'

'No, not at all,' Iris said sharply. 'He always brushes his teeth and gargles with mouthwash before he comes back to bed.'

Her mom was easily the most practical person she had ever met, Stella decided. That's what her dad must have been doing in the bathroom before he went back to bed the night before; he was brushing and gargling. 'Oh, so as long as he's a considerate smoker this is all right with you?' Stella said, completely astonished.

'Stella!' her mother snapped. 'After what you've done, I don't think you have any right to be giving lectures about what's right and what's wrong!'

Iris picked up two of the cups of coffee and went into the lounge, leaving Stella shocked and gaping in the kitchen.

POPPY

Poppy and Buck strode a path through the casino, weaving their way between the machines. Poppy tried to take everything in. Lights flashed and bells rang; people whooped around them; some celebrated, others sobbed and others simply sat and fed their machines mechanically, as if they themselves were machines.

'This is the craziest place on earth,' Poppy said, nudging Buck and pointing towards an absolutely enormous lady who was wearing a giant Hawaiian shirt stretched over a pair of luminous pink cycling shorts. The shorts managed to highlight every roll of fat and every pucker of cellulite on her lower half, of which there were many, and the whole look was rounded off with a pair of luminous pink Crocs, a pink visor cap and pink lipstick. The lady was so incredibly fat that she couldn't fit on just one stool and so, as they watched, she hefted herself onto two neighbouring stools. One for each fat buttock. Poppy shook her head in disbelief.

'My uncle Ernie is an interior designer, back home,' Buck said. 'And he told me some stuff about casinos. You know why they have these crazy, patterned carpets no matter where you are around the world?'

Poppy shook her head and looked down, he was right, the carpet was a deep red with a repeating pattern of a fan of brightly coloured gambling chips. It hurt her eyes just looking at it.

'My uncle said that the casinos insist on these carpets for a reason. They know that their regulars are completely obsessive and often totally superstitious. So, like, if they're busy playing and they get on a roll, they don't ever want to have to take a break or leave the table, or change anything that might screw up their luck. He says they can sit in one spot for hours, through the night even, as long as the luck is going their way. And the casino guys will bring them food and water and whatever else they need to keep on going. So, if they need to, you know, *go*, rather than move and upset a winning streak, they'll just go in their pants, right there in the casino.'

'No way, dude,' Poppy shrieked. 'That's crazy!'

'It's true!' Buck nodded. 'He knows it for a fact, 'cos his firm worked on the interior at Montecasino in Joburg. They need the carpets to be as indestructible as possible, so that they can get the stains out.'

Poppy looked down at her feet. 'That's the most disgusting thing I've ever heard.'

'Yeah,' Buck said. 'You'd think if those gamblers were so clever they'd buy some of those adult diapers or something, then at least nobody would know they'd gone to the toilet in their pants, and nobody would have to clean up after them.'

'Gross, man!' Poppy said, turning her nose up at him.

They walked on in silence for a couple of minutes, circling back on themselves around the casino floor.

'So, where should we play?' Poppy eventually asked.

'Maybe the tables,' Buck said, pointing towards them. 'Definitely not the slots, they're way too depressing, and they don't even have the arms you can pull any more. They shouldn't be allowed to call them one-armed bandits. They should call them soul-sucking cash-eaters instead.'

'Yeah, I know what you mean. How can you just sit and press a button? What about blackjack, or roulette?' Poppy suggested. 'At least then we have some control over our own destiny.'

'Roulette,' Buck said, his eyes sparkling. 'You can win a ton of cash on roulette.'

'Have you played it before?' Poppy asked.

'Not in a casino, but in junior school a friend of mine had one of those toy gambling kits with a roulette wheel, and we used to play that all the time. So I have had a little experience. Anyway, how hard can it be, right? All you have to do is pick some numbers. We can do that easily enough.'

Poppy took the wad of money they'd gathered out of her pocket. She counted out fifty bucks for the cab fare to the airport and split the rest of the money evenly between them. They had roughly a hundred and fifty bucks each.

'What about that table?' Buck asked, pointing out one of the tables after they'd circled the room a couple more times.

'Nah, I don't like the look of that croupier,' Poppy said. 'You should never trust a man with a moustache.'

'Okay, what about that one, then?' Buck asked, pointing out an adjacent table. As he pointed at it someone at the table yelped at a big win, and the whole table applauded.

'No way,' Poppy said. 'Someone just won there. What are the chances of two big wins, one after the other?'

'Jeez, Poppy, come on, you can't have a problem with every single table in this place!' Buck said.

'What about that one?' Poppy asked, pointing out a table at the far end of the floor. 'I don't mind the looks of that one.'

Buck shrugged his shoulders. 'What makes you like that one?' he asked.

'Well, I don't know much about feng shui, but I'm sure it's a good sign that it more or less faces the front door of the casino. And, look, it's got two empty seats. I bet that's a sign. That's our lucky table.'

'Whatever,' Buck said, rubbing his hands together. 'Come on, let's do this thing.'

They sat down at the table and watched a couple of spins to acquaint themselves with the general rules of the game and get a feel for the table. Then they nodded to each other, both ready to exchange their money for chips. Buck waited till the table was between spins and then he held a handful of money out to the croupier.

'Can you exchange this for chips, please?' he asked politely.

'Please put the money down on the table, Sir,' the croupier said with a tight smile.

Buck looked at her and cocked his head, confused.

'You're not allowed to hand the money to me directly, Sir,' she said, smiling at him again politely, but clearly bored. 'It's against the rules, Sir. If you lay your money down on the table I will pick it up and exchange it for you.'

Poppy blushed for Buck and instantly laid her money down on the table, not wanting to also look like a rookie. The croupier smiled at her politely and nodded, then she reached for the money. Counting the money carefully, she dropped it into a slot in the table before counting out a small stack of chips which she slid over the table towards Poppy.

The other punters fiddled with their chips and some even began to place them on the table as Buck also laid his money down. Poppy looked closely at the croupier as she repeated the process of changing it into chips. She was a tired, bored-looking brunette in her late thirties. She had her hair pulled back loosely in a ponytail and she wore the standard croupier's uniform of a pair of black pants, a white shirt and a black waistcoat. A name badge on her breast announced to the world that her name was *Carmen*. She had the deeply lined face of a woman who had started smoking early, been disappointed young and seen altogether too much.

'So, how are we going to do this?' Poppy whispered to Buck, adrenalin pumping through her veins. Her hands were shaking with the sheer excitement and potential foolishness of what they were about to do.

'I'm going to put it all on black,' Buck said.

'All of it?' Poppy squirmed. 'On one roll?'

Buck nodded.

'Are you sure you want to do that?' she asked.

'A hundred per cent,' he said. 'Black's my favourite colour, and the way I see it, in this situation it's all or nothing. Let's be rock stars, Poppy! For once in our lives!' He beamed and his eyes shone. Then he pushed his entire pile of chips across the table and placed them on the little black diamond.

Poppy's eyes went wide. She studied the table, focusing on the numbers, to see if anything jumped out at her. The thirteen looked good, but so did her age, twenty-one.

'Place your bets,' the croupier yelled, spinning the wheel.

Poppy's heart felt like it was going to burst out of her chest it was beating so hard. The number thirteen loomed large in front of her, the number itself heaving as if it was breathing, getting bigger and smaller in front of her eyes. This was it, it would be thirteen black, she was sure of it. In fact, she had never been more sure of anything in her life. The number thirteen filled her brain; it had to be some kind of sign.

The bored croupier dropped the small white ball onto the rim of the spinning table. 'Final bets,' she called, eyeing Poppy, whose hand still hovered above the table, clutching her chips.

The other players at the table blurred in her vision as they placed their final bets. The thirteen loomed large in front of Poppy's eyes, warping and receding, still calling out to her.

Poppy took a deep breath, if she was going to do this, it was now or never. She felt she had to honour the strong feelings she was having about the thirteen. She pictured a scene where she didn't place her bet and the ball came to land neatly on thirteen, thinking about how devastated she would be. Then she cupped her small pile of chips in her palms, kissed them and then placed the entire lot directly onto the middle of the thirteen. The square was empty, nobody else at the table seemed to have felt the power of the thirteen, but whether that was a good thing or a bad thing, Poppy had no idea.

'No more bets,' the croupier called and Poppy snapped her now empty hand back off the table and crossed her arms in front of her chest, burying her fingers in her armpits and blinking quickly, shocked by her own spontaneity.

Time slowed as the little white ball raced round and round the rim of the wheel, bouncing as it went. Poppy followed it, fully focused on its journey. She straightened her arms and gripped the table, digging her fingernails into the padded edging. The ringing bells and crowds and shouts and screams in the background faded, everything seemed to be in slow motion, except for the beating of her heart, which raced in her chest at a million miles an hour. The only other sound she could hear was the deafening bounce of the little white ball and the *whir whir whir* of the quickly spinning wheel. The ball popped into red sixteen, bounced out again violently, then plopped into black thirty-three, bounced out of that too, landed on red seventeen, bounced out of it and then slipped neatly into black thirteen with a small thunk. Poppy's heart screamed in her ears. Then just as quickly the little white ball bounced one last time. Out of black thirteen to settle comfortably and securely in the pocket of red number three.

Poppy heard Buck suck in his breath and she let out a little barely audible whimper herself.

'Fuck!' Buck swore.

Poppy dropped her head onto the table and bashed her forehead repeatedly into the padded edging. The casino had obviously thought about this too – it was padded for a reason.

When Poppy eventually looked up Buck had a deranged smile on his face.

'What the fuck are you smiling about, Buck?' Poppy cried. 'We lost the lot! We didn't even gamble for five minutes and we lost everything!'

'Go big or go home!' he said, shaking his head and grinning his deranged grin.

Poppy was suddenly so irritated with him that she couldn't look at his stupid face for another second. She wanted to slap him silly. 'This is all completely your fault,' she cried. 'I wasn't ready to put all my money down. I should have waited for the next spin. You hurried me, Buck! I should never have listened to you!'

'Poppy, chill, this was the plan. We lost, it sucks, but it's nobody's fault,' Buck said.

'We could have carried on travelling for another couple of weeks on that money.' Poppy felt hysterical. 'We could have seen more things, had more adventures, and now we're just screwed, it's all over. We've got nothing left! We're going to have to get up the day after tomorrow and go to the airport and go home and all you can say is "go big or go home"!'

The other people at the table were staring at them, but Poppy was so upset she didn't care. All she wanted to do was shout at Buck.

'Poppy, this is the way it was meant to go,' Buck said. 'You chose the table, and I didn't force you to put all your money down on one number – you did that all by yourself. It's not my fault you picked a fish number and I picked the wrong colour.'

'Fuck you, Buck!' Poppy swore, kicking at the leg of his chair below him.

'What's your problem?' he asked her sarkily. 'There was always a chance we were going to lose, you knew that. That's why it's called gambling, not investing!'

'Fuck you twice,' she said, unable to think of anything more intelligent to say. 'We didn't have to bet it all at once, we should have done it slowly, figured out some kind of system. Discussed it properly before we just went and did it.'

'That's ridiculous!' Buck said. 'We lost, that's life. Tomorrow is another day and we'll deal with that when it comes. If it means we have to go home, then we have to go home. I'm going to bed!' Buck got up and strode a couple of steps away from the table. Then he turned to see if she was following him. 'Coming?'

'I can't look at you right now,' Poppy said. She knew she was being irrational and that it wasn't entirely his fault, but she was angry and she needed someone to blame, someone to take it out on. And he was closest.

'Suit yourself,' Buck said, shrugging his shoulders and disappearing into the crowd.

Poppy dropped her head back onto the cool, padded leather on the rim of the table and closed her eyes, the spinning wheel and the small white ball bouncing out of the number thirteen playing itself over and over on the back of her eyelids.

STELLA

Monday morning Stella sat at her desk feeling bleak. She still hadn't spoken to Lucy since The Incident or to Max since the ensuing Evening Of The Outing Of The Incident at Violet's house. She took a few deep breaths to calm her nerves, picked up her phone and dialled Lucy's number.

'Hi, you've reached Lucy. I can't take your call right now, so please leave a message and I'll get back to you as soon as possible. Stella, if that's you, don't bother leaving a message, I won't listen to it.' *Beep.*

Next Stella dialled Max's number, a nauseous feeling in the pit of her stomach. His phone also rang several times and then went to voicemail. Stella left a long, garbled message that started with an apology, rambled tearfully through remorse and over into pathetic-ness before the phone cut her off with a beep mid-sentence. She said a little internal prayer that the beep had deleted the entire disastrous, unplanned mess from his voicemail and put the phone down.

It was hopeless. Neither of them would ever talk to her again. Ever. Stella felt like she was starting to come apart at the seams without either of them in her life. Without Lucy she was half a person, and without Max she was half a person. Essentially, without both of them, there was nothing left of her.

Stella reached for the small stack of unwritten wedding thank-you notes. She picked up her pen and began to write the first one. Maybe if she acted as if nothing bad had happened, if she just carried on, things would go back to normal.

Dear Aunty Sheila and Uncle Gerard,

Thank you so much for the wonderful coffee maker you gave us for our wedding. Max and I will cherish it, together with all the magical memories we have of our special day. We will think of you both every time we use it, throughout the long years of our marriage.

Love, Stella and Max

As Stella signed the note a fat tear dropped off her cheek and landed on the card with a splash, directly over the word marriage. The ink slipped and skidded across the page, the letters all moulding into each other, rendering the entire thing illegible.

Stella attacked the pile. By lunchtime she'd made a pretty good dent in the thank yous. As she had in every moment since this whole nightmare had begun, she ached to phone Lucy and tell her.

Stella couldn't eat lunch. Her throat felt thick and constricted and her stomach churned. In a haze of grief she sifted on autopilot through some of the Dr Dee letters that had begun to stack up on her desk, picking out a few for the website. She chose two very different letters. One was quite sweet and innocent, the second one more risqué. That should keep the spectrum of her readers happy, she thought. With her selections made she got to work and typed the first one into her system.

Dear Dr Dee,

My best friend in the whole wide world is a gay guy. I am a straight girl. I really truly believe that he is my soul mate. We just get along so well. We share all the same interests and love spending time together. I really believe that I am in love with him. When we're not together I miss him so much my heart aches. The other reason I know that he's my soul mate is because I also find I'm very turned on by him. He spends a ton of time in the gym and he has an amazing body. It's so beautiful that I can't take my eyes off him. I once watched him for an hour and a half when he fell asleep while we were watching a DVD together. What do you think I should do about it? What are the chances he has bisexual interests and maybe I have some kind of shot at getting to be with him?

Fag Hag

Stella dashed off her response.

Dear Fag Hag,

Your friend is gay. He likes cock. And so do you. That's why you have so much in common and get along so well, you dimwit! He probably only spends all that time with you because he wishes he could wear those pink stilettos you bought last time you went shopping together, and there's a good chance that he wonders if he might be able to turn some of the guys who try to pick you up while you're out together.

Get a grip, Fag Hag, either that or a penis, because that's the only way he's ever going to look at you 'that way' twice.

Love, Dr Dee

Stella concealed a snicker behind her hand; she was always amazed at how much better writing the biting, cynical responses made her feel. But the reward was always fleeting and she felt almost immediately guilty about being so nasty.

Hitting the return key a number of times, Stella got to work on the real response. She would answer as best she could and try to help this poor girl, despite her own personal cloud of misery. Perhaps by doing something even just a little bit 'good' for someone else she could start to undo the wad of bad karma that must by now be piled up, waiting for her on her doorstep.

Dear Fag Hag,

I'm so pleased you've found someone you identify with so closely, and it's quite natural for you to have such strong feelings for the special friends in your life. However, as I think you're beginning to see, things do get a lot more complicated once you start having sexual feelings for someone.

You have a few choices in this situation. You could choose to preserve your relationship as it is by ignoring the attraction you feel. However, I would be concerned that in time this will create feelings of resentment, frustration and dissatisfaction for you.

I personally feel you owe it to yourself and your friendship to be honest with your friend. But that conversation has to happen with the understanding that there's a strong possibility that he may not reciprocate your feelings, which might lead to some awkwardness.

Another strategy might be to bring up bisexuality in a casual conversation, and see how he reacts. It would be a more subtle way for you to test the water. But bear in mind, chances are he already suspects you're interested in him, since these emotions are often tricky to hide.

I'm afraid at some point you need to ask yourself which is more important, having your friend remain your friend or possibly turning your relationship into a romantic one.

Good luck, I'm holding thumbs for you.

Love, Dr Dee

Satisfied that she'd crafted a friendly, supportive response, Stella moved on to the second, more risqué letter. In the past this would definitely have been a letter Stella would have phoned Lucy over, it was so out-of-the-norm crazy that they would have laughed over it together for weeks. Stella felt her heart constrict as she typed the letter into her system, sad that she didn't have anyone to share it with.

Dear Dr Dee,

I have a rather strange question for you. But I have no one else to turn to because I feel too awkward to ask our family doctor about this. So here goes.

I was wondering if it's at all possible for a woman who isn't pregnant and has never been pregnant before to lactate?

And if it is possible I would like to know what the best way to stimulate the lactation is? Because I would love to please my new husband with this.

Curious Newlywed

Just as she'd finished typing the letter into her computer her phone rang.

'Dr Dee speaking,' she said.

There was a brief silence. Then, 'Stella, it's Violet.'

Stella held her breath and wished she hadn't answered the phone. She was furious with Violet and hadn't planned on speaking to her for a while. Violet needed to know how wrong she'd been. How could she betray Stella's trust by telling Daisy about what had happened with Jake? Stella felt her anger bubbling up anew at the thought of it.

'Stella, are you there?' Violet asked. 'I've been trying to get hold of you for days, but your phone goes to voicemail every time.'

'I'm really angry with you, Violet. I don't want to talk to you right now!'

'I'm really sorry, Stella,' Violet said. 'I feel awful about what happened. I wanted to make sure you're okay.'

'Violet, why did you tell Daisy? How could you do that to me?' Stella whined, close to tears.

'I don't know why I told her. I'm exhausted, Stella. The boys never sleep and somehow all three of them end up in our bed most nights. I haven't had a full night's sleep in going on seven years, Stella. I wasn't thinking clearly. I never, ever thought she'd tell anyone, I swear. I had no idea she was so vulnerable and that she was about to come out of the closet to everyone. How could I have known?'

'Well, everything's really screwed up now, Violet, and it's partly your fault. What the hell am I going to do?'

'I think the important thing is to stay calm and keep breathing. Mom says you're staying with them temporarily. How's that going?'

'Oh, you wouldn't believe me if I told you,' Stella said, an image swimming across her vision of her father sitting at the kitchen table in his pyjama bottoms, dragging on a cigarette in the middle of the night.

'Stella, I really feel terrible about everything that's happened, and I know it will take you a while to trust me again, but I want you to know that I'm here for you. If there's anything I can do …'

Stella shook her head silently.

'Stella, are you still there?' Violet asked again into the silence.

'Yes.'

'How's work going?' Violet asked.

Stella could hear the desperation in Violet's voice. And as furious as she was with her, she still loved her sister and she really needed someone on her side, someone she could talk to and confide in.

'Work's ridiculous. You wouldn't believe one of the letters I got today, it's absolutely crazy.'

'Well, crazy is a relative term,' Violet said, the relief that Stella had let her off the hook evident in her voice.

'No, this is seriously crazy, Vi,' Stella said. 'This chick wants to breastfeed her husband! Have you ever?'

'Sounds to me like typical codependent behaviour,' Violet said seriously.

'No, Vi, what are you talking about? It's typical crazy behaviour!' Stella shrieked. 'Can you believe there are such freaks out there? Imagine wanting to breastfeed your own husband? Even worse, imagine breastfeeding! Yuck!'

'Actually, I can believe there are people like that out there, Stella,' Violet said seriously. 'If there weren't I'd be out of a job. Also, we don't really like to use the term freak.' Stella could hear Violet writing notes on the other side of the phone. 'Some people just have different urges and needs, and that doesn't make them crazy or freakish, it just makes them a little bit different.'

Stella chewed on her lip; this wasn't quite the conversation regarding this letter that she'd had in mind. She and Lucy would have laughed and laughed, and Max would have chuckled overly loudly in that way of his, and told her again how lucky she was to have such a cool job. Violet was just too analytical for all of this, she sucked the fun right out of it.

'I know, I know,' Stella said. 'Look, Vi, I'm going to go now, I've got a ton of work to do.'

'Sure, Stella,' Violet said, then she paused. 'So we're all right?' she asked tentatively.

Stella took a deep breath. 'I shouldn't be talking to you for at least another ten days, you deserve at least two weeks of cold shoulder for what you've done, you know. You're just lucky I don't have anyone else to talk to right now!'

'You know I'm sorry about all this, Stella …' Violet said quietly.

'Yes, I know,' Stella said, wiping a tear off her cheek. 'I'm sorry too.'

After she put down the phone, Stella picked up the letter and read and reread it several times. The world was full to the brim with freaks. She couldn't believe the kinds of things people came up with. She tapped at the keyboard, putting down her first response with a smile.

Dear Curious Newlywed,

You've got to be kidding me! You want to breastfeed your husband! What the hell? Have you completely lost your mind? Seriously! That's not acceptable. If your husband wants milk he can get up and go to the kitchen like all the other men in the world, lazy bastard!

Love, Dr Dee

Stella read over her response and smiled. It was perfect. It was only a pity that it was going straight into the trash and nobody would ever get to see it.

Then she got busy with the real response. She picked up a medical journal and ran her forefinger down the index, looking for the section on lactation.

As she turned to the correct page Stella imagined a conversation around the dinner table, the kind of conversation she'd had with Max a hundred times over the past two years:

MAX: How was your day, honey?
STELLA: Well, I advised a woman on how to induce lactation so she could breastfeed her new husband, what about you, darling?
MAX: Well, I taught my class about isosceles triangles, and then we played rounders during PE. Stephen Savoy stuck chewing gum in Carla Levitt's hair again. And we ran out of sugar in the teachers' lounge.

Stella came back to reality with a bump. She shouldn't fantasise about the conversation she would be having that night with Max at the dinner table, because she knew perfectly well she wouldn't be having any conversation with Max that night, or any other night in the near future for that matter, the way things were going. And she only had herself to blame.

Stella read through a couple of medical journals, made a call to a physician she knew, whose number she kept in her crazy file, and once she'd completed her research she hit the return key a couple of times and typed up her response.

Dear Curious Newlywed,

Believe it or not, although rather rare, it is actually quite possible for women who aren't pregnant to lactate. The most successful cases of women who haven't just given birth lactating usually include a combination of hormone therapy and physical stimulation of the breasts and nipples.

However, I would suggest that you consult with your gynaecologist or physician on the subject before you make any decisions as not everyone is a suitable candidate for the treatment.

Love, Dr Dee

Stella's cellphone rang again as she was signing off the letter. She looked down at the screen and saw it was Max. Her entire body broke out in an instant sweat.

'Hello, Max,' she said breathlessly.

'Stella,' he said. His voice tight and quivering.

'Thank you so much for calling me back, I've been desperate to talk to you since Friday, I've left you dozens of messages. It's horrible not being able to talk you.'

'Where are you staying?' he asked, his voice still controlled.

'I'm at my folks; it's awful. Max, will you let me see you?' she asked, well aware of the fact that her voice sounded weak and pleading.

'Stella,' he said sternly.

She hated the tone of his voice. It was cold, angry, disappointed and unyielding.

'I only called because I want to ask you one thing,' he said.

'Of course, anything.'

'Why did you do it?' he asked. 'Just tell me honestly, Stella. I need to know.'

Stella paused and took a deep breath. Tears were pouring down her cheeks and she blew her nose on her sleeve, which was the nearest available thing. 'Max, I don't know, I can't tell you why. It just happened ... I'd been drinking and ...'

'Since when do you drink?' Max asked, sounding angry and confused.

'Listen to me, Max, something happened at work, okay. Something else I need to tell you about. It's what started all of this in the first place,' Stella sobbed.

'What happened?' he asked, his voice a whisper.

Stella couldn't speak. Her heart pounded in her chest. This was the moment she'd been avoiding. She felt sick to the stomach and eyed out her dustbin just in case she needed to vomit, noticing for the first time that it was one of those wire mesh ones, which meant vomiting in it wasn't really an option.

'Tell me what happened, Stella!' Max said through clenched teeth.

'Max, that day we went to La Perla to celebrate, I didn't actually get the promotion at work.'

'But you told me you got it?' Max said, sounding confused.

'I know. I can't explain it. Everything just spiralled out of control. Some other girl got it, some student straight out of Rhodes. I was so upset, Max. And then on the phone you were so excited that you just assumed I got the promotion, and I didn't get a chance to correct you because the bell rang and you had to go. Then I planned to tell you later on, when we met for drinks to celebrate at La Perla. I was going to tell you straight away, but you and Lucy went and planned that amazing party, and then the thing with the sprinklers happened, and after that I just couldn't find the right time to tell you. And the longer I left it the worse things got. It was all such a mess. That's why I was drinking that afternoon; I needed Dutch courage. I was supposed to meet Lucy for lunch. I was going to tell her and then I was going to come straight to the school and tell you, and then tell everyone else. But Lucy didn't turn up and I drank too much, and I was too drunk to drive. So I walked up to Lucy's place instead, because I was in Sea Point. I was going to tell her and try and sober up a bit before I came home. But then Jake came in, and he thought I was Lucy, and then it just sort of happened. I'm so, so sorry, Max. I was out of my mind drunk. I didn't know what I was doing.' She was howling now, pleading with him for forgiveness.

There was a long silence on the other end of the phone.

'Max, are you still there?' Stella asked.

'That's two lies, Stella,' Max finally said in a very quiet, faraway voice. 'In such a short space of time. I thought we weren't ever going to lie to each other. That's what we always said.'

'I know ...' Stella said. 'I never meant for any of this to happen, and if I could go back in time and undo it, I would do it in a heartbeat ...'

'I don't quite know how to process all of this, Stella,' Max said, cutting her off. 'I don't think you should come home right now. I can't deal with this. I don't know how you could do this to me, Stella. I don't think I can ever trust you again.'

'Will you at least let me come and see you, so we can talk about this face to face?' she pleaded.

'I can't, Stella. Not yet. It's all too much. We've only been married a month, for crying out loud.'

'Hey, I finished the thank-you cards for the wedding presents,' Stella said forlornly, trying to rescue what was left of the conversation.

'I wouldn't send them off quite yet,' Max said. 'We may have to send all the gifts back.' Stella heard the school bell in the background. 'I've got to go, Stella,' he said, putting the phone down in her ear.

Stella collapsed onto her desk, sobbing loudly.

When Stella eventually looked up, both sleeves sodden and covered in mascara, someone had anonymously delivered a cup of tea and a roll of toilet paper to her desk. She did her best to try and dry her damp cheeks, but before she could make her way to the bathroom to freshen up properly her desk phone rang again. Wary of who it might be this time, she sucked in a few breaths and tried to compose herself before she answered.

'Hello,' she said, trying hard to sound together and professional.

'Stella, it's Ebrahim, in typesetting,' a voice said down the phone.

'Hi, Ebrahim,' Stella answered, her voice shaking with relief.

'Stella, we have no column and we're about to go to print,' Ebrahim said. 'I've got some filler editorial I can place if you're not ready.'

'Oh no, Ebrahim, what time is it?' Stella asked.

'It's quarter past three and we go to print at half past,' he replied.

Stella looked at her watch – her deadline was every Monday at two thirty, for the issue that would come out two weeks later. She'd never missed a deadline before. In fact she was usually early, because she would prepare each week's column towards the end of the week before.

'Oh no, oh no, oh no,' Stella said, half to herself and half to Ebrahim.

'It's no problem,' Ebrahim continued, 'we have enough editorial for filler.'

Stella stared at her screen. There was no way she was going to let her column give way to editorial. That would simply add insult to injury. Not only could she not get into editorial, but now she couldn't even do her own column. She thought about the work she'd done that morning for the website. She ran her eye over the document briefly. The column would be a little thin compared to normal, but she thought she probably had enough content with the two letters she'd worked on – she could send those and she would be out of danger for another week.

'Nope, it's cool, Ebrahim. I'm going to email the document to you right now, this very second, is that okay? Sorry it's so late, we've had some technical problems up here,' she said, crossing her fingers behind her back as she lied.

'Sure, but you need to hurry up,' Ebrahim said. 'We're going to print in exactly fifteen minutes, and I still need to drop the copy in and set it.'

'No problem,' Stella said. 'I'm sending it down as we speak. I'm clicking send right now, I promise.'

'Okay, I'm waiting for it at my computer,' Ebrahim said, putting the phone down.

Stella blew her nose with a wad of soggy loo paper, then she sat up straight and began preparing her document for print – her breakdown was going to have to wait until after she'd sent off her column.

Saving the working document under a work in progress title, Stella returned to the original document, carefully deleting all the dodgy faux responses. She read through it a couple of times and cleaned up her grammar and punctuation, then she also ran the spell check on her document, just to catch any stray mistakes. As she worked, her conversation with Max played over and over in her head. She'd never heard him sound so angry with her before. Another tear of self-pity trickled down her cheek.

Ordinarily Stella would have spent at least half a day copy-checking and crafting the document that would go to print, but it would have to do as it was for now, she simply didn't have the time. But she felt confident it would be all right, she'd been doing this column for so long now it had become almost second nature. She could do it with her eyes closed.

Stella wiped the tear from her cheek with her sleeve, then she closed all her documents, opened up her email, added her column as an attachment, tapped Ebrahim's email address into the mail and hit the send button. Then she slumped back in her chair, shattered.

Thank goodness for Ebrahim, she thought. Denise would have freaked out if she had missed her deadline. And even worse, her column would have been replaced by editorial. Which, knowing her luck at the moment, would have been Yolanda's copy.

One disaster cemented, and another one averted, Stella called it a day and snuck away from her desk just after four. However, it was only as she slowed down on De Waal Drive, so as not to get caught by the permanent speed camera set up before the Gardens turn-off, that she suddenly realised that she was in such an unfocused dwaal that she was driving home to their flat in Vredehoek, instead of to her temporary home at her parents' place in Claremont.

Stella clicked her tongue in irritation and tapped at her indicator so she could throw a U-turn and head back to the Southern Suburbs, but at the last minute she changed her mind and carried on driving, taking the off-ramp that would take her towards the flat. She wasn't sure what she wanted to achieve – her conversation with Max earlier had been disastrous, so she couldn't go to their apartment – but she didn't want to go home to her parents' house quite yet, and she had nowhere else to go.

Tapping her finger on her steering wheel nervously as the Gardens Centre shopping mall appeared on her left-hand side, Stella wondered what she was doing. She didn't have an answer. She was just driving, aimlessly. She had nowhere to go. She was homeless, and soulless and husbandless and hopeless.

Stella cruised past The Mount Nelson and drove towards town, still unsure where she was going. She drove past the Long Street Baths and Depasco, an upmarket deli-type restaurant, where she and Max had gone every now and then. She wondered how she could ever bring herself to live in Cape Town without him. Everywhere she looked there was a Max memory. Right there, on Long Street, was Royale, where Max insisted they made the best burgers in town. And there was the old Big Issue seller dude that they always bought their Big Issue from, on the corner of Buitensingel and Buitengracht. The same place where Max had taught Stella how to do a proper hill-start back when she was seventeen and practising to get her driver's licence. She waved at The Big Issue salesman as the robot changed and she pulled past him. He waved back at her, but it was quite obvious that he didn't recognise her without Max. She could relate, she thought, she didn't recognise herself without Max either.

Stella drove down the length of Buitengracht. As she crossed over Strand

Street she put on her left indicator and moved into the centre lane, so she could head straight out back onto the highway, which would take her in a massive loop over the city and back towards the Southern Suburbs, to her parents' house. But as the light changed and the cars around her surged forward Stella froze. She really didn't want to go to her parents' house. The cars piling up behind her began to hoot impatiently, urging her to move forward. Instead Stella suddenly flicked on her right indicator and leapt across two lanes, turning right, throwing a U-turn.

'Sorry, sorry!' Stella yelled out her window as she swerved to miss a bakkie and almost took out a very orange Opel Corsa, holding her hand up in the rear-view mirror to pacify the hooting and swearing, her heart pounding in her chest at the near miss.

Stella drove back along Buitengracht, going back the way she'd just come. When she pulled up at the next set of red lights she tried to ignore the death stares from the Corsa which had pulled up on her right, and the bakkie that was idling on her left. She looked down in her lap, twisted her wedding ring, then adjusted her rear-view mirror and checked her cellphone, her cheeks red, anything to avoid making eye contact with the angry drivers she could sense in her peripheral vision.

When the lights changed Stella breathed a sigh of relief and pulled off slowly, allowing the other cars to move ahead of her. She looked at the clock on the dashboard, it was half past five. Max would be home from work soon. She wondered what he would do, who would make him dinner? She wondered if he missed her. The urge to see him was overwhelming, making itself known as a dull ache in her body.

Thirteen minutes later Stella pulled into Davenport Road, the street that ran up the side of Victory Court, the small apartment block where she and Max lived on the second floor. She checked in the rear-view mirror twice to make sure there were no cars behind her, and slowed down to a crawl, craning her neck to try see into their apartment. Then she pulled into a parking space a block away in Bellair Road, hoping her car would be hidden from view under a big leafy tree, should Max look out the window.

Stella turned off the car engine and slunk down as low as she could in her seat. She wasn't sure why she'd come. She definitely didn't want Max to see her there, and she knew there was no way he would talk to her, but for some reason she felt a desperate need to see him. She gazed up at their apartment on the second floor. From where she was parked Stella could just see the entrance that Max would use to get into the block, and she could also see their lounge window, kitchen window and bedroom window. All the lights were off in the apartment and there didn't seem to be anybody home.

A few hours later Stella was still slumped down low in the front seat of her car. It was almost eight o'clock and Max still wasn't home. Worry ate away at her. Where on earth was he? Her stomach grumbled. She was hungry and incredibly thirsty, and her legs were starting to cramp from crouching low in her seat for so long.

Just after eleven o'clock, when there was still no sign of Max, Stella decided to give up and go home. It had been a truly terrible day. Max had put the phone down on her, she'd almost missed her column deadline and she'd spent the last six hours stalking her own husband, who didn't seem to be coming home. Stella felt pathetic and alone. This was an all-time low. Even for her.

'Stella, get up,' Iris said, prodding her sharply in the ribs with a pointy finger.

'What, what's that noise?' Stella moaned, trying to cover her head with her pillow.

'It's your alarm clock,' Iris said.

Stella opened an eye as Iris fiddled with the alarm clock that was bleating loudly right next to Stella's head.

'I can't get this thing to turn off,' Iris yelled. 'It's five in the morning, why is your alarm set for so early?'

Stella sat up and smashed her fist down hard on the alarm clock to stop it squealing. 'Sorry, Mom, I took a couple of sleeping pills, so I could sleep,' she said, rubbing her eyes.

'Why are you getting up so early anyway?'

'I need to go into the office early,' she lied.

Iris grumbled under her breath and shuffled out of the room in her slippers, shaking her head.

At around six a.m. Stella pulled into her now familiar parking space under the tree in Bellair Road, a block away from Victory Court. The street was quiet that early in the morning, but Stella wasn't taking any chances. She'd brought a baseball cap, a pair of oversized sunglasses and a scarf, to help ensure that Max wouldn't spot her. Her disguise in place, she slunk down in her seat, to wait out her husband.

Just after seven a light came on upstairs in their apartment and Stella breathed a sigh of relief. His car wasn't parked in the street, so until the light had come on she'd had no idea whether he was even home. Stella had tossed and turned half the night, worried about where Max was and wondering who he was with. Which was why at around three a.m, before popping two sleeping pills, and setting her alarm, she'd planned this undercover operation.

Stella sucked in a breath and ducked even further down in her seat when she caught her first glimpse of Max sometime after seven thirty. He was late for work, she thought as he emerged from the front door of the apartment looking tired and unshaven, his untied tie dangling loosely around his neck. He had his briefcase in one hand, a full black garbage bag in the other and half a piece of toast rammed between his teeth.

Stella felt a sudden rush of emotion when she saw him. At least he was eating breakfast, she thought, slipping even further down in her seat, so just the peak of her cap would be visible if he happened to look her way. She wondered how she would explain herself if he caught her. But Max seemed to be in too much of a hurry to notice anything. He tossed the bag of garbage into the big black bin waiting on the kerb and then made his way to his car in the garage. Stella was surprised to see him taking out the rubbish, she always had to nag him half to death before he would remember to do it, and here he was doing it of his own free will. Was he better off without her? Did he even need her? Stella wondered, the self-pity welling up inside her again.

Stella waited a couple of minutes once Max's car disappeared around the corner, then she opened her own car door and pulled her scarf closer around her face. Creeping up Bellair Road and into Davenport, she made her way towards Victory Court. When she got there she flipped open the lid of the bin and grabbed the full black garbage bag that Max had just thrown away. Looking both ways to make sure there was nobody watching Stella pulled the bag all the way out of the bin and returned to her car. She opened the boot and shoved the garbage bag inside, then looking both ways once more, to make sure nobody had seen her, she jumped back into the driver's seat, adjusted her peaked cap and sped off.

Stella drove around the neighbourhood looking for a quiet side street or cul-de-sac. When she eventually found one she drove to the end of it, parked and retrieved the bag from her boot.

Crouching on the pavement beside her car, Stella untied the top of the bag. She hadn't yet stopped to think about what she was doing or wonder why she was doing it. She was operating out of pure desperation. She had to know what Max had been up to since she'd left, and if it meant going through his trash, then that's just what she would do.

When Stella opened the bag the stench of rotting garbage floated into her nostrils and she dry heaved as the bile rose in her throat. Taking a few deep breaths to try and settle her stomach she stuck a cautious hand into the bag and poked around. There were a few greasy old pizza boxes, and some stale pizza crusts. She also identified Chinese takeaway packaging and tossed-out noodles. She dug deeper, sticking the other hand in now too. Elbow-deep in the bag Stella sifted through more old noodles, a ton of empty beer cans, an empty bottle of shampoo, some orange peel and a thin layer of crumpled-up bills and junk mail. Towards the very bottom of the bag Stella started to recognise garbage from when she had still been living in their apartment with Max – some leftover stir-fry and some tampon wrappings. The further down into the bag she got, the worse the smell.

Finally satisfied that she'd been through everything and that there didn't seem to be anything out of the ordinary, Stella pulled her hands out of the bag and tied a knot in the top of it. She felt relieved. She didn't know what she'd thought she was going to find, but whatever it was it wasn't there. Standing up she brushed some stray trash off her blouse and trousers and glanced at her watch. It was already after eight. If she didn't get a move on she'd be late for work. Again.

Stella picked up the garbage bag and dropped it off in one of the black bins on the side of the road in the street she was in, then she jogged back to her car, trying to wipe off her filthy hands. But the smell of garbage clung to her and it wouldn't let go.

Back in the driver's seat Stella rolled down the window to try and air out the smell of rotting garbage. She shook her head as she pulled away from the kerb. She hadn't really learnt anything by going through Max's trash, other than what she probably already knew deep down inside. One, that she might be going just a little bit crazy. And, two, that if she didn't nag him, and just left him to his own devices, he would take out the trash all by himself, in his own time.

Dear Dr Dee,

A few months ago I noticed these strange little bumps on my penis. At the time I thought nothing of it, and decided to just leave it in the hope that it would go away by itself. But it's been four months now and the little bumps are still there. They're on the shaft of my penis and I also have some under my pubic hair.

I feel too shy to go to the doctor, but recently I have begun to notice a bad smell coming from the area as well as the bumps. Do you think I have genital warts, or some kind of STD? And what should I do about it? I knew I shouldn't have slept with that girl I met at the Rand Show.

Worrywart

Stella sighed and sniffed. This guy was complaining of a bad smell, and that was something she could relate to. She'd been running so late by the time she'd finished stalking Max and going through his garbage, that she hadn't had time to go home and change. She'd washed her hands as soon as she'd got to the office, but her clothes were a different matter entirely. It wasn't like she tipped the bag over her head or anything, but somehow her clothes stank of garbage. Stella had kept her cardigan on and buttoned up the front, but it was a warm day and the heat of her body underneath the jersey had only managed to increase the smell of hot, rotting garbage that wafted off her and sat in the air in a green, noxious haze around the office. Her colleagues shot curious glances in her direction and whispered amongst themselves. Somebody opened a window. Somebody else sprayed air freshener. Somebody else sent an email to say that whoever left rotting food in the fridge needed to clear it out before the end of the day.

After work, Stella found herself driving back to Davenport Road on autopilot again. She couldn't stop herself. She pulled on her peak cap and the dark glasses and wrapped the scarf back around her neck, then she cruised slowly down the street past Victory Court. There was no available parking in the street, so she went around the block twice, and then pulled into a parking space two blocks away in St James Street. Getting out of the car she crept through the lengthening shadows towards their apartment, hiding behind each street pole along the way and checking to make sure Max wasn't looking out of a window.

Once she'd made it to Victory Court Stella crouched behind one of the now empty black bins standing in front of a house across the street from their flat, using it as cover. Looking up she saw a light go on in the apartment. Stella pictured Max in the lounge, with sovereign power over the remote control. Her heart ached. She wanted desperately to go up there and climb onto the couch, in her spot, next to him, she on the left hand side, him on the right hand side. But she knew it was too late for that.

Suddenly she pictured an alternative scene, one in which Max had someone over, and that other someone was curled up in Stella's spot. She took a deep sobering breath, looked both ways and tentatively crossed the street towards the front entrance to their apartment block. She would go up there and talk to him, she thought. Then another scene started to play itself out in her mind, in this one Max was shouting at her at the top of his voice, saying terrible things, and never wanting to see her again. Turning around she crossed the road again, going back to hide behind the dirt bin. She didn't think she could handle more rejection from Max, and, anyway, how would she explain the terrible stink of garbage?

Stella prowled in the shadows for another hour, then she slunk back to her car and drove home to her parents' house. She hated herself. She was an awful human being – what she'd done to Max was unforgivable – and on top of it all she now knew that she was also a coward.

POPPY

Poppy felt a hand press down on her shoulder. 'I won! I won!' a voice bellowed in her ear as she looked up to see who was touching her.

A man was standing next to her. He looked somewhere in his mid-forties, but he was tall and well-built and he'd aged well. His greying hair was cut short and he had a charming smile and green eyes, which were creased nicely in the corners. There was something George Clooney-esque about him, Poppy thought as she took in his well-pressed dark blue, almost black denim jeans and a plain white button-down polo shirt.

'I won! You made me win,' he shouted, smiling kindly into her tear-stained face.

Poppy looked across the table and watched as the croupier counted out stacks and stacks of purple chips, piling them one on top of the other. Then, using her croupier stick, she shunted the pile across the table, placing them on the red twenty-three, where they joined another large pile of purple chips.

'See,' the man said, leaning forward and pulling the piles of chips in his hands along the baize towards his chest. 'These are all mine now. Look what you did. You made me win,' he repeated, beaming at her.

'I don't understand,' Poppy said, looking back at him shyly. 'I didn't do anything. I don't even know you, how could I have made you win?'

He pointed a finger at the table where Poppy's purse was lying in front of her. Next to it lay the key ring with her hotel room key on it. The shiny brass tag had the number twenty-three embossed on it in sharp black letters, surrounded by a red circle. Poppy's eyes went wide and she looked back up at the guy and then back down at the key ring again.

'I saw your key, and I thought it was a sign, so I bet on twenty-three red, and we won!' He smiled, clapping his hands together and then rubbing them. Then he picked up one of the oblong purple chips and dropped it into Poppy's hand. 'Here, this is for you, my very own lucky charm.'

Poppy looked down into her open palm and saw that it was a thousand dollar chip. She gulped and then looked back up at the guy, holding her open palm back out to him, with the chip lying in the middle of it. 'I couldn't ... I can't ... I mean, it's not ...' she stuttered.

'Don't be ridiculous,' he said, pushing her hand away from him and winking. 'The gambling gods would never forgive me if you didn't take it, and then I'd be jinxed. Anyway, I made six grand on that spin alone, I'd say that's your fair cut, Lady Luck.'

Poppy looked down into her palm again and closed her fingers around the chip. She loved the feeling of the bevelled edge against her skin. Then she brought it up to her face and smelled it. She was sure it smelled of happiness. 'Thank you,' she said, slipping the chip into her pocket.

'You're not leaving, are you?' the man asked, looking panicked. 'You can't, not yet, you're my lucky charm. I hadn't won a single spin tonight until you came along.'

'I don't know,' Poppy said, looking around to see if Buck was still anywhere in sight. 'My friend has gone off to bed.'

'Excellent, so you'll stay then?' he asked. 'Just for a little bit. Please. No strings attached, I promise!'

Poppy eyed him out again. He seemed nice enough, but then the serial killers you saw on TV always looked nice enough, right up until the moment they chopped your boobs off.

'I'm Carl,' the man said, putting his hand out to shake hers with a big friendly grin on his face. 'How about you hang out with me a bit, Lady Luck? It will be great fun, I guarantee it.'

Poppy stared at him, unsure of what to do.

'Come on, you're in Vegas! Take a chance. What's the worst that can happen? We might just win some money and have some fun,' Carl said, with a cheeky smile.

Poppy thought about it. He was so good looking and so charming, he was almost impossible to refuse. And he was right, she thought. Why the fuck not. 'Nice to meet you, Carl. I'm Poppy,' she said, reaching out to shake his hand.

'Nice to meet you, Poppy, would you like some champagne?' Carl asked.

Poppy shrugged, her cheeks still flushed with the excitement of the thousand dollar chip nestling quietly in her pocket.

A peroxide blonde waitress appeared seconds later with a large bottle of champagne and poured them each a glass of bubbles.

'To my lucky charm,' Carl said as they clinked glasses.

Poppy smiled and nodded. 'And to my luck,' she said, sipping the champagne. She'd never tasted proper champagne before, well, at least, not the expensive corked kind, and it tickled her nose and throat in the most delicious way.

'So what number's looking good to you now?' Carl asked, jiggling a pile of chips in one hand and pointing at the table with the other.

Poppy eyed the numbers on the table for inspiration. 'I feel I should warn you,' she said, 'in the spirit of full disclosure, that about ten minutes ago my best friend and I lost every cent we had to our names on this very table because of the number I chose, so I'm not so sure you want to go with whatever I suggest. Maybe choose the opposite number or something.'

Carl laughed and sipped his champagne. 'No way, Poppy, I've got a good feeling about this. I think you're way luckier than you give yourself credit for.'

'Okay,' Poppy said. 'It's your money.' Then she eyed out the table again, seeking inspiration. 'How about seven?' she asked quietly, with a tentative, raised eyebrow.

Poppy watched nervously as Carl reached over and placed a large pile of chips on and around the seven. Then he placed a few more small piles of chips on various other numbers. When he was done he turned to her and winked.

The croupier spun the wheel and dropped the ball into the well, repeating her earlier routine of calling for last bets just as the wheel hit mid-spin. Poppy closed her eyes and held her fingers crossed under the table where Carl couldn't see them. She could hear the ball spinning and then bouncing in and out of a couple of holes before it bounced one last time and then everything went still. Only when she heard the crowd cheering collectively did she open her eyes. The ball hadn't landed on the seven, but it had landed on an adjacent number on the table and the croupier paid out another enormous pile of chips to Carl.

Carl grinned widely. 'Good job,' he said with a beaming smile.

'But I don't understand,' Poppy said. 'We didn't win. It didn't even land on seven, so how come you still got paid out?'

Carl pointed to the table. 'I put some of the chips on the corner of seven, which also covers number twenty-eight. And number twenty-eight is where the ball landed, so we win. It's not as big a win as if the ball had landed on our number seven, but a win's a win and we take 'em when we can get 'em. See, that's two wins in a row, you are my lucky charm, I told you so.'

With some quick lessons between spins from Carl, Poppy slowly picked up the rules of the game. His strategy seemed simple enough, each spin he would lavish the table with so many chips in so many different little squares, that he ensured himself a win in some form or other on just about every spin. After watching the game a bit the foolishness of her and Buck's strategy made her blush.

Carl consulted with her before every spin, asking her what looked good, or what number she liked, or if she was feeling anything specific. Whenever they won Poppy shrieked with delight, jumping up and down in her place next to the table. Gambling with someone else's money was way more fun and a lot less stressful than gambling with your own, and in her experience it seemed to last longer, too. The waitress returned often to fill their glasses and after about half an hour Carl handed Poppy a small stack of chips of her own.

'Here, Poppy, why don't you play a little yourself,' he said. 'It's the least I can do.'

Poppy eyed the chips he'd handed her; it looked like about five hundred dollars. She gulped audibly. 'I couldn't!' she said. 'If I lost there's no way I could ever pay you back.'

'I don't care,' he said, pointing to the growing pile of chips that lay in front of him. His pile had doubled, tripled, potentially even quadrupled since they'd started playing. Perhaps, she thought, she really was his lucky charm. She shrugged and thanked him. She would play her chips carefully and cautiously, she thought, closely mimicking his moves, but on a much smaller scale.

'More champagne?' the waitress asked her.

'Oh, go on then,' Poppy said, with a smile.

STELLA

Stella had *SYPHILIS*.

SYPHILIS, for eighty-seven points. She, Violet and Daisy were playing Scrabble outside next to the pool. It was Sunday, late afternoon. Her dad had made a big braai for lunch and now Violet's kids were splashing around shrieking and screaming in the swimming pool with Stewart. Lucy had declined their parents' invitation to come for lunch because she was still refusing to be in the same room as Stella, let alone speak to her.

Stella never won when they played Scrabble. It was one of the things about her family that drove her crazy. The fact that she was the writer in the family, as well as 'the organised one' and she could never win at Scrabble had become a bit of a family joke over the years.

She chewed on her lip and stared at her tiles hopefully. If she could just pull this one off it would be one small victory in the sea of defeat her life had become. If she could somehow break her Scrabble curse, Stella thought, then maybe she could break the curse that seemed to have fallen on her life too. It would be satisfying, quenching, like rain after a very long drought. She smiled, enjoying the glow of the potential win she could see just ahead of her on the horizon.

Violet had just had her turn and she'd played *GOOSE*, for eighteen points. Now it was Daisy's turn and then it would be Stella's turn. As long as Daisy didn't put something down in Stella's space, she would be able to place her *SYPHILI* down on the board alongside the *S* of Violet's *GOOSE*, over a triple-word score, which would give her a whopping eighty-seven points, putting her in the lead by far, with very little chance at this late stage in the game that anyone else would be able catch up with her. And then she would finally win.

Stella held her breath and tried to wait patiently while Daisy shuffled her tiles across her tile-holder. She tried not to stare at the *S* on the board too obviously, for fear that Daisy might see her and play defensively, but she didn't want to take her eye off the *S* either, in case it somehow disappeared.

Eventually Stella couldn't help herself. 'Violet, please tell Daisy that it's her turn!' she said through gritted teeth, her foot tapping nervously on the ground.

Daisy looked up, irritated. 'Stella, how many times must I say I'm sorry! I've told you, I'm really sorry! I didn't mean to rat you out! It was an accident. I was totally freaking out! How much longer are you not going to talk to me for?'

Stella glared at Daisy and then turned to Violet. 'Violet, please tell *your* sister, Daisy, that what she did is unforgivable, and breaks all the codes of sisterhood, and I have every right not to talk to her for as long as I deem fit. And you can also tell her that it's her turn, and she needs to move already, I don't have all day!'

'I know it's my turn, I'm not retarded, Stella!' Daisy snapped. 'And there's no time limit, I can take as long as I want. So I'll go when I'm ready, okay!'

'Let's not say "retarded", shall we,' Violet cut in. 'It shows very little understanding of an incredibly complex issue.'

Both Daisy and Stella turned from glaring at each other to glare at Violet. They all hated it when she got all psychiatristy on them.

'Look, Stel, I really am sorry, okay,' Daisy said, her voice softening. 'How many times do I need to say it? Like I said, everyone was staring at me, and Mom and Dad were spinning out, I had to do something.'

'Just play your move already,' Stella said to her sharply, not quite ready to let her off the hook yet.

Daisy went back to her tiles and made a big show of sipping on her Savanna slowly. Stella knew she was stalling on purpose now, just to irritate her. She took a deep breath and counted back from ten, looking off into the corner near the braai where her parents were standing. It looked like they were having some kind of argument.

As Stella looked back down at her rack quickly, to make sure she still had SYPHILIS, there was a loud smash from the direction of the braai. Turning to see what had happened, Stella saw that her mom had somehow dropped her wine glass on the floor, the glass shattering into a million little pieces on the paving. 'That's it,' Iris shouted. 'It's time you all know the truth. I'm tired of pretending that everything is okay! You're all old enough to know what's really going on around here.'

Stella stared at her mother in horror.

'Iris!' Hylton said, grabbing his wife's arm.

'Get away from me, Hylton!' Iris shrieked, shaking his hand off her arm and stepping away from him, her shoes crunching through the broken glass. 'I'm sick and tired of this, and I won't do it any more. Everyone, your father and I are getting a divorce!' Then she whipped past the table and disappeared into the house.

The three girls sat in shocked silence for a moment, nobody knowing what to say or do. They could only gape as their father stormed past them, following Iris into the house.

'Oh shit!' Daisy mumbled, breaking the shocked silence. 'Do you think it's because I'm gay?'

From where they sat the girls could hear their parents screaming at each other inside the house. Then there was a loud crash and the tinkle of porcelain; somebody must have thrown something.

'Game's over!' Violet said. As she stood up she accidentally bumped the Scrabble board, knocking her rack of tiles over and sending the words PATIO, HIPPY and Stella's precious GOOSE skittering across the board.

'Dammit!' Stella said. 'Look, I have syphilis! For once I was actually about to win!'

'That's it, Stewart. Come on, we're going home!' Violet said, walking over to the side of the pool.

There was more shouting from inside the house and the sound of something else smashing.

Entirely unaware of the chaos, Stewart raised his head up out of the water with a laughing child clinging to each arm and Luke attached to his back like a backpack. 'What's going on?' he asked, oblivious to the drama that was busy unfolding inside.

'My parents are having a screaming match, and we're going home,' Violet said, her words punctuated by the noise coming from the house.

'Stella, do you want to stay at ours tonight?' Violet asked, looking back at her over her shoulder as she pulled one of the boys out of the pool and started to towel him off.

'Oh, thank goodness ...' Stella said. 'Thanks, Vi, just give me two minutes to pack a bag.'

POPPY

'Carl, I'm really sorry,' Poppy said, her mouth turning down at the corners.

'It's really fine, Poppy,' Carl insisted, smiling his sexy smile at her again. 'Come on, don't frown,' he said gently, 'you're so beautiful when you smile and we're having such a great time.'

'I know but I've managed to lose just about all that money you gave me. I told you I was bad luck.'

'Now that's not true,' Carl said, indicating his own pile, which was now simply bordering on ridiculous. 'Look how lucky you've been for me. I don't care about a couple of hundred dollars, look at all of this!'

'I can't believe how well you've done,' Poppy said. 'How'd you do that?'

'Ah, you're my lucky charm, I told you,' he said, smiling again. 'Also,

I've been betting a lot more than you, remember, so when I do win, I win a lot more.'

'I feel terrible, to have wasted your money,' Poppy said. 'Do you know how much five hundred dollars is? Me and Buck, he's the friend I'm travelling with, we could live off that for months if we had to!'

'Have you had fun?' Carl asked her.

'Sure, it's been absolutely amazing,' Poppy said, nodding her head.

'Well then, it wasn't a waste, was it? Anyway, there's no way I could have made all this without you by my side. And I've got to tell you, this is the most fun I've had in ages.'

Poppy smiled at him, grateful for his kind words, and comforted by the close touch of the thousand dollar chip still nestling safely in her pocket. She would come out of this night a winner, regardless of all her losses, she thought. 'So what's a guy like you doing in a place like this, anyway?' she asked Carl coyly.

'Can't a guy head out to Vegas for a weekend with some golfing buddies?' he said, with a sexy smile.

'Oh, you're here with mates,' Poppy asked, craning her neck and looking around the casino.

'Oh, please, they went to bed hours ago,' Carl said, dismissing them with a gesture. 'All of them are married. Translation: boring!'

'What about you?' Poppy asked.

'Nope, I'm not boring at all.' Carl winked.

'No, man. I mean, are you married?' Poppy asked, blushing at her own forwardness.

'Nope,' he said smoothly. 'Not married, and no kids. I've been too busy making money over the last fifteen years to find someone to marry.'

'Reeheeeheeeeaaaalllly,' Poppy said. She was beginning to like this guy more and more. 'So what is it that you do, moneybags?' she asked, taking another sip of champagne.

'I invented the flash drive,' he shot back at her.

'What do you mean?' Poppy asked, furrowing her brow.

'Exactly that,' he said. 'You know that little computer sticky thing that you stick in your computer to move data around?'

Poppy nodded.

'Well, I invented it.'

'Wow!' Poppy said. 'That's pretty impressive.'

'Thank you,' Carl said. 'But it was really more a mixture of luck and good timing than anything else.'

'You seem to be a pretty lucky guy,' Poppy said.

'Let's see how lucky I really am,' he said. 'How about we go play something else for a bit?'

'Sure,' Poppy said. 'What do you want to play?'

'Have you ever play craps before?' Carl asked.

'Nope.'

'Come on then, let's go play some craps.'

Poppy looked around for a clock, but couldn't see one anywhere. She figured it must have been well after three in the morning, but she'd never felt more wide awake. It must be the adrenalin pumping through her body, she decided. She'd drunk what felt like buckets of champagne, but she only felt slightly giddy.

The croupier gave Carl two small black trays and together they stacked all his chips neatly into the little slots in them. Then they crossed the floor to the craps tables, the waitress chasing behind them with their ice bucket and what was left of their most recent bottle of champagne. Halfway there, feeling happy and confident, Poppy slipped her arm into the hook of Carl's arm, allowing him to escort her. She liked this guy. What wasn't to like? He was good looking and incredibly charming, and he seemed polite, gentle, friendly and very generous. So what if he was double her age? Look at Demi Moore and Ashton Kutcher. Age didn't matter any more.

Poppy had never even seen a craps table before, so when she climbed onto the stool next to Carl to watch him play she had no idea how it worked. Carl talked her through the basic rules and within a couple of throws Poppy was blowing on the dice and cheering with every won round, and booing the lost ones. Whenever they won it was Poppy's job to help Carl sort through his piles of chips and stack them up neatly in front of him in their denominations, while he laid his next bets and rolled the dice.

'This one's for my lucky charm, Poppy,' he shrieked as he rolled another seven and the croupier paid him out.

Poppy looked around and reached for the bottle of champagne to fill up their glasses. She could get used to this, she thought. Travelling the world with an amazing, wealthy guy; filling his champagne glass, working hard at looking beautiful and blowing on his dice when the need arose. It was fun and exciting, and kind of sexy and she imagined there would never be a dull second.

As she crunched the almost-empty bottle of champagne back into the ice bucket, she saw a man walking towards the craps tables. 'Take a look at that,' she said, nudging Carl.

Carl turned to look. The man was incredibly short and excessively wide; his stomach a fat ball, leashed in by a straining belt. Minus twenty kilos he could have been Danny DeVito's stunt double. A six-foot blonde hooker on each arm, he wore a black-and-white pinstriped suit and the shiniest black-and-white patent leather shoes Poppy had ever seen. The whole look was rounded off with a fat unlit cigar which was shoved between his fleshy pink lips.

Poppy snorted at the ridiculous sight of the trio. But soon it became clear that the posse was heading straight for their table. When the threesome eventually reached them the small man hefted himself up onto the vacant stool next to Carl's at the table and the two girls positioned themselves on either side of him, cooing and batting their eyelashes.

The man looked at Carl and Poppy. 'Hey, whatchu playing?' he asked, clutching his cigar between two fat fingers. He had an American accent but his voice was small and wheezy, almost like a woman's.

'It's craps,' Carl said.

'Howdya play?' he asked.

'It's pretty easy,' Carl said. 'You place your bet here,' he pointed out the various betting areas on the table, 'and then for this round if you're the shooter, you need to throw a seven or an eleven to win.'

Poppy smiled, Carl was so sure of himself, so suave and calm, she found it incredibly attractive.

'Gimme a go,' the guy said, reaching into his inside front pocket and pulling out a wad of cash so thick he could barely get his short fingers around it. It was wrapped in an elastic band which he whipped off and wrapped around his porky wrist for safe keeping. Then he pulled off layer after layer of notes.

Poppy's eyes went wide, she had thought Carl had flashed a lot of money around, but this was in an entirely different league. She had never seen so much money all in one place.

As the waitress furnished the trio with their own shiny silver ice bucket stand, full of expensive French champagne, Poppy did some quick calculations and tried to guess how many rands this crazy guy was holding in his hands. No doubt ten years' worth of living expenses for the average South African back home.

The guy slammed an enormous stack of bills onto the table. His every move was emphasised and comedic, and Poppy had to stop herself from laughing out loud, she didn't want to offend anyone.

The croupier casually counted out his money and then slid a huge stack of chips back towards him. He was so short he couldn't reach across the table, so he barked orders out to each of the girls, who bent over the table for him, flashing their enormous fake boobs and placing his bets as he instructed them. Poppy saw flashes of nipple on numerous occasions. She nudged Carl repeatedly and he laughed at her innocent open-eyed gawk.

Eventually, when everyone was settled, the croupier slid the dice across the table and laid them in front of the strange little man. He picked them up and then proceeded to shake them vigorously in both hands.

'Dice be nice!' he shouted in his wheezy girl's voice. 'Baby needs a new pair of shoes!' Then he made a massive performance of getting both of the hookers to kiss the dice and blow on them, before, finally, standing up on the front rung of his stool to get maximum height and leverage, he threw the dice, over-arm, from behind his head, like a baseball pitcher. 'Seven!' he shrieked hopefully at the top of his lungs as he released the dice, the girls clapping and shrieking their support.

The dice flew through the air at high speed, two small square bullets. They didn't even bounce on their table, they simply flew over the back edge of it, sailing through the air and landing on the next table along, in the middle of someone else's game.

Poppy stood on her tiptoes and craned her neck over at the next table, so she could see the numbers on the dice. It was a five and a two, it was indeed a seven.

'It is a seven,' Poppy said slowly and with surprise.

The hookers went crazy. Screaming and shrieking, jumping and hugging the guy, their breasts slipping dangerously from their tiny dresses. The croupier and the players at the next table looked up in shock at the mysterious dice that had landed in the middle of their game. And the croupier at Poppy's table gaped, open-mouthed, at the spectacle.

'Yeah, baby! Yeah, baby!' the man shrieked, producing a box of matches to light the cigar in his mouth.

'Um, Sir,' the croupier said, 'I'm not sure that's allowed.'

'I just won sixty grand, lady!' he yelled. 'I'm gonna light up my cigar!'

'No, Sir, I meant the throw. You need to throw the dice on your own table!'

'Who says!' the man shouted aggressively.

Poppy looked up and saw a barrage of casino suits heading towards them, and at the same time the pit boss arrived at the edge of their table, looking serious.

'Come on, I think it's time to get out of here,' Carl whispered in Poppy's ear, piling the chips he'd been gambling with back into the two trays the croupier had given them earlier before grabbing her hand.

'That's the craziest thing I've ever seen!' Poppy shrieked as Carl pulled her across the casino floor. Her eyes felt like they couldn't go wide enough.

Turning back towards the table she saw that things had deteriorated. The guy was yelling at the pit boss, stabbing the air with his smoking cigar, the bulky men in dark suits standing by, ready to jump.

'What do you think's going to happen over there?' Poppy asked. 'He did throw a seven. It just wasn't on the right table!'

'I have no idea.' Carl laughed, squeezing her hand. 'Ten strokes of madness if you ask me. I doubt they'll pay him out in full, but they'll have to comp his stay or something.'

They reached the edge of the casino floor, still holding hands. Poppy twisted his arm and looked at the watch on his wrist. It was just after four a.m. The casino was still packed; it could have been eight o'clock at night instead of four o'clock in the morning.

'So, what do you want to do now?' Poppy asked, her eyes shining.

'I don't know,' Carl stuttered. 'I mean, it's so late, I thought that you would probably want to call it a night.'

'No way!' Poppy shrieked. 'I couldn't sleep now, I'm too amped.'

'Weeeeell,' Carl said, dragging the word out, as if in thought. 'We could go somewhere to watch the sun rise over Vegas, if you wanted to?'

'That's an awesome idea,' Poppy said. 'Where should we go?'

'I know we only just met, and this probably sounds incredibly forward, but my suite is on like the hundredth floor here, and it has an amazing view. We could go watch it from there?' Carl suggested, raising an eyebrow.

'Hmmmm,' Poppy said, scratching her chin. 'Tell me you've got one of those big fancy suites filled with complimentary baskets of fruit and views of the whole of Vegas?'

'As a matter of a fact, it just so happens that I do,' Carl said, smiling at her.

'Show me your room key.'

Carl furrowed his brow, then fished in his pocket with his spare hand and pulled out his key.

'Hang on one second,' Poppy said, eyeing it. 'Wait here, and don't move a muscle.' She ran a couple of steps and then turned around again. 'I mean it, don't move!' she said, wagging her finger at him.

Running over to the hotel reception desk she asked the concierge for a pen, a piece of paper and an envelope. She scribbled a note, looking back to make sure Carl was still standing there waiting for her. He was. He stood on the spot, clutching his trays of casino chips, smiling at Poppy warmly.

Buck,

It's me. I've gone up to room 1489 with a man named Carl. If I'm still not back at our room by lunchtime tomorrow please go directly to the police. If you don't know where I am, chances are he's taken me hostage and done terrible things to me, like chopping my head off and putting it in a ziplock bag in the bar fridge.

P.S. Before they take away my body be sure to take the thousand dollar chip out of my right front pocket.

Poppy signed her name, sealed the note in the matching envelope and wrote her room number on the front. Then she handed it over to the concierge together with strict instructions to deliver it to Buck in their room. Finally she made her way back to Carl, who was now standing with his back to her, looking in the window of the hotel gift shop.

Poppy shoved her hand into her pocket and fingered the chip. It had been the night of a lifetime and she didn't want it to end. She appraised Carl, tipsy on champagne and high on winning and excitement and wondered what it would be like being with a man like him permanently. Would she be able to handle a life of luxury, being at the beck and call of an older, richer man? Poppy wondered. Women all over the world did it all the time. Her parents would freak if they knew she was going up to a strange man's hotel room, she thought. But then they didn't have to know, did they?

Poppy joined Carl where he was standing, eyeing out a pair of silver cufflinks in the shape of a pair of dice. 'Right, I'm ready,' she said. 'How about that sunrise and a cocktail, then?'

'One sunrise and one cocktail coming right up,' Carl said, taking her hand again and leading her to the bank of hotel elevators off to the side of the casino.

In the elevator Poppy thought nervously about what she was doing. She hadn't decided yet whether she would sleep with Carl or not, but she did know that she didn't want the night to end yet. She thought about how all of this might look to a stranger looking in. A very handsome and charming older man had given her a ton of champagne and a bit of money and now she was going up to his hotel room with him to do who knew what. She wondered if that made her anything like the hookers on the casino floor with the short, fat whale. No, she concluded, looking at herself in the mirrored walls of the elevator, she was very different to them, her boobs were real for starters.

As the elevator dinged up the floors she smiled at Carl and wondered how a guy like him was still single, and how a girl like her, with pink hair, covered over with Purple Haze, had gotten so lucky. Reaching out she put her hand on his shoulder. 'That was so much fun, Carl,' Poppy said gratefully. 'Thank you.'

'My pleasure, treasure,' he said, smiling at her, then he took her hand in his and squeezed it gently. 'I had a really amazing time too.'

Poppy beamed and felt butterflies in her stomach. This tall, charming stranger made her feel like she was the most important person in the world. 'I've never really gambled before, well, not properly anyway,' she said.

Carl lifted her hand to his mouth and kissed it gently, still clutching the trays of chips in his other hand. 'It's been an incredibly special night for me too,' he said, looking into her eyes. 'I feel like the luckiest man in Las Vegas.'

Poppy smiled and blushed.

STELLA

Dear Doctor Dee,

Does the clitoris really exist?

I'm only asking because I hear people talking about it all the time, and I've looked and I've looked but I just can't find my girlfriend's.

Do you think it's medically possible that she was born without one? The other night, after I'd spent another twenty minutes unsuccessfully trying to find 'it', I told her that I thought maybe she didn't have one, and she should see her doctor about it. That made her really angry, and she stormed out, so we didn't end up finishing having sex, which I thought was very unfair.

Anyway, please can you help me. I've looked everywhere and I really don't think she has one!

Tired of Searching

Dear Doctor Dee,

I just found out that my boyfriend cheated on me. He had sex with his dental hygienist. He says it was an accident and a mistake, and just a once-off thing that will never happen again, because he is going to change dentists now.

This isn't the first time he's cheated on me. At the beginning of the year I found out that he'd had sex with his ex-girlfriend this one time.

When I tried to break up with him he told me it wasn't his fault and that he couldn't help it because he has a sexual addiction. He promises me over and over again that he won't ever do it again, but I just don't know if I can trust him any more. What would you do if you were me? I really love him and he is the father of my two-year-old daughter. Should I leave him, or should I forgive him and give him another chance?

I mean, if he really does have a sexual addiction then he can't help it, right? Like, it's not his fault?

What would you do?

Cheater's Girlfriend

Stella put down both the letters and twirled her wedding ring on her finger. As much as the people who wrote these letters were freaks and lunatics, she was starting to wonder whether she had more in common with them than she had previously liked to admit.

If she was in a position where she could say whatever she wanted in her responses, she would tell both letter writers that things were entirely hopeless. That *Tired of Searching* should just give up his hunt – if he hadn't found it by now, he was never going to find it. After all, if Stella could barely find her own clitoris, how on earth was she going to be able to help some strange loser dude find his girlfriend's.

And as far as *Cheater's Girlfriend* was concerned, well that was more complicated. The professional side of Stella wanted to tell this girl to dump her cheating boyfriend and move on immediately, but how could Stella preach when she was the one in the cheating boyfriend's position.

There was no way she could answer either of the letters, she decided, looking at her watch, relieved to see that it was almost home time.

The evening stretched ahead of Stella endlessly. She thought about driving past Victory Court to see if Max was home, but then what? Would she just park outside and waste another evening, watching for any sign of Max? She picked up the phone and dialled Lucy's number. It rang once and then went to voicemail, as it had every time Stella had called since The Incident. Stella hung up, she knew what she wanted to say, but she couldn't say it in a message, she needed to look Lucy in the eye and say it to her face. More than anything, not being able to talk to Lucy was killing her. Her marriage had fallen apart. Her parents' marriage was falling apart. And she had nobody to talk to about any of it.

Stella made her way through the rush-hour Cape Town traffic towards Lucy's flat. Tapping her finger on the steering wheel she nervously considered what the best plan of action might be. She would wait outside Lucy's apartment for her to come home after work, then she would corner her and beg Lucy to talk to her. She nodded her head – it was a good plan with only a few flaws. The first being that she wasn't sure whether Lucy was actually going to be coming home straight after work. Stella pushed the thought aside. She didn't care if she had to wait. It wasn't like she had anywhere else to go and she knew she had to speak to Lucy in person. This freeze-out was getting ridiculous and Stella knew it was high time she grew a pair of balls and did something about it. The situation wasn't going to rectify itself and they couldn't carry on not speaking to each other forever, that would be ridiculous, especially over a guy. They'd never fought over a guy before.

Stella parked on High Level Road and crossed over to Lucy's block. She rang the buzzer, but nobody was home, so she sat down on the steps in front of Lucy's building and waited. She patiently watched every car that passed, looking out for Lucy's black VW, all the while plotting exactly what she was going to say in her head when she was eventually face to face with her twin.

Stella mapped out her apology word for word, tapping her foot anxiously on the ground as she practised it over and over to perfect every nuance of it. Finally, with no sign of Lucy, she dug around in her handbag until she found an old piece of gum. Picking the hairs and lint off it she popped it into her mouth. Forty minutes later the gum was completely stale. It was like chewing on an old piece of rubber, so Stella spat it out back into the wrapper and dropped it in her handbag.

As she waited a familiar sensation began to creep up on her. It was her bladder and it was full.

By the time Stella had been waiting for Lucy for almost an hour she needed the toilet desperately. She still had her key to Lucy's apartment, but there was no way she could use it. If Lucy came home and found her in her flat she would be even more furious. She would think that she was stalking her or something. No, the last thing she needed was Lucy furious about something. Stella squeezed her legs together and thought about her other options. She could abandon her position on the front steps of Lucy's block, drive down to Sea Point Main Road and find a restaurant where she could pee. But, she thought, if she did that she might miss Lucy coming home, and then the last hour would all be in vain. She needed the element of surprise, Lucy would never let her in if she rang on the buzzer, she wouldn't even take her calls, so why would she let her into her home. Stella squeezed her legs together even tighter and looked around for a more appropriate and immediate solution.

The apartment block was one of the old art deco-style blocks on High Level Road. Visitors and residents came off the street, up a small brick flight of stairs, at the top of which was a door with a buzzer pad. The block had a small but pretty garden, made up of a few hibiscus bushes and a tree or two, which wrapped around the building. Stella made a snap decision. She couldn't think properly on a full bladder. She needed to relieve herself in a hurry.

Looking both ways to make sure no one was coming, Stella hobbled quickly down the stairs and into the garden, knyping her legs together as tightly as she could. She surveyed the bushes, there was only one that might be big enough to provide her with enough protection from the traffic driving by and the neighbouring blocks of flats, but if anyone were to climb the stairs and look to their left they would definitely be able to see her. But there was no time to worry about what ifs, if she didn't relieve herself within seconds she knew her body would take over and then even all the control in the world wouldn't be able to help her.

Stella dashed behind the biggest hibiscus bush, hurriedly unbuckled her belt, undid her jeans and pulled them down, then she squatted down behind the bush. The relief was instant. But having held it in for so long she had a lot of liquid to get rid of and it felt like the longest pee in history. It tapered off for a second and she thought it was finished, but then it gushed out again full stream. Stella pulled a contented grimace; there were few feelings as satisfying as going when you're desperate.

Suddenly Stella saw a head appear at the bottom of the stairs; it was Lucy arriving home at last. She panicked. This was not how she wanted Lucy to discover her. It would be a pathetic and embarrassing ambush. She closed her eyes briefly, hoping it made her invisible, and pushed, willing her bladder to empty quicker. When she opened her eyes again Lucy was standing at the top of the stairs looking down at her, mouth agape and a horrified look on her face.

'Stella!' she shouted, 'Oh, my God, what on earth are you doing?'

Stella finished weeing and jumped up, fumbling with her pants, trying to pull them up as fast as she could.

'Jesus, Stella, what on earth is going on with you? First you fuck my boyfriend and now you piss in my garden! What's next, shit in my bed?' Lucy shrieked.

'Lucy, I'm so glad you're home. I've been waiting here for you for over an hour, I needed the toilet desperately and I didn't want to miss you, I didn't know what else to do. I had to pee and this was the only place!' she said, gesturing back towards the bush. 'It's totally hidden from the street, I checked,' Stella finished off weakly.

Lucy stared at her, completely shocked. There was an awkward silence as the girls appraised each other, neither quite sure what to do next. Stella decided to make her move while she still had the benefit of the element of surprise. 'Lucy, it's really nice to see you, you have no idea how much I've missed you,' She said, running up to her sister.

Lucy took a step back, to avoid any physical contact. 'What do you want, Stella?' she said coldly. 'I thought I made it clear, I don't want to talk to you.'

'Please, Luce, you have to talk to me. Please let me in. I promise, just five minutes, then if you still want me to leave I will, you have my word. Just five minutes, that's all. I'm begging you,' Stella said, holding her hand up and flaring her fingers desperately to indicate five minutes.

Lucy shifted her handbag and readjusted her gym bag, which was clearly digging into her shoulder. She was also carrying two heavy-looking bags of shopping. She thrust the shopping bags into Stella's hands and turned to open the front door to the apartment block with her keys. 'All right, you can have five minutes,' Lucy snapped, 'but only because I need someone to carry my shopping, not because I want to speak to you.'

Stella beamed from ear to ear at the small victory and followed Lucy into the apartment block and up the stairs towards her front door on the fourth floor. 'Thank you, Luce,' she said, 'I really appreciate you giving me this chance.'

Inside the apartment both girls avoided the kitchen, which held too many awkward memories, and instead made their way into the lounge. Lucy dropped her bags and turned around to face Stella, crossing her arms across her chest. 'Right, what do you want, Stella? You've got four minutes and fifty seconds.'

'Um, can I have a glass of water?' Stella asked as she placed Lucy's shopping bags onto the floor gently. Her mouth was suddenly very dry.

'No, Stella, you can't,' Lucy snapped. 'What did you come here to say? Four minutes, thirty seconds.'

Stella paced a couple of steps in each direction and then looked up at Lucy with tears in her eyes, her entire practised speech instantly forgotten. 'Lucy, all I can say is how sorry I am,' she choked. 'You know I would never do anything to hurt you intentionally ...'

'But you did, Stella,' Lucy cut in harshly. 'I don't understand it. I don't understand why you did that. Did you plan it?'

'No, of course not!' Stella said emphatically. 'I don't know how it happened. I came over that afternoon because I wanted to tell you that I never actually got the promotion at work. I lied to Max about it, and then he went and told you, and then you guys threw that amazing party. I tried to tell you downstairs in the bathroom at La Perla, but the opportunity just wasn't there and then everything snowballed out of control. Now you know everything!' The words tumbled out of her mouth. 'I hate lying to you Lucy; it was killing me, eating me up from the inside. I needed to tell you the truth, and that's why I got drunk on stupid Bacardi and Coke when I was waiting for you at Bistro. I needed some Dutch courage before you arrived so that I could tell you everything. But you never arrived. And then I came over, you know, that afternoon and the rest, well ...' Stella trailed off.

'What do you mean you never actually got the promotion at work?' Lucy asked, her arms crossed in front of her chest and an astonished look on her face. 'And since when do you drink Bacardi and Coke?'

'I didn't get the promotion. I lied about it,' Stella said. 'I don't know why I did it. It was just in the heat of the moment. This other girl got it. This pretty, newly graduated student from Rhodes! I was devastated, and when I called Max to tell him, he thought I was calling to say that I'd got it. And somehow I just couldn't find the words to tell him the truth, and so he thought I got the promotion and I never corrected him. But I never expected it to get so out of control.' She sniffed. 'I didn't think Max would tell you so fast. I was going to tell him the truth straight away that night, the second I saw him at La Perla. I swear I was!' Stella was feeling terribly sorry for herself again, and the tears were pouring out generously. 'It was just a little white lie, but it all spiralled so badly out of control.'

'Stella!' Lucy said. 'That's terrible! Why would you lie about something like that? And why would you lie to me? We tell each other everything! Well, at least, we used to! I feel like I don't know you any more.'

'I know,' Stella said, dropping down onto the couch and sinking her head into her hands. 'But that's why I was here that night. I came up here to confess. And I was just looking for something to eat in the fridge, because I was really, really drunk. Like drunker than I've ever been before, Luce. You know that I barely ever drink. And then Jake came in, and he must have thought I was you ... and ... Well, you know the rest.'

'But I still don't understand why you didn't just stop him when he started touching you? Why didn't you say something?' Lucy asked. 'I mean, you're married, for Christ's sake!'

'I think maybe sometimes I wish I was you,' Stella said earnestly. 'Your life is so fabulous, Lucy. The awesome job, the great promotion, the amazing men – it always sounds so exciting around here. And my life is just so boring. It felt really good to be you, even for just a couple of minutes.'

'What are you talking about, Stella?' Lucy said. 'You have an amazing life. Look at you and Max, what you guys have is incredible. Don't you ever think that sometimes maybe I'd like a little bit of what you've got, Stella?

The stability and the trust. It's kak being on your own all the time. I live here all by myself, Stella!' Lucy said, indicating the apartment. 'Sure, it looks all fun and glamorous from the outside, but it's not always that easy. Do you think I want to be alone my entire life? I'd also like to have what you've got with Max, Stella. Who wouldn't want a soul mate? And I thought I'd finally found him, and then you fucked it all up for me! Literally!'

Silence fell as they both stared at the carpet. 'So, how are you and Jake …?' Stella finally asked.

'Fucking over, Stella! What do you think?' Lucy flared up again. 'He was completely freaked out; he couldn't bear to look at me. He didn't even stay long enough to do up his pants. He left right after you and I haven't heard from him since. He must think we're some kind of psycho twins or something. He hasn't even contacted me to come and get his stuff, and he won't take my calls. And I'm terrified that he's going to tell people in the industry what happened and then everyone in advertising will think I'm a complete freak! It's a fuck-up, Stella!'

'Oh, Luce, I'm so, so, so sorry. Please, believe me, I really never intended for this …'

'No, of course you didn't, Stella. You never intend for anything! You know what, you need to grow the fuck up and get your own fucking life. Mine isn't up for rent!' Lucy drew in a deep, shuddering breath. 'All right, you need to go, I've given you your five minutes, and now I want you out of my flat!'

'But can't we just …?' Stella asked.

'No, Stella, we can't just anything. I don't want to look at you. I can't stand the sight of you. It's over between you and me. I'm done with you!'

'No, don't say that, Lucy, you don't mean it,' Stella said through her tears.

'I do mean it, Stella,' Lucy said. 'You've gone too far. I don't think I'm going to be able to forgive you.'

'Not even in time?' Stella asked desperately.

'I don't know, Stella. I don't know anything right now.'

Defeated, Stella picked up her bag and limped towards the front door. When she got there she turned to face Lucy. 'Hey, did you hear that Daisy's gay now and Mom and Dad are getting a divorce?'

'Yeah, Violet told me,' Lucy said morosely.

They stood in silence staring at each other for a minute and then Stella left, closing the front door forlornly behind her.

'It's a beautiful evening, hey?' Iris said, staring up at the stars.

'Not really,' Stella said, taking a sip of her wine.

'Well, at least you spoke to her,' Iris said. 'That's progress, isn't it?'

'I suppose, except she told me to get a life, and that she never wants to speak to me again.'

Iris nodded. 'You can't really blame her, though, can you?'

Stella nodded sadly and they sat at the patio table in silence for a few minutes.

'Mom, can I ask you a question?' Stella asked.

'You just did,' Iris said.

Stella rolled her eyes. 'I know you and Dad have always bickered, but I always thought that it was just the way you were together. But now this; a divorce; it seems really extreme. Especially at your age. I thought you were happy.'

'Oh, you know, darling, happy is relative. We've been together a very long time, but we've also been apart now for a long time too. And once you start drifting, there's really no turning back.'

Stella thought of her and Max and wondered if there really was no turning back. She felt a chill in her heart at the thought of it. 'But I don't understand, what suddenly brought all of this on?' Stella asked.

'Stella, I didn't want to tell you this, and please don't tell your sisters, all right?'

Stella nodded.

'Promise me,' Iris said.

'I promise. You have my word,' Stella said, nodding again.

Iris took a sip of wine and a deep breath. 'About three years ago I went to the chemist to pick up my hormone pills ... it was sometime around June or July. Anyway, when I went to the till I noticed that they were charging me full price for my medication, so I went back to the chemist. He checked on the computer and said that it was because we were all out of medical aid funds for the year, that we'd already used them all up. I remember thinking how strange it was, because it was still only the middle of the year, and we usually only run out of funds around November. So I told the chemist there must be some mistake, and I insisted he double check. So he went back into his records and printed out all our transactions, and then he combed through every single purchase. And then he said, "I'm sorry, Mrs Frankel, but you've used up the bulk of your funds this year buying your Viagra."'

'Ew, gross, Mom! I don't want to hear about that!' Stella shrieked, covering her ears with her hands.

'Well, dear, there's nothing to hear about. Your father and I stopped doing that kind of thing on a regular basis a very long time ago, so I knew there must be someone else, and I also knew right then that it was over between us. It's just taken us till now to really get used to the idea of it all being over.'

'Dad? Really?' Stella asked.

'Really,' Iris said.

'I had no idea. Who is she?'

'Oh, just some opportunistic woman,' Iris said.

'Sheesh, I didn't realise he was such a cliché!' Stella said. 'That's awful, Mom! I'm so sorry.'

'I know,' Iris said. 'That's one of the reasons I've been so angry with you for what you've done to your sister and to Max. It's terrible to hurt another human being like that, Stella.'

'I know, Mom, and I am really sorry for what I've done. I can't explain it, it's like I haven't been myself ...'

Stella watched as her mother sipped at her wine. 'So, this other woman ...' she eventually asked.

'Oh no, dear, she's long gone,' Iris said. 'Your dad was devastated that I'd found out. He said it was over before it really began and that it was the biggest mistake he'd ever made, some kind of late-life crisis or something. Blah, blah, blah. You know, all those pathetic excuses that men make. And he's been trying to make up for it ever since.'

'So then I really don't understand why you're getting divorced,' Stella said. 'If it was just once, a few years ago, and he's sorry, then maybe ... Can't you just maybe try to forgive him or something ...' Stella trailed off.

'Well, dear, it's not as simple as that. There may not be another woman any more, but there most certainly is another man.' Her mom smiled mischievously and squeezed Stella's hand.

'I think I need a refill,' Stella said, getting up from the table with her empty glass. 'Want one?'

'Why not,' Iris said.

Stella leaned against the fridge, her mind racing. Her parents were ancient. This was ridiculous. She poured two glasses of wine and carried them back outside.

'I can't believe we're having this conversation,' Stella said, handing Iris her glass.

'What do you mean?' Iris asked.

'Well, my whole life has been so utterly normal, so completely pedestrian and average and boring until now. And suddenly everything's gone crazy. My marriage is a wreck, Lucy and I are in a shambles, and now this stuff with you and Dad. It's crazy. I feel like my life has just been hanging out on the sidelines, waiting, storing up all the surprises for just the right moment to drop them all on my head at once.'

Iris nodded. 'Life can be like that,' she said.

Stella settled back down at the table next to her mom and they sipped on their wine. 'You know, Mom, I never even noticed anything was wrong around here with you two when I moved back in a few weeks ago. I mean, I noticed a few things, like Dad sleep-smoking and you guys bickering all the time, but I never thought for a second that it was this extreme. I just never clicked. I suppose I was so busy dealing with all my own stuff.'

'It's okay,' Iris said, 'we've become quite good at hiding it over the years, but now we figure we shouldn't have to hide things any more. You lot all have your own lives, and we've both moved on already and we're better for it. We'll always be friends, I think.'

'So Dad's all right with all of this?' Stella asked.

'Well, he's coming to terms with it slowly,' Iris said. 'But he knows it's all his fault. He's the one who started this whole thing in the first place, and he's terribly sorry about it, but regret doesn't buy you a do-over. And then I got together with Pete ... I suppose we're both realising that it's maybe for the best that we get divorced. We're both just so angry with each other. And it's exhausting being angry with someone all the time.'

'Pete, is that the ...' Stella wasn't quite sure what to call her seventy-two-year-old mother's boyfriend.

'Yes, actually you know him,' Iris said, sipping her wine.

'I do?' Stella said, taken aback.

'Yes. He's your old homeroom teacher from school.'

'Mr Davies!' Stella shrieked. 'Have you gone absolutely mad!'

Iris didn't answer. Instead she looked out over the garden and the darkened swimming pool.

Her father was on Viagra and her mother was sleeping with her old homeroom teacher, Stella thought. Had the world gone insane? 'But Mr Davies was such a chop! He would never give me an A,' Stella said. 'The highest I ever managed to score in his class was a B-minus, no matter how hard I tried. I always thought he didn't like me.'

'Oh, don't be ridiculous, Stella. He's a lovely man.'

'Does he still have that awful beard and those stupid glasses?' Stella asked, slightly sulkily.

'The glasses are still there, but I got rid of the beard a long time ago.' Iris smiled.

'Mom, you do know this is completely mental, don't you?' Stella said. 'You and dad have five children and so much history together. I'm struggling to fully understand why you're doing this?'

'Stella,' Iris said gently. 'I want you to look at me and listen very carefully, there's something I need to say to you. Life is very short, Stella. You have to do everything you ever wanted to do right now, there isn't a second to spare. Your father and I should have left each other years ago, but we didn't. We were too scared. We were cowards. And we didn't want to upset anybody. And we had all you kids to think about. But now here we are, finally doing it. I wanted to see what it was like to be with a younger man, and I found Pete, who makes me very happy ...'

Stella cringed, the thought of her mother with anybody, let alone her old homeroom teacher was really grossing her out. 'Gross, Mom,' she said again, waving her hands in front of her face to try and get her to stop.

'Stella, I'm trying to tell you something that you need to hear – you need to sort things out with Lucy and decide if you want to sort things out with Max or not. Whether you choose to stay with him or go your separate ways, it doesn't matter. The only thing that matters is that you follow your heart and do everything you've ever wanted to do right now, because you'll regret it if you don't.'

'Basically, what you're saying is that I need to get a life,' Stella said.

Iris nodded. 'Yes, exactly. You need to get a life. But, you also need to make sure that it's the life that you want.'

Stella nodded. Her mom was right – there were so many things she wanted to do, so many things she'd always stopped herself from doing, because she hadn't wanted to disappoint anyone: her parents, Lucy, Max. And now here she was in a position where she could change things, really shake them up and do all the things she'd ever wanted to do, but instead she was climbing into bed at nine every night like an old lady, moping around her parents' house in her pyjamas, feeling sorry for herself, stalking Max and Lucy like a lunatic, as if it was the end of her world, when in fact it was really only just the beginning.

'Maybe I need to see everything that's been happening to me as an opportunity, rather than a curse.'

'Yes, exactly. Everything happens for a reason,' Iris said.

'Hang on. I'm going to get a pen.'

Stella returned from the kitchen with the rest of the bottle of wine and the small pad of paper from next to the telephone and a pen. She topped up their glasses again, her mind buzzing with a million thoughts.

'What's that for?' Iris asked.

'I think I need to make a list.'

'You always did like a list.'

'You know, I've never done anything even vaguely interesting or exciting before,' Stella said, tapping the pen against her lip.

'So put something exciting on your list, then. But you will be careful, won't you?' her mother said, sounding concerned.

'Of course, Mom,' Stella said, smiling as she looked down at the empty page.

'At least now you've got a plan.'

'Yup,' Stella said. 'I am going to get a life.'

POPPY

Carl walked through the door of the suite and dropped his room key and the two trays of chips on the table just inside the door. Then he held a hand out to Poppy to welcome her inside. Looking around Poppy felt surprisingly underwhelmed by what she could see of the suite. She had expected something enormous, something lavish like the penthouses you saw on television – with jukeboxes and pool tables, with indoor swimming pools in the lounge and tigers in the bedroom.

The room wasn't anywhere near as bad as the one she was sharing with Buck, but it also certainly wasn't anything phenomenal. There was a short passageway which quickly led to a smallish lounge area, with a couple of couches and a flat-screen television set. On the other side of this a pair of double doors opened onto a medium-sized bedroom with a king-size bed on a small raised platform, which made it seem to

Poppy like the bed was on a stage. Smiling at the thought, Poppy noticed that the suite's windows overlooked the main Las Vegas strip, where the sun was starting to rise, lending it a beautiful predawn glimmer. The room she was sharing with Buck was over on the cheap side of the hotel, overlooking the dumpsters and the alleyways. Vegas was a city of two sides, Poppy thought, and you just rolled the dice and hoped to land on the right side.

'Right, so I believe I owe you a cocktail,' Carl said, clapping his hands and then rubbing them together.

Somewhere in the suite Poppy heard a toilet flush. She glanced at Carl, surprised, but as she opened her mouth to ask him what was going on she heard a woman's voice shouting from the bedroom.

'Carl, is that you?'

'Fuck!' Carl whispered. Then he reached over, placed his hand on top of Poppy's head and pushed down hard, till she dropped down onto her hands and knees behind the couch.

Poppy looked up at him, shocked and confused.

'Carl?' came the voice again, closer this time. 'Who are you talking to? Is there someone with you?'

Putting his finger to his lips, his face panicked and pleading, Carl darted away from Poppy. 'Lucille, is that you?' he asked, moving towards the bedroom. 'What on earth are you doing here? Jesus, you almost gave me a heart attack.'

'Carl! What the hell is going on?' the woman said. 'Where have you been all night?'

'What are you doing here, Lucille? I don't understand,' Carl said. Poppy could tell he was trying hard to remain cool.

'Well, I thought I'd surprise my husband,' the woman replied, her voice raised. 'I left the kids with my folks and drove all day to get here. The hotel concierge let me in . . .' She paused to take an irate breath. 'Where have you been all night? Your phone's been off and I've been worried sick! I checked with the front desk to see if maybe there was some kind of conference function tonight, but they told me that there's no accounting conference for your firm here at all this weekend! You'd better tell me what the hell is going on, Carl! I thought you were here on a conference? I came to surprise you and I've been waiting for you all night! You'd better tell me you haven't been gambling!'

'No, no, of course I haven't been gambling,' Carl said, his voice quivering. 'I know how strongly you feel about gambling, darling ... But, wow! It's just such a surprise that you're here! I'm shocked. I don't know what to say!'

Fucking bastard, Poppy thought. Fucking lying bastard. He wasn't single, and he hadn't invented the flash drive. He was married and he had children and he was an accountant. Fucking bastard. Poppy shook her head, furious at herself for being so naïve.

'I can explain everything,' she heard Carl say, an edge of desperation to his voice. 'About the conference, about everything, but look we're missing the sunrise. Have you seen the view from the bedroom, it's quite something. Come, I want to show you. I'm so glad you're here, babe, I've really missed you.'

Poppy could hear their voices getting softer. Carl must have led Lucille into the bedroom, as far away from Poppy as he could manage. She crawled forward on her hands and knees and slowly stuck her head out from the side of the couch. She saw Carl standing with his arm around Lucille's shoulders in the bedroom. They were looking out of the bedroom window, with their backs to the lounge. Poppy took the opportunity and leopard crawled as quickly and quietly as she could towards the front door.

Reaching the entrance to the suite Poppy silently pulled down on the door handle to open the door. Then, just before she slipped out of the room, she reached out and grabbed one of the two trays of casino chips off the little table by the front door. If, as he'd told Lucille, the lying, cheating bastard hadn't done any gambling, she thought, he certainly wouldn't miss some of his chips that he 'hadn't won'.

As the door to the suite clicked shut silently behind her, Poppy stood up and took off, running as fast as she could down the passage towards the elevator, clutching the tray of chips to her chest for dear life. She pumped the button with her finger, looking back down the hallway nervously, to make sure the suite door was still closed and there was nobody coming after her.

Only once she was safely ensconced in the elevator, heading for the ground floor, did she burst out laughing.

STELLA

Stella sat in her small office cubicle and unfolded the piece of paper that contained the list she'd made the night before. She smoothed it out on her desk with the flat of her palm to iron out the creases. So far her list had four items on it:

- go skinny dipping
- go bungee jumping or skydiving
- get tattoo
- have orgasm

Looking at the list again in the cold light of day, Stella could see that it had clearly been written by someone who'd had far too much wine. It started off okay, but it got progressively more crazy. She drew a line through the bungee jumping and skydiving one. She was terrified of heights, why would she do that to herself? She twisted her wedding ring around her finger, scratched her head and went to make herself a cup of coffee.

When she settled back at her desk Stella considered the neat blue line she'd drawn on the list. 'Why not at least try it?' she mumbled to herself. Hell, people do it all the time, she thought. And you don't want to remain the same boring old Stella for the rest of your life, do you? She raised an eyebrow and thought about it. If she was really serious about embracing a more exciting lifestyle she knew she was going to have to step out of her comfort zone a little bit. She sipped on her coffee thoughtfully, then she scribbled the item back onto her list.

Stella evaluated the list again. It was a good list, and if it didn't prove how committed she was to embracing a new and more exciting lifestyle, then nothing would. She felt proud of herself. At last she was doing something to get a life, and it was going to be a pretty exciting one by the looks of things. If only Lucy could see me now, she thought.

Stella doodled around the last item on the list. It had been over a week since she and Max had last spoken and she'd had no choice but to come to the conclusion that her marriage was probably over. She had tried to call him a dozen times but he was still ignoring her, either that or he'd turned off his cellphone completely. She and Max had never talked about what would happen if one of them ever cheated, but she knew Max, once he made a decision about something he very rarely changed his mind – he could be incredibly stubborn – and all the signs pointed to the fact that for him their marriage was over. What Stella had done was such a massive betrayal that she wouldn't be surprised if he never wanted to talk to her again. And she knew in her heart that sooner or later she was going to have to move on. Her mom was right – she was going to have to seize the moment, whether she liked it or not.

Stella turned her attention back to the items on her list. She felt sad and embarrassed that she'd never had an orgasm. For years she'd convinced herself that other girls probably exaggerated about their orgasms. That they couldn't really be all they were cracked up to be, it was just the contraction of a couple of million nerve endings, that was all, it couldn't be that great. But then when she'd seen Lucy and Jake having sex that night in the guest bathroom it had made her re-evaluate everything she believed. Now she wanted what other women, like Lucy, got to have. And why shouldn't she get it, didn't she deserve to have a toe-curlingly good time too?

Stella chewed on the end of her pen. That only left one problem – how to achieve it – where would she get her orgasm from? That was the tricky part. She was sure she could walk into any bar in the city and find someone willing to sleep with her. Women did it all the time. But that plan presented its own problems. How could she be sure whichever guy she met would know how to give her an orgasm, firstly? And, secondly, it wasn't safe. What if the guy turned out to be an axe murderer? Stella didn't know what to do.

This would be easy if she was a guy, she thought. A guy in her situation would just find a prostitute – no questions asked, no strings attached. Stella wondered about male prostitutes. At least sleeping with a prostitute would be a sure thing, she thought. She'd have full control of the situation and if she wasn't satisfied she could just say so.

The more she thought about it, the more interested Stella became in the idea. The way she imagined it, for the first time in her life she could have a guy do exactly what she wanted, when she wanted, no questions asked. He would be entirely focused on her the whole time. And, of course, he wouldn't just fall asleep afterwards, she would make sure of that. Maybe she would ask him to tell her what he was thinking, or tell him to go and make her a cup of tea and bring it to her in bed, if she really wanted to get her money's worth. Her wish would be his command; it was an appealing thought.

Other things about the idea tantalised her too. Like the fact that his satisfaction would be derived purely from her satisfaction. And then he would leave and she would never have to see or hear from him again. The thought gave her an excited shiver. A couple of hours of pampering were exactly what she needed. In fact, she thought, if she were her own doctor, that's precisely what she would prescribe. She needed to take her mind off everything that was going on and for once just focus on herself. Whichever way Stella looked at it, it felt like the perfect solution to her problem.

Millions of people did it every day, didn't they? So what if they were mainly men. She would look into it, she thought, just out of curiosity. It could even be research for her column, she rationalised, just in case at some point somebody wrote in with a query on the subject, at least then she'd be well equipped to deal with it.

Stella went to reception and picked up the newspaper, then took it back to her desk and flipped to the classifieds section.

The escorts section was eight columns long. Tina was looking for 'fun any way you like it'. There were plenty of young Asian girls up for grabs, and there was even a he-she or two and a couple of transvestites. Stella wondered where transvestites fitted in. Would they be considered a male or female prostitute?

Finally Stella found what she'd been looking for, right at the bottom of the page, tucked away in a corner. In contrast to the female escort section, male escorts were a little thin on the ground. In fact, there were only four listed, lined up, waiting for her perusal.

Straight male escort available to accompany you on business engagements, dinner dates, to parties, shows or just for good company. I will give you an exciting and sensual full body message that you will never forget.

The first chap couldn't spell massage properly in his ad, so Stella moved on to the next ad. Bad spelling was a major turn-off for her.

Allow me to guide you through a universe of pleasure. Exploring the paths of passion and sensuality. Satisfaction guaranteed. Discreet and caring.

The second guy offered discreet services and guaranteed satisfaction. Stella drew a circle around that one. She liked the idea that his service came with a guarantee, like when you buy a television or a fridge. Stella looked up from her desk, hot and blushing, as she suddenly realised what she was doing. Had she and Lucy been on talking terms she'd have called her immediately, and Lucy would have talked her down off the ledge. But she couldn't call Lucy; that was out of the question.

Stella peered over the top of her partition, to make sure nobody was watching her. Her breath was shallow and her palms were sweaty. The fear of being caught doing something so objectionable was acute. She took a deep breath to calm herself. If anyone came across her circling ads for male escorts she would simply tell them she was doing research for a pro-active editorial piece she was working on, she decided. But she needn't have worried; she was isolated in her cubicle in her very own department of one.

The third ad read:

23-year-old white male, athletic body, tanned skin, 1.54m tall, green eyes, short brown hair. Easy, safe, professional and fun.

He also sounded quite nice, although he was a little on the short side for her. She ran her eye over the last ad:

For ladies only. Massages, full house, unrushed pleasure. Please enquire for any other services. Travel and all nights offered. Available 24/7.

Stella was pleasantly surprised by the options available to her. She wasn't sure what she'd been expecting, but this was a little like going to a restaurant and choosing something to eat off the menu. She ran back through her choices and compiled a new list of options on a clean sheet of paper:

1. Spelling mistake
2. Discreet, satisfaction guaranteed
3. 23 years old, athletic, but short
4. Massage and unrushed

She considered the list carefully. Each option, other than Mr Typo, had something that appealed to her. Only hypothetically speaking, of course, if she was actually going to go through with something crazy like this, and not just doing research for a potential future article.

Stella scratched her head and wondered how one made such a decision. She decided to be brutal and drew a line through number three. She felt bad for being so superficial, but he was short, and if she was going to pay for it, she would want someone taller than her. She also put a line through number one; he'd spelt himself out of a sale, poor chap.

That left 'satisfaction guaranteed' and 'slow massage'. Number two or number four. It was a tough choice. Stella tapped the end of her pen on the page and made her hypothetical decision: she could get a massage any day of the week, but guaranteed satisfaction, that was something that was harder to come by, and it was also exactly what she needed. In fact, she thought, if her satisfaction was guaranteed, like it said in the ad, then she'd be assured of being able to tick an item off her list. No mess, no fuss.

Stella wondered what one of these guys might cost. It was natural to be curious now that she'd started doing the research. She reread the ads for any sign of price, but couldn't find any. She wondered if they were unionised and charged a standard fee, or did it depend on how much experience they had? But then, how could one prove experience? She wasn't sure. Or perhaps they charged by the orgasm, or by pleasure given, although there were probably too many variables to be able to do that. Maybe she would just call this guy, this 'satisfaction guaranteed' one, to see how much he would charge. All in the name of research, of course. She would need that kind of information if she was going to write a piece on it.

Fully empowered by her curiosity, Stella picked up the telephone and dialled the number quoted in the ad.

'Hello.'

It was a man's voice. Not young- or old-sounding, just average. She couldn't tell from just the one word, but he seemed to have a slight Afrikaans accent. Stella froze and moved to put the phone down.

'Hello, anybody there?' the voice asked, with a gentle smile.

Stella changed her mind at the last minute and picked the phone up again just before it hit the cradle. 'Hi,' she said, her voice a half-whisper so that nobody in the office could hear her.

'Hi,' the voice said back, still smiling.

Then there was quite a long pause.

'Hi,' she whispered again, awkwardly.

'Hi.'

There was another silence. Stella didn't know what to say.

'Can I help you?' the man asked.

'Um, yes, well ... I don't know, um, maybe,' Stella said.

The man laughed. He had a kind laugh and it made her feel more at ease. 'You don't need to be nervous,' he said. 'I won't bite, you know. Well, not unless you want me to.' And then he laughed again.

Stella also laughed this time, although her laugh was more nervous than anything else. 'So I was calling about your ad,' she said, with a sudden burst of confidence that she hadn't known she possessed.

'Great,' he said. 'My name's Patrick.'

'Hi, Patrick, my name's Stel ... um, Cindy.'

The man laughed again and Stella smacked herself on the forehead and rolled her eyes at her own stupidity.

'I was wondering how much you charge?' Stella asked.

'It sort of depends on what you're after,' Patrick said. 'But for a standard appointment, you know, nothing fancy, no bells and whistles, so to speak, you can have me for a thousand rand an hour.'

Stella sucked in her breath and tried to cover it up with a fake clearing of the throat, not wanting him to hear her shock. That was way more than she'd expected.

'So, is that a standard rate?' Stella asked, trying hard to sound nonchalant.

'Pretty much,' he said. 'In this industry it ranges from about four hundred and fifty rand to around one thousand five hundred for an hour. But, trust me, you don't want a five-hundred-rand guy, that's just wham, bam, thank you ma'am, you know. No finesse, no skills.'

Stella nodded at what he was saying; her mom had always warned her and her sisters that in life you got what you paid for.

'I was also wondering about the guarantee that you mention here in your ad?' Stella said.

'It's pretty simple,' Patrick replied. 'I guarantee your satisfaction. That is, if you don't orgasm, I'll give you your money back.'

'Wow,' Stella said, blushing at his casual use of the O-word. 'That's pretty impressive. But how will you know for sure if I've had an ... an ... you know ... one of those?' she asked. 'What if I'm really, really quiet when it happens?'

'Don't worry, Cindy,' he said with a confident smile in his voice. 'I'll know if you've had one.'

Stella blushed again; she had already forgotten that she'd told him her name was Cindy. 'Well,' she continued, nodding into the phone, 'about your guarantee, you see, I've never actually ...' She paused, unable to continue.

'Yes, go on.' Patrick said, urging her on gently.

'I've never, well ... You see, I think I've sort of had one, but I've never actually, you know ... I've never really, you know, done that. I mean, I've done *that*, you know, *it*, but I've never actually had like an actual orgasm before.' She said the word orgasm quietly, in a full whisper.

'That's okay,' Patrick said. 'You'd be amazed at how many women out there tell me that. You're not alone. But like it says in my ad, satisfaction guaranteed. I've never once had an unsatisfied customer.'

Stella took a deep breath; there was something comforting about hearing that she wasn't the only woman on the planet who'd never had an orgasm before. She thought about everything Patrick had said while he waited patiently on the other end of the phone. She cast her eye back over The List. She had to start somewhere if she was going to actually change her life for real. And this was as good a place as any to start.

'I suppose you're busy tonight?' she asked, holding her breath, hardly able to believe what was coming out of her own mouth.

'Actually, funny you should ask, a spot's just opened up for tonight,' Patrick said smoothly. 'Where do you live?'

'Oh crap!' Stella said. 'I forgot, I actually live with my parents, so you won't be able to come to me.' Stella smacked her hand against her forehead again – she must sound like a complete loser, she thought. 'No, I mean, I don't *live* with my parents, not exactly. I've got my own place, of course. But I'm just staying with them for now, you know, temporarily, until I get a few things sorted out.'

'Cindy, Cindy, don't worry, I completely understand. We could always go to a hotel. Although I'm afraid you'd have to pick up the bill,' Patrick said.

'How much do you think that would cost?' she asked, chewing her lip.

'I tell you what, Cindy, you sound like a nice girl, and you sound like you could really do with my help. I've got some connections at the Holiday Inn in town, the room will cost four hundred rand, and I'll drop two hundred rand from my fee, as a new client discount and because you sound like a sweetheart. That way the whole thing will only cost you an extra two hundred bucks, and I'll throw in a bottle of sparkling wine as an added bonus, just to set the mood. How does that sound?'

Stella nodded. 'That's really generous of you, thank you, Patrick.'

'Hey, what can I say? I'm a generous kind of guy,' he said.

'Yes, that sounds generous ...' Stella said, her voice tapering off.

'You sound unsure.'

'No, no,' Stella said. 'I'm not unsure, it's just that this is a big step for me, I've never really done anything like this before.'

'Yes, it's a big decision,' Patrick said. 'I completely understand if you're a little scared and you'd like to think about it a bit, weigh up your options, be a little more conservative, I totally understand. Another time perhaps ...'

There were those words again, 'scared' and 'conservative', they meant boring, staid, frigid. The words caught in Stella's throat. It was all the things she so desperately didn't want to be any more.

'No, wait, Patrick!' Stella snapped. 'I want to do this! Let's do it. Tonight is good for me. What time would you like to meet?'

'Excellent,' Patrick said. 'I'm at your beck and call. You tell me what time to be there and I'll be there. After all, from now on, your wish is my command.'

Stella smiled. She liked the sound of that. 'How about eight thirty?'

'Perfect. One last thing,' Patrick said. 'I have a strict cash-on-arrival policy, and no cheques or credit cards, all right. Cash only.'

'Absolutely,' Stella said, taken aback by his sudden businesslike tone.

'See you at eight thirty, then,' Patrick said. 'At the Holiday Inn just off St George's Mall?'

'Absolutely,' Stella said again, unable to find any other words.

'Bye, Cindy, I'm really looking forward to meeting you and giving you satisfaction, guaranteed.'

'Bye,' Stella whispered, suddenly feeling terrified.

Putting down the phone Stella rubbed her face in disbelief at what she'd just done. She hadn't actually meant to book him. She was only going to ask him a few questions about his prices and how the transaction would take place, she wasn't going to go through with the crazy scheme.

And then a new realisation dawned on her, she'd been so busy negotiating she hadn't even asked him what he looked like. She chewed on her lip and reached for the phone. She would cancel. This was crazy. Nice newlywed girls who liked their socks pulled all the way up did not sleep with male prostitutes, not ever. Or none that she'd ever heard of. Stella lifted the phone to her ear and hovered her finger over the numbers. She started dialling and then put the phone down. Then she picked it up and started dialling again, but Patrick's phone didn't even ring – it went straight to voicemail. Stella hung up. It was a sign. She could do this, she thought. She could get a life. No more conservative, boring, frigid, un-orgasmed Stella. She would show them all. She looked back at her list, resolve filling her veins. She would tick everything off her list, she told herself. And she would do it all by herself.

By the time Stella arrived at the hotel she felt ill. Her stomach was a big swimming knot of nerves and her mouth was filled with saliva, as if she might vomit. She made her way to the toilet in the lobby and leant against the wall in the stall, letting the cold tiles cool her flustered cheeks. She couldn't believe she was doing this. She dipped her hand into her pocket and fingered the wad of cash. One thousand two hundred rand in hundred rand notes. The daily withdrawal limit on her bank card was only a thousand, so she'd had to borrow the rest from her mom with promises to pay it back the following day. When Iris asked what it was for Stella considered telling her the truth, but instead told her mom she was going for dinner with some old girlfriends. Iris shrugged and handed her the notes from her purse, eyeing Stella suspiciously over the top of her spectacles.

Stella wondered what Max would think when he saw that the amount in their savings account had dropped by a grand. It was money they'd been saving to put towards a deposit on a house, although the only thing they would probably need it for now, Stella thought, was a good divorce attorney.

Stella wiped her face with toilet paper and exited the cubicle. She washed her hands and poured cold water on her wrists to try cool her blood, then she looked at herself in the mirror, trying to calm her nerves. There was excitement somewhere in there too, wrapped up in the nerves. Excitement at the fact that she, plain old Stella, Stella Frankel, the boring one, was actually about to do something daring for a change. Something edgy and out of character and completely and utterly insane. For the very first time in her life Stella was out of control with crazy and it felt good.

She had almost lost her nerve and called Patrick to cancel over a dozen times during the course of the day, but she was here now and she was going to go through with it. The nausea receded slightly and she pushed through the bathroom door with resolve and headed back out through the lobby. Patrick had SMSed her with their room details, so she walked across the lobby of the hotel with purpose. She felt like everyone was staring at her, like she had a siren above her head, but when she took a quick look around the lobby nobody made eye contact. It was all in her mind, she told herself, everybody was way too busy worrying about themselves to even notice bland old Stella.

Getting into an empty elevator Stella pushed the button for the fifth floor, adjusting her dress and fiddling with her hair nervously as the doors closed. Arriving at her floor she made her way out of the lift and down the carpeted hallway. A gaudy mirror hung on a wall and Stella stopped to make sure her hair was looking okay. She was about to wrangle her fringe back into place when it dawned on her that it didn't actually matter how she looked. This man was here for her, and not the other way around. She could have been wearing tracksuit bottoms and a pair of Crocs and not have showered or shaved under her arms for over a week, and he would still have to pretend to find her attractive, that was his job. She smiled at her reflection and stopped fiddling with her fringe, but she did check her teeth. Having stuff stuck between your teeth was unacceptable, even when you were paying someone to sleep with you.

Stella's nerves raced themselves to the finish line as she found herself outside the door to the hotel room. She raised a knuckle to knock, then she dropped her hand back down to her side. She couldn't do it. She flexed her clenched fist open and closed again. Yes, she could, she urged herself forward. She made a fist and then raised her hand and knocked, but so quietly that even she could barely hear it. Maybe he wouldn't hear, she thought. Maybe he wouldn't answer and she could just turn around and walk away from this crazy idea, having at least given it a good bash.

Stella was about to turn and run when the door opened. 'Hi, I thought I heard a knock,' a man's voice said as he opened the door all the way and stepped back to welcome her into the room. 'You must be Cindy, I'm Patrick. I'm so glad you came, and may I say that you look absolutely gorgeous this evening.'

Stella eyed Patrick out. He was about the same height as Max and he was very broadly built. He had brown eyes, a slightly receding hairline, glasses and a moustache, and he was wearing a brown patchwork leather jacket. He looked the way Stella imagined a plain clothes detective in the South African Police Service might look.

'Come in, come in,' he said, turning around and walking back into the room, where he picked a bottle of J.C. Le Roux up out of an ice bucket and began fiddling with the foil covering.

Stella froze at the door with a fake smile pasted on her face. He was absolutely nothing like what she'd been picturing in her mind all day. She didn't know what to do. She hovered at the threshold of the room, trying to decide on a plan of action. She desperately wanted to leave, but she couldn't just run away, that would be incredibly rude. She knew she was going to have to go into the room and talk her way out of this one. She stepped tentatively inside, still smiling her big fake, nervous smile.

Stella wasn't sure if it was the brown patchwork leather jacket, the moustache or the glasses, but something about him reminded her of Mr Davies, once her homeroom teacher from high school and now her mother's boyfriend. She shuddered at the thought.

Once inside the hotel room Stella hovered awkwardly with her arms crossed protectively in front of her chest, taking it all in. It was a typical, badly decorated Holiday Inn room, with a bed covered in an ugly patterned bedspread, an ageing television set and a pine table with two matching upholstered pine chairs. Stella also noticed a brown leather briefcase propped up next to the bed.

'So, how about a nice glass of champagne, Cindy?' Patrick asked, popping open the bottle and pouring it into two plastic cups.

Stella nodded gratefully at his offer and accepted the cup.

Patrick made arbitrary small talk, saying something about the champagne and then something about his friend who was a manager at the hotel, but Stella didn't process a word of it. Her breathing had sped up and she suddenly felt incredibly nauseous again. Beads of sweat started to form under her arms and saliva filled her mouth; she was going to have to tell him she wasn't interested, and she didn't know how.

'Please, excuse me, I'll just be a minute,' she said, escaping into the bathroom in the middle of Patrick's story.

Stella leaned against the counter and panted into the mirror. Images of Max slipped through her mind and she suddenly felt achingly guilty. Even if her marriage was all but over, this just wasn't something she could actually go through with. There was no way in a million years she would ever be able to sleep with this strange man. He seemed nice enough, but after only ever being with Max she just couldn't imagine him touching her, or herself naked next to him. It was never going to happen. She wondered what she'd been thinking? Had she really thought she would be able to go through with this? She pictured herself ten minutes from now, lying naked on the bed with this strange man above her, the skin under his leather jacket would be doughy and pale white, she was sure of it. Nausea engulfed her. She couldn't do it, and she wouldn't do it, she needed to get out and away.

Taking a couple of deep breaths, Stella stood up straight and wiped her forehead with some toilet paper, clearing her throat. She clutched her purse tightly with resolve and returned to the room.

Patrick was sitting on the edge of the bed, but he stood up when she returned. He'd taken off his brown patchwork leather jacket and draped it over a chair, revealing a brightly patterned shirt. 'Everything okay?' he asked, clearly sensing that she was having second thoughts.

'Patrick, I'm so sorry,' Stella said. 'I've made a terrible mistake. I'm not going to be able to sleep with you tonight. I'll pay you of course ...' She reached for the notes in her pocket, held them up for him and then placed them on the edge of the hotel room table, next to the TV guide and the remote control. 'I don't know what I was thinking. This is madness. I'm really sorry! You see, I just got married. I mean, I've only been married for, oh, I don't know, about one thousand one hundred and something hours. My husband and I had this massive fight, and my sister isn't talking to me, and my parents are getting a divorce, and you're wearing a brown patchwork leather jacket, and my name's not really Cindy, it's Stella, and I just think I got a little confused. I think I went off my path a little, without entirely realising it. But now I realise that there's just no way I'm going to be able to have sex with you. I'm really sorry, Patrick. I thought I was going to be able to do it, but I just can't ...'

'Oh,' he said as her ramble slowly came to an end. He sat back down on the edge of the bed with a disappointed look on his face. 'I've never had an unsatisfied customer, you know. You would be the first.'

'Again, I'm really so, so sorry!' Stella said, turning to leave. 'I really didn't mean to ruin your record, I swear.'

'Well, you don't have to go yet, do you?' Patrick said. 'I mean, you only just got here. Why don't you finish your champagne, at least?'

He seemed so disappointed, and the thought of hurting his feelings even more, and the fact that she'd ruined his untarnished record weighed heavily on Stella's conscience.

'Okay, why not, sure. Just a quick drink and then I'd better get going,' Stella said, sitting down on one of the chairs, just across from where he sat on the edge of the bed. She took a big sip of her cheap sparkling wine, and then another one. It helped ease the tension from her shoulders. She felt better now that she'd told him she wasn't going to stay. It wasn't that he'd done anything wrong; it was just that she clearly wasn't this kind of girl. She really was just boring, conservative old Stella after all, she thought.

'I'm sorry to hear about your husband and your sister and your parents,' Patrick said gently.

Shame, he was sweet, Stella thought. He was probably a lovely chap. 'That's okay, it's not your fault,' she said.

They sat in silence for a couple more minutes, drinking their champagne.

'Do you mind if I ask you what's wrong with my jacket?' Patrick finally asked, breaking the silence and pointing to his jacket.

Stella grimaced. 'Well, to be honest, it's just not … well, it's kind of … it's just that it's not the most fashionable item of clothing these days, if you know what I mean? You could try a normal suit jacket, or maybe even a blazer, or something like that,' she said, trying to put it as delicately as possible. 'Or even just a normal leather jacket, without the pattern, if it has to be a leather jacket. I would imagine in your industry it's all about image, right?'

Patrick nodded slowly, taking in her advice.

They sat in silence for another couple of minutes.

This time Stella broke the silence. 'So, what's in the briefcase?' she asked, nodding at it where it lay on the floor.

Patrick looked at the briefcase and then looked at her and shook his head, smiling. 'I'm afraid that's classified information, Ma'am. If you don't go all the way with me, you don't get to know what's in the briefcase. Let's just say those are just a few of the little tricks I have up my sleeve,' he said and winked at her.

'Oh, for satisfaction guaranteed?' Stella asked.

'It's not too late to change your mind,' Patrick said with a friendly smile. 'All leather jackets look the same when the lights are out.'

'I'm afraid unfortunately it is too late for me,' Stella said, getting up to leave.

'Fair enough,' Patrick said. He stood up and went over to the table where he reached for the money she'd left for him. He thumbed through it and then he held out a few of the hundred rand notes to her. 'Here you go,' he said. 'Let me pay for the room, at least.'

'No, really it's fine,' Stella said, pushing his hand holding the money back towards his chest. 'I'm the one who chickened out. You shouldn't be out of pocket.'

'No, you should take it,' Patrick said, holding it out to her again until she took it and nodded her thanks. Then he picked up the remote and returned to the bed. 'I think I'll stick around and watch a bit of TV if you don't mind, we've still got the room for another forty-five minutes.'

Stella shoved the cash into her pocket gratefully and walked towards the door.

'You sure there isn't something I can do to try change your mind?' Patrick asked, looking at her hopefully. 'Last chance?'

Stella took in his black suit pants and his cheap patterned shirt and his thick brown moustache and shook her head. 'Thanks anyway,' she said. 'It's not you, it's me.' Then she turned and let herself out of the hotel room.

Stella shook her head as she walked back towards the lift. She wondered if things would have worked out differently if she'd selected the short guy or the massage guy or even the spelling-mistake guy. Whether she still would have been walking down this passageway with her orgasm virginity intact? She shook her head again. She just didn't think she was the paying-for-sex kind of girl, no matter who the guy was.

Maybe this was too big an item to start off with, she thought. Perhaps she should have gone a little easier on herself and started with something simpler, something that didn't require as much guts. Like skinny dipping or bungee jumping, or even the tattoo. Baby steps were what was called for here, not giant leaps into the unknown.

POPPY

Poppy opened the door to their hotel room silently and tiptoed inside. The curtains were pulled closed and the room was in darkness, full of the smell of sleep. Buck was dead to the world, lying spreadeagled on his stomach in nothing but a pair of boxer shorts. His one yeti-sized foot had slipped off the edge of the bed and was dangling above the floor, half-socked.

Tiptoeing over to the window Poppy pulled the curtain partially open. She stared out at the now pink and orange sky, a sky that hinted at the beautiful day that was about to bloom in Las Vegas. She'd been awake all night but she didn't feel the slightest bit tired. A renewed thread of energy surged through her body at the reality of their massively revised situation. Seeing Buck start to stir, she bounded over to his bed and leapt up onto it. 'We're rich! We're rich! We're rich!' she shouted, jumping up and down.

Buck rolled over onto his back and rubbed his eyes as he opened them slowly and looked up at her, half asleep, half awake.

'Wake up, dude! There's no time to sleep when you're filthy, stinking rich!' Poppy yelled as she sank her hands into her pockets and began to pull out wads and wads of cash.

Poppy had exchanged the chips she'd taken from Carl's room in the casino ten minutes earlier, before she'd made her way back up to their room, situated in the cheaper, viewless back wing of the hotel. The cheap rooms couldn't have been further away from the more expensive suites like Carl's, even if the architects had tried, Poppy had thought as she'd trudged down identical corridor after seemingly endless identical corridor. It was clear the rich and famous had no desire to bump into the riff-raff when entering or exiting their suites. But what did Poppy care? She wasn't riff-raff any more!

Poppy threw the notes in the air and watched as they rained back down on the two of them. When all the notes had come fluttering down onto the bed and the floor she knelt down next to Buck and swept the money up in her cupped hands, tossing handfuls up in the air so that crumpled bills rained down on the bed again.

'Look, we're rich, you motherfucker!'

'What the fuck, Poppy?' Buck asked, sitting up and rubbing his eyes. 'Am I dreaming? What's going on?'

'Look at all this money, Buck,' Poppy shouted.

'I don't understand,' Buck said, picking up fistfuls of cash and holding them up in front of his face to make sure they were real. 'How much is it?' he asked.

'Nine thousand four hundred and ninety-two dollars!' Lucy shrieked.

Buck looked at her and then down at the money and then smiled. 'Did you rob a bank or something?' he asked. 'Do we need to get out of here in a hurry and come up with disguises?'

'Nothing quite as illegal as that, but it's probably a good idea if we head out of here pretty soon.'

'Jesus Christ, Poppy, what have you done?' Buck asked, looking worried.

'Let's just say it involved a fat midget, some hookers, an accountant who lied about inventing the flash drive and a woman named Lucille! Come on, up and at 'em, moneybags, we need to get out of here.'

'I can't wait to hear this story,' Buck said. 'Are we Poppy and Clyde now?'

'Hurry up,' Poppy said, starting to scoop up the cash. 'Let's get out of here. I'll tell you everything at breakfast, I'm starving.'

'With money like this we could go just about anywhere in the world,' Buck said with awe.

'Hey, I've got an idea,' Poppy said. 'Let's go somewhere that's the complete diametric opposite of this place.'

STELLA

Stella tapped on her indicator and took a left turn, following the signs to get off the highway. It had been a long drive and she felt anxious to get it all over with. When she'd left Cape Town four and a half hours earlier she'd been excited and amped, but with every passing kilometre the excitement had made way for the nerves and dread which bullied her bravado, slowly shoving it out of the way.

She parked her car in the dusty parking area and got out, stretching her nervous shaky legs. The bridge was a couple of hundred metres away and she could hear people shouting out the countdown back from ten.

Stella took a deep breath and walked towards the bridge, her stomach doing flips. As she approached the gorge she grasped hold of the railing tightly with both hands, looking down onto the sandy river bed, which was very far below her. She sucked in her breath and took a big step backwards, away from the edge, fighting off the sensation that she was already falling, helplessly out of control. It all felt like a bad dream.

A friendly looking guy with a big open smile pasted on his face approached her holding a clipboard. 'So, are we doing the bungee today?' he asked.

'Yes ... No ... I think so. I don't know. No, maybe ...' Stella responded.

'Ah, so you've decided then?' He laughed at her playfully. 'Hi, I'm Sam,' he continued, holding out his hand and shaking hers. 'And I gather you're really nervous?'

Stella looked down at her open palm and saw that it was slick with sweat. 'Sorry!' she said, swiping her hands down the front of her jeans. 'It's just that I've never done anything like this before and I'm kind of scared ... no, wait, make that absolutely completely terrified of heights!'

'I gathered. Well, there's nothing to worry about, okay? You're in very safe hands here,' Sam said. 'And today's a perfect day for a bungee. See, no wind and quite a short queue. I'd say your timing couldn't be better. Today is a great day to do something new for the first time. You're going to love this, I guarantee it. You'll be hooked. Just about everyone who does this once says they would definitely do it again.'

Stella nodded numbly and allowed Sam to escort her towards a small table set up under an open-sided tent, near the bungee station.

'So who did you come with?' Sam asked, looking over her shoulder towards the car park. 'Is anyone else in your party wanting a jump, or is it just you?'

'No, I came alone,' Stella whispered. 'This is kind of a personal thing, just for me. I didn't want to bring anybody and nobody actually knows I'm doing it.'

'Oh, sure, I can understand that,' Sam said, still smiling warmly. 'Well, let's get you signed in and paid up, and we should have you ready to jump in a matter of fifteen, twenty minutes.'

This would be over in minutes Stella thought. She just had to stay focused and not lose her nerve.

Stella filled in her details numbly. Name, age and weight, address and phone number. Then she signed the lengthy consent and liability forms after skimming over the small print lightly. All the consent and liability forms in the world wouldn't bring her back if she was dead, she thought.

Once she'd finished filling everything in she handed the clipboard back to Sam and her credit card to the lady sitting behind the table. She waited, tapping her foot nervously on the ground and chewing the inside of her cheek, twisting her wedding band around on her finger over and over again. Then she signed the slip with a shaky hand. Another purchase out of their house deposit fund, she thought. She shrugged her shoulders. It would make up for all the thrills Max had never given her in the bedroom, she decided.

Sam led her over to the back of the queue and left her to go help out in the middle of the bridge where the jumpers were all headed. Stella leaned against the bridge's railing, holding tightly onto it with both hands. Then she took in her surroundings for the first time, taking deep gulping breaths to try and calm her nerves. The old bridge she was standing on stood parallel to the new bridge, which was how vehicles now crossed the Gouritz River. These days, since they'd built the new bridge, the only thing this old bridge carried was adrenalin junkies.

'So, how are we doing over here?' Sam asked, reappearing at her shoulder, still clutching his clipboard.

'Um … I don't know …' Stella mumbled. 'Sam, how high is this bridge?'

'The jump itself is only about seventy metres,' he told her, gesturing down towards the river bed.

'Only!' Stella said, feeling a little hysterical.

'Yeah, well, the highest one in the country is a hundred and sixty metres, so this is nothing in comparison. But, really, I promise, you're going to love this, you have my word.'

'Has anyone ever fallen?' Stella asked him, panic rising in her voice.

'Sure,' Sam said. 'People fall every day, but generally we make it our business to catch them.'

Stella knew he was just teasing her, trying to ease the tension she felt, but at that moment she couldn't find the humour in his words. Her insides felt frozen. She nodded at him, her face contorted with anxiety. 'Sam, I'm completely terrified of heights. Even standing here, holding onto this railing is hard for me,' she whispered.

'I can see that,' Sam said gently, rubbing a hand over her white knuckles.

'Listen, you need to just relax and breathe and let go. Everything is going to be amazing, trust me. Seriously, I know what I'm talking about.' Someone called out his name from the middle of the bridge and he looked up. 'Okay, I just have to go help them out with this next jumper,' he said. 'Try to relax and enjoy your surroundings. Look, isn't it gorgeous here?'

Stella nodded as he turned and made his way back to the middle of the bridge where a tall thin guy with a ponytail was getting ready to take his jump. Stella marvelled at how calm the guy looked, he was even smiling.

Stella looked down at the river bed below. Even though the railing was chest-height and there was no way she could fall over, when she stood near the edge she still felt that familiar vertigo she'd had her whole life. Her stomach lurched, her legs wobbled and she thought for sure this time she was really going to be sick. She breathed deeply and tried to distract her brain which was trying very hard to convince her to run very far away.

The shrieks of the countdown rang out across the valley and out of the corner of her eye Stella saw the man with the ponytail swan dive off the side of the bridge with grace that belied his size. He howled with excitement as he plunged towards the river bed. She leant forward and watched his trajectory, unable to stop herself. He fell, fell, fell, and then he bounced back up again on the giant elastic attached to his ankles. Then he fell back down again still shrieking and whooping with delight. Stella looked away, her stomach turning, still trying hard to distract herself from the desperate desire to first run away, and then vomit. Or vomit first and then run away.

She had to tick something off her list, she told herself, even if only to prove to herself that she could do it. After the debacle with Patrick she had decided to choose what she thought would be one of the simpler things on her list to do next, and this had been it. It had only been once she'd seen the bridge that the reality of the situation had really hit home.

Stella wondered if she'd made a mistake not bringing someone along to egg her on and force her to jump, but she wasn't sure who she could have brought. The only people she wanted to be doing something like this with were Max and Lucy. They were the only people in the world who would understand the full significance of Stella actually bungee jumping. To Daisy this wouldn't be something scary at all. In fact, she would relish the opportunity. And Violet would only be able to relate to it on an intellectual level, in terms of dealing with a phobia. But Max and Lucy would get the kind of sacrifice Stella was making to prove a point and to try and get a life.

What would happen if she died? Stella wondered. Max and Lucy would feel terribly guilty. She pictured them both howling at her funeral, Lucy wearing something simple and black, Max inconsolable. Both berating each other for not forgiving Stella sooner and by doing so, forcing her to jump off a bridge to her untimely and tragic death. They would never recover, she thought, a small smile turning up the corners of her mouth. That would teach them.

'Ready? It's your turn next.' Sam was by her side again. He looped his arm in hers and led her forcefully over to the side of the bridge. 'This is where we'll be suiting you up and getting you ready,' he said, showing her to a small, open-sided tent in the middle of the bridge.

Stella's hands were shaking and her pulse raced loudly in her ears.

'And then this is where you'll jump from,' Sam added, showing her a scaffolding structure attached to the side of the bridge. 'Remember, I'll be right here with you the whole time. There's absolutely nothing to be scared of, okay?'

Sam led her back into the tent where a group of guys started to strap her into a complicated harness. But the closer Stella got to actually doing the jump the more sure she was becoming that she was making the biggest mistake of her life. She wondered what she thought she would be proving to anybody by doing this, particularly since there was nobody there to witness it. She suddenly realised how foolish her plan had been. Nobody who knew her would ever believe that she'd actually done a bungee jump and she hadn't brought anyone along to act as a witness, she hadn't even thought to bring a camera to help gather evidence. She shook her head. She knew that this was a ridiculous attitude, after all, hadn't she been telling herself for the last four and a half hours that she was doing this for herself and not for anybody else. Stella suddenly needed the toilet very badly. She wondered what would happen if she literally wet her pants while doing the jump. Compared to this, sleeping with the prostitute would have been easy, she thought. You couldn't pee your pants in public and then fall to your death while sleeping with a prostitute.

Once she was all strapped up Sam led Stella to the scaffolding at the edge of the bridge. Bystanders stepped aside and let them through, clapping their hands and cheering her on. Sadly, their bravado did nothing to urge Stella forward. She wished their enthusiasm was more contagious.

Once they reached the platform Sam held her elbow and helped her step up onto it. Then he walked with her calmly and with purpose towards the launching platform, holding her arm tightly in his grasp, as if she might get away if he held her too loosely. Stella suddenly realised he had been talking to her the entire time, but she hadn't heard a word of it. What if he had been giving her advice and instructions and she'd missed something vital? The blood was rushing so loudly in her ears that she couldn't hear anything. Panic gripped every part of her body. She couldn't breathe. She couldn't think. She could barely even speak.

'Right, you're almost ready to go,' Sam shouted in her ear.

'I don't think I can do this!' Stella shouted back, in a shrill, high-pitched voice. 'I didn't hear a word you said just now, I wasn't listening. I'm not prepared. What if I missed some important piece of information? I don't know what to do!'

'There's nothing to do,' Sam said, squeezing her arm again gently. 'All you have to do is fall, enjoy the sensation and the view and we'll pick you up down at the bottom a changed person. Take a deep breath, now, Stella. Everything is going to be fine. All you need to do is remember to breathe.' Then Sam stepped forward, but Stella didn't follow him. Instead she stood bolted to the spot, staring at the gorge spread out in front of her. 'But what if I die?' she called out, desperately afraid, a tear lodged firmly in the corner of her eye.

'Stella, you won't die. There's something like a one in a million chance that something goes wrong.'

Stella looked at him, horrified. 'Well, there was something like a one in a million chance that I was going to become a sex columnist, and there must have been something like a one in a million chance that I would end up having sex with my identical twin's boyfriend and have to move back home to my parents' house. And both those things happened to me.'

Sam smiled at her soothingly. 'No, Stella, listen to me, you came to do this and you're going to do it and you're going to love it. Everyone gets scared, but you can do this, I know you can. Now take a deep breath ...'

Taking hold of her arm again Sam pulled Stella forward towards a small gate that led onto the jumping platform right on the edge of the bridge. There was now only about two metres between Stella and the drop. 'Please don't let me go, swear you won't let me go!' she shrieked pathetically, gripping Sam's arm tightly with both of her hands.

'Right, Stella,' Sam said, swinging her around so that she was closest to the drop, 'are you ready to jump?'

Ignoring him, Stella carried on gripping his arm tightly.

'You'll need to let go of my arm,' Sam said, trying to ease her fingers off his flesh. 'I think I'm bleeding now.'

'No way, take me down!' Stella shouted.

'But you aren't even near the edge yet.' Sam said calmly. 'Stella, listen to me. You can do this. Everyone gets scared, you just have to let go and let it happen ...'

'No, I can't. I can't let go. I can't. I'm not doing this. Pull me down! Pull me down, Sam!' Stella shrieked hysterically, tears pouring down her cheeks.

'Are you absolutely sure?' he asked. 'You know you'll regret not doing it.'

'I'll also regret dying before I've made things right with Max and Lucy. I don't want to die! I don't want to die!' Stella howled dramatically as the gorge swam in and out of focus below her. 'Pull me down, right now, goddamnit!'

'There are no refunds if you quit,' Sam said.

'I don't care!' Stella shouted. 'Please pull me down!'

She felt Sam pull her back a couple of steps, off the platform, then he leant back and shouted at the top of his voice to the rest of his team: 'We've got a quitter!'

'Quitter, quitter, quitter,' the word echoed down through the gulley and bounced back up at her ad infinitum.

One of the guys pulled the gate closed behind her and manhandled Stella's limp, exhausted body back into the tent, where they started unstrapping her harness. Nobody spoke to her and Sam was no longer by her side. When she looked up he was on the platform ledge, talking calmly to the next jumper, who was poised on the platform.

When Stella was eventually free she stumbled away from the tent and sat down on the tarred kerb. Dropping her head into her hands she sobbed into her fingers. She felt like the biggest loser on the planet. She had failed at two items on her list now. She wondered if she was destined to be the most boring woman on the planet for the rest of her life. Her shoulders shook. Perhaps she wasn't built for happiness or excitement, she thought, wiping her fingers across her nose and sniffing as she sobbed.

The crowd around her began to shout out the countdown for the new jumper about to launch herself off the platform. She listened to it closely: 'Ten, nine, eight, seven, six, five …' A small part of her wanted the jumper to either not go through with the jump or, better still, to do the jump but to die a horribly gruesome death in the process. 'Four, three, two, one …' the onlookers shrieked. 'Bungee!' they yelled as the jumper launched herself off the platform, shrieking as she fell into the gorge.

The jumper's shrieks died down as she dipped far away, down into the depths of the gorge. Stella listened closely, waiting for the blood-curdling screams of the onlookers as the jumper's body smashed into the river bed. She imagined how those who had judged her earlier would pat her on the shoulder and tell her how lucky she was that she had decided not to jump, how it could have been her lying dead seventy metres below, how she must have a guardian angel. How she must be the luckiest girl alive and the fact that she was a little boring had probably saved her life in the end.

But all she heard was the shouting and clapping of the spectators, and the loud echoing shrieks of a successful bungee jump bouncing off the sides of the gorge.

Stella stood up and wiped the tears from her face. Then she walked back towards her car. She unlocked the door, climbed in and drove away, never once looking back at the old, unused bridge that she would forever remember as The Bridge of Disappointment.

On the long drive back to Cape Town Stella had a lot of time to think about what had, or rather what hadn't happened. By the time she hit the bottleneck at the beginning of Sir Lowry's Pass she had decided two very important things. Firstly, that she definitely would not be telling anyone that she had driven almost nine hours not to jump off a bridge. And, secondly, that she was going to go through with whatever it was that she selected next on her to-do list, no matter what. Failure was not an option.

POPPY

Poppy ran a hand over her shaven head. It had been four days since the monk had taken the razor to her scalp and she could feel the regrowth tickling the tips of her fingers. She'd never had a shaven head before and she was surprised at the odd shapes she'd felt as she ran her hands across her skull, familiarising herself with the bumps and inclines, nooks and crannies.

Poppy had once read somewhere about phrenology. It was the art of understanding a person's personality by reading the shape of their head, a sort of scalp astrology. But she knew zero about the technique, and she wondered what a phrenologist would make of her head.

Buck's shaven head was hilarious. It was completely white, in contrast to the rest of his body, which had become darker and darker during their travels. Poppy had also noticed for the first time that he had a ginormous forehead; it was like a ledge on the top of his face, where he'd be able to store things if he wanted to. He also had a longish pink scar just behind his right ear, which to Poppy made it look like he had a thin pink pencil wedged permanently behind his ear, ready to grab whenever he needed to take notes or fill in his lottery ticket. When he was done being shaved by the silent monk Poppy had pointed at him and stifled a giggle behind her hand. 'I don't know what you're laughing at, baldy!' he'd said crossly. 'Just wait till you see yours.'

That had shut Poppy up quickly, but as there were no mirrors at the temple she still had no concept of how she looked without hair. She'd tried using the side of a metal tap as a mirror, but it distorted her shape so badly that she'd given up on it.

Just eight days earlier she and Buck had landed in India after a direct flight from Las Vegas. Then they'd taken a sweaty three day bus ride to a town called Kandy. Then they had taken another bus to a place called Galaha Pass Nilambe Office Junction. From there it had been a steep seventeen kilometre hike through a jungle-like forest to get to the Tushita Buddhist Meditation Centre.

Back in Vegas, with their new found wealth, they'd decided to go to the most diametrically opposed place they could think of to Vegas. And once they had made that decision, an ashram in India seemed the only suitable choice.

On their arrival they'd been stripped of their backpacks, and all their clothes and possessions, and had each been given a floor-length white robe to wear. Then they'd been shown to their quarters.

Boys and girls slept separately at the ashram – Poppy assumed it was for reasons of modesty, to minimise distractions and aid successful meditation – so she had no idea what Buck's room was like. Hers, however, was one of a dozen other small concrete rectangles, all identical in every way and all devoid of both furniture and comfort. Previous residents had stuck small pieces of paper all over her walls, each one covered with meditations or thoughts, like *Be at one with your spirit*, *Quiet your mind* and *Let it go*, a mantra which she had soon discovered was one of the core teachings of the monks at the meditation centre. In the back corner, in amongst the other messages, one joker had written *For a good time call Susan*, followed by a phone number. It was on a dirty piece of paper that looked like it had been torn out of an old exercise book. Poppy badly wanted to pull it off the wall, screw it up and dispose of it, it was so incongruent with the entire experience, but after considering it she had decided not to remove any of the little slips of paper; she was only passing through this place and she didn't want to change anything. That was the Zen way, she felt.

The monk who had shown them around had given her a sleeping mat and a thin blanket, and that was it. She didn't even have a pillow, and she smiled as she remembered her complaint just days earlier that their room at the hotel in Vegas was dodgy. Compared to this, their room in Vegas was eight starred. They'd even had an en suite! In the ashram a short pathway outside her room led to a communal toilet that was no more than a hole in the ground and a bucket she had to fill with water, if she wanted to flush.

They had both known from the start that there would be no talking, no music and no technology, and that they would have to follow the temple's strict vegetarian diet, but the sheer sparseness of the ashram had shocked Poppy. She hadn't been expecting luxury, but she'd never considered it would be like this. She imagined the look on Buck's face when he'd seen his room for the first time and it made her smile.

In comparison to the starkness of her room, the view was spectacular. They were located in the middle of a vast, lush forest. Poppy breathed in slowly and then breathed out again, focusing on the calming effects of the incredible mist-enshrouded vista. If she was going to get through this she needed to give in to the ways of the temple, she decided for the umpteenth time, otherwise she would never make it.

The first day had been spent settling in, and having briefings with various monks to discuss what would be required of them in the days ahead, particularly once they took their oaths of silence.

Life in the temple followed a simple routine. They were woken by bells every morning at a quarter to five, had group meditation at five, tea at six, health yoga at six thirty and breakfast at seven thirty.

Right from the beginning Poppy had found the meditating part of the programme excruciatingly difficult. Calming her mind was impossible.

Sitting in the lotus position the way the monks had shown them, with each of her heels balanced on an opposite knee, wasn't a problem, but remaining focused on her breathing was almost impossible. All she had to do was breathe in and consider it, then breathe out and consider that. That was all that was required of her. However, after less than a minute she found stray thoughts creeping into her mind. She would bounce from thinking about her family back home, to thinking of an adventure from her travels with Buck, or worse, she would suddenly become aware of an acute itch on her elbow or on the tip of her nose. After seconds the itch would become all she could think about, crippling her until she gave in and scratched it. Then she would try to refocus, pushing all the thoughts out of her mind and returning to her breathing. Breathing in and considering it, breathing out and considering that.

Of course this focus would only last another couple of seconds before her brain wandered off again without her. She would wonder how Buck was managing and ultimately she would find herself slowly opening one eye just a slit to look over at him. So far he'd always seemed intent and focused, eyes closed, breathing deeply, but Poppy was convinced that he was really just asleep sitting up.

An hour had never seemed all that long before, but meditating for more than five minutes on that first day had been impossible for Poppy. By the third day she had managed to stretch it out to about eleven minutes, but she was crap at it, and she knew she'd need a lifetime to make it to forty-five minutes, let alone an hour.

After group meditation every day, it was time for tea, which wasn't really tea. Rather, it was a cup filled with a bitter concoction of sticks and bark and leaves that didn't taste anything like tea, or none that Poppy had ever had before. After 'tea' there was more yoga till seven thirty, then breakfast, which consisted of fruit and a small portion of a stodgy porridge-like mix. Other meals at the temple included things like beans and tofu, and a variety of other unidentifiable organic vegetarian or vegan treats that tasted nothing like food as Poppy knew it.

Then at eight thirty every morning working meditation began. First they were instructed in Anapanasati, the mindfulness of breathing, and then they would spend till eleven sweeping, which was what the monks considered working meditation. The monks would hand out brooms made from bamboo and twine, and Poppy and her fellow initiates would be tasked with meditating while they swept the grounds of the temple from corner to corner. The idea was 'to gain mindfulness of the sensations arising and ceasing in the body', as this would apparently lead to a better understanding of themselves and inner peace, or something like that. Poppy was desperately bad at the sweeping, and surprisingly bad at the breathing as well, which she thought odd, considering it was something she'd been doing her entire life.

And so the day would continue, with lunch, if you could call it that, more meditation, and then some quiet time – which Poppy couldn't quite understand since when you've taken a vow of silence all time was quiet time. Then there were lectures in the afternoon, more meditation and dinner, or something that vaguely resembled dinner, if you lived on cardboard. And then it was early to bed, so they could wake up before five the following morning and do it all again.

Poppy sat on the floor alone in her room, feeling up her head and watching a spider crawl across the ceiling. She'd named the spider Bob on their second day at the meditation centre, and over the last two days he had become her friend and confidant. She had long silent conversations with him in her mind. At this point she hadn't as much as cleared her throat in three days. At first she thought that she would find the whole vow of silence thing easy, but it was much trickier than she'd thought. She'd just about forgotten what her own voice sounded like and the temptation to clear her throat out loud with a good 'ahem' had become almost unbearable.

Poppy opened her mouth to say something to Bob, and then closed it again. She had come so far. She was on day four, they were here for six more days; she wasn't sure she could do it, but she was going to try.

On the night of day five, halfway through their stay, Poppy lay on her mat and stared at the ceiling. She had no idea what time it was. After dinner she'd come down to her room and gone to sleep, but had been woken up some time in the middle of the night by the deep, echoing grumbling in her stomach. Poppy was starving. She'd never felt this hungry in her life before. She came from a big Jewish family, where food was a priority. If you were happy, you ate; if you were sad, you ate. Something to celebrate? Here, why not have a little something to eat?

Poppy stared at Bob on the ceiling in the dark – she could just make out his outline – and wondered what spider tasted like. The silence of the night was deafening. Over the last day or so the silence at the ashram had slowly become almost too much to bear. It was the loudest silence Poppy had ever heard, only ever punctuated by the screeching of the monkeys or the chiming of the bells.

Poppy lay and thought about food. If she could eat anything in the world what she would eat? Maybe a hamburger, with fries and a shake, or her mother's roast chicken and rice, that was her favourite. Her stomach growled again, turning itself inside out in the search for something, anything, to digest. Poppy wasn't going to be able to fall asleep like this, she was just too hungry. She got up and went to the door of her small room, staring out into the night. There was no electricity in the rooms, electricity at the ashram was reserved for the main buildings and the kitchen, but a full moon hung in the sky, illuminating the buildings and the forest canopy behind them.

Poppy thought about the kitchen and her stomach rumbled again, saliva filling her mouth. She'd never been in the kitchen, but she was sure that there must be food in there. Maybe an apple or some sprouts, anything would do. Wearing nothing but her panties and a small vest she slipped on her sandals and started walking from her room up towards the main building, driven forward in the dark by the grumbling hole in her stomach.

Poppy broke into a sweat as she reached the main buildings, it was partly nerves, but it had also been incredibly hot at the ashram the entire time they'd been there, and even the short walk to the kitchen had left her covered in a sheen of perspiration. She turned around to make sure nobody was following her, and satisfied she was all alone she tiptoed up to the entrance to the kitchen. What if it was locked? Poppy wondered. But then reassured herself with the thought that it would surely be un-Zen to lock something in an ashram.

Poppy's heart was racing, her stomach churning in anticipation. She reached out and grabbed the door knob and turned it slowly to the left. Nothing. Then she turned it to the right, and it gave, the door opening. Poppy's heart soared and she stepped through the door, fully focused on her quest to find something, anything to eat.

Inside the kitchen was pitch dark, the only light coming from the full moon outside, but Poppy could see that it was lined with huge stainless-steel counter tops. Quietly, she tiptoed towards the back of the kitchen, looking for anything edible, anything at all. Suddenly she heard an almighty clunk as she bashed her shin hard on something cold and sharp. Swearing in pain, she grabbed at her leg as the enormous pot she'd walked into toppled over and the lid rolled around on the concrete floor, the metal ringing loudly like a set of cymbals that had been thrown down a flight of stairs.

Eventually both the noise of the pot lid and the pain in her shin subsided and Poppy stood upright, listening to hear if anyone was coming to investigate. When she was sure that all she could hear was the quiet of the night, some crickets and her own shallow breathing, she continued tiptoeing forward, now with a slight limp.

At the back of the kitchen Poppy came across another door. Reaching for the handle she opened it and found herself in a large pantry space. Supplies were stacked high against the walls: piles of spices and chopsticks and plates and cups. Then Poppy saw what she'd come for – the giant walk-in fridge, glinting at the back of the pantry. She smiled, unable to stop herself, and limped forward, reaching for the large, stainless-steel fridge handle.

The metal of the handle was blissfully cool to the touch and as she opened the door frosty air seeped towards her, enveloping her hot, sweaty body. Ignoring the light switch she reached for the nearest jar and opened the lid, peering inside. She saw large squares of white tofu, swimming in liquid. Then she reached for the next container and opened that too. It was full to the brim with sloppy, slushy, reddish beans. Poppy dipped her right hand into the tofu container and grabbed a slab of it, which she shoved into her mouth, whole. Chewing as fast as she could she reached out her left hand and dug that into the second container, scooping up a handful of sticky, mushy beans, which she also shoved into her mouth. Swallowing hard, she shovelled in mouthful after mouthful of tofu and beans, the food dripping down her chin and the front of her vest.

Suddenly the lights came on in the pantry and Poppy froze where she stood, her back to the door, her eyes blinking as they adjusted to the sudden fluorescent brightness. She heard nothing except her own breathing. Slowly she pivoted on one foot and turned to face the door. Four monks faced her in their robes, staring at her with horrified looks on their faces.

'What type of crazy person gets kicked out of an ashram for breaking into the kitchen and stealing food?' Buck shouted in mock horror, kicking a stone down the hill.

They were headed the seventeen kilometres back down the slope, in the sweltering heat, to get the bus at Galaha Pass Nilambe Office Junction.

'I'm sorry, okay!' Poppy wailed. 'I don't know what happened. It wasn't me, the devil made me do it!'

'Tofu and beans, Poppy, really?' Buck asked her. 'Gross, man! How could you want to eat that stuff? It's like cardboard and tasteless mush!'

'I know, Buck! Don't rub it in. Weren't you hungry? I was starving!'

'That monk who gave us back our stuff when they asked us to leave said it's the first time in the one hundred and seventy-seven year history of the ashram that anyone's broken into the kitchen and stolen food in the middle of the night!'

'They don't know that!' Poppy said, blushing. 'They don't lock the doors. I bet you tons of people have done it before, but they just didn't find out about it because those people didn't trip over a pot and make such a massive noise.'

'Yeah, I still don't know how you managed that either,' Buck said. 'That pot was like three feet tall!'

'I don't know, all right!' Poppy said. 'It was dark in there and I was hungry, goddamnit!'

'Don't stress, Pops,' Buck said. 'I'm only teasing you. I don't know how much longer I could have taken all that Zen stuff either. How's your leg?'

'Sore! Hey, isn't it nice to be able to talk again? I missed you, you big dummy,' Poppy said, nudging him gently.

'Yeah, I missed you too,' Buck said. 'Nice haircut, by the way.'

'So, where to next?' Poppy asked.

Buck shrugged and they walked on in silence for five or ten minutes, both immersed in their own thoughts. Eventually Buck spoke, breaking the silence, 'Hey, I know,' he said, 'what about Amsterdam?'

STELLA

The butterflies in Stella's stomach were performing live and unplugged. She took a deep breath, pushed the door open and stepped inside. The lighting inside the shop was low, with a bluish tinge, creating the kind of ambience one would typically find in a nightclub. A woman behind a counter next to the door glared at Stella. She was huge, easily weighing over a hundred kilos. Despite, or perhaps in spite of which, she wore a tiny vest, with her bra and boobs sticking out in a million different places. The woman's face was pasty white while both her arms and her entire chest were covered in tattoos. Butch was an understatement. Stella placed the woman somewhere in her early forties, although she had the look of someone who woke up to ten cigarettes and half a bottle of brandy every morning, so she could have been younger. Her hair was a wild fake red colour and her nails were painted a clashing dark blue.

'Oi oi', she said, nodding at Stella, snapping on her chewing gum loudly.

Stella pulled the two sides of her cardigan closer together. 'Hello', she said with a nervous smile.

'Chop or pop?' the woman asked her.

'I beg your pardon?' Stella asked, her eyes wide.

'Chop or pop?' the woman asked again, this time much slower, spreading out each syllable as if Stella was from special school.

'I don't know what you're saying?' Stella said, asserting herself a little. This was a hard enough thing to do already; she didn't want to be made a fool of at the same time.

'I'm asking', the woman said, straightening up a little and putting on a fake posh English accent, 'whether Madam is interested in getting a tattoo or a piercing from this fine establishment?'

'Oh, I see. A tattoo. I'd like to get a tattoo.'

The woman eyed her up and down, nodded and then hefted herself off her chair and craned her neck into the back room. 'Oi, Simon', she yelled. 'There's someone here for you!'

'I'll be out in ten', a man shouted from the back room.

'Don't take too long, gorgeous', the woman called, pushing through the beaded curtain into the back room without so much as a backward glance at Stella. 'This one might not keep.'

Stella turned around and took in her surroundings properly; she found it easier to focus now, without the woman glaring at her. The room was square, the walls covered with hundreds of images and designs. A few chairs lined one of the walls and a waist-high wooden shelf lined another wall, filled with dozens of photo albums. Stella took a closer look at some of the images pasted on the walls. Dragons and Celtic symbols, peace signs and yin-yangs, wolves and roses and wolves covered in roses. She eyed the door leading to the street, wondering if she should take the opportunity and make a run for it. Instead she breathed deeply and forced herself to sit in one of the chairs. She'd already failed at the first two items on her list, there was no turning back now. And anyway, she wasn't going to give the annoying woman the satisfaction.

Stella rubbed her arms, suddenly feeling very cold and nervous. She didn't really regret pulling out of the bungee jump at the last minute that much, and she didn't regret not sleeping with the prostitute in the end at all. Both decisions had been pretty easy to make, but Stella knew she was going to have to tick something off her list to validate it very soon. If she didn't push herself to do this next item and at least tick off one thing, she was worried she'd just be the same old, plainer, less-fun, more anally retentive twin forever, and the only thing that would have changed would be that she would have lost her husband and her best friend. So, more than anything, she needed to go through with this.

A man appeared from the back room. He was so tall his head almost reached the ceiling, and he was almost as wide as he was tall. He wouldn't have been out of place in the Springbok scrum – everything about him was enormous; each of his arms was as wide as Stella's waist. He was dressed in full leather from head to toe, and he was covered in tattoos, even his bald head had a large spider on the back of it, with its hairy legs reaching all the way behind his ears. Stella shuddered.

As she tried not to stare a much smaller guy appeared from behind the giant. 'You the one here for a chop?' he asked Stella.

Stella nodded. 'Uh, yes, I think so.'

'Cool, I'll be with you in under a minute,' he said, walking the big guy to the door. 'So, you'll need to keep an eye on it, all right, Tiny?' he said to the giant. 'You know the drill, usual story, try not to get it wet for a couple of days, and put that antibacterial cream I gave you on it whenever you think of it, preferably a couple of times a day, okay? Not like last time, when you forgot!'

Tiny grunted, pumped Simon's hand in a handshake and disappeared through the door, ducking so as not to hit his head on the lintel.

'Jesus!' Simon moaned as the door closed behind the giant, cradling his crushed hand. 'He always does that,' he said, turning to face Stella, shaking his hand out. 'His handshake could crush rocks and I always forget until it's too late.'

'Are you going to be okay?' she asked nervously.

'Yeah, yeah,' he said with a little reassuring smile. 'Good thing I'm a leftie, hey?' He held up his untouched left hand and flexed the fingers for her. 'But you don't mind if we don't shake, do you? I'm Simon, nice to meet you.'

'Hi, I'm Stella,' she said, clearing her throat nervously.

'So, Bertha says you're in for a chop, right?'

Stella looked at him, confused.

'Bertha, the lady you spoke to when you came in.'

'Oh, yes, is that Bertha?' Stella asked.

'Yeah, don't mind her, she's as harmless as a kitten once you get to know her. Well, as long as you don't nick her cigarettes.'

Stella laughed nervously, even though what he'd said wasn't funny. Then she felt foolish and blushed awkwardly.

'So,' Simon asked, pretending not to notice, 'what are you thinking about getting?'

'Um, I told you,' Stella said, looking at him like he was crazy. 'A tattoo.'

Simon laughed at her. 'Ah, yes, I thought we'd established that. I meant what would you like to get a tattoo of?' Now it was his turn to look at her as if she was crazy.

Stella blushed from the tip of her toes to the very last hair on her head. 'Oh, sorry, sorry!' she stuttered. 'Um, I've never done this before, you'll have to excuse me, I'm a little bit nervous.'

'No need to be nervous,' Simon said, leading her back to one of the chairs against the wall, 'I've been doing this for almost twelve years, I could give you the perfect tattoo with my eyes closed. I promise I'll keep them open, of course, but just so you know, I could do it with my eyes closed if I wanted to. Now, tell me what you're thinking of getting.'

Stella blinked a couple of times. She'd never actually thought this far into the process. Her thinking had always stopped at getting a tattoo. 'Oh crap!' she said, blushing again. 'I have no idea. I haven't really thought about it.'

'Oh,' Simon said, cocking his head. 'Well, that's a new one for me. I don't think I've ever had someone come in without even an inkling of what they want to get. But, no worries, let me show you some of my work, and we'll figure something out.' He strode over to the shelf on the opposite wall and paged through a couple of the albums, choosing two to take back to Stella. 'So, Stella, what about geography? Do you have any idea where on your body you want to get this tattoo?'

Stella raised her eyebrows. 'Um, no, not really,' she said in a small voice. 'Like I said, I've never really thought about all of this in too much detail before.'

'Okay,' Simon said, dragging out the word. 'Well, it just means we've got more choices to make than usual. No problem, this will be fun.'

Simon sat down next to her and opened up the first album half on his lap and half on hers, so they could look through it together. His leg touched her leg and his arm brushed hers as he turned the pages. 'Any special names in your life? A boyfriend whose name you'd like to ink?' he asked, pointing to a photograph of a woman's arm in the book with *Ronan* beautifully scripted on the inside of her wrist.

Stella shook her head. 'Nah, I don't think that's such a great idea. I've got a husband ... Well, I had a husband. Long story. I don't think I should get his name put on me. At least, not permanently.'

'Okay, okay, I feel you,' Simon said.

They carried on paging, Simon pointing out dozens of other designs, none of which seemed to grab Stella. When he got to the end of the first album he turned to the second one without any urgency or impatience, and continued paging. 'What about this one?' he asked, pointing to a small daisy on a woman's hip, just to the right of her bikini line.

'That's quite nice,' Stella said, 'only my sister's name is Daisy.'

'Are you and her close?' Simon asked hopefully.

'Well, sort of. Only, you see, she just came out the closet, so I'm not so sure that's the best idea.'

Simon nodded and closed the album shut on his lap with a *thwack*, then he dropped both albums on the floor and turned to face Stella. 'I tell you what ...' he said.

'What?'

'Will you try something for me?' he asked.

Stella nodded nervously.

'Right, first close your eyes. I promise, you're perfectly safe, I won't hurt you.'

Stella blinked twice and then nervously closed her eyes.

Simon smiled at her as she squinted one of them open again. 'If this is going to work you need to relax a little bit,' he said gently. 'You're really tense, like, your whole body is stiff, and this won't work unless you're relaxed. Now, close your eyes properly. Trust me, it's okay.'

Stella nodded and squeezed her eyes shut.

'Relax,' he said.

With her eyes still closed Stella leaned back in her chair and shook out her shoulders, trying to relax.

'Now,' Simon said. 'Take a very deep breath.'

Stella did as he said.

'I need you to take your time, just breathe. And then, when you're ready, tell me what you see. There will be a lot of images that will flash past your eyes, that's perfectly normal. Just let them do their thing. Think about images and things that are significant to you. Just let your mind run free for as long as it takes, I'm not in any hurry. But ultimately your mind should settle on something. Try that, okay?'

'Okay,' Stella said. She took a deep breath and let the images come. And they did, flashing through her mind's eye like slides. Some of them were repeats of all the images she'd just seen in the albums, but others were more personal images. The things she often doodled, or pictures that she liked. She saw a favourite pendant she often wore, a childhood photograph of her and Lucy standing next to each other at the age of six, identical in white dresses with purple flowers; Stella on the left with her socks pulled all the way up, Lucy on the right with her hair dishevelled and a smile on her face. She saw an old teddy bear and other paraphernalia from her childhood. Then something came to her mind, and the second she saw it she knew that was what she wanted, it was perfect. Slowly she opened her eyes with a small smile on her face. When her focus returned she saw Simon walking towards her, holding a pen and a sketch pad in his hand. 'Would you like to draw it yourself, or would you like to describe it to me and I can try drawing it?' he asked.

Stella shook her head. 'How did you know to do that?' she asked.

'I told you,' he said. 'I've been doing this for a very long time.'

Stella took the pen and sketch pad out of his hand and balanced it on her lap. 'It's very simple,' she said as she began to draw. 'It's a little, perfectly formed red heart, but it has a thick black outline.'

Simon looked at her drawing; it was so simple it had only taken her a couple of seconds to complete.

'I like that,' he said. 'I think it suits you. A full, open, pumping heart, with a bit of a dark edge to it.'

Stella smiled. He thought she had a dark edge. Really? Her, Mrs Stella Pull Up Your Socks, Count The Hours, Never A Hair Out Of Place De Villiers? There was something she really liked about this guy.

'So, where do you think you want it?' Simon asked, taking the image from her and studying it closely.

'How about on my hip?' she said, pointing to her bikini line. 'Where that lady had that daisy? I think that's a cool spot, and nobody else will know it's there.'

'Excellent,' Simon said. 'Come with me.'

Stella followed Simon into the back room. She wasn't sure what she had been expecting, but this wasn't it. It looked exactly like a dentist's room. There was a white leather dentist's chair in the middle of the room, with a big bank of bright lights hanging directly above it. A small stool sat next to it, and next to that was a table on casters, which was covered with equipment.

'There you go, make yourself comfortable,' Simon said, pointing to the chair. 'But you're going to want to take your pants and panties off first.'

Stella shot her head up in shock and took a step backwards. 'What do you mean I have to take my pants off?' she asked, her voice quivering.

'Well, you want a tattoo on your hip, don't you?' he asked with a wry smile.

Stella nodded.

'Well, how do you expect me to do it with your pants on?'

Stella blushed again. 'I just hadn't thought … I mean, I didn't think … I hadn't thought this far, you know?' she stuttered.

'Everything's going to be fine,' he said, patting the chair. 'C'mon, I swear, I've seen it all before, and I promise to be the perfect gentleman.'

Stella walked over to the corner of the room with as much dignity as she could muster. Slipping off both her shoes she slowly undid the button on her jeans and then the zip and then she slipped them down her legs as quickly as possible. 'I'm not taking my panties off,' she said, pulling her top down to cover her panties. 'You'll have to work around them.'

'Fair enough,' Simon said, nodding his head, a huge grin plastered across his face. 'But you can't blame me for trying, right?' Then he patted the chair again.

Stella laughed nervously, shuffled across the room and climbed onto the chair. As she sat down the gravity of what she was about to do hit home and her heart started to race. 'Is this going to hurt much?' she asked.

'That depends,' Simon said, 'on what your definition of hurt is?'

Stella suddenly wasn't so sure about this at all.

'Listen,' he said, making her jump nervously as he put his hand down on her naked calf to reassure her. 'Everything is going to be fine. It might hurt a bit, but it will be over before you know it, and then you'll love it forever.'

His hand was soft and strong and Stella's calf burned where he touched it. This, she thought, looking at Simon, was the kind of guy mothers had been warning their daughters about for centuries. Hot, funky, funny, charming and the most appealing characteristic of all: dangerous.

'Right,' Simon said, reaching over to his table and picking up a pen and some paper. 'This is how this works. This paper I'm about to use is a special kind of transfer paper. I'll draw your design, so that we can agree on the dimensions and get everything just right, and then I'll transfer that directly onto your skin, and use it as a template. Make sense?'

Stella nodded, scared to talk in case her voice shook.

'So, what I'm saying is that you need to make sure you're happy with what I'm doing here. Because once the ink goes on, that's it, it's permanent, like, forever, like, for the rest of your life, for always. You know what I'm saying?' he asked her, looking serious for the first time since they'd met.

Stella felt scared, but also oddly safe in his hands. She loved how seriously he took his work; it was clear that he knew exactly what he was doing. It was a massive turn-on.

Stella nodded at him, finding her tongue at last. 'This is crazy. I can't believe I'm really going through with this,' she said. 'If Lucy or Max could see me now, they'd never believe I was doing this.'

The mere fact that she was going through with it on her own, without their support or approval made it all the more appealing to her. She thought back and realised that this was the first time in her life that she'd done anything of any great importance without either Lucy or Max by her side. Could it be possible, she wondered, that she'd never done a single thing by herself, ever? The realisation further steeled her resolve to go through with the tattoo.

'So, how's this?' Simon asked, holding the image up for her approval.

'That's okay,' Stella said, 'but I think it's too perfect. Like, the one side of the heart should be ever so slightly bigger than the other side, and also I think that it's too big, it should be a little smaller.'

Simon redrew it and held it up for her approval again.

'Cool,' Stella said. 'The shape is much better, but I still think it should be smaller.'

Simon drew it again and then held it up for her once more.

'Still smaller,' Stella said.

Simon raised his eyebrows and drew it again.

'That's it,' Stella beamed, 'that's perfect!' It was the tiniest little imperfect red heart, with a thick black outline.

Simon smiled, got up and walked across to what looked like a photo-copier, standing in the corner of the room. Seconds later he was back at her side with a copy of the drawing. 'I'm afraid you're going to have to let me in there,' he said, pointing to where she was still nervously clutching her shirt to her thighs.

Stella took a deep breath and slowly raised her shirt with shaking fingers, revealing a pair of old, almost-still-pink, cotton tanga panties. 'I didn't know I was going to do this today,' Stella said, blushing puce. 'Otherwise I would have worn more appropriate underwear ...'

'Well, I would say those are pretty perfect,' he said with a cute wink.

Simon placed the heart in a couple of different places, trying to find the perfect spot on her bikini line.

'A little to the left, down a bit ...' Stella said, guiding him.

Simon had to pull the top of her panties down a centimetre or so to reach the spot she wanted. Stella closed her eyes when he touched her panties, her face boiling over. Then he swabbed the spot with some kind of liquid and pressed the paper directly onto her skin, transferring the outline onto her bikini line. She could feel his breath on her hip as he leant in to place the transfer and goosebumps rose on her flesh as his fingers met her skin. He smiled at the goosebumps, which were impossible for her to hide, and all she could do was blush, yet again.

Once the image was positioned perfectly and Stella had nodded her approval, Simon picked up his tattoo gun and began to prepare it. Stella's eyes went wide; it wasn't anything like what she'd expected. She had imagined a small pen of some kind, like a ballpoint, but this was an entire mechanical contraption. The front end of it looked like a pen, with a sharp needle, but the back end contained capsules and wires, cords and buttons. Stella felt weak as she looked at it, and when Simon turned it on and she heard its electric buzzing her heart sank. Could she really do this? Could she, Stella de Villiers, really get a tattoo? She thought she was going to be sick.

Simon must have noticed her suddenly off-colour cheeks and her shallow breathing because he turned off the gun and put it down. Then he put his hand on her arm and leaned in close. His touch was soothing, but exciting at the same time, and his breath was warm, not fresh, but not stale either, just masculine and almost inky. 'You okay?' he asked. 'Listen, this is going to be over in just a few minutes and it's going to be fine. Just take a few deep breaths. And maybe you shouldn't watch. Why don't you look over there and try think of something nice.' He pointed towards the opposite wall.

Stella nodded and turned her head. His comforting hand and his calm voice together with a bit of deep breathing did the trick and she nodded for him to begin.

She heard him pull on a pair of surgical gloves and then the machine came back to life again. She squeezed her eyes shut tightly as she felt a slight pressure on her hip. 'Ow! Ow, ow, ow!' she shouted.

The pressure receded. Then she felt it again, the same slight pressure on her hip, and the drilling sound of the tattoo gun. 'Eina! Ow, ow, ow!' she shrieked again.

'Stella!' Simon said gently, a smile in his voice.

She opened her eyes slowly and turned her head to face him.

'I haven't even started yet!' he said. 'That pressure you felt was my hand. I haven't touched you with the needle yet, look!'

She looked down and saw that he was telling the truth, he hadn't started yet. She blushed and smiled, feeling ridiculous.

'Hold on a second,' he said, 'I'll be right back.'

Stella lay and stared at the ceiling, feeling foolish. A second later Simon returned with a full bottle of Jack Daniel's. He twisted off the lid, cracking the seal and he held it out to her. 'Here, take a slug,' he said.

'Do you have a glass?' she asked.

He widened his eyes at her. 'No, man, stop being such a wuss, just take a slug!'

Stella looked at him and took the bottle, holding it up to her lips, then she raised the bottle slightly and took a tiny little sip. She coughed and pulled a face as the whisky burnt its way down her throat and tried to pass the bottle back to Simon.

'And another one,' he said, refusing to take the bottle back.

Raising the bottle to her lips once more Stella took another sip, a bigger one this time. This one also burned as it went down her gullet, but it wasn't an entirely unpleasant sensation, it warmed her stomach instantly and she felt it trace its fiery way through her body.

'There's my girl,' Simon said, sitting back down on his stool and picking up the tattoo gun again. He flicked the switch and the machine buzzed into life. 'Now, you just hold onto that bottle,' he said. 'Take a sip if you need one, but remember I need you to stay as still as possible. This will all be over before you know it. Okay?'

Stella nodded and turned her head to face the wall once again, squeezing her eyes tightly closed, the bottle cradled in her arms.

'Okay, first I'm going to do the outline,' Simon said. 'And then I'll colour in the inside. The colouring in will probably be the sorest part, because it's just over the bone, but it's not going to take long, so I need you to be brave, and just breathe and work through the pain.'

Stella nodded, her stomach buzzing with whisky and adrenalin. She was ready for this, she told herself. She couldn't be more ready. This was it. This was the moment when she actually did something for herself. When she, Stella de Villiers, got herself a life.

She gasped as the needle bit into her skin. Gritting her teeth, she squeezed her eyes tightly shut against the pain.

'Easy there, girl,' Simon said.

Stella opened her eyes and turned to look at him. He was completely focused on his work, his face was intent, and Stella reflected that he wasn't good looking as much as he was rugged. He had several tattoos sneaking out from behind his grubby white vest, and she saw another tattoo snaking out the bottom of his jeans and onto his foot. She'd noticed earlier that he also had a number of scars scattered around his body. One on his cheek, another on the back of his shoulder and a third across the bridge of his other foot, the one without the tattoo. She gritted her teeth to try and clear the pain, which was now close to unbearable. It was a searing hot heat; it felt like there were a million needles being stabbed into her hip bone.

'So, tell me, what's a nice girl like you doing in a place like this?' Simon asked her as he worked, his face dangerously close to her crotch.

Stella thought he was sweet to try and distract her from the pain.

'Well,' she said, through her still gritted teeth, 'it's kind of a long story, but the short version is that my whole life I've always been the good one ... You know, good at school – good grades, good behaviour, good attitude. Always done the right thing, never upset anybody, and I'm kind of sick of it. So I made a list of all the things I want to do, and this is one of them. Actually, it's the first thing I'm really doing for real off my list.'

Simon stopped what he was doing and looked up at her. 'Wow, cool,' he said, reaching across her body and taking the bottle of whisky from her. He took a big swig and then handed it back to her as she looked down at his progress on her hip. He was just over halfway done. The area he was working on was quite swollen and there were small pricks of blood across it, but she could see it was going to look cool. She smiled and nodded at him, encouraging him to continue. The whisky was starting to work and she felt a little tipsy, the pain and worry receding a little in her mind.

'So, what are some of the other things on this interesting-sounding list, then?' Simon asked, wiping the whisky off his mouth with the back of his gloved hand and getting back to work.

'Well,' Stella said, 'There's skydiving and skinny dipping ... You know, that kind of stuff. You'd probably think some of the things are silly.'

'I don't think it's silly at all. In fact, I think it's very interesting,' Simon said, a naughty grin lighting up his face. 'Perhaps I can help you tick one of those off?'

'You already are,' Stella said, nodding down at the almost completed heart and smiling coyly, her cheeks flushed, half with booze and half with courage.

POPPY

'Hey, let's go in there,' Buck said, pointing into a shop window.

Poppy loped over and joined him where he was standing. She followed his finger. Behind the shop window a very tall, buxom woman wearing a large red mane of a wig was sitting on a bar stool, posing dramatically for the benefit of the people walking past on the street. The room was bathed in the glow of the red light that shone from the ceiling.

The woman was wearing the skimpiest lingerie Poppy had ever seen. A red-and-black lace bra, which did little to hide her nipples, a tiny skirt, a garter belt, fishnet stockings and a pair of very high heels. She was muscular, almost manly looking.

Professional that she was, she'd already noticed that she had Buck's full attention and she was doing everything in her power to close the sale. The woman ignored Poppy, staring straight at Buck as she licked her lips and spread her legs wide.

Poppy covered her mouth with her hand and gasped. 'Jeez, Buck, she's forgotten to put her knickers on! You can see what she had for breakfast!'

Buck simply gaped.

Poppy slapped him on the arm, but he didn't flinch, he was mesmerised.

Next, the woman in the shop window stood up and raised one leg, placing her foot on the side of the bar stool, turning slightly so that Buck got a slight view of her rear end. Never taking her eyes off him for a second, she pretended to pull up her stocking, running her hands up her leg. Then she swapped legs, and did the same with the other leg. Once she was finished she stood up straight, took a step closer to the window and pointed a finger at Buck. She licked her lips again and curled her finger, summoning Buck with it.

Buck took a step forward, to get closer to the window.

'Buck!' Poppy yelled, grabbing the back of his shirt and wrenching him back towards her. 'I've got a much better idea. Let's go in there.'

Reluctantly Buck turned away from the window to look where Poppy was pointing. It was a coffee shop diagonally across the street called De Tuin.

Poppy dragged Buck along behind her, taking charge of crossing the road; Buck was so distracted that he probably would have stepped right into the path of an oncoming tram.

'So what do you think happens back in there?' Buck asked Poppy as they settled around a table in the coffee shop, craning his neck to see if he could still see the woman's shop window from where they were seated.

'Well, we're in the red light district in Amsterdam and that woman standing in that shopfront isn't wearing any knickers ... So, I'm just taking a wild stab in the dark here, but I'm guessing that what happens in there is that you go inside, hand over a pile of cash and then she takes you back into a grubby room behind that shop window, that doesn't look anything like the front of house looks, and then she'll make all your dreams come true for about nine and a half minutes. After that, and I'm just guessing here, but I would imagine that after that she gives you about thirty seconds to get your pants back on, and then she hurls you back out on the street again without as much as a kiss goodbye. I'm also guessing she gives you a mean case of something you really don't want. Like I said, it's just a guess, but I'm pretty sure that's what happens in there.'

Buck nodded slowly and rubbed his hand over his shaven head. 'Poppy, I don't think we're in India any more,' he said.

'No kidding,' Poppy said. 'Check out this menu. They've got seven different kinds of hash, and weed from just about every country!'

'Ha!' Buck yelled. 'Look, they've even got Durban Poison! Rad!'

Poppy laughed. 'Funny that we have to travel all this way to smoke dope that was grown at home.' The whole one side of the menu offered every imaginable form of weed, served however you wanted it, even baked in cakes, cookies and brownies. And the other half of the menu was an ordinary menu just like one you would find in any restaurant; burgers, pizzas and toasted sandwiches, alongside coffees, teas and cooldrinks.

Eventually the waitress ambled over to their table. She was friendly, but in no real hurry to provide any kind of service. She had thick multicoloured braids and she was pierced in every available space across her body. A horn stuck out of her chin and her earlobes sagged under the weight of her silverware.

Poppy imagined that if the waitress were to drink a glass of water the liquid would spout out of her as if she were a hose with holes in it. She would be like a fountain.

'So, we were wondering how you serve your dope?' Buck asked the waitress.

'It depends which one you want to order,' the waitress said. She had a very strong Irish accent and Poppy was surprised, somehow she had imagined that she would be Dutch.

'We just want ordinary marijuana,' Buck said, his eyes wide.

'Well, love,' the waitress said, 'you can have it any way you like, just like you have your eggs. You can have it in a pipe, in a joint, in a cake or in a brick. You can eat it, smoke it or inhale it.'

Poppy and Buck shook their heads at all the options, spoiled for choice.

'Let me guess,' the waitress said with a smile. 'This is your first time in Amsterdam?'

Poppy and Buck both nodded simultaneously, their heads buried in their menus.

'Well, then,' she said with an evil glint in her eye. 'Allow me to make some recommendations. I'm almost positive you won't be disappointed.' Once she had discussed their options and taken their orders she disappeared off into the depths of the coffee shop with a knowing smile across her face.

'Hey, Poppy,' Buck said. 'I just realised that De Tuin means "the garden" in Afrikaans.'

Poppy laughed. 'I suppose that makes sense then. What else would you expect them to sell in a shop called De Tuin, other than grass?'

Poppy and Buck lay on their backs on a blanket on a patch of grass in Vondelpark. Poppy was staring up at the wispy clouds floating across the ceiling of sky above her. It was a sunny winter's day. The sky was mostly blue and clear, but the air was icy, and when they spoke it looked like they were smoking. They should have felt cold in their summer hemisphere jackets, but they were too stoned to feel anything.

Poppy was trying to decide if the cloud directly above her looked more like a leopard or a watering can.

'Hey, Poppy, that was really funny,' Buck said, starting to laugh.

'What was?' Poppy asked.

'That joke you made.'

'Which joke?' Poppy asked.

'You know, that one about De Tuin selling grass.'

'Buck.'

'Yes, Pops.'

'That was two days ago.'

'Really?'

'Yup.'

Poppy rolled over onto her side so that she was facing Buck, staring him straight in the ear. Even though he was way taller than her, the way they were lying meant they had their heads directly in line with each other. He also rolled over onto his side and faced her. They were so close she could smell the marijuana on his breath.

She knew his face so well; every line was etched into her mind. Maybe she was still stoned but she felt like she'd never known anybody as well as she knew Buck, maybe not even herself. They both lay there, staring into each other's faces. The weight of their shared experiences balanced in the air between them. Nobody else would ever be able to understand what they'd been through; nobody else would ever be able to comprehend the depths of their friendship.

'Everybody here rides bicycles,' Poppy said randomly in response to a bicycle bell she heard somewhere in the distance. 'I don't think I've ever seen so many bicycles in one place, like, ever.'

'I know,' Buck said. 'Totally.'

'Why do you think that is?' Poppy asked.

'I dunno,' he said. 'Maybe because it's so flat?'

'And you know what else is weird?'

'What?'

'None of them wear helmets or anything.'

They lay in silence, staring into each other's eyes for a couple more minutes.

'I don't know how to ride a bicycle,' Poppy eventually said.

Buck blinked and touched her nose gently with the very tip of his finger. It was an incredibly intimate gesture. 'That's weird,' he said softly. 'How come?'

Poppy shrugged.

'What kind of person doesn't know how to ride a bicycle?' Buck asked again. 'That's like not knowing how to swim, or not knowing how to read.'

'I guess it's because I'm the youngest of five kids. I suppose my parents weren't expecting to have any more children when I came along, and they were kind of over it by then. You know. They'd done it four times already. I think parenting bored them by then.'

'What about your sisters, how come they never taught you?' Buck asked, lifting his finger off her nose at last and moving it onto a freckle on her forehead before trailing it in a feathery-light movement straight back down her nose and over her lips and onto a freckle in the middle of her chin, joining the dots.

'I don't know,' Poppy said, furrowing her brow.

Buck returned his finger to her brow and smoothed out each of the furrows, one by one. 'I could teach you here,' he said. 'Right here, on this lawn.'

'Maybe,' she said. 'Or maybe it's too late for me.'

'Hey, did you know that these freckles over here look exactly like the Southern Cross?' Buck said, trailing his finger over the bridge of her nose and then tapping each individual freckle to connect the constellation.

Poppy breathed in, then, propping her head up on an arm, she leaned forward ever so slightly and kissed him on his mouth. Their tongues entwined. She felt his eyelashes flickering on her face. He had the eyelashes of a giraffe, she thought, they were so impossibly long. She'd always coveted them. She also marvelled at how soft Buck's lips were; it took her by surprise. But in contrast to the softness of his mouth, his stubble chafed across her chin like the coarsest grade of sand paper. They stopped kissing and then opened their eyes and lay blinking at each other in the weak sunlight for a few moments.

Then Buck leaned forward and he was in charge of kissing her this time. The air was chill and the lawn smelled fresh and icy green. Somewhere two birds tweeted in agreement and some children screamed and laughed in the distance. Bicycle bells rang, dogs barked and they kissed.

Finally they both pulled back simultaneously, as if the kiss had been called off by some mutual agreement or silent buzzer. They remained, lying on their sides staring into each other's eyes, their expressions unchanged for a moment, both unblinking.

Then, in unison, they both scrunched up their noses.

'Not really, hey?' Poppy said.

'Nah, I don't think so,' Buck agreed, nodding.

'You could shave some time!' Poppy said, rubbing her red, beard-chafed chin.

'Dude, brush your teeth once in a while!' Buck retorted.

Then they both rolled around on the blanket, laughing hysterically. Poppy laughed so hard her stomach hurt and Buck laughed so hard he farted, and that got them laughing all over again, this time even harder.

STELLA

Stella dug her feet into the cool sand and wriggled her toes around in it. It felt good. All the Jack Daniel's she'd had felt good too. It was the first time in weeks that she wasn't feeling guilty or nervous or miserable and panicky or all of them at the same time. She raised the bottle to her lips and took another big sip.

'Hey, leave some for me,' Simon said, running up behind her. 'How's the tattoo, any pain?'

'What pain?' Stella asked, with a smile.

'See, I told you,' he said, wriggling his fingers in front of her. 'I've got magic fingers. So, you coming or not?' He pulled his vest off over his head and then started to unbutton his jeans.

Stella looked up and down the beach. It was a perfect night and Camps Bay beach was empty on both sides, with a big full moon hanging in the middle of the sky, lighting the beach and casting a sheen over the ocean. When she turned and looked behind her she could just see the lights and action along Camps Bay Main Road, but the tide had dug into the sand and left them a dip on the beach which hid them from the restaurants and bars.

'You do know it's going to be absolutely freezing!' she said.

'That's the wonderful thing about Jack Daniel's; it does a great job of warming you up again afterwards,' Simon said, grabbing the bottle from her.

Somewhere between the tattoo shop and the beach they had managed to lose the bottle top. Well, if Stella was being honest, they hadn't lost it; Simon had thrown it out of the car window with a whoop as he'd driven her up Kloof Nek Road. Stella couldn't believe how daring she was being, heading to the beach with this stranger and a bottle of whisky.

Simon tossed his jeans onto the blankets they'd brought with them from the tattoo shop and then bent down to drop his boxers. Stella blushed, she barely knew this guy. She didn't want to make a big fuss about looking away in case she came across as a prude, but it also felt quite rude not to at least avert her eyes, she couldn't openly stare at his naked body, could she?

'Don't be shy,' Simon said, turning to face her. 'Please don't tell me you've never seen one of these before.' He grinned his naughty grin and then turned and darted off down the beach. 'Come on!' he yelled back at her. 'Last one in is a vrot banana!'

Stella watched Simon go, his entire body shone white in the moonlight, but his bum somehow managed to be even whiter. She thought he was damn cute and he had a naughty streak as long as the beach. Max was the only man she had seen naked before, Stella realised as she watched Simon plunge into the ocean. What twenty-five-year-old woman had only ever seen one man naked, she thought, it was pathetic. She shook her head at her own limited experience. It was time she broadened her horizons.

Thinking about Max brought on a sudden surge of nostalgia. She wondered what he was doing, and what he would think if he knew that she was drinking and frolicking on the beach with a naked man. He probably wouldn't have been that surprised, she decided. He would probably just see it as the next in a long string of betrayals. Stella shook her head in amazement at her behaviour. It felt like her life was totally out of her control these days, running on its own momentum, like a runaway train. But it was too late to stop what was happening and what had already happened. She had to put Max out of her mind; this was no time for going backwards, this was a time for going forwards.

Stella was feeling a nice, steady buzz, her cheeks were flushed and she wasn't feeling any cold or pain, but she put the Jack Daniel's to her lips and took another big swig just to make sure. Bending down and wedging the open bottle into the sand she pulled her shirt and her cardigan off over her head, ignoring the buttons. Then she slipped off her bra and covered her breasts with one arm, looking up and down the beach nervously once again. What would happen if someone stole their clothes? Stella wondered. They'd be left cruising the Camps Bay strip stark naked, that's what. The thought made Stella shudder.

'Come on, it's amazing,' Simon screamed out to her.

Stella looked up; he was waist-deep in the water and had turned to face her. What the heck, she thought, she had wanted experiences and life didn't offer up much more of an experience than this. Quickly, she undid her jeans and pulled them off, leaving her panties on. Having dropped her trousers on the pile of blankets next to the bottle and Simon's discarded clothes, Stella bent down, dug a small hole and buried her car keys just underneath the corner of the blanket. At least if someone nicked their clothes they could leopard crawl naked to the car and drive out of there.

Satisfied that she had a plan B in place, Stella raced towards the water. The fresh sea air on her naked skin was invigorating and excited goosebumps puckered up across her body. She knew caution in this situation was not the answer – whichever way she did this it was going to hurt – so she raced right into the ocean.

The water was so cold it knocked the breath right out of her, it was like ice, but she carried on moving until she reached Simon. He grabbed her hand when she got to him and dragged her forward into the waves. Then, letting go of her hand, he dived under an oncoming wave. Closing her eyes tightly, Stella followed him. Seconds later they both burst out of the water, whooping with the cold.

'Oh, my God,' Stella shrieked, her lips shivering – she was sure they were bright blue. She felt excruciatingly alive; every nerve ending and muscle on fire with the shock of the cold water.

'That's just about enough for me,' Simon said, his teeth chattering. 'You ready to get out?'

Stella nodded insistently and Simon grabbed her hand and they waded out of the water together. Back on the beach, Simon wrapped first her and then himself in a blanket and then he rubbed his hands up and down her arms as fast as he could on top of the blanket to try restore some warmth to her body. Slowly the blood started to pump back through her veins and Stella smiled at him like a crazy woman, her hair stuck to her face in a wet, tangled mess. 'Man, that was amazing!' she shrieked.

Simon secured his blanket around his waist, like a towel, reached down and grabbed the bottle of Jack Daniel's, wiping the sand off of the neck of it before he handed it over to her. 'Here, have a sip, it'll warm you up.'

'Thanks,' she said, her teeth chattering as she took a big gulp. Stella could almost track the flow of the liquid through her pipes, as it heated her body from the inside out.

'Come on,' Simon said, seemingly oblivious to the cold he must have been feeling. 'Let's get you warm and into some dry clothes.'

Simon lived in a small bachelor flat just off Green Point Main Road. Stella glanced around briefly as they bundled themselves inside, wrapped in the now damp and sandy blankets. The apartment was sparsely furnished. The mattress from a double bed lay on the floor and some DJ decks stood up against one of the walls, surrounded by piles of records, and that was pretty much it.

'Why don't you have a hot shower,' Simon said, pointing her in the direction of the bathroom. 'Don't worry, I'll go after you. There should also be a cleanish towel in there that you can use.'

The bathroom was small but functional. Stella dropped the soggy, sandy blanket and her panties at her feet and climbed into the shower. The hot water was amazing and she let it cascade down her body, watching as the sand disappeared past her toes, down the drain. She wondered why the Atlantic had to be so cold, fantasising about how nice it would have been to be able to frolic in the water with Simon, instead of having to race in and out so quickly.

When she started to feel human again Stella rinsed her hair and then bundled it in a bun on top of her head, securing it with a band she'd had wrapped around her wrist. Then she climbed out of the shower, dried off and put her clothes back on. All except the damp, sandy panties, which she shoved into her pocket. This was the first time in her life that she'd not worn panties, and the sensation was thrilling. She tried to clean up after herself, folding the damp sandy blanket neatly and dropping it in the corner, then she slipped back out into the apartment where Simon was busy putting on some music. When she appeared he looked up at her and smiled. 'Better?' he asked.

She nodded. He'd ditched the blanket and was kneeling on the floor at his decks in nothing but a pair of fresh white Calvin Kleins. Stella felt a little lost for words. She hadn't had a chance to study all his tattoos properly in the moonlight on the beach but now, with his back half-turned to her and his concentration wholly on the decks, she took the opportunity to stare as much as she liked. He had a dragon snaked down his back with one claw reaching all the way up the back of his neck and almost into his hairline. He also had a tattoo on his calf. It was some kind of Celtic design that spilled over his ankle and down onto the bridge of his foot.

Stella stepped towards the door, reaching for the bottle of Jack Daniel's that Simon had put down on the counter when they'd walked in. Picking it up she sucked some back. She barely recognised herself, standing in a strange, half-naked boy's bachelor flat drinking from a bottle of Jack Daniel's. But, she reminded herself again as she took a second, bigger sip from the bottle, she was the one who had wanted adventure.

'Did you do those?' Stella asked, pointing at Simon's tattoos.

'I did this one,' he said, running his hand over his calf. 'But I could hardly do this one, could I?' He pointed at his back and laughed. 'Would be kind of tricky to reach, don't you think?'

Stella blushed. 'Of course, yes, I meant, yes, well, obviously,' she said, suddenly feeling foolish. She took another sip from the bottle to ease her embarrassment.

Simon walked towards her and reached for the bottle, taking it out of her hands. He stood squarely in front of her, so close that their bodies were almost touching, and threw his head back, taking a few sips in a row, as if the whisky was a soft drink.

'So,' he said, wiping the back of his hand across his mouth, 'tattoo, tick. Skinny dipping, tick. What's next on that list of yours?' Then, without waiting for a response, he reached an arm around Stella's back and pulled her into him, kissing her hard. Her body was warm from the hot shower, but his was still cold and sandy, his mouth and tongue tasting of the ocean – salty and fresh, mixed with the strong taste of the Jack Daniel's. She felt the course rub of the sand on his face, arms and body on her skin where he touched her. It was the most passionate kiss Stella had ever experienced. Hard. Desperate. Hungry.

'Hey, hang on a second,' Simon said, pulling back from her. Turning around he bent down in front of a black backpack that lay on the floor up against the wall.

Stella admired the rip of his back and the dance of the dragon across it as he moved, cursing the end of the kiss that she would have liked to have gone on forever.

Unzipping the front pocket of his bag Simon pulled out a tube of something, a roll of plaster and a small pair of scissors. 'What's that for?' Stella asked, looking at him wide-eyed.

'I have to look after my favourite client,' he said, moving back towards her.

When Simon reached where she was standing he wiped his fringe out of his eyes, gave her a naughty smile and sank to his knees. Stella's heart raced as he placed his hands on her waistband. 'I think I should take a look at that tattoo, it probably needs a new dressing after our swim,' he said, slowly unbuttoning her jeans, then pulling the zip down and carefully easing her jeans down her legs. He let out a small, pleasantly surprised breath when he found her not wearing any panties.

Stella bent forward over his crouched body and traced the tattoo across his back with a finger, running the line of it. As she did so her hair fell out of its band, draping down his back, small drops of water dripping from it, down the length of his body and onto the floor. When she stood up straight again he put a hand on each hip and examined her tattoo closely, suddenly all business, then he carefully covered the tattoo with cream, and replaced the original plaster which must have come off during their swim. Stella rocked gently to the music as he worked, enjoying the sensation of his hands and his breath close on her hip.

Finished with his running repairs, Simon stood, his one hand snaking around her waist, the other under her hair. Leaning into her, he gently bit her neck and then her earlobe. Stella groaned with intense joy and threw her head back with her eyes closed – she couldn't remember feeling more turned on in her life. He seemed so sure of himself, so completely in control. The whole time she'd been with him she hadn't had to think too much about anything; he'd gently talked her through each new experience.

Breaking away from her, Simon reached down and lifted her shirt off over her head. She felt the water from her hair drip slowly, cooly down her back as he moved closer again, his hands moving up to unclip her bra. Stella's knees buckled a little as his mouth found hers and he ran his strong, sandy fingers over her breasts. She could feel him pressing hard against her thigh and when he put his finger up to her mouth she sucked on it – skin had never tasted so good, so salty and inky.

Finally Simon took Stella by the hand and led her to his unmade bed. They lay down and carried on kissing, Stella running her hands endlessly over the planes of his body until he stopped her. Turning her over onto her stomach Simon straddled her and began to massage her back, leaning forward and kissing her neck as he did so, alternating tenderness with gentle bites that sent goosebumps raging down her thighs. Stella stretched her body out as far as she could, every muscle melting as his fingertips worked their way down from the top of her neck to the very base of her spine, arching her back at the sensation. Then she rolled back over onto her back and reached her hands up, pulling Simon down onto her and wrapping him between her thighs, loving the feeling of the weight of his body on hers. Throwing his head back Simon reached over to the backpack on the floor next to the bed and pulled out a condom. He put it on and then leaned back over her; the sensation of skin on skin, and the music that matched her pulse, and the feeling of being entirely filled completely overtaking her. Stella moved in time with him and the music, riding wave after wave of joy until her body was arched and taut, and then the strangest thing happened – she had an orgasm. She didn't completely recognise the sensation, but it was almost unbearable as she reached her climax, so pleasurable it bordered on pain as she shuddered it out, her body slick with sweat, tears rolling down her cheeks. Her knees shook as she squeezed her thighs around Simon, digging her fingers into his back and holding him inside her as tightly as she could, realising she'd been crying out loud, but not caring and never wanting the sensation to end. His body also went taut and then, just as quickly as the intensity had overtaken her, it was gone, and she loosened her grip on him.

He bit into her shoulder gently as the moment passed, and Stella shuddered again as an aftershock of pleasure rippled through her body. Then he rolled over onto his side, and after looking at her for a moment, he pulled her in towards him and held her tightly as ripple after ripple of post-orgasmic thrill shuddered through her body, each one slowly lessening slightly in intensity.

'Wow!' Stella said, when she finally regained the ability to speak, every hair on her body still tingling.

'Tick, tick and tick,' Simon said with a self-satisfied smile.

Stella drove home slowly through the dark, quiet streets of Cape Town. She felt a deep-seated calm pervading every cell of her body as she thought about what she had just done, savouring each delicious wave of memory as it washed over her.

So that was an orgasm. She finally understood what all the fuss was about. She now knew what it was that shattered empires and made men and women the world over do foolish and often illegal things. She shuddered at the idiotic and unbelievable rendition of it that she'd unknowingly acted out over the years. In comparison to the real thing her attempts had been so lacklustre and so deficient in feeling that she wondered how Max could have ever bought into the performance, believing that she had actually orgasmed with him for real. Was he that unaware? Stella wondered. Could he have been that unplugged in? Or did he know she was faking all along and just gave in to the charade, happy that at least one of them was coming.

Stella imagined a life in which she hadn't become a compulsive liar and slept with her twin's boyfriend, a life in which she only ever slept with Max for the rest of time, and never once got to experience an orgasm of the magnitude she'd experienced that night. That would have been a tragic situation. And while she felt a truckload of guilt at the trouble she'd caused, she couldn't find an ounce of regret.

POPPY

Poppy and Buck landed in Hamburg on time. That's just how Germany is. Even if your plane was due to land at two a.m., because you'd bought the cheapest seats on the cheapest airline, because you were just a couple of kids travelling around the world with nothing but backpacks. Even if the flight was so cheap you had to pay to use the toilet onboard, even if it was cheaper than the train, even then the plane would still land in Germany on time. At precisely two a.m., not a second earlier, or a second later.

'You've got to love the Germans,' Poppy said as they slouched through the terminal, dragging their backpacks behind them.

Buck grunted. He was too tired to respond. They'd been on the move now, schlepping around the world for so long that they were both physically and mentally exhausted. They were at the point in their travels where the shape of their backpacks was practically indented into their backs.

They exited the airport terminal and stood on the side of the road, trying to figure out what to do next. Overnight it had suddenly become winter in Europe. Amsterdam had been crisp and cold, but now the first of the European winter snow had fallen, and their breath made smoky shapes in the freezing night air.

'Okay, so I reckon we need some kind of cheap B. & B. arrangement. I don't know about you, but I can't face another backpackers,' Poppy said, rubbing her hands together to try keep them warm. 'I'm over it. I just want my own room, with a real bed.'

'Bed,' Buck moaned. 'I need a bed.'

Poppy looked around, there was a single taxi parked at the very end of the taxi rank with its lights off, the driver slumped in his seat. Other than that they seemed to be the only people around. The airport was quiet at this time of morning. No cars drove past and there wasn't a soul in sight. It was the graveyard shift at Hamburg Airport on a cold winter's night, and everybody else had done the smart thing and gone home to bed.

'There's a taxi,' Poppy said, looking over at Buck, who was sleeping standing up, leaning against a lamp post. 'Urgh, whatever, fine. You sleep, I'll deal with it.'

Poppy walked the hundred metres over to the cab and bent down to look in the front window. The driver was fast asleep with his head leaning against the car window. He had a big fat stomach and an enormous strawberry-blond handlebar moustache, of which Poppy thought he must be particularly proud.

Poppy knocked gently on the window right by his ear and watched in amusement as the cab driver almost jumped out of his skin with fright. She glanced back at Buck who was still sleeping standing up, then back at the cab driver, trying to look as cold and vulnerable and desperate and friendly as possible.

The cab driver rolled his car window down and assaulted her with a barrage of thick German. Poppy couldn't grasp a word of it. 'Sorry, no German,' she said, holding both hands up at him, palms facing outwards. 'English?'

'Nein,' he said emphatically, shaking his head grumpily at her.

'We want to go to a B. & B.,' Poppy said.

Again the cab driver shook his head; he clearly had no idea what she was talking about. Poppy looked around to see if she could spot someone who might be able to translate, but they were still all alone.

'We need a B. & B., bed and breakfast,' she said again, this time articulating every single word, dragging out each of the syllables.

The cab driver shook his head again and rattled off a couple of sentences at her in German.

Poppy spoke again, this time acting out the words elaborately, jumping around and gesturing with her hands. 'That is my friend,' she said pointing at Buck. 'Friend, amigo,' she repeated, finding the only foreign translation of the word she could think of. 'We want to drive with you.' She mimed gripping tightly onto an imaginary steering wheel in front of her and turning it maniacally. 'We want to drive with you to a bed and breakfast, capiche?'

Poppy was starting to sweat despite the cold; it was about thirty degrees under all the clothes she was wearing. 'Hold on a second,' she said mid-mime, putting her hand up in an imaginary stop sign.

Pulling off her backpack and dropping it on the floor by her feet, Poppy shrugged herself out of the jacket she was wearing and pulled her jumper off over her head. Once she'd managed to strip off her top two layers she wiped the sweat off her forehead and continued with her performance. 'My friend and I,' she said, pointing back to Buck, 'need you,' she pointed at the cab driver, 'to drive us,' she pointed back at herself and then at Buck and then mimed the driving thing again, 'to a hotel.' She put her hands together and held them under her ear, bending herself head against her hands as if they were a pillow. 'Where we can sleep and eat,' she said, miming the act of eating with an imaginary knife and fork. Then she dropped her hands by her side and looked at the taxi driver pleadingly, hoping he'd grasped at least some of her pantomime.

'Aaaaaah,' he said, nodding and smiling as he twisted one side of his handlebar moustache in thought.

'You take us in taxi?' Poppy asked, pointing at the car.

'Ja, ja, gut, ja,' the cab driver said, climbing out of the car and going round to the back to open the boot.

'Thank fuck,' Poppy said. Running back to Buck she woke him up with a swift punch to the shoulder. 'C'mon, I got us a cab, lazybones,' she said.

Buck opened one eye and evaluated her, then he grunted twice and ambled over to the cab, hoisting his pack into the boot and nodding at the cab driver, who was smiling widely at them both.

Poppy tried to stay awake for the cab journey, to get a feeling for the city, but she couldn't hold out. Her eyelids were so heavy she could barely keep them open, and the warm air in the cab and the lulling sound of the engine pushed her over the edge. She fell asleep with her head balanced on Buck's shoulder as they drove through the icy night.

The driver woke her with a few sentences in his thick German. Poppy pried her eyes open and tried to get her bearings. She had zero idea of how long he'd been driving or where they'd been driven to, and everything outside was dark and snowy. 'Wake up, Buck,' she said, nudging him with her elbow.

He opened just one eye and checked her out.

'We're here,' she said. 'At our B. & B. Soon you'll be in a real bed, come on.'

Half asleep, they grabbed their backpacks from the boot of the car and paid the taxi driver by holding out a wad of cash and letting him take what he needed, too tired to negotiate or try to understand him. Then they followed him up the snow-covered path to the front door of a darkened house. The taxi driver rang the bell three times and eventually, after a couple of minutes of stamping their feet to keep warm, the door opened and Poppy and Buck were faced with a porky-looking woman in her late fifties, sleepily pulling her robe across her body to protect herself from the cold night. The woman and the cab driver clearly knew each other and they had a brief conversation in German. Then the woman waved goodbye to the cab driver and turned back into her house, indicating for Poppy and Buck to follow her. Grateful to have finally arrived somewhere they followed the woman inside, waving their own goodbyes to the driver as he disappeared back down the pathway to his cab.

The woman chattered away to them in German as they followed her down the passage to a door. She opened it and showed them in. It was a simple but perfectly adequate room with a double bed and a small en suite bathroom. The woman gestured to the bathroom and gabbled on in German. Poppy nodded at her, but the pretence was futile. 'No German, only English,' she said loudly at the end of a particularly long sentence, smiling as politely as she could, but the woman seemed intent on showing them every detail of the room and giving them detailed instructions in German, whether they understood or not.

Buck had already taken off his shoes, lain down on the bed and was snoring by the time the woman was done with her exhaustive tour and left the room with a friendly smile in Poppy's direction. Poppy covered him with a thick blanket she found in an otherwise empty cupboard and then pulled off each of her shoes, her jacket and three more layers. Taking her bra off, but leaving her vest on, she went to the toilet, washed her face and brushed her teeth before collapsing into the bed next to Buck. They would deal with payment and everything else when they woke up later, she thought. She had no idea how much the room cost, but she didn't care, right then she would have paid a million euros to stretch out on a real bed. The B. & B. owner had been really kind to let them in so late at night without a booking, and Poppy's last thought before she dropped into a deep sleep was that whatever the room cost she would be eternally grateful for the woman's kindness.

Poppy woke up first. It was the smell of frying bacon that did it. There was no better smell to wake up to, she thought as she rolled over and tried to prise her eyes open. She had no idea how long she'd slept – her grasp on time had become completely warped and the room was still dark – but the smell of the bacon told her that it was definitely morning.

Poppy sat up and put both feet on the floor. She was starving and the smell of bacon was only exacerbating the situation. She went to the toilet and then examined their room. It had no windows and since they'd arrived in the dead of night she had no clue where she was. She looked over at Buck, who was still snoring loudly. She wondered whether she should wake him or not. By the looks of things he hadn't moved an inch from where he'd fallen face down the night before. She decided against it. She needed to get some breakfast and then get some bearings and then, if he still wasn't up, she'd wake him.

Poppy was still wearing the same clothes she'd been travelling in the night before but she didn't care, food was the only thing that mattered. She put her shoes back on over her disgustingly filthy socks and pulled a T-shirt on over her vest. Then she opened the door as quietly as she could, so as not to disturb Buck.

Closing the door behind her Poppy found herself in a long passageway with a wooden floor. It was punctuated with big wooden doors that obviously led off to the various bedrooms. Poppy heard voices and followed them, walking towards an open door at the end of the passage, which looked like it stood a good chance of leading to a kitchen or a breakfast room.

Poppy stepped cautiously through the door into an enormous wooden farmhouse-style kitchen and gaped, her jaw dropping in horror. Off to her right was a huge old-fashioned stove, in front of which the woman who had let them in the night before was standing, frying eggs and turning bacon. Further in the kitchen became a large open-plan dining room, and there were five or six large round tables spread out across the floor. Each table held a variety of people of all shapes and sizes, casually eating their breakfast, drinking juice, reading the newspaper and chattering away amongst themselves in German. And this was all fine, Poppy thought, and exactly what you might expect to find in any B. & B. anywhere in the world in the morning, except that every single person in the room, of which there must have been close to twenty, was completely and totally naked. Other than the odd hat or pair of shoes, none of them was wearing a stitch of clothing. Even the proprietress, standing in front of the stove, was nude, with the exception of a tiny white apron which she had tied around her waist.

'Fuck me!' Poppy said, covering her mouth with her hand.

The dining room suddenly became very quiet as everyone turned to stare at the only woman in the room wearing any clothing. The proprietress turned to face Poppy too, waving her spatula, with a broad, welcoming smile on her face, but the smile died on her lips as quickly as it had appeared as she took in Poppy's lack of lack of attire.

Just then Buck appeared in the doorway behind her, rubbing the sleep out of his eyes. The crowd gasped anew when they saw a second person who had the audacity to be fully dressed in front of them.

'Fuck me!' Buck said as he took in the spectacle in front of him, his mouth wide with shock. 'What the ...?' he added, tapering off.

'I have no idea!' Poppy stammered back at him. 'But it's all a bit much before I've had a cup of coffee.'

'Why on earth is everyone here naked?' Buck asked, taking a step backwards.

'It must be a nudist B. & B.,' Poppy whispered to Buck. The naked people were still staring at them in wonder and surprise and she felt like she was at a zoo, but one where the exhibits thought they were the visitors.

'Ya think?' Buck responded, sarcasm dripping off his tongue.

Poppy glared at him, but then her expression changed as a terrible realisation stole over her. 'Oh shit, Buck,' she said, her hand going to her mouth. 'I think I know how this happened.'

'Yes?' Buck said, trying to shield his sleep-sappy eyes from the terrifying view in front of him.

'You know when I got us that cab last night at the airport?' she said. 'Well, the cab driver didn't speak any English at all, I mean, not a word. So I had to act out that we wanted to go to a B. & B., you know, mime it out for him. But I was wearing two jerseys and a jacket and while I was jumping around, trying to play charades for him, I got really really warm. So, while I was trying to tell him that we needed him to take us to a B. & B. I took off my jacket and my top two jerseys.'

'So what?' Buck asked.

'What do you mean "So what?", dummy! Don't you see? He thought me taking off my clothes was part of the mime for where I wanted him to take us. That's why he's brought us to a nudist B. & B.!' Poppy finished off, gesturing into the room full of ugly naked flesh.

'Oh shit!' Buck said.

'Shit on a roll!' Poppy said.

'My eyes hurt!'

'Mine too.'

'Hey, do you think they'll let us have breakfast before we check out and find somewhere normal to stay?' Buck asked.

'That depends ... Are you willing to get your kit off?' Poppy asked.

'Well, I like bacon,' Buck said, eyeing the room one last time and considering it for a moment, 'but not that much.'

STELLA

Stella cut her car engine and freewheeled into her parents' driveway, turning her car lights off as soon as she could, so as not to wake anyone up. She looked at the dashboard. It was twenty past four in the morning. She smiled to herself. She couldn't remember when last she'd come home at four a.m. Probably never. And certainly not after a night like the one she had just experienced. She looked into the rear-view mirror and her hazy reflection eyed her back. Stella knew she was in for some form of disastrous hangover. She wasn't a seasoned party animal, but she was still well aware of the fact that a girl couldn't just go out partying the way that she had without some sort of payback. Fun was never free; it always came at a cost. She felt all right now, but she wondered how she would be feeling in five hours' time, sitting at her computer answering ridiculous letters. The only upside was that now she would at least feel like slightly less of a fraud. Maybe answering those dreadful letters would be a little more enjoyable, Stella thought, now that she had experience of at least some of the things people were always asking her about.

Parking outside the garage, Stella climbed out of the car, locked it and then wove her way up to the front of the house. Fumbling with her keys at the front door, she raised her nose and sniffed the air. She was sure she smelt smoke. She sniffed again. Someone was making a braai or something. Turning around, Stella looked up and down their street to see if she could see any smoke, but all was quiet in the predawn light.

Stella finally got the right key into the lock and pushed the front door open, still wondering why someone would be braaiing at four in the morning. The smell of smoke was much stronger now, she realised as she stepped into the hall and batted her hands in front of her face, surrounded by a light haze. Stella wondered if she was imagining things, but as she walked through the house the smell of smoke only intensified and her eyes began to sting.

Rounding a corner, she caught a glimpse of her father. He was sitting at the kitchen table in nothing but a pair of fireman-red underpants, his legs crossed in front of him, casually smoking a cigarette, while behind him flames licked at the kitchen curtains. Stella rubbed her eyes, but she wasn't imagining things, her parents' kitchen was really on fire and her father was really sleeping right through it. She remembered what she'd read about not waking sleepwalkers and instantly weighed up her options: he could die from a house fire or he could die from being woken up. She would take her chances with the latter.

'Dad! Dad!' she yelled, running into the kitchen. 'Wake up!' She grabbed a dishcloth and started beating at the fire with it, coughing as she sucked in a huge mouthful of smoke. 'Dad!' she shrieked, grabbing him by the arm and shaking him to wrench him back to consciousness.

He blinked once and then opened his eyes wide, suddenly awake. 'Stella?' he said, sounding surprised.

'Dad, there's a fire, come on, wake up, you've got to move!'

Hylton looked down at the cigarette in his hand in absolute shock, then he looked around at the flames that were getting bigger by the second, a massively confused look on his face. 'What the hell? Get your mother! Call the fire department!' he yelled at Stella, dropping the cigarette into the ashtray like it was poisonous and jumping up to grab a second dishcloth.

Stella raced down the passage, the smoke in the kitchen was getting thicker by the second but it thinned out somewhat as she ran towards the bedroom at the other end of the house. 'Mom! Mom!' she yelled at the top of her voice, bursting through her parents' bedroom door.

Her mother sat up like a shot. 'What? What's happening, Stella?' she asked, rubbing her eyes.

'There's a fire!' Stella gasped, feeling panic clutching at her throat. 'In the kitchen. Dad was sleep-smoking, and I think he set the kitchen curtains on fire. We need to call the fire department!'

'I'll call them, you go help your father,' Iris shouted, lunging across the bed for the telephone.

Stella raced out of the bedroom and back to the kitchen, where the smoke was now so thick that she had to cover her face with her arm. Her father was standing in his red underpants near the wooden central island, slapping at the licking flames with a dripping dishcloth. 'We need wet towels!' he shouted at Stella.

He was trying not to cough, but Stella could see that the smoke was starting to overwhelm him. She turned around and raced back to the linen closet just off her parents' bedroom, pulling armfuls of towels out of the closet.

'Here, give me some of those,' Iris shouted, coming up behind her. 'The fire department's on their way.'

'It's really bad in the kitchen, Mom!' Stella shouted, tossing piles of towels into Iris' open arms. 'We need to soak these.'

Running into the bathroom they turned on all the taps full blast, dousing as many towels as they could carry, water overflowing and splashing onto the tiles. Then they raced together back to the kitchen, dragging the dripping towels behind them.

'Oh, my God! Hylton, are you okay?' Iris shouted as Stella tossed him a sopping towel.

'Did you call the fire department?' Hylton shouted, coughing as the flames snuck closer to him.

'Yes, Mom did, they'll be here any minute,' Stella said, wrapping a wet towel over her face. She looked around for her mom, but she wasn't in the kitchen. 'Dad, it's moving too fast, there's too much smoke,' she shouted through the towel, tears pouring down her cheeks. 'I don't think we can fight it any longer ...'

Suddenly water started to pour into the kitchen, coming through the windows that had shattered in the heat.

'Come on, Stella, let's go,' Hylton said, grabbing Stella by the arm and pulling her backwards out of the kitchen as the water continued to splash through the window.

Stella followed her dad out of the kitchen, through the house and out of the front door, where they both collapsed, sucking in lungfuls of cool early morning air.

'Are you okay, Stella?' Hylton finally asked when he could speak again, his eyes streaming from the smoke, his voice hoarse.

'Yes, I'm all right. Are you okay?'

'I think so, but where's your mother?' he asked, a look of panic crossing his face.

Climbing to their feet, they both started around the house, calling out for Iris. It didn't take them long to find her. As they turned the corner that led to the back of the house, Stella saw her mom, standing in her nightie outside the kitchen window. She was holding the garden hose, which was pointed directly at the flames licking from the blackened kitchen windows. Iris stood with one hand on her hip, dousing the flames as if she was watering her roses on a Sunday afternoon. 'Are you two all right?' she shouted as soon as she saw them.

'I think we're okay.' Stella said. 'Dad, are you burnt?'

'Just a couple of small ones, I'll be fine,' he said, holding his arms around his chest, his teeth starting to chatter with shock.

'Stella, get your father a blanket or a jacket or something,' Iris ordered, stepping forward with the hose, to try reach some of the furthest flames.

Running back around to the front of the house, Stella grabbed a couple of jackets and a scarf from the hall, then quickly made her way back to her parents.

'Here, Dad,' she said, draping one of the jackets over his shoulders. His singed hair was standing on end and he was covered in black soot from head to toe. Stella's mother, on the other hand, looked quite calm and seemed to have the fire under control.

Stella heard a siren in the distance, slowly coming closer. 'That must be the fire engine,' she said, heaving a sigh of relief. 'Everything's going to be okay.'

'What happened?' Hylton asked, his voice still rough and raspy from all the smoke. 'I don't understand.'

'You burnt my kitchen down with your infernal smoking, you old fool!' Iris shouted.

'What are you talking about?' Hylton shouted. 'I don't smoke.'

'You do, actually!' Iris yelled, angling the hose at another batch of flames. 'Boxes and boxes, sometimes as many as three whole cigarettes a night! You're addicted!'

The three of them stood together in a clump. Her mother in her nightie and bare feet, her father with crazy hair and wild, disbelieving eyes and Stella in the same clothes she'd worn the previous day, with a monster hangover beginning to make itself known as the morning light cleared the smoky sky.

Stella stared into the smouldering kitchen as her parents bickered next to her. It was a blackened, smoky mess. The microwave had melted and there was nothing left of the wooden island in the centre of the kitchen. Anything that had gotten in the way of the flames had been destroyed. It all felt so surreal, she thought as firemen poured into their house.

'How can it all be my fault if I didn't even know that I smoked!' Hylton was shouting at Iris. 'You could have told me!'

'I didn't want to wake you up!' Iris screamed back. 'You know how grumpy you get when you get woken up!'

'Well, I think you should probably wake me up if I'm on fire, Iris!' Hylton cried. 'What's wrong with you, woman?'

Stella felt a deep exhaustion set in as she listened to her parents yell at each other.

'Not only do you destroy our marriage, but now you're trying to destroy our home too!' Iris shouted. 'This is all your fault, Hylton Frankel! You and that home wrecker!'

'Well, at least I'm not sleeping with my daughter's homeroom teacher!'

he spat back.

Stella couldn't bear it any more. 'Will you two just stop fighting for one second!' she shouted. 'You both could have died in there! You're lucky I came home when I did. This could have been way worse.'

'Yes, and that's another thing. Where have you been, Stella?' Iris asked angrily. 'Since when do you come home at four in the morning?'

Her parents both looked at her intently.

'I don't want to talk about it, if you don't mind,' Stella said, suddenly at a loss for words.

Silence descended as they watched the firemen putting an end to what was left of the fire. Stella couldn't remember ever feeling so exhausted. 'I could do with a cup of coffee,' she said. 'Anyone else?'

Her parents ignored her, seemingly transfixed by what was happening to what was left of their kitchen.

Stella stepped forward and peered through the kitchen window onto the counter where the kettle normally stood. But in its place stood a charred lump of smoking black plastic. 'Well, the kettle's boiled,' she mumbled, 'so that's the end of that idea.'

POPPY

'Poppy, why do you think this place is called Hamburg?' Buck asked, scratching his stubbly chin. 'And do you think they called the burger after the city, or the city after the burger?'

'Dunno,' Poppy said. 'Hey, do you think I have time to find a toilet before the train leaves?'

'I kind of feel like a burger now,' Buck said, ignoring her question. 'It would almost be wrong not to eat a hamburger in Hamburg, don't you think?'

'Will you wait here for a minute and keep an eye on my backpack while I go? I'm so over dragging it everywhere, it weighs a fucking ton.'

'Need to spend a penny, eh?' Buck asked, raising an eyebrow.

'Okay, seriously, I really need to go now. Will you just watch my backpack for me for five minutes?'

'Got to see a man about a dog?' Buck asked.

'Buck, I swear ...'

'Need to make lemonade?'

'Buck, for fuck's sake. Come on, you're killing me over here! Will you watch my backpack or not?'

'Well, with all this talk of pissing, now I gotta punish the porcelain myself,' Buck said.

'You're a real piece of work, you know that!' Poppy huffed, pushing her hair out of her face. 'Fine, don't bother, I'll take it with me. Our train leaves in twenty minutes, and the platform is over there,' she said, pointing through the crowds. 'So meet me back here as soon as you're done, okay?'

'Sure, see you back here as soon as I've siphoned my python,' Buck said, sauntering off with a smile on his face.

Poppy looked around, spotted a ladies loo sign and headed towards it. She loved Buck, but sometimes he could be such a doos, she thought as she followed the signage into a thin tiled passageway.

The signs led to the top of three narrow flights of stairs. Poppy groaned. She was already sweating like a pig from lugging her backpack around all day and now this. Her bladder was full and the backpack was just so flipping heavy.

'I'm sorry, I'm so sorry, I'm so, so sorry,' Poppy said, apologising to the other women on the staircase as she began her descent. The stairs were so narrow and her backpack was so wide that nobody could get past her in either direction. At least she was going down, she thought. She didn't want to even imagine what it would be like coming up again.

Finally, knees trembling, Poppy arrived at the bottom of the stairs, in a small area that led into the public toilet. She really needed to wee badly now and she shifted her weight from foot to foot as she eyed out the turnstile at the entrance to the toilet. A woman carrying a crying baby squeezed past her and slipped a euro into a slot on the turnstile and went into the bathroom.

'Fuck, fuck, fuck!' Poppy muttered, realising that she was going to have to pay if she wanted to pee. She thought back to the orange juice she'd drunk with breakfast earlier that day. It had cost her a euro. She'd paid to put it in and now she was going to have to pay to let it out again. That was capitalism for you. She fished in her pocket, pulling out a ten euro note. It was the only money she had on her.

Another woman struggled past, making for the turnstile. 'You don't have any change, do you?' Poppy asked in desperation, but the woman just shook her head at Poppy and disappeared into the bathroom.

Poppy turned around and eyed the stairs back up to the platform; she was going to have to drag her stupid backpack all the way up to the top, get change from one of the shops in the station and lug it all the way back down again. She couldn't just leave it at the bottom of the stairs because someone would think it was a bomb, and then they would call Hamburg Station security, and Hamburg Station security would do something stupid like blow it up. But it wasn't a bomb; it was all her worldly possessions. Every last one. And there was no way she was letting it out of her sight.

With no other choice, Poppy ignored her pulsing bladder and began to heave herself and her backpack up the three flights of stairs.

Back up on the platform, dripping in sweat, Poppy made a beeline for the closest shop. Grabbing the first thing she could find at the till, which was a pack of gum, she slammed it down on the counter, together with her ten euro note, hopping desperately from foot to foot, her backpack shifting awkwardly on her back. The shop assistant took the gum and the note and spoke to Poppy in German, asking her a question.

'I don't understand. I just need one euro! Please!' Poppy pleaded, holding up one finger and squeezing her thighs together tightly, a tear of desperation forming in her eye.

The cashier eyed her nervously as she handed over her change, but Poppy didn't care. Grabbing the coins out of the cashier's outstretched hand she walk-ran as quickly as she could back towards the toilets, dragging her backpack along the floor behind her.

Poppy bustled back down the skinny tiled corridor and down the three flights of stairs that would take her back to the turnstile, clutching the precious euro in her sweaty hand. There were two women in front of her, so she hopped from foot to foot as she waited her turn to slip the coin into the slot. But as soon as she got her chance the coin fell back out again. Poppy groaned, grabbed at it and slipped it back into the slot. She could hear it rattling through the innards of the machine, before it clattered out the bottom once more. 'Fucking coin!' Poppy swore, not caring who heard her. 'Goddamnit, I need to pee,' she shouted, sweat dripping down her face.

Finally the machine accepted the coin and the turnstile gave. Poppy breathed a sigh of relief and pushed forward, but she didn't get far. Her backpack was too wide; it wouldn't fit through. Poppy wanted to cry. She needed to pee so badly it literally hurt. If the backpack hadn't contained absolutely everything she owned, she would have just left the stupid thing there. Poppy swore at Buck again, under her breath. If the bastard had only watched her bag for her for one lousy minute, she would have already finished peeing by now. She heard somebody running a tap ahead of her in the bathroom. It sounded like Victoria Falls and her need to relieve herself instantly doubled. She gritted her teeth as a woman standing behind her cleared her throat impatiently. 'I'm sorry. It won't fit. It's going to have to go over,' Poppy said to the woman, pointing at her backpack and then at the turnstile.

The woman shrugged and said something to Poppy in German.

Planting her feet, Poppy began to manhandle all thirty kilos of the backpack over the top of the turnstile. Sweaty and desperate she grunted loudly as she manoeuvred the bag, shoving it viciously over the top of the turnstile, then letting it fall with a loud *whump* onto the floor on the other side.

Sighing with gratitude Poppy pushed through the turnstile, grabbed the backpack and dragged it along the floor to the first available cubicle she could find. The bag was too big to fit in the cubicle with her, but by now she was beyond caring. Dropping it at the open door she hopped from foot to foot as she struggled to undo her jeans, her fingers not working fast enough. Eventually she made it onto the toilet, and not a second too soon. She heaved a huge sigh of relief as her bladder finally began to empty, not able to remember ever feeling a greater sense of relief in her entire life.

It felt to Poppy like she peed forever. The cubicle door was open and women stared at her as they passed by, but she didn't care, the relief of finally being able to pee overrode everything else. At least she was getting her money's worth, she thought as, still peeing, she pulled some of the half-ply toilet paper from the roll and mopped up her sweaty forehead.

Having finished in the cubicle, Poppy checked her watch – she didn't have long. She quickly washed her face and her hands before dragging her backpack through the toilet's exit gate and back towards the stairs, noticing for the first time a special entrance gate, right next to the turnstile, specially designed for people carrying big backpacks or other things like prams. Poppy had been so desperate and so focused on not peeing her pants that she hadn't noticed it on the way in. As she shuffled past the gate, swearing under her breath, a cleaning woman mopping the floor caught her eye and smiled cruelly.

Poppy shook her head and dragged her backpack back up the three flights of stairs for one last time. Then she lugged it over to where Buck sat waiting for her.

'Take your time!' Buck said. 'We've still got four minutes!'

'I fucking hate you, you know that,' Poppy said.

'What? What did I do?'

'Turns out it's people like me who make working in the public toilets in Hamburg Station a fun job to have!' Poppy said grumpily as they made their way to the train.

STELLA

Stella sat on the edge of her unslept-in bed and considered taking a duvet day. She felt like she needed to sleep for a year at least.

All of a sudden her bedroom door opened and two old ladies and an old man shuffled into her room.

'Hello, can I help you?' Stella asked with surprise, trying to figure out if she knew them.

'No bother, dear,' one of the old ducks said, 'we're from number seventeen.'

'Just down the street,' said the other old lady, pointing out the window with a crooked finger.

'We heard about the fire and we thought we'd just pop in and offer our condolences,' the first lady said.

'This is a nice room,' the old man shouted as he shuffled around in a circle, taking in the room. Stella noticed a hearing aid wedged into his ear. 'See, Audrey, they get the morning sun,' he yelled, 'we don't get the morning sun.'

'No, dear, you're right, we don't get the morning sun,' the second old lady said.

'They get more morning sun, but our house is still nicer,' the old man shouted as if Stella wasn't even there.

'Okay, well, thanks for visiting,' Stella said loudly, stepping forward and herding them out of her bedroom.

The passage that ran down the middle of the house was buzzing with people: neighbours and well-wishers and, by the look of things, people who had just wandered in off the street. Closing her bedroom door behind her, Stella herded the neighbours towards the lounge and what was left of the kitchen, where a group of insurance assessors were busy taking notes.

Stella found her father sitting in his chair in the lounge. He'd showered and put on clothes, but his hair was still scorched and standing on end. Daisy was standing next to him, holding hands with a butch-looking woman. 'Oh, my goodness, Stella, are you all right?' Daisy asked as soon as she saw her sister. 'We were so worried.'

Daisy's friend was very tall, she had short hair and a nervous smile played on her lips.

'Daisy, hi. Yes, no, I'm fine, just quite tired and a little shaken. We were lucky. It could have been much worse.'

'Stella, this is Lisa, my girlfriend,' Daisy said, still not letting go of her girlfriend's hand, but instead raising it up as if she was the winner in a boxing match.

Stella glanced at Hylton, but he was just sitting, staring into space vacantly, clutching his newspaper in his hand. Maybe he was still in shock after the fire, Stella thought. Or maybe he had finally realised that some things are more important than who your daughter chose to love.

'We came over as soon as we heard,' Daisy said, smiling nervously. 'We're just so glad everyone is okay.'

'Nice to meet you, Lisa, sorry about the mess,' Stella said, indicating the scorched remains of the kitchen.

'Aunty Stella …!'

Stella felt a painful thud on her back as Luke jumped up onto her and threw his arms around her neck, bashing her windpipe and throttling her in the process. Lowering him to the ground, she choked in a breath and turned around just in time to see Violet arriving with the other two boys in tow. 'Aunty Daisy! Aunty Stella! Aunty Daisy!' they yelled, charging around the lounge as if powered by nothing but sugar.

'Why's Aunty Daisy holding hands with a girl?' Nathan asked.

'Because she's a lesbian, dummy,' Luke said, smacking his brother.

'What's a lesbian?' Nathan asked.

'Lesbian, lesbian, lesbian,' Jack shouted, jumping up and down on the couch.

But even this did nothing to break Hylton out of his trance.

'Stella,' Violet said, putting her arms around her sister and giving her a hug. 'I thought I'd bring the boys. You know how excited they get about fire engines. And I also thought it was important for them from a cognitive perspective, to see the damage and understand the cause and effect of playing with fire.'

Stella looked over at the boys, who were now climbing all over Lisa. 'Aren't they supposed to be in school?' she asked.

'This is school, Stella. It's the school of life,' Violet said.

Stella rolled her eyes.

'So how are you holding up?' Violet asked.

'Yeah, I'm good, but I'd better get to the office,' Stella said, suddenly desperate for the peace and quiet of her little cubicle.

Despite all the chaos, Stella managed to shower and leave the house some time just after nine. Not bad for someone who hadn't slept in almost twenty-four hours and had been involved in fighting a house fire, she thought as she climbed into her car. Although, if she was honest with herself, she'd never felt worse. Lack of sleep mixed in with a hangover had left her in a very bad mood. She felt like death warmed up.

At her desk Stella chewed on her pen, thinking about the events of the night before. Getting tattooed and her general debauched foolishness with Simon felt like it had happened decades ago. She sighed and shook her head at her own outrageous behaviour as delicious memories of her first ever orgasm flooded her mind and a warm wave washed over her, making her severe hangover feel worth it, just for the moment.

Her desk phone rang, shooting her back to reality. She grabbed the receiver and held it to her ear. 'It's Connie,' a voice said sharply on the other end of the line. 'Denise wants to see you.'

Stella sat up straight. Denise wanted to see her. Her heart raced. She wondered why. Maybe Denise had seen her come in late? Stella panicked. No, that couldn't be it, she reassured herself, she was just being paranoid. She imagined explaining herself to Denise: 'I'm sorry I was late this morning, but last night I went out and got a tattoo and skinny dipped in the ocean. And then I got shit-faced and had sex with a stranger and had my very first real orgasm. And then the kitchen at my parents' place, where I'm staying right now because my marriage is falling apart, burnt down. So I'm sorry I couldn't make it in on time, but I'm sure you understand!' At least she had a good excuse.

At the thought of the tattoo Stella ran her hand over her hip. It felt quite tender and she worried about it for a second, but then she dismissed her concerns. It was probably going to be quite sore for a while, she told herself, after all, she had just got a tattoo.

Turning her thoughts back to Denise, Stella stood up and looked over her partition. A bunch of the girls from editorial were crowded around one of the desks, poring over something. A couple looked over at her and then returned to the cluster, whispering furiously.

Maybe she was finally getting her promotion, she thought, smoothing down her hair. That could be what they were all gossiping about. Crouching back down, Stella grabbed her bag and scuttled out of her cubicle, heading for the bathroom. She wanted to make sure she was looking her best for Denise, which considering how she was feeling was going to be a near-impossible feat.

Stella stared at herself in the bathroom mirror. She had reapplied her make-up, doing her best to hide the damage from the night before, but there was nothing she could do about her bloodshot eyes. Now that she was standing up her hip seemed to be more painful than it had been at her desk, and she lifted her skirt to examine her tattoo. It was still covered by the dressing Simon had put on for her the night before, so she couldn't see the tattoo itself, but the skin around the dressing was red and raised and hot to the touch. Dropping her skirt back into place, she smoothed it down. There was nothing she could do about it now, she would change the dressing and clean it up when she got home later, after celebrating her promotion for real, of course.

Stella suddenly wished that she hadn't told Max that she'd lied about the promotion. Now that she was actually getting it she realised that she could probably have avoided all the added angst if she'd just sat tight for a couple of weeks. Hindsight really was twenty-twenty, she thought as she pushed open the bathroom door and made her way to Denise's office.

'What took you so long? She's been calling for you since seven thirty this morning!' Connie hissed as soon as she saw Stella, waving her through the door to Denise's office.

'Stella, sit down!' Denise said, in a curt tone. As usual she was wearing all white, and a milky white cappuccino sat untouched in front of her on her desk. Next to that her phone was lit up like a Christmas tree. Every line was flashing silently with a waiting call. Stella eyed it and then eyed Denise, but Denise was reading a thick document, ignoring Stella and all the calls.

Stella sat down and winced, feeling the pain in her hip again. 'Denise, I'm so sorry I was late this morning,' she apologised. 'I've had some problems at home and ...'

'Stella, I want to read something to you,' Denise said abruptly, cutting her off mid-sentence.

'Okay,' Stella said, settling back into the chair.

Denise put down the document she had been reading and picked up the latest issue of the magazine, opening it in front of her face dramatically. Stella hadn't seen the new cover yet, and she studied it carefully as Denise found the page she was looking for. The issue must have only just come off the presses the night before and been distributed first thing this morning. In fact, Stella thought, just as she'd been arching her back in Simon's bed the vans would have been delivering the magazines to news-stands and shops around the country.

Having found the right page Denise appraised Stella over the top of the magazine, then she began to read out loud in a slow, controlled voice: 'Dear Dr Dee,' she read. 'I have a rather strange question for you. But I have no one else to turn to because I feel too awkward to ask our family doctor about this. So here goes. I was wondering if it's at all possible for a woman who isn't pregnant and has never been pregnant before to lactate? And if it is possible I would like to know what the best way to stimulate the lactation is? Because I would love to please my new husband with this. From Curious Newlywed.'

Stella wondered why Denise was reading out her column, she'd never taken an active interest in it before. Perhaps the content was too risqué and Denise had gotten into trouble with the shareholders or the advertisers. It only took one shareholder or director to have a prudish wife and a column like Stella's was toast. Or perhaps Denise was simply pleased with Stella's choice of letter, something this risqué could only increase readership figures and that was the be all and end all for any publisher.

Stella chewed on her lip, her stomach boiling as Denise carried on reading, moving on to the response: 'Dear Curious Newlywed,' Denise read, pausing and looking up at Stella once again over the magazine. 'You've got to be kidding me! You want to breastfeed your husband! What the hell? Have you completely lost your mind? Seriously! That's not acceptable. If your husband wants milk he can get up and go to the kitchen like all the other men in the world, lazy bastard! Love Dr Dee.'

Stella's heart crashed. She wished desperately that she had decided to take her own advice and stay in bed, and that this was all some kind of nightmare brought on by too much Jack Daniel's, but she knew it wasn't. Somehow this had happened. Somehow in the confusion of the moment the wrong response had been emailed to Ebrahim and they'd gone to print with it. And nobody had bothered to proofcheck it; there just hadn't been enough time. Stella gulped loudly and her face went crimson.

'Do you need me to remind you what you said to the poor girl who has a crush on her gay best friend, or do you remember that one?' Denise asked sarcastically.

Stella shook her head vigorously, looking down at her feet in horror as Denise laid the magazine down gently on her desk and folded her arms in front of her, her white fingernails tapping on her sleeves. 'What have you done, Stella? she asked.

Stella blinked and looked at Denise's furious face. 'Oh, my goodness, Denise, I have no idea how that happened, that's not my response,' she gabbled.

'You mean you didn't write this response?' Denise asked, her voice angrily curious now.

'No, I wrote it,' Stella nodded, 'but I didn't send that one to print. There was another response, the right response.'

'Well, someone printed it,' Denise roared, smashing her hand down on the open magazine, her ring cutting through the page, tearing a gash across it.

'Yes, I know, but I can explain,' Stella said, her voice high and shaking.

Denise looked at her and raised an eyebrow, waiting for her explanation.

'You see, I always write two responses. You know, one is just a joke. I mean, I don't show it to anyone, it's just for myself. And then I write the other response, the serious one, and that's the one we publish. But I must have gotten it wrong,' Stella said, her voice wobbling.

'You think this is a joke?' Denise raged. 'I don't think our readers are going to think it's a joke, and I don't think the Curious Newlyweds are going to think it's a joke. And I certainly don't find it particularly funny.'

Stella rubbed her face with her hands, tears only a second away.

'I knew you wanted out of the column,' Denise said, standing up and pacing around the office, 'but I didn't know you wanted out of it this badly.'

'No, I didn't do this on purpose, I swear,' Stella said, feeling desperate. 'Denise, I am so, so sorry. Can we retract it? Or maybe we can print an apology? Isn't there anything we can do?'

'We'll have to print an apology,' Denise said, 'but I'm afraid the damage has already been done.'

Stella pictured the tens of thousands of South Africans who would pick up the magazine that day and for the rest of the week, until the next issue was published the following Monday. She imagined their faces as they read her column. The Mother Grundys would be up in arms about this one. Stella usually got a handful of complaints every week from Bible-bashers and prudes around the country, but the sentiment in those letters would pale in comparison to the wrath that this new set of letters would contain. So much for her writing career, she thought, wondering what she would do now. Telesales, perhaps?

Suddenly the job that Stella had hated for so many years felt incredibly important to her and she wondered why she hadn't embraced it while she'd had the opportunity. It was all she had left. She'd overlooked all the pros. The fact that she was being published every week and actually being read by people. The fact that the readers relied on her to answer their questions and help them with their problems. She'd ignored all of that, and now she'd never have it again. She should have had the good sense to enjoy it and make the most of it while she had it.

'So, I guess I need to pack up my desk then?' Stella said quietly, hanging her head in shame and disappointment.

'Not a chance!' Denise said, turning to face her. 'There's no way you're leaving me to deal with this mess on my own!'

Stella cocked her head and stared at Denise, confused. 'I don't understand, Denise?' she said.

'You're going to stay and answer the calls, my dear!' Denise said sharply, indicating the flashing red lights on her phone. 'Every single one of them. Every single person who calls to complain or cancel their subscription will be put through to you. And the calls you can't take or have missed this morning, you will return over the next couple of days. I'm collating a list of our advertisers and shareholders and you will call every single one of them and apologise in person and let them know that you made this mistake and assure them emphatically that something like this will never, ever happen again. And then I want you to follow up each of the calls to our advertisers with a hand-written letter of apology, do you understand?'

Stella eyed Denise's telephone, the lights were still flashing red on every single line. 'You're joking, right?' she asked.

'Only as much as you were joking when you wrote this response,' Denise said, pointing back down at the magazine. 'Connie will divert these calls to your desk when you leave this office. You will take each one and apologise and explain what you did. And then, when the calls start to die down, sometime next week I would imagine, and when you've finished calling up all our advertisers and writing the letters of apology to each and every one of them, then you can pack your desk and go. Understood?'

Stella nodded her head.

'That is all!' Denise said curtly.

Stella stood up to go. She looked back over her shoulder at Denise, wanting to apologise, to somehow try and make things right, but Denise had already turned her back on Stella and was staring out of the window, shaking her head.

Bile rose up in Stella's stomach as she thought of what she had done, and her face was suddenly awash with sweat. She needed to be sick. 'You'd better get a move on,' Connie yelled after her as she ran down the passage towards the bathroom, her hand covering her mouth to hold in the vomit. 'I've just put half a dozen calls through to your phone.'

Once she'd cleaned herself up, Stella walked back to her cubicle with her head hung low, not making eye contact with anyone.

Back at her desk, she found her telephone just as lit up as Denise's had been. There were ten lines in total on her phone, but she'd only ever used two of the lines at a time, on the odd occasion that she'd been on the phone with Lucy and Max had called, or her mother had called when she was on the phone with Max. She looked at the phone nervously. One of the flashing red lights went dark, but then, only seconds later, resumed its frantic flashing.

Stella sat down at her desk and reached for the phone gingerly. She put it to her ear and pressed one of the buttons. 'Dr Dee,' she said softly, in the hope that the person on the other end of the phone might not hear her. But she wasn't going to be that lucky.

'I want to speak to the person who wrote this week's agony aunty column,' a woman's voice said.

'I'm afraid that's me,' Stella said.

'You know, I've been a nurse for almost fifteen years, and I couldn't believe what I read.'

'I'm so sorry, Ma'am,' Stella said. 'I didn't mean what I wrote, it was a mistake, they printed the wrong responses.'

'What about those poor people who wrote in?' the woman asked. 'You should be ashamed of yourself.'

'I am and I wish I could apologise to them too,' Stella said, but the line had already gone dead.

Stella sighed deeply and reached for the button to activate the next line. 'Dr Dee speaking,' she said.

'Are you the lady who writes the agony column?' a man's voice asked.

'Yes, I am,' Stella said. 'And please, before you say anything, let me apologise. There was a mistake when we went to print, and they published the wrong responses. I really didn't mean to say those things, I swear it. I'm so very, very sorry.'

'Have you accepted the Lord Jesus Christ as the Saviour in your life?' the voice asked.

'I'm afraid at this stage I doubt even he'd have me,' Stella said, shaking her head into the phone.

'It's never too late to find redemption,' the voice said.

'Thank you,' Stella sighed, desperate for the call to end. 'And I'm sorry. Goodbye.'

The calls continued relentlessly for the remainder of the day. Stella started counting them just before lunch and the grand total came to sixty-eight separate calls. She was sworn at, shouted at and damned to hell by sixty different people. The remaining eight calls had been from Daisy, Violet, Stella's mom and a handful of Stella's friends who had all heard about the debacle. But conspicuous by their absence were Lucy and Max. She wondered what Max would think when he read her column. Was it possible that he could think even less of her than he already did, or would he simply feel sorry for her. Then she wondered what Lucy's reaction would be. She doubted Lucy would feel sorry for her. Lucy would probably roar with laughter at the sweet justice of the situation. One ruined life for one ruined life, it was only fair.

Stella drove straight home to her parents' house after work, completely drained. She sank into a deep, hot bath, but even under the water she could still hear the words of callers ringing in her ears. When she climbed out of the bath she carefully changed the dressing on her tattoo. The skin around it was still red and angry and small sores had started to form where the skin had been broken. She covered it with a thick layer of antibacterial cream and applied a fresh plaster.

Her mother had gone out somewhere in a sulky huff and their kitchen was a big blackened hole, so she and Hylton ordered takeaway pizza, which they ate in the lounge.

'So, what did they say about the kitchen?' Stella asked as she chewed on a slice of pizza.

'The insurance guys said it's going to need a complete rebuild,' her dad said, looking at her with sad eyes. 'They won't be able to save any of it. We were lucky you came home when you did and we managed to contain the fire in the kitchen. We could have lost the whole house, Stella.'

'What are those?' Stella asked, pointing at a series of small white patches that ran all the way up both of her dad's arms.

'They're nicotine patches. I thought they might help put a stop to the midnight cigarette cravings.'

'That's a good idea,' Stella said. 'Why do you think you do it?'

'I have no idea,' her dad said, shrugging his shoulders. 'All I know is that at seventy-three years of age I'm going to have to quit smoking, when I never even knew I smoked to begin with.'

Stella smiled at him weakly and wiped her mouth.

'What about you? Are you okay, Stel?' he asked her gently.

'Oh, you know, I've been better,' she said. 'Work's a mess and I don't know what's going to happen with Max. And Lucy, well ...'

Her dad patted her on the arm gently. There was nothing he could say to make it better and he knew it.

Stella got up and kissed him on the forehead. 'Night, Dad, I'm going to have an early night,' she said. 'Hey, do us a favour, don't burn down the rest of the house tonight, okay?'

Stella climbed into bed and stared at the ceiling. It was only five past seven, but she was more than ready to call this day a day. Her ears burned from answering the phone all day and her stomach was constantly full of bile at the thought of the disaster that her life had become.

Stella closed her eyes and did some basic calculations. She had now been married for just over one thousand, two hundred and fifty-four hours, separated from Max for a little under three hundred and ninety hours, and it had been just about thirty-seven hours since she'd had any kind of real, solid sleep. The events of the last three weeks played themselves out in the theatre of her mind, refusing to stop for an interval. She saw herself as if from the outside looking in. She saw herself watching Jake and Lucy having sex, lying to Max, allowing herself to be seduced by Jake, Max finding out about her infidelity, almost sleeping with the prostitute, not bungee jumping, getting the tattoo, skinny dipping and having sex with Simon and then coming home to find the kitchen burning down, shortly followed by the end of her career as a writer.

Maybe it was just because she was so incredibly worn out and hung-over and she felt so rotten, but suddenly Stella realised that she missed the quiet comfort and predictable slow pace of her old life with Max. She missed her bed and her couch and her kitchen. Maybe calm, average and boring were good. Maybe adventure and excitement and wild sex and staying up all night were overrated. She wondered if she was having an epiphany. She needed to get hold of Max and see how things felt between them, she decided. Maybe if she begged he would be prepared to listen to her, and maybe even to forgive her. And then she could go back to her old life and try to patch together some sort of happiness for the two of them. Or maybe by now he had come to the conclusion that he could never trust her again and their marriage was over. Either way, she needed to know.

Stella couldn't sleep. She tossed and turned, agonising over the decisions she needed to make. She had nobody to talk to. More than anything she missed Lucy. She needed Lucy back in her life; there was no way she could go on without her. She tried to imagine what Lucy would say if she were talking to her right now. Perhaps she would remind Stella that losing her job wasn't the end of the world, and that she would be fine without Max, and then they would laugh together and see the funny side of things. But seeing the funny side of things right now was something that Stella just couldn't do on her own.

Stella was up and out of the door early, before either of her parents was up. She stopped off at Vida in Cavendish, to grab a cup of coffee and some breakfast, then she made her way through the early morning traffic to Violet's rooms in Newlands.

Walking into the shared waiting room, Stella was relieved to see that the light above Violet's door wasn't on. She tried the door, but it was locked. Violet obviously wasn't in yet, so Stella sat quietly sipping on her coffee, perched on a badly upholstered couch that smelled of dust and old people, and waited for her to arrive.

Stella was woken by a gentle tap on her arm, closely followed by a second, slightly less gentle pinch. She opened her eyes and wondered where she was. It took her a couple of seconds to realise that she'd dozed off curled up on the couch in Violet's reception and that she'd been in a deep and dreamless sleep. She wiped the drool from the side of her mouth and sat up straight.

'Stella,' Violet said, dropping her briefcase and her *Cape Times* on one of the chairs. 'How are you holding up?'

'Not so good, to be honest, Vi,' Stella said, starting to cry. 'Things are really bad, and I haven't been sleeping.'

'I'm not surprised,' Violet said, sitting down next to her and rubbing her back gently. 'With everything that's been going on that's perfectly normal.'

'Vi, I need a favour,' Stella said.

Violet raised an eyebrow. 'Sure, anything you need.'

'I was wondering if you could prescribe me a little something to take the edge off?' Stella asked.

'No, Stella, anything but that!' Violet said, standing up, obviously irritated. 'I'm not that kind of doctor. I'm a psychologist, Stella. I can't prescribe drugs, that's a psychiatrist, you know that!'

'I know,' Stella said, 'but I thought maybe you know someone, or you could pull some strings or something. I wouldn't ask if I wasn't desperate, you know that. It's just that I've run out of sleeping pills. I'm barely sleeping at all, I'm not managing at work and everything has spiralled out of control. I just need something to tide me over in the short term ...'

'Stella,' Violet said sharply, 'I know this isn't what you want to hear, but you don't need drugs. What you do need is a reality check! You need to sort things out with Lucy, find another job and go back home to your husband. And you look terrible, by the way.'

'Aw, gee, thanks, Vi,' Stella said sarcastically, getting up and grabbing her things. 'I feel better already. I can see now why you're such a good shrink. Brilliant, thank you!'

Stella stormed across the waiting room and slammed her way out of the office. 'Family,' she huffed to herself, shaking her head furiously as she stomped across the parking lot.

Traffic going to her office was completely backed up as it always was during rush hour. As Stella waited for the car in front of her to inch forward half a centimetre she ran a finger over her hip, distracted by the throb. The pain had reached new heights this morning and when she'd examined the area after her shower she'd noticed that the small sores were starting to look a little pussy. Her life was not a pretty sight and now she had a hip to match. It was remarkable that such a tiny little imperfectly shaped heart could manage to cause her so much pain. She was going to have to get it looked at sooner rather than later, she thought.

Waiting for the car in front of her to budge, she tapped her finger on her steering wheel anxiously, and contemplated some of the calls she was going to have to deal with during the course of the day. She wouldn't be surprised if the devil himself called, just to have a bit of a laugh at her expense.

By some unimaginable fluke Stella arrived at work only fifteen minutes late. She panicked when she pulled into the parking garage and saw Denise's car already in its space, but then she shrugged her shoulders, what were they going to do to her for being late anyway, fire her? She snorted at the absurdity of her reaction, panicking at the thought of being late for a job she'd already been fired from.

As Stella walked towards the bank of elevators she saw someone step into the furthest lift. 'Hold the lift!' she shouted, picking up her pace and run-walking towards it.

The person inside the lift either didn't hear her or decided to ignore her and the lift doors started to close.

'I said hold the lift!' Stella shouted a second time, this time louder, picking up her pace. Suddenly catching the lift became very important to her, it would be a little victory in a sea of losses – Stella needed something to go right, even if it was something as small as catching an elevator.

Stella sprinted at full speed towards the lift and slid up to it with her arm extended just before the doors shut completely. The doors bashed closed against the top of her arm twice and then juddered open again. She would definitely have bruises on her arm by lunchtime, she thought as she tried to catch her breath after her hundred metre dash.

As the lift doors opened all the way Stella stepped inside, rubbing her arm, and got her first glimpse of the person inside. It was Yolanda. Stella's stomach turned, and she gritted her teeth, immediately regretting her sprint across the parking lot. Why hadn't she just waited for the next lift, she berated herself, she was always competitive in all the wrong places. There were three elevators; it wasn't like she would have waited that long for the next one to come along.

'Oh, hi,' Yolanda said, awkwardly. 'Sorry, I didn't see you coming.'

'Sure, no problem,' Stella said, wincing once more on the inside and rubbing her bruised arm. She pressed the already lit button for the sixth floor and they stood uneasily in an uncomfortable silence, trying not to make eye contact.

Please don't mention the column, please don't mention the column, please don't mention the column, Stella prayed over and over again as they stood in self-conscious silence while the lift ascended slower than she thought mechanically possible.

'Sooooo,' Yolanda said, breaking the silence eventually. 'I heard about what happened ... You know, with your column ... Wow! That's just crazy!'

Stella half nodded at her a couple of times and tried to force a smile.

'You know, you shouldn't worry too much about it,' Yolanda continued in a matter-of-fact tone. 'I suppose it could have happened to any one of us.'

'I suppose so, I guess I was just the unlucky one,' Stella said, fighting to keep her rage from boiling over.

'You know, we were talking about it in features,' Yolanda said. Stella cringed inwardly at the mention of features, the team she had so desperately wanted to be a part of for all these years and that Yolanda had so easily fallen into. 'It may not be a bad thing, you know, a little profile never hurt anyone in our industry.'

'I really hope you're right,' Stella said, nodding at Yolanda again and then looking at her feet, scared at what she might do if she made eye contact.

In her rational mind Stella knew that none of this was actually Yolanda's fault. It was quite possible that the young woman who stood before her in yet another gorgeous designer outfit was a really lovely person who had never done a thing to hurt another human being in her entire life. And it was also quite possible that she was immensely talented and had deserved that job, but in her irrational mind Stella wanted to blame Yolanda for everything. Because, surely, if Yolanda hadn't come along and stolen her job with her degree and her perfect designer wardrobe, then none of this would have ever happened to Stella to begin with. She bit her lip to keep her mouth closed and when the elevator finally dinged open on their floor she realised she'd been holding her breath for four floors.

At her desk Stella's phone lines were already going berserk, the red lights lighting up both sides of the phone. She ignored them for a couple of minutes, putting down her handbag, taking off her jacket and booting up her computer, trying to remain calm. Finally she settled at her desk, straightened some papers, sharpened a pencil and counted up the hours of her marriage (one thousand two hundred and sixty-eight) and then the hours of her separation (four hundred and two, give or take an hour or two). But she soon realised that she wouldn't be able to ignore the calls forever. At some point in the very near future she was going to have to answer not just one of them, but all of them. She took a deep breath and reached for the phone. 'Hello,' she said unenthusiastically.

'Is that Dr Dee?' said a woman's voice.

'Speaking,' Stella responded, closing her eyes tightly.

'My name is Evelyn Mercer, and I'm calling from LACSA, Lactating Couples of South Africa. We're a non-profit organisation, formed by myself and my husband in 1989.'

'Hello,' Stella said, dread knotting itself tightly in her stomach.

'I was hoping to have a moment of your time to discuss your most recent column regarding lactation. Would that be possible?' the woman asked. Her voice sounded tight, as if she was gritting her teeth while speaking.

'Absolutely,' Stella said, eyeing the rest of the angry flashing red lights desperate for her attention. 'I am so sorry about what happened and I hope you'll let me explain ...'

'You know, at LACSA, Lactating Couples of South Africa, we really don't appreciate being ridiculed,' the woman said, cutting Stella off. 'LACSA, Lactating Couples of South Africa, is actually a legitimate organisation formed to help people who find themselves stuck in a society which doesn't understand both sides of the story.'

'Yes, I absolutely understand,' Stella said, wondering why Evelyn insisted on saying the acronym first if she was then going to follow it with the full name of the organisation each time. 'There's been a terrible mistake and I never actually meant ...'

'It's hard enough getting over the stigma of being an organisation that supports couples who wish to enjoy the perfectly natural act of lactation together as a physical representation of their love, but then you people come along and destroy thirty years of hard work.' Evelyn barely stopped to take a breath. 'Enjoying lactation is actually perfectly natural. It can be a beautiful thing. And articles like yours do nothing to assist those who are curious about it. It's a crying shame when something like this happens! Here you are, in a position to help people, and instead you damn our good name ...'

'Absolutely,' Stella said, jumping in quickly. 'And please let me tell you how terribly sorry I am that this has happened. I just wish there was some way I could make it up to you folks at LACSA.'

'Oh,' Evelyn said, obviously surprised to hear an apology. 'Well, you know the cornerstone of LACSA, Lactating Couples of South Africa, is tolerance. It's in our manifesto. Perhaps you'd consider joining us at our next meeting?'

'Oh,' Stella said, horrified at the thought of it.

'We meet on the first Thursday of every month at the Observatory Community Centre at seven o'clock. If you came we could enlighten you with some of the facts, so that next time you're faced with a query you'll be able to respond in a more, well, let's just say in a more educated and respectful manner.'

The thought of going to one of their meetings made Stella want to commit suicide immediately. Not only would she be forced to discuss lactation, but she could only imagine the scalding looks she'd get from the crowd once they found out that she was the person who had bad-mouthed their beloved hobby. But if she turned them down and Denise found out she'd be in even bigger trouble, and if she were ever to attempt to reconstruct her career in journalism it was a good idea not to burn any more bridges. At this point she could do with as much goodwill as she could muster.

Stella took a deep breath. 'Sure, of course, definitely,' she said, jotting down the details on the pad in front of her. 'And, once again, Evelyn, I'm dreadfully sorry.'

Stella put the phone down and let out a big depressed sigh. She laid her head down on her desk and tried to ignore the ten other lines which were flashing at her angrily. It was going to be a very long day.

POPPY

Poppy followed Buck down the train's slim corridor, her backpack scraping and bouncing against the walls. She watched as he slid open a cabin door, stuck his head inside and then pulled it out again almost immediately, sliding the door closed again. 'Two old ducks,' he said, looking back at Poppy and scrunching up his nose.

They walked on to the next compartment, where Buck repeated the performance, sticking his head inside and snapping it back out again. 'Either somebody eating bad cheese or they just took their shoes off,' he said, pulling a face and carrying on down the passage.

Eventually, as they reached the last of the compartments towards the back end of the train, or the front end, depending which direction you were travelling in, Buck pulled a door open, stuck his head inside and then pulled his head out, beaming at Poppy. 'Empty,' he said triumphantly, holding the door open for her.

Poppy heaved a huge sigh of relief. She was exhausted. Being on the road all this time and lugging her stupid backpack halfway across the planet had really taken it out of her.

Inside, the cabin was small and snug. There were benches on both sides of the cabin, which folded out into makeshift beds, and a piece of wood was attached to the wall in between the benches that could be raised and bolted in place to make a makeshift table. 'Well, it's no Orient Express,' Poppy said, eyeing out their new home, 'but at least it's ours.'

Poppy dumped her backpack and sank down gratefully onto the bench, watching as Buck also sloughed off his backpack and collapsed on the bench directly across from her, stretching out his long legs.

Seconds later the compartment door slid open again and Buck and Poppy turned just in time to catch a glimpse of a full head of crazy black curls. The head disappeared out of the door just as fast as it had appeared, the door sliding partially closed, and Poppy heard furious whispering outside in the corridor. Seconds later the door slid open all the way and two girls stepped into the compartment.

'G'day,' the bushy-haired girl said in a strong Australian accent, 'mind if we bunk with you? All the other compartments are full, and some guy down there is eating something that smells really bad!'

The other girl had straight blonde hair and she nodded furiously in agreement with wide, pleading eyes.

Poppy looked at Buck and shrugged her shoulders. 'Hulle lyk goed,' she said. 'En hulle is beter as oue mense, of iets.'

Buck nodded at Poppy. 'Sure, come in, make yourselves at home,' he said, dragging his backpack out of the way before crossing over to sit next to Poppy on the opposite side of the cabin.

Just then the train came alive, lurching forward. The curly-haired girl lost her balance and stumbled forward, landing directly in Buck's lap. She scrabbled around trying to get her balance and Poppy watched with amusement as she landed a flat palm straight in Buck's crotch. Both Buck and the girl blushed from head to toe. 'I'm so sorry!' she said, finally managing to steady herself and leaping off Buck as fast as she could. 'I wasn't expecting the train to move like that!'

Buck burst out laughing. 'Really, it's fine. Are you okay?' he asked her.

'Yes, fine. I didn't hurt you, did I?' she asked, making her way carefully over to the bench and sitting down next to her friend.

'No, no, really, I'm fine, it's fine ...' Buck stuttered. 'Although girls normally make me buy them dinner first.'

All four of them burst out laughing and Poppy smiled at Buck, only he could break the ice like that.

As the train gathered speed and left the station the girls busied themselves, stowing their bags and stripping off their heavy coats.

'I'm Poppy,' Poppy said as soon as they were settled, sticking her hand out towards the curly-haired girl first.

'I'm Nancy,' she said.

'And I'm Shirley,' the blonde girl said. It was the first time she'd spoken and she also had a thick Australian accent.

'Buck,' Buck said, shaking hands with both girls.

Nancy clapped her hands together in relief. 'You can't believe how close that was, we almost missed the train, eh, Shirley?'

'Oh, yeah, too tight. It was your fault, though, I told you it was eight o'clock, not eight thirty,' Shirley said, looking accusingly at her friend.

'So where are you guys from?' Nancy asked, appraising them both across the compartment.

'Cape Town, South Africa,' Poppy said, smiling and nodding at the girls' backpacks, which looked as well-worn as hers and Buck's. 'Have you guys been on the road for long?'

'A couple of months,' Nancy said. 'We've been touring Europe. We're heading to Paris now, just to see what all the fuss is about.'

'Us too!' Buck said. 'We figure you can't come to Europe and not swing by Paris, right?'

'That's what we thought,' Nancy said. 'It's supposed to be the most romantic city in the world, so I guess you never know what could happen there, right?'

Poppy might have been imagining it, but she was sure Nancy was giving Buck the eye.

'So where in Australia are you guys from?' Poppy asked. Their accents were so thick there was no hiding their origin.

'We're from Melbourne,' Shirley said. 'We're taking a gap year.'

'Hey, us too,' Buck said, grinning.

He must have noticed Nancy fancied him, Poppy thought, there was no other explanation for his enormous cheesy grin.

'It's going to be a long trip,' Poppy said, more to break the silence that had fallen than anything else. 'I suppose we'd better get comfortable.'

Poppy bent over her backpack and pulled out a jersey which she balled up and shoved against the window like a pillow, leaning her head against it. The motion of the train was incredibly soothing and she was so tired that she quickly lapsed into a trance, watching the streets flash by outside the window as they slowly made their way towards the outskirts of the city. Across from her Shirley dug in her own backpack and pulled out an iPod, which she plugged into her ears. Poppy could hear Nancy and Buck chatting away. Buck had discovered that Nancy and Shirley had also been to Amsterdam and they were busy comparing notes, chatting about where they'd stayed and which coffee shops they'd gone to. Poppy could hear Nancy giggling and flirting. She turned her focus back on the scenery and it wasn't long before her tired mind blocked out their natter altogether.

Poppy must have fallen asleep, lulled by the motion of the train, and when she eventually opened her eyes it took her a second to figure out where she was. It was pitch dark outside and it was only when she heard the Australian accents of the two girls that she remembered that she was on a train on her way across Europe. She sat up and turned her neck, trying to stretch out the crick that had developed from sleeping with her head over to the side. Looking around the cabin, she saw that Buck, Nancy and Shirley were playing cards. They were playing something that looked like snap, and every time someone put down a similar card they all shrieked with excitement. A bottle of red wine and a couple of paper cups had appeared from somewhere and they were passing the bottle around, filling their cups liberally between rounds.

'Morning, sunshine,' Buck said.

'How long was I asleep?' Poppy asked.

'Only about an hour.'

Poppy stood up and stretched out. 'Mmmm, just going to find a loo,' she said, slipping past Buck and nipping out of the compartment.

By the time she returned the game had become even more raucous. She slid back onto the bench and watched the rest of the hand.

'Wanna play?' Nancy asked, raking in all the cards and shuffling them. 'It works better with four, anyway.'

'Sure, why not,' Poppy said.

'It's as easy as pie,' Nancy said, starting to deal out the now shuffled cards. 'We divide the cards up evenly between all of us, and then everybody turns a card over at the same time. If two or more of you have the same card then you shout out WAR and lay out three more cards. You each then turn one of them over, and the person with the highest card wins all those cards. And the person left with all the cards at the end wins. See, like I said, easy.'

Poppy nodded, not entirely sure of the rules, but how hard could it be, she thought, she would pick it up as they went along.

Nancy dealt out the cards and Shirley first filled her own paper cup with wine and then held the bottle up to Poppy, 'Want some wine?' she asked. 'We bought it here in Germany, their wine is soooo good. We bought tons of it.'

Poppy smiled. 'Thanks, that would be great.'

'Everybody ready?' Nancy said as Shirley pulled out a spare paper cup and poured some wine for Poppy. 'Then let's go.'

The game was simple and Poppy soon caught on; every time someone had a match the compartment erupted.

'Hey, I've got an idea,' Nancy piped up, after they'd played a couple of hands. 'Let's make it a bit of a drinking game. Every time you get a matching card with someone else, you both have to drink.'

They bantered a bit and then got to playing again. It was a quick, fun game and Poppy found herself drinking and refilling her cup a number of times. At one point she looked over at Buck and noticed that he and Nancy were touching legs under the table. She nudged him and when he looked at her she smiled a silly, naughty smile. It felt strange to see Buck engaging with someone else; they'd become so close over the last couple of months that she couldn't imagine him spending time with anyone other than her. She wasn't jealous, or at least she didn't think she was, she just wasn't used to it.

As they played they swapped travelling stories. Buck told the story about Poppy and her 'winnings' in Las Vegas, and Shirley told them about their pathetic attempts at skiing in Germany.

'I mean neither of us has ever seen anything even close to snow before,' Shirley said. 'Where we come from winter is when it doesn't go above twenty-nine degrees for a month or two. You should have seen this one.' Shirley pointed a finger at Nancy. 'She almost killed herself. You know those ski lift things? Well, when we reached the top of the mountain, and you had to jump off, I jumped off and rolled down the hill and landed face first in the snow, but when I look up, she's still on the chairlift. Somehow she managed to get her windbreaker caught on the chair. They had to stop the entire machine, leaving everyone else dangling, and some guys had to climb up and help her off!'

'We gave up in the end. Reckoned we'd be better off going to the bar and drinking Glühwein instead,' Nancy said. 'Fortunately you don't need to learn how to ski to drink Glühwein!'

Poppy realised she was suddenly quite drunk. She hadn't eaten since lunchtime and the wine had gone straight to her head. She rummaged in her backpack and pulled out a small loaf of bread and some ham and cheese they'd bought in Hamburg. 'It's no five-course meal,' she said as she offered it around. 'But it might help soak up some of this wine!'

They played cards for a few more hours, polishing off another three bottles of wine between them. Some hours later, when Poppy had lost track of the game altogether, she tossed her cards into the middle of the table. 'That's me done,' she slurred drunkenly. 'I need to lie down before I fall down!'

Everybody shouted loud protests, but Poppy was too drunk to care. 'G'night,' she slurred, shoving her jersey against the cool window of the compartment and closing her eyes as the rhythmical movement of the train rocked her into a drunken coma.

Poppy woke up to somebody prodding her hard in the shoulder.

'Mademoiselle, mademoiselle,' said a voice with a thick French accent. 'C'est arrive.'

Poppy peeled her eyes open. Her mouth felt like it was fleece-lined and it tasted like she'd eaten a mouldy shoe. She sat up and nodded at the conductor, hoping that it would be enough to get him to stop speaking so loudly and poking her so hard. Luckily her plan worked, and as soon as he was sure she was awake he disappeared out of the compartment, leaving the door open.

Poppy looked out of the window. The train had stopped, and it was early morning. She saw a sign that said *Gare du Nord* outside her window. They must have arrived in Paris, she thought. The platform was alive with activity. People were busy dragging their luggage off the train and heading en masse towards the exit.

A searing pain shot through her brain and she suddenly recalled the litres of red wine they'd drunk. Looking around she saw that Buck was passed out on the seat next to her. He had his mouth open and his eyes shut and he was snoring loudly. Poppy stretched her arms above her head. Her entire body ached, mainly from her hangover but partly also from having slept half slouched down, half sitting up, with her neck cricked to one side against the cold glass window. She stretched her neck out and it cracked loudly; she must have been so out of it that she hadn't moved a muscle in hours. Suddenly Poppy noticed something. The opposite bench was empty. She wondered where the Aussie girls had disappeared to. Her memory was hazy, but Nancy was the forward one with the black curly hair. What was the other one's name? The quieter one; the one with greasy blonde hair; the one who had been sitting opposite her? Poppy racked her brain. She could see her face in her mind's eye, but she couldn't remember her name. Standing up, she kicked Buck gently on the leg and when he didn't budge she kicked him again, this time harder and slightly higher up, right below his knee. 'Oi, Buck,' she shouted, kicking him a third time, this time nailing him right in the middle of his shin. 'Get up! We're here. We're in Paris.'

On the fourth kick Buck grunted and opened his eyes slowly, rubbing them and stretching out his body. 'Fuck, I feel like crap!' he said, his voice thick with sleep. His lips and teeth were stained red, which only reminded Poppy again of just how much cheap red wine they had both had to drink. She winced at the thought of it. 'Yeah, not the best we've ever looked, if I'm honest,' she said, stretching her arms again, as high above her head as she could without bashing into the roof of the compartment. 'Hey, did you hear the girls go?'

'No, I was dead to the world, I didn't hear anything,' Buck said. 'Do you think they got off and didn't say bye? That's a bit rude, don't you think?'

'Maybe they didn't want to wake us,' Poppy said. 'Shame, Buckie-poo, are you sad that your girlfriend didn't give you a kiss goodbye? Is your heart broken?'

'Hey, where's my backpack?' Buck asked, turning around a full three-sixty degrees.

Poppy looked around the compartment. Strangely, she couldn't see her backpack anywhere either. There were empty bottles of wine and empty cups strewn everywhere, but no backpacks. Her heart skipped a beat as she felt panic set in. 'Fuck,' she said. 'Where the fuck are our bags?'

'Maybe a porter took them when we arrived?' Buck said, checking carefully under the benches.

Poppy darted out of the compartment and caught sight of a conductor coming out of one of the compartments further down the train. She raced over to him. 'Excuse me, Sir. Our bags are missing,' she said in a panicked voice. 'Is there any way one of the porters has carried them outside onto the platform?'

The conductor looked up at her with uncomprehending eyes, 'Je ne parle pas anglais,' he said, shrugging his shoulders.

'Fuck, fuck, fuck!' Poppy swore, racing back to Buck who was standing in the middle of the compartment with both hands on his hips and a perturbed look on his face.

An hour later Poppy and Buck stood on the platform trying to explain to a pair of French policemen what had happened, the language barrier making things much trickier than they needed to be.

'By the time they understand what you're telling them those girls will be in Spain,' Buck grouched, crossing his arms angrily across his chest. 'Fuck, man!'

'Two Australian girls,' Poppy said, starting her story again from the beginning, holding out her fingers to indicate the number two. 'One had crazy curly black hair.' She shot her hands away from her head to indicate wild, curly hair.

'Zese gels, did zey ave ze weapon?' one policeman asked Poppy in heavily accented English.

Poppy shook her head. 'No,' she said, 'but we think they must have drugged us with sleeping pills or Rohypnol or something, and then we think they just got off the train while we were passed out and took our bags with them. Don't you have CCTV cameras or something? We could identify them for you!' Poppy waved her arms around like a crazy woman. 'You should be chasing them now! They're getting away! You have to stop them!'

'Mademoiselle was not watching ze luggage, non?' the policeman asked, ignoring the entire second half of Poppy's comments.

'No, of course not, we were sleeping!' Poppy said, deciding not to mention the three bottles of wine that had been a precursor to the sleeping.

'But ze conductor, he say this girls were your friends, non?' the policeman said, his face scrunched up in confusion.

This was useless, Poppy thought. Letting her arms drop by her sides she turned to look hopelessly at Buck. If this cop ended one more sentence with the word 'non' she might have to throttle him, or maybe just breathe on him, which would probably be worse.

'What's the point?' Buck said to Poppy, shrugging his shoulders, dejected. 'They're long gone, and so is our stuff.'

'I can't believe you let your girlfriend steal our stuff!' Poppy shrieked. She knew she was being irrational, it wasn't his fault, they had both been equally drunk and stupid, but she needed to blame someone. 'All our money, our clothes, our passports, everything, all gone!' she wailed, tears rolling down her cheeks. 'You shouldn't have told them about the Vegas money. I bet that's why they took our stuff.'

Buck took her in his arms and gave her a big bear hug as she cried. He stank of red wine and body odour.

'Paris sucks!' Poppy sobbed. 'And I don't care what anybody says, it's not even the least bit romantic!'

STELLA

'Has it been really awful?' Iris asked.

Stella nodded, not trusting herself for a moment to speak without crying. She snivelled and looked down into her lap. 'I had to field calls from so many angry readers, Mom.' She took a deep breath. 'There were all these furious church groups, ten different non-profit organisations and every gay rights activist in the country. You can't believe how angry everybody is at me. And it's been a week. I mean, I thought the calls would have died down by now, but they're just as hectic as they were on Monday. And you can't believe all the letters of apology I've had to write ...'

'Oh, Stel, I am sorry. But I don't really understand what happened with your column, dear?' Iris prodded gently. 'Why would you say those things?'

'I told you a million times, they printed the wrong copy,' Stella said, her lips turned down at the corners, her voice quiet and shaky. 'I would never say those things in public, Mom, you know that. It was a mistake. And now I keep wondering if it's even worth pulling together my CV. My name is mud. I don't think anyone else will ever hire me. What am I going to do with my life now?'

They sat in silence for a couple of minutes.

'I'm sure you feel terrible right now, Stella, but you know, it may not actually be the worst thing that's ever happened to you,' Iris said matter-of-factly.

'What do you mean, it may not be the worst thing that's ever happened to me?' Stella said angrily, wiping away her tears. 'I lost my job! I got fired, Mom! How is that not the worst thing that's ever happened to me?'

'Well, let's be honest, you never really liked that job, Stel,' her mom said gently. 'Did you?'

Stella looked at her.

'You were always complaining about it, and it's not like it's what you really want to do for the rest of your life, is it? But if this hadn't happened, then what's the betting that you'd still be doing it in three years' time and still be hating it, probably even more than you do now.'

Stella didn't respond. She just wiped her leaking eyes with her fingers.

'At least now you don't have a choice, Mother Nature or karma or fate, or whatever has forced you to get out there and find a different job. Maybe something that you actually like,' Iris continued. 'See, it could be a good thing.'

Stella thought about it. Her mom wasn't entirely wrong. Mothers seldom were. 'I suppose you've got a point,' Stella said. 'I just wish it didn't have to happen like this.'

'But it *had* to happen like this, Stella,' Iris said. 'Don't you see? And anyway, you wrote under the pseudonym Dr Dee. In a little bit things will die down, and after that nobody ever has to know it was you.'

They sat in silence again for another couple of minutes.

'Are you going to be all right here on your own tonight, Stella?' Iris asked, glancing at her watch. 'Do you want me to cancel my plans? Your father's gone out with some friends and I don't know when he'll be back.'

'Where are you going?' Stella asked, looking up at her mom with a pathetic look on her face.

'I have a date, dear,' Iris said, bending down and kissing her on the top of her head.

Stella cringed. The thought of her mother with Mr Davies was nauseating. 'No, go!' she said, shuddering. 'I'll be fine. I'm exhausted. I'm going to try and get an early night.'

'Chin up, love,' Iris said. 'There are microwave meals in the bar fridge on the dining room table, and Violet loaned us a microwave. Things could be worse.'

Stella prodded at her broccoli, shuffling it around the tray till it disintegrated. There is nothing more depressing than a microwave meal for one, she thought as she sliced through a piece of chicken breast and popped it into her mouth. It tasted like the packaging it came in.

Stella wondered what Max was doing for dinner and whether he was also having a meal for one, or whether he was out, it was a Friday night, after all. The one upside of no longer living with him was that she didn't have to do all the shopping and cooking every single night. It was the one side effect of their separation that she thought she could get used to. Cooking every day was exhausting, particularly when the person you're cooking for has a mother who's pretty much made everything before, and seemed to have made it perfectly. It had been a lot to live up to.

Stella chased a pea around the plastic container before stabbing it with one of the tines of her fork. It popped and deflated instantly, like a plastic beach ball with a hole in it, going limp and mushy. As much as she enjoyed not being pressured to cook every night, she hated eating alone, it was soul destroying. She ate a few more mouthfuls of plastic chicken, then pushed her lukewarm, half-eaten meal for one away from her with her fork. Getting up, she grabbed her car keys and headed for the front door. Halfway there she stopped, turned around and went back to her bedroom to fetch her cap, scarf and sunglasses.

Stella did three drive-bys on Davenport Road. She hadn't been back to the apartment since the morning of the garbage raid, but nothing much seemed to have changed. The flat was dark, except for the bluish-green glow of the television coming from the lounge.

Stella yawned as she pulled into an empty parking space. It had been a long, tiring week. She turned on the radio, 5FM was playing the latest Katy Perry, KFM was belting out something by Whitney Houston and Good Hope FM was playing an R & B track she couldn't identify. Then she tuned into 567, the talk radio station. Max had always called it Nerd Radio, and had teased her whenever she listened to it. But Stella liked it. It was informative and comforting. Except tonight they were talking about animal abuse and that was too heavy a subject for her after the kind of week she'd had, so she turned off the radio and sat in silence, tapping her finger on the steering wheel.

Her hip throbbed and she scratched at it over the top of her jeans, but it stung when she touched it. Stella yawned again and wondered what Lucy was doing. She missed her so much. There was a huge Lucy-shaped chasm in her life.

Stella turned on the car and pulled out of the space. She trawled down Davenport Road two more times, and then she left.

Stella drove down High Level Road in Sea Point, slowing down outside Lucy's apartment block. It was just after eleven, but in spite of the late hour there were no parking spaces available on the busy road directly outside Lucy's apartment, so instead Stella pulled into a bus stop a little way down the street. Craning her neck to see into Lucy's lounge, she noticed that there was still a light on. She wondered what her sister was doing, whether she had a hot date over or maybe just some friends for dinner.

Moments later Stella was surprised to see the lounge light go out. Lucy must be going to bed, she thought. Sitting up straight Stella turned the key in her ignition; it was time to go home. But before she could ease out of her parking space the front door of the apartment block opened, and someone stepped out. It was Lucy. Stella gasped and slunk down as far as she could in her seat, pulling her peak cap down over her face. She was pretty sure that she was parked far enough away from the block of flats that Lucy wouldn't be able to see her, but she stayed as hidden as she could and kept her car lights off, just in case.

Lucy was wearing a pair of black jeans, a black top and her black All Star Hi-Tops; her hair in a casual ponytail. Stella watched her walk down the front steps of the apartment and get into her car, which was parked directly outside on the street. She wondered where she could be going at eleven o'clock on a Friday night – she was too casually dressed for a bar or a nightclub or any kind of party. Starting her car, Lucy turned on the lights and flicked on her indicator, waiting for a break in the traffic. Maybe she was going to the 7-Eleven to get milk and a chocolate or something, Stella thought.

When Lucy eased into the flow of the traffic Stella waited for a couple of cars to come past and then she pulled out too, following Lucy's car down the street from a safe distance. Her sister remained on High Level Road, going towards town, driving past the turn-off that would have taken her to the corner shop at the bottom of Glengariff Road. Then, when she hit the top of Strand Street, she drove on into the centre of the city. 'Where on earth are you going?' Stella said out loud, tapping a finger on the steering wheel, still slunk down in her seat as far as she could go. This was hardly the time of night to go for a scenic drive.

Crossing Adderley, Lucy drove past the Golden Acre and the train station. Stella was flummoxed, she didn't know anyone who lived out this way, and Lucy was starting to head into a dodgier territory.

As Lucy cruised past the Good Hope Centre, Stella furrowed her brow. 'Woodstock!' she muttered. 'Lucy, what the hell are you doing in Woodstock?' Her nerves were on edge. Why would Lucy be driving into such an awful area on her own so late at night?

Stella had to be extra careful now, because Lucy was slowing down each time she drove past a street. Stella figured that she was reading the street signs, trying to find the right side street, and sure enough a few streets into Woodstock Lucy took a right turn into a small, dark side street. Stella slowed right down, she couldn't follow her straight away, Lucy would definitely see her then as they would be the only two cars driving up the narrow side street. Pulling over, she counted to twenty, her eyes wide with the thought of what she was doing – her knuckles white on the steering wheel.

As soon as she'd finished counting Stella pulled back onto Woodstock Main Road and turned into the road Lucy had turned into. As she turned she caught sight of Lucy in the distance, taking a left into a road that ran parallel to the main road. Stella drove achingly slowly, not sure if she was more terrified of Lucy discovering that she had followed her or of what might await them in one of the most dangerous areas of Cape Town late on a dark Friday night. Stella eyed the street nervously, even though it was completely deserted, and took a left into the street Lucy had turned into. Lucy's car was about three hundred metres ahead of her and Stella pulled over at the kerb a safe distance away, turning off her lights as she watched her sister do the same.

On Stella's left was the back of some kind of factory and on the right-hand side of the street was a small row of old, mostly derelict houses. Looking nervously in her rear-view mirror again, to make sure there wasn't anyone behind her, Stella leant as far forward in her seat as she could, straining to get a better view of what her sister was up to. Up ahead Lucy was already out of her car, and Stella watched as she looked up and down the street before hurrying over to one of the houses directly across from her parked car. Stella couldn't see the house itself, as it sat safely behind an unpainted eight-foot wall topped with broken glass, but she could see the entrance to the property – a battered door covered in peeling paint – and it was clear that Lucy was headed straight for it. Perspiration beaded on Stella's top lip and her heart thundered in her chest as she peered into the night to try and see what her sister was doing.

Seconds later the door opened a little and a tall, thin coloured man stuck his head out and eyed Lucy up and down. They were quite far away, so Stella had to squint to see what was going on, but it looked like they were having some kind of conversation. The man said a few words to Lucy and Lucy responded, standing casually, her arms by her side.

Conversation complete, the man opened the door just wide enough to let Lucy in. 'Don't go in there alone!' Stella whispered as her sister disappeared inside, squeezing the life out of her steering wheel. 'No, Lucy, are you crazy?'

As soon as she was sure the door was closed Stella started her car. Keeping her headlights off she drove down the street and pulled in behind Lucy's car. She was so scared now that she didn't care if Lucy knew she was there. The only thing she cared about was whether Lucy would still be alive long enough to care that Stella had stalked her.

Stella covered her face with her hands and wiped the sweat off her lip and forehead. Then, nervously, she looked up and down the street once again. Her hands were shaking uncontrollably and she was finding it hard to breathe. She didn't know what to do. What if Lucy was in danger? What if someone was murdering her right this second while Stella sat outside in the car doing nothing? She realised that she was in the middle of what could potentially be one of the worst moments of her life. Worse than lying to her husband or sleeping with her identical twin sister's boyfriend. Worse than having to move back home and losing her job. This moment, she thought, could surpass everything else.

Stella maintained her watch and tried to manage her breathing. She focused on the door, only taking her eyes off it long enough to check up and down the street at regular intervals, praying desperately for it to open and for Lucy to trot back out in one piece. She willed it to happen, but after what felt like eons with no sign of Lucy she went into full scale panic mode. Whatever Lucy was doing in there was taking way too long, she thought. Something had almost certainly gone horribly wrong.

Slipping the keys out of the ignition Stella climbed out of her car and closed the door silently behind her. Looking both ways she crossed the road, listening closely for anything that could be a shriek or a scream or a gunshot.

Stella stood in front of the door and tried to decide what to do next. There was no handle on the outside and the only other means of access she could see was a small white doorbell nailed onto the door jamb. Making up her mind she pressed it once, quickly, and then pulled her finger away from it. The buzzer made no sound, so she considered pressing it again, but she wasn't sure whether it was broken or if it was one of those bells that only rings inside the house, so she waited a couple of seconds, looking up and down the street again nervously.

The door opened just a crack, and the same tall coloured man who had let Lucy in earlier stuck his head out. 'Ja?' he said.

Stella noticed that he barely had any of his own teeth left. His gums had a large gap along the top row, which she could see his pink tongue through.

Stella cleared her throat. 'Um, yes, hello, Sir,' she said, her voice wobbling and her knees shaking. 'I'm so sorry to bother you, Sir. I'm looking for my sister; you just let her in a couple of minutes ago. She looks like me, we're twins.'

The man stared at Stella for a second without changing his expression, then he looked out into the street and craned his neck to see if there was anyone coming or going. Satisfied they were alone, and she wasn't of any immediate danger, he opened the door and let her in. 'Quickly,' he said, sounding irritated at the disturbance.

Having made it through the door, Stella followed the tall man nervously up a concrete path that led through the middle of a dusty patch of dirt and unkempt weeds, to a wooden front door. As the man held the door open for her she noticed that there was a trellis door on the outside of the house as well as another metal security door on the inside. Stella knew it was a bad area, but this kind of security seemed like overkill, she thought, as she made her way inside reluctantly.

Once she was inside the man pulled all three doors closed. Stella heard first the metallic slide of the trellis door and the *klunk* as the lock caught, then the wooden *thunk* of the actual front door before, finally, the metallic groan of the inside door. Oh, my God, Stella thought, what have I done? We're locked in. Now we're both going to die.

'Excuse me, Sir …' Stella said, her voice a nervous whisper.

'In here,' the man said sternly, ushering her into the very first room on the right-hand side of the hall. 'Your sister's busy now with Oupa! You must wait here, nè. She's coming now.'

As the man pushed past her and sat down on one of the couches Stella looked around the room. She counted six other people sprawled over the couches and the chairs that it held. Two of them were haggard-looking women of indeterminate age, who, judging by their outfits, were probably hookers. The rest were men, ranging in age from around eighteen to somewhere near forty. Like the guy who had let her in, she noticed that very few of them, including the women, had any real teeth of their own. The other thing she noticed was that they were all completely stoned out of their heads. Two of the men were having an intense conversation on one of the couches, speaking so quickly that Stella was unable to keep up, barely waiting for the other to finish before speaking again. In fact, it was less like they were talking to each other and more like they were talking at each other. The other guy was a kid of about eighteen, slouched listlessly on the second couch. As she watched the man who'd let her in slapped the kid on the head, forcing him to shove up so there was enough space between them in the middle of the couch for Stella to sit down. Stella really didn't want to sit down on the disgusting couch, the thought of it made her skin crawl. She wanted to stay standing, ready to run, or hide, or kick, or take some kind of action when things went bad, but she also didn't want to be rude. She would have much rather remained standing, shifting from foot to foot nervously in the doorway, ready to bolt at the first sign of danger, but Stella knew that upsetting any of the people in this room might be seriously bad for her health.

Briefly she craned her neck and looked all the way down the corridor in the desperate hope that she might catch a glimpse of Lucy, but she couldn't see anything, the corridor was pitch black. What could she possibly be doing in this house? Stella wondered. And how could it be taking so long? It felt like Lucy had been in the house for decades.

Stella looked skittishly back into the room, running her fingers nervously over her pockets to check that her cellphone was there. Not that it would help; she didn't have anyone she could call if things suddenly got out of hand. How could she explain that she'd been stalking her sister and had then followed her into a derelict house in the middle of Woodstock for God knew what? She didn't even know where she would start to explain their situation.

Stepping forward into the room Stella sat down in the spot on the couch between the two men. Satisfied that she had settled in, the two hookers slipped into a quiet, slurred debate about who owed who a cigarette. Their eyes were red and glassy and they spoke slowly and incoherently. Stella wondered what they were on, but she didn't know enough about drugs to even guess.

Stella glanced down at her watch nervously, amazed to discover that it had been less than ten minutes since she'd first pulled up to the house behind Lucy's Golf. Looking up again, she made accidental eye contact with the kid and he smiled at her lasciviously. She half-smiled back nervously and then looked away as fast as she could, her foot tapping nervously on the stained carpet. She mustn't make eye contact with any of them again, she told herself, eye contact would only lead to some kind of conversation and she couldn't handle that.

Stella heard a door open and close in the bowels of the house. Holding her breath she watched the door to the room carefully, listening out for footsteps. Finally Lucy appeared just outside the room and Stella jumped off the couch and raced over to her. She'd never been more relieved to see anyone in her entire life.

'Stella, what the fuck are you doing here?' Lucy said, looking surprised, caught completely off guard.

'Thank goodness you're okay!' Stella whispered.

'But what are you doing here?' Lucy asked again, her face a picture of confusion.

'That's what I should be asking you!' Stella said. 'What the hell are you doing here? I followed you ...' Stella blushed. 'I mean, I came to your flat earlier because I wanted to talk to you,' she said, the lie falling out naturally. 'But as I pulled up I saw you come out the flat, so I just followed you. I thought maybe you were just going to the shop to get milk or something, and that I would surprise you. But what the hell are you doing here? What is this place?'

'I can't believe you fucking followed me,' Lucy said, her face angry and astonished. 'And then you came inside?'

'Please can we get out of here first, before you shout at me!' Stella said. Then she turned and spoke to the man on the couch who'd let her in. 'Thank you for having us, Sir,' she said politely, but he wasn't listening – he had become involved in the cigarette conversation with the two hookers, informing them that they actually both owed him a cigarette, and so he barely even looked up as Stella left the room and followed a fuming Lucy as she stomped down the passageway.

'Thank God you're all right,' Stella whispered as they reached the front door. 'I was terrified something was going to happen to you!'

'I can't believe you followed me in here!' Lucy hissed. 'What's wrong with you?'

'I was worried about you, okay? Plus, I didn't like being out there in the car by myself. It's dark and scary,' Stella whispered. 'Please can we talk about this outside? I really want to get out of here.'

The tall, thin man suddenly appeared in the corridor behind them. He must have won his argument as he had an unlit cigarette between his lips and another tucked neatly behind his ear. Stella watched him striding towards them purposefully down the passageway. Fear overwhelmed her as he approached and she squeezed her eyes shut as tightly as she could as the guy stretched his hand out towards her. There was a moment of silence and then she heard the sound of the first security door opening. She unscrewed her eyes and saw that the man had simply reached across her to open the door for them. Once that was open he unlocked and opened the front door and then he unlocked and slid open the outside trellis door. Holding all three doors open he ushered them both outside. Then, once they were over the threshold, he shut everything behind them without a word. As Stella heard the clicks and clunks of all three doors being shut and securely locked behind them she couldn't help but breathe a sigh of relief. They were both still alive; she couldn't believe it. They were outside the house and there was just the short pathway down to the door in the wall, and then they would be on the street again and safely in their cars.

Shaking her head Lucy pushed past Stella and began to stride down the path ahead of her, then, abruptly, she stopped and turned to face Stella, her eyes flashing with a furious anger. 'You couldn't just leave me alone, could you?' she shouted, her face red with rage. 'Are you that pathetic that you had to follow me?'

'Lucy, what is this place?' Stella whispered, ignoring Lucy's questions. 'What are you doing here?'

'If you must know, Stella, this is where I buy my dope!' Lucy shouted, throwing a small bank bag at Stella.

'Drugs?' Stella asked, bending down and picking the bank bag up off the floor. 'Jesus, Luce, do you know how dangerous it is out here?'

Tossing the bag back to Lucy, Stella pushed past her sister and made for the door. She couldn't believe Lucy could be this stupid, and that she would be idiotic enough to follow her.

'Yeah, but it's worth it,' Lucy said, opening the small bag in her hand and dipping her fingers in. 'This is the best Malawi Gold money can buy.'

'Can we please just get out of here?' Stella hissed, grabbing the door handle and pulling it open.

She stopped dead in her tracks.

'Oh, don't be such a scaredy-cat,' Lucy said mockingly from where she still stood on the path. 'You're pathetic. I bet you've never even smoked dope. You're always such a goody two-shoes. It wouldn't do you any harm, you know, to have a little fun. And this is the best place in town to get it.'

'Lucy,' Stella hissed, interrupting her, her voice shaking.

'Hey, they even gave me a bit of a discount tonight. Said it's 'cos he recognised me from the last time, he said I'm now a preferred customer and ...'

'Lucy!' Stella whispered, louder now and more urgently.

Lucy strode over to where Stella had stalled at the open door. 'What, Stella!' she asked, irritated. 'What the hell is it now?'

But Stella couldn't answer. She was speechless. The street was full of police cars and four policemen were standing right in front of her, each one pointing a gun directly at her head.

'Oh shit!' Lucy said, dropping the bag of weed on the floor, where it spilled out at her feet. Then both Lucy and Stella slowly raised their arms in the air above their heads.

The cell stank. Stella lifted her knees up to her chest, pressed her feet onto the wooden bench and leaned back against the cold cement wall. Then she pushed her face into her knees to try and block out the smell. It was a mixture of sweat and urine and human excrement and vomit and despair.

'It really stinks in here,' she whispered as quietly as she could to Lucy.

'What did you expect, the One&Only?' Lucy said, her voice cold.

'I can't believe we're in prison!' Stella hissed.

'I can't believe you followed me!' Lucy said.

'I said I was sorry, okay!' Stella whined. 'I was worried about you.'

'Whatever!' Lucy said, looking away.

There were twelve other women in the cell with them, all in various states of dress, sobriety and mental competency. One homeless-looking lady was curled up asleep on the floor in a corner, although Stella was only assuming she was asleep, she may just as easily have been dead, particularly since Stella couldn't imagine how she could fall so soundly asleep on the cold, hard, filthy concrete floor. Besides the smell, the noise was unbearable. The men's drunk tank was next door to their cell and it sounded like it was full; it had obviously been a very busy Friday night at the cop shop.

A tall, fat policeman appeared at the cell door and eyed the inhabitants warily, making sure nobody was making too much trouble. 'Frankel!' he shouted.

Both Lucy and Stella jumped up simultaneously and raced to the door of the cell, clutching the bars.

'Which one of yous is Frankel?' the cop asked, looking at them both with bored, red-rimmed eyes.

'We both are,' Stella said, excited at the prospect of getting out of the cell.

The cop looked down at his clipboard and then back up at them, confused. 'It says here that there's only one Frankel,' he said.

'Well, technically I'm a De Villiers now, that's my married name, but I used to be a Frankel, and really I still am because I'm not with my husband any more,' Stella said, sounding desperate.

'Look, lady!' the man said sternly through his bushy moustache. 'Yous not a Frankel. Yous a De Villiers. Where's Lucy Frankel?'

'That's me,' Lucy said, raising a hand.

'Yous can make a telephone call now,' the officer said, letting Lucy out of the cell. 'And don't yous give me any more trouble, hey, lady!' he added, pointing a fat finger at Stella.

Stella watched nervously through the cell bars as Lucy disappeared with the officer.

As Stella returned to her seat and slumped back down again a very dark-skinned woman got up from a bench across the cell and approached her in a slow and deliberate manner. She was wearing a minuscule miniskirt, a revealing top and a big curly black-and-purple wig; even without shoes she was almost six feet tall.

The woman sat down next to Stella, who tried to slide away from her as inconspicuously as possible. She didn't want to offend the woman, but she was also terrified.

'They took shoes,' the woman said to Stella in broken English, pointing at her bare feet.

Stella looked down between her knees and studied the woman's large bare feet. Her toenails had been painted a burgundy colour, but it wasn't the badly applied polish that caught Stella's attention, it was something else. Something was different. Something was wrong. Stella couldn't figure it out at first, but after a couple of seconds she realised that the woman only had four toes on her right foot. Her baby toe was missing.

'They don't want let me wearing stilettos here,' the woman said. 'To can be use as weapon.'

Stella wasn't sure if she was required to respond, so she just sat still and wished she was invisible.

'Cigarette?' the woman said, raising her voice slightly.

'No, thank you, I don't smoke,' Stella said politely.

'No! Give me cigarette,' the woman reiterated, her voice loud, gruff and demanding.

'Sorry, I don't smoke,' Stella said in a scared half-whisper, chewing her lip nervously. She knew it was important not to exude fear, but she also knew that she would be no match for the woman, with or without stilettos. If she happened to take a dislike to Stella for whatever reason, Stella was sure she would be dead long before the cops came to rescue her.

'I like shoes,' the woman said, pointing with a long purple fingernail at Stella's feet.

Stella nodded at her.

'I say, I like shoes,' the woman said again, this time a little more aggressively, pointing down at Stella's takkies again. 'They me size, I think.'

Stella looked at her again. The woman had shifted even closer to her and their bodies were now touching. She had an angry, intent look on her face, and she licked her lips as she moved her gaze slowly between Stella's face and her shoes, her finger still pointing down at Stella's takkies.

'Oh!' Stella said, understanding where the conversation was going. 'I understand. Would you like them?'

'Good, yes!' the woman said to her, nodding slowly.

Stella was unsure what to do next, but she realised that the only way she might get rid of the woman without getting injured would be to hand over her shoes. Slowly she bent down and undid the laces on each shoe, then she slipped them off and handed both of them over.

The woman slipped them on, first the five-toed foot, and then the four-toed foot. They seemed a slightly tight squeeze, but with a little pushing and pulling she managed to get them on and lace them up. Then she held each foot out in front of her, admiring her new footwear as if she were in a shoe shop. Satisfied, she then shifted a couple of inches away from Stella and looked away, ignoring her completely, as if they'd never spoken.

Stella looked down at her socked feet, then back up at the cell, trying to act casual even though she was shaking with fear and rage. After a first initial sweep she took a deep breath, relieved that none of her other cellmates looked like they posed any imminent threat.

Eventually the policeman with the impressive moustache returned with Lucy. Stella jumped up and ran to the cell door.

'Where are your shoes, Stella?' Lucy asked as the guard let her back into the cell.

'Excuse me, officer,' Stella whispered as quietly as she could. 'That woman stole my shoes!'

The guard laughed at her, a rough unfunny kind of laugh. 'Lady, if you want to use the phone, now's your chance, hey,' he said. 'Or would you rather stay here and report the shoes?'

'No, no, let me out, I'll make my call now,' Stella said, desperate to be anywhere but in the cell.

Iris answered on the second ring.

'Mom, Lucy and I are in big trouble,' Stella said, starting to cry the second she heard her mother's voice.

'Oh, Stella, Lucy just called your father. What on earth is going on? What have you stupid girls done now?'

'It wasn't me,' Stella said pathetically. 'It was Lucy. I went to her flat. I wanted to talk to her, but then I saw her leaving, so I followed her, and she went to this place in Woodstock.' Stella looked up at the policeman who was standing next to her, listening in on her conversation. She didn't want to say anything that would implicate either of them, so she turned her head away from the policeman and whispered into the phone, covering her mouth and the mouthpiece with her free hand. 'I was so scared for her, Mom, and I didn't know where we were or what she was doing, so I followed her inside. It's such a dodgy area, and I wanted to make sure she was safe … And then the police came … And they put us in the back of a police van, Mom!'

'Are you both okay?' Iris asked, her tone practical and businesslike.

'We're fine,' Stella said, sniffing like a child. 'They've got us in a cell at Caledon Square. You and Dad have to come and get us out, straight away. Mom, I'm so sorry, everything is just such a mess right now!'

'Your father is on his cellphone with our lawyer, and we'll come down as soon as we can,' Iris said. 'But, Stella, listen to me, you need to pull yourself together, all right. Crying won't help anything right now, okay? You need to be brave.'

Stella sniffled. 'Okay,' she said in a very quiet voice. 'Mom, I need you to bring some antibacterial cream when you come, and also a pair of shoes.'

'Shoes and antibacterial cream?' Iris asked, sounding confused.

'Yes, this huge scary girl in the cell stole my shoes, and I've got this … this … this … thing on my hip, and I think it must have gotten infected or something, because it really hurts.'

'Really, Stella, I don't know what's gotten into you girls. Just try to be brave, and look after each other, and your father and I will come down as soon as we can and try sort this thing out, okay?'

Stella snivelled into her sleeve and nodded into the phone. 'Mom, I've got to go,' she sniffed as the policeman tapped the phone, indicating that her time was up. 'Please don't forget the shoes, okay? And please hurry.'

Reaching for the receiver, the policeman pulled it out of her hand and hung up before she could say goodbye. Then he led her in her socks back towards the cell.

'I really need the toilet,' Stella said to the cop, desperate to prolong her freedom.

'Lady, there's one in the cell. Don't give me any trouble, hey,' he said, giving her a warning stare.

'Can't we just wait out here,' she pleaded. 'Just me and my sister. We're not criminals. We won't try to run, I promise. You can lock us in an office or something.'

The cop looked at her like she was crazy. 'That's not how it's working, lady,' he said, taking hold of her arm. 'Come now, stop wasting my time.'

Stella walked compliantly back to the cell, her shoulders slumped low in defeat. She would have dragged her feet if she'd been wearing shoes.

The officer opened the cell and Stella stepped inside, scanning the room for Lucy. She spotted her sitting on the bench next to the woman in the yellow miniskirt who had stolen Stella's shoes. Stella's adrenalin kicked in instantly. They weren't on great terms, but Lucy was still her sister and Stella would do whatever she had to do to protect her. Courage she never knew she had bubbled up inside her at the thought of somebody hurting Lucy, but as she got closer she saw that Lucy and the hooker were chatting comfortably. Lucy looked up as Stella approached, and the hooker made a comment, and both Lucy and the hooker burst out laughing.

Stella slumped down on the bench on the other side of her sister. 'What did Dad say?' she asked Lucy.

'They're on their way,' Lucy said. 'I believe you've met Grace,' she added, pointing towards the hooker, who nodded politely.

'Your sister give me shoes,' she said with a sly toothless grin, holding up her feet in Stella's shoes.

Stella looked down at her filthy white socks that were sagging around her ankles, she wanted to pull them up straight, but for the first time in her life she just didn't have the energy. 'How can you be so calm, Lucy!' Stella groused, wiping her red eyes with her damp sleeve. 'We are so screwed!'

'Just relax, Stella, everything's going to be all right,' Lucy said, crossing her arms in front of her body. 'It was just a bit of weed. It's not like we were selling crack or anything. I spoke to Dad, and he'll get hold of his lawyer, and then they'll come and get us out, okay. Everything's going to be fine.'

'Fine!' Stella said, horrified. 'How will everything be fine? We were arrested. We're in jail!'

'Stella, I'm sorry you got caught up in this, but I didn't know you were following me. It's not my fault you were there.'

'Lucy, I just wanted to talk to you. That's why I was at your flat. I've missed you so much. Then I saw you leaving as I arrived, so I don't know why, but I just followed you. I'm sorry, all right. I'm sorry for everything that's happened …'

But Lucy wasn't listening. Instead she shook her head and leant back against the wall, closing her eyes and rubbing the bridge of her nose with her fingers as if she had a headache.

Stella was constantly amazed by her sister. She never seemed to get scared of anyone or anything, and people like Grace responded well to her confidence. Stella knew that if she hadn't been with Lucy in the cell the other girls would have picked her clean in under an hour. First her shoes, then her jeans, her T-shirt and finally even her socks and underwear. And there wouldn't have been anything she could have done to stop them.

Time passed slowly in the cell. Over the next couple of hours more girls came into the cell, but none of the girls left; it seemed they were all in for the night. The homeless lady continued either sleeping or being dead in the corner and Stella's hip ached dully through her jeans.

From what Stella could gather their cellmates were mainly low-class hookers and drug addicts, or harmless but drunken bergies. It was clear that they had all pretty much been here and done it all before.

'What do you think will happen to us?' Stella whispered to Lucy, finally breaking the silence.

'I think we'll be okay,' Lucy said. 'I don't think they're looking for people like us. I think they're after the big guys, the ones who are actually bringing the drugs into the country and then dealing them out to the smaller operators. And anyway, I was only buying a bit of dope, that's barely even considered a real drug these days. We were just in the wrong place at the wrong time. I'm sure they'll keep us here overnight to try and scare us straight and then they'll let us go.'

'You think we'll be here all night?' Stella asked, horrified. She'd been sure they'd be sprung as soon as their parents arrived.

'I doubt there's anyone here who can process us in the middle of the night,' Lucy said. 'I'm sure we'll have to wait till morning for them to release us. Then we'll have to go to court in a couple of months to fight the charges.'

'Charges!' Stella shrieked, garnering evil stares from some of their more lucid cellmates.

'Shhh!' Lucy hissed at her.

'Lucy, I can't get a record!' Stella whispered. 'It's bad enough I've gone and lost my job, but it's going to be even harder finding a new one if I've got a criminal record. It's okay for you, you work in advertising, having a criminal record is practically a requirement! But I'd be screwed! What am I going to do?'

'I'm sorry, okay!' Lucy said. 'But you're not the only one with a ruined life. I'd say you did a pretty good job of fucking me over too! Remember?'

'Lucy, how many more times am I going to have to tell you how sorry I am?' Stella wailed. 'I never meant for it to happen. It was all a horrible mistake. I would never do anything purposely to hurt you, you know that. Do you really think I've been happy about all of this? Everything's a complete disaster. I've lost my husband, my job and my sister, who's also my best friend. I screwed up. I'm really, really sorry, Luce.' Stella was crying again, her face a picture of wretched misery. 'All I know is that my life is totally screwed up without you in it,' she continued, pathetic, exhausted, lonely tears dripping down her face. 'I just don't function properly. I can't. I'm only half a person without you. You have to forgive me, Lucy.'

Lucy stared at her, her jaw set and her arms still crossed on her chest.

'Please can we not do this any more, Luce?' Stella looked pleadingly at Lucy, noticing for the first time that her eyes were also sad and tired. 'I'm exhausted. I take full responsibility for what happened, and I'm willing to do whatever it takes to make it up to you. No matter how long it takes. But you have to know that I didn't do it on purpose, and I didn't do it to hurt you. I think I did it because I hated my life.'

Lucy sighed deeply and then put an arm around Stella. 'Oh, Stella, what a fucking mess!'

Stella sobbed, so grateful to feel her sister's arm around her.

'Well, you fucked my boyfriend and I got you a criminal record, I suppose we could consider it quits,' Lucy said finally, a small smile playing across her lips. 'If you forgive me, I guess I could forgive you.'

Stella wiped her eyes. 'Oh, thank God,' she said, throwing both her arms around Lucy. 'I've missed you so much you can't believe it! The last month has been the worst month of my life.'

'I know, I've missed you too, Stel,' Lucy said, returning her sister's hug. 'Who would have thought we'd have ended up in jail?' she added, laughing.

Stella wiped a tear from the corner of her eye and leant back against the wall.

'I saw your column,' Lucy said, smiling widely. 'What a disaster!'

'I know, it was a mistake, they printed the wrong letters!' Stella replied. Lucy's smile was infectious and she couldn't help but reciprocate. 'I've been so unfocused I made a mistake.'

'I gathered,' Lucy said, shaking her head. 'That reply to the Curious Newlyweds was classic, though.' She giggled at the thought of it. 'So, what do you think you're going to do?'

'About a job or about doing time in jail for drug trafficking?' Stella asked, laughing for the first time in what felt like years.

'No, about the job, idiot. Have you thought about what you want to do with your life yet?'

Stella shrugged her shoulders. 'I don't know. But I think I miss Max.'

'You do?' Lucy asked.

'I don't know. Maybe. I just don't think I'm cut out for a wild life,' Stella said. 'I've been trying to get a life, you know, like you said. I've been trying new things and expanding my horizons these last couple of weeks. And it's been fun, but I'm not sure it's my thing. I think I'd just like my ordinary, boring old life back again.'

'Okay,' Lucy said, nodding her head thoughtfully. 'But you should make a hundred per cent sure it's what you want, Stella. Because once you're back with Max, that's it for the rest of your life. And the rest of your life may be a very long time.'

'Not if we stay in here much longer,' Stella said, eyeing one of their newer cellmates, a tall woman wearing a long curly black wig and exceptionally high wedge heels. She was wearing a short, luminous pink dress, which left little to the imagination, but things were obviously not entirely as they seemed because she was standing in front of the metal toilet in the corner of the cell, urinating into it. Lucy covered her mouth in horror and laughed.

'I do miss my home,' Stella said. 'And I miss knowing there's someone to come home to. I miss normality. But I also know that I need things to be different with Max and me. Not crazy or anything, but more interesting and definitely more honest.'

'As long as that's what Max wants too,' Lucy said, looking serious.

Stella nodded and thought a bit about what she'd just said. She'd said it without thinking, but she realised that it was what she'd been thinking for a very long time now, she just hadn't been able to verbalise it before.

Lucy rested her head on Stella's shoulder and closed her eyes. But Stella couldn't relax like her sister. She sat with her eyes wide open, fighting sleep, watching the women around her closely in case one of them decided to shank her or Lucy. She wasn't completely naïve, she'd watched both seasons of *Prison Break*.

'Frankel and De Villiers!' a voice shouted.

Stella had been nodding off sitting up for a couple of minutes at a time and then waking up with a start all night. The voice that woke her belonged to a female police officer, a short, stocky woman who shouted in short, sharp blasts. 'Frankel, De Villiers!' she shouted out again.

Stella grabbed Lucy's arm and shook her awake. 'That's us,' she said. 'They're calling us. Come on, let's get out of here.'

They were led out of the cell and down several long corridors before they finally arrived in an office where they were instructed to sit down at a desk. The policewoman, Constable Motlale, then pulled out some paperwork. 'You've both been released on bail,' she said, starting to fill in the forms. 'The state will be in contact with you regarding your court date, which will be in a couple of months' time.' She handed her clipboard across the table and had them both sign it. 'There are just a few more forms you need to sign in front, together with the party who posted bail, and then you are free to go.'

With the paperwork completed Constable Motlale led them towards the front section of Caledon Square Police Station. As they reached the end of a corridor Stella could see her parents in the distance, waiting for them on a row of wooden benches that lined the wall of the charge office. She felt an instant surge of relief, but she also noticed that Iris was leaning on Hylton, her head resting gently on his shoulder, and they were holding hands, something Stella couldn't remember seeing since she was a little girl.

When they caught sight of their daughters Hylton and Iris jumped up out of their seats and ran to them with relieved looks on their faces.

'Are you two all right?' Iris asked, hugging both girls. 'Your father and I were worried sick!'

'Sir, we just have a little more paperwork we need you to sign before we can release them,' Constable Motlale said to Hylton.

'I'll go with him,' Lucy said, following Hylton and the constable to the counter.

'Here are your shoes,' Iris said. 'Dad and I have been here half the night, but they wouldn't release you until their sergeant came on duty this morning.'

'I'm so sorry, Mom,' Stella said. 'What a nightmare.'

Sitting down on one of the wooden benches Stella put the shoes on gratefully. She would have to burn the socks she was wearing, she thought as she cast a glance over to where her father and Lucy were deep in conversation with Constable Motlale, discussing some of the paperwork.

'Mom, I know it's not really any of my business, but I noticed you and Dad were holding hands,' Stella said.

'Well, we've been here all night, and it kind of gave us an opportunity to talk,' Iris said.

'But you live together.'

'Yes, but we don't really talk any more. Except for when I shout at your father and when he shouts at me. We haven't really talked properly in a very long time. I know it wasn't under ideal circumstances, but it gave us an opportunity to connect for what feels like the first time in years,' Iris said, her eyes misting up a little.

Stella looked at her and felt hopeful. 'Oh, Mom,' she said with a small smile.

'You know, Stella, I love your father, and I always will, the stupid old fool. Can you believe he burnt my kitchen down?'

'Mom?'

'Yes, dear.'

'What about Mr Davies?' Stella couldn't bring herself to call him by his first name. He would always be her homeroom teacher, Mr Davies.

Iris eyed Stella carefully. 'Stella, I need to tell you something. But you're not to tell your father or any of your sisters. I will tell your father when the time is right, and the time may never be right, but it has to be my choice.'

'Of course, Mom. What is it?'

'Mr Davies doesn't really exist,' she said softly.

'Of course he does, he was my homeroom teacher in Grade Ten. He refused to give me an A because he hated my guts.'

'No, Stella, of course he exists, but he doesn't exist with me. He's not my lover. I haven't seen him since you finished school.'

Stella looked at her mom, feeling confused. 'I don't understand.'

'It's always been your father, Stella. There's nobody else for me. What do I want with somebody else? But when I found out he'd cheated on me I was so hurt that I wanted to get back at him. I wanted to force him to realise what he'd ruined, and Mr Davies was the first man who popped into my head.'

Stella sucked in a breath. 'Wow, that's pretty devious, Mom. I've known you my entire life but until now I didn't realise what an evil genius you are.'

'Thank you, dear, that's very sweet,' Iris said, smiling.

'So, do you think you and Dad could make things work again?' Stella asked.

'You never know,' Iris said. 'Anything can happen. I mean, look at you. I bet you never thought you'd spend a night in jail, and here you are.'

'Come on, let's get out of here. This place gives me the creeps,' Lucy said, ambling over and handing Stella the few belongings the police had confiscated from them. Then Lucy walked out of the police station into the morning air, and Stella, Iris and Hylton followed her outside.

'So, what did we miss out on in the real world?' Stella asked as they congregated on the pavement outside the police station. 'Please tell me you didn't burn down the rest of the house while we were gone?'

'No, the house is still standing,' Hylton said with a tired, embarrassed smile.

'Yes, well, the house may still be standing, but you're not going to believe what happened to your other sister,' Iris said, shaking her head.

'What now?' Stella asked, sighing and rolling her eyes. 'Daisy?'

'No, Poppy,' Iris said.

'Oh?' Stella raised her eyebrows.

'Is she okay?' Lucy asked.

'Yes, she's fine. Come on, we'll fill you in on the way home,' Iris said.

Stella caught Lucy's eye and raised an eyebrow. 'What do you think Poppy did now?' she asked as their mother and father began to walk off up the street.

Lucy shrugged her shoulders. 'Never a dull second around here.'

'Hey, are you two coming?' Iris shouted over her shoulder. 'We've got bagels for breakfast and the good coffee.'

'Oh bugger, where are our cars?' Stella asked, her eyes panicked.

'They're probably still in Woodstock, where we left them,' Lucy said. 'Come on, let's go up to Mom and Dad's, have a shower, get something to eat and then we'll go pick them up.'

Stella smiled and nudged Lucy. 'Look,' she said, pointing up the street at Iris and Hylton, who were holding hands as they walked towards their car.

Stella stood under the shower and let the water wash over her. She'd never felt so disgusting and so filthy. The second they'd arrived home she'd taken off all her clothes and dropped them straight into the bin, but the smell of the cell seemed to have seeped through her clothes and permeated deep into her pores.

After washing her hair four times, and scraping under her nails, and scrubbing her face and body obsessively Stella finally climbed out of the shower and dried herself. The throbbing in her hip had gained momentum through the night and the whole area now felt much worse than it had before; it was hot and sore and itchy, but she was too scared to look at it. Instead, Stella fantasised about lying down in her clean bed and sleeping for a hundred hours. She was physically, mentally and emotionally drained, and with everything that had been going on she couldn't remember the last time she'd had a full, uninterrupted peaceful night's sleep in an actual bed.

Stella wrapped her dripping hair in a towel turban, wound a thick, thirsty bath sheet around her body and stepped out of the steamy bathroom. She made her way to her bedroom, peeking into the living room where she saw her mom and dad sitting drinking coffee together, chatting and laughing at the dining room table. She couldn't remember the last time she'd seen them look so happy.

'Hey, I hope you don't mind, I borrowed some clothes,' Lucy said as Stella opened the bedroom door and stepped inside.

'Luce, can I show you something quickly?' Stella asked, a worried look on her face.

'Sure,' Lucy said, plonking herself down on her old bed across from Stella's. 'I can't believe you're staying here,' she added, smoothing down her old pink bedspread. 'It must be weird.'

'Yeah, it's been very strange,' Stella said. 'But I didn't have a choice; it's not like I had anywhere else to go. It was either this or stay in a hotel.'

There was an awkward silence, neither of them wanting to bring up the events that had caused Stella's eviction again.

'So, what do you want to show me?' Lucy asked.

'Okay, I need your help. I've been too scared to look at it myself, so I need you to do it for me. But before I show you, you have to promise not to freak out, okay?' Stella said.

'Oh shit. What did you do now, Stella?' Lucy asked with wide, worried eyes.

'Promise you won't freak out and I'll show you,' Stella said.

Lucy looked at her as if seeing her for the first time. 'Okay, I promise I won't freak out,' she said.

'All right, but remember, you promised. I did this last week, before the fire ...'

'Just show me already!' Lucy snapped. 'I'm dying over here!'

'Okay, okay. I got a little tattoo, but I think there's something very wrong with it – it hurts like hell.'

'You got a tattoo!' Lucy shrieked, clapping her hands together. 'I've always wanted one!'

'Shhhh, you promised you weren't going to freak out!' Stella said.

Lucy ignored her. 'Show me, show me,' she squealed. 'I can't believe you did it without me, you cow!'

'Shhhh, man! I don't want Mom and Dad to hear!' Stella snapped.

'Oh, please,' Lucy said, 'they've just bailed us out of jail, I would imagine they'd be surprised if you hadn't got a tattoo! Now show me already!'

Stella dropped her towel and stepped forward towards Lucy so she could get a closer look at it. She covered her eyes with her hands, not wanting to look down.

'Ew, gross, Stella! Is that a tattoo? What a mess. Who did it, Helen Keller?' Lucy said. 'Does it hurt?'

'Yes, like a lot. All the time. It started out as just a small throb, but now it's really, really sore, and totally itchy. Is it bad? I can't look.'

'It's really bad, Stel,' Lucy said, sounding worried. 'I can't even see what it's of, it's just a big pussy open wound, and the skin around it is all red and swollen. I think we need to get you to a doctor right away.'

'Dammit!' Stella cursed.

'Come on, put on some clothes and I'll take you down to the emergency room and then we can go get our cars,' Lucy said.

'What, now?' Stella asked, horrified.

'Yes, now!' Lucy said. 'It's certainly not getting any better while you stand there. What's it supposed to be of anyway?'

'It's a little red heart with a black outline,' Stella said, slipping on a pair of panties, careful to avoid her sore hip.

'My wild and crazy sister!' Lucy said with a proud smile. 'I can't believe you got a tattoo! What have you done with Stella?'

'Did it hurt a lot?' Lucy asked, pointing at Stella's hip. 'Like how sore was it on a scale of one to ten? Ten being something like childbirth without an epidural and one being a splinter.'

'How should I know, I've never gone through childbirth,' Stella said. 'It was very sore getting it, but it's even more sore now. And it's really, really itchy.'

'I still can't believe you did it. I thought you were terrified of needles?' Lucy said.

'I've done a lot of things you wouldn't believe over the last couple of weeks. Hey, stop fiddling with the bed, you're going to break something!' Stella hissed urgently.

'Okay!' Lucy snapped back. 'Sheesh! So, I still don't understand, what made you decide to get a tattoo? It just seems like the last thing you would ever do. It's so out of character.'

'I know, but that was kind of the point, I guess,' Stella said, shrugging her shoulders as if it was no big deal. 'Mom and I got talking and I realised that I wanted to do all the things that I'd never done before. I've always felt like you were the only one having any fun, you know. Because I've always been the good one. And you'd told me I should get a life, so I did. I made a list of some of the things I've always wanted to do, or been curious about, and then I went out and did some of them.'

Lucy appraised her and nodded her head slowly. 'Did you try sushi?' she asked.

'No, not yet, but I definitely need to add it to my list.'

'You really do, I've been trying to get you to try it for ages,' Lucy said.

'I know, I know, and I'm going to be more adventurous from now on, and not be such a big wuss all the time.'

'That would be cool. But promise you'll take me with you next time you do one of these crazy list things, okay?'

Stella nodded at her and smiled. It was good to have her other half back.

Lucy started fiddling with the handle on the side of the bed again. 'He's kind of cute, don't you think?' she said absent-mindedly.

'Who?' Stella asked.

'Don't pretend you didn't notice!'

'Shhhh, one of the nurses will hear you,' Stella whispered. 'These are just curtains you know, not walls.'

'And he was totally flirting with you,' Lucy carried on, ignoring Stella completely.

'What? No! You're crazy!' Stella said, stretching out on the hospital bed, careful not to let anything touch her throbbing hip. 'Anyway, it doesn't matter, I'm married, remember!'

'You could have fooled me,' Lucy said, pointing at Stella's hand. 'I noticed you aren't wearing your wedding ring.'

'I kept twisting it around my finger, till I rubbed the skin here raw, look,' Stella said, pointing out the peeling skin on her finger. 'And anyway, I haven't really been feeling particularly married lately.'

'So, what do you plan on doing about that?' Lucy asked. 'Have you decided yet?'

'I don't know. He's not taking my calls, so I'll probably have to go over there and see him. I guess it's up to me to try and fix things, though I'll probably have to beg him to take me back,' Stella said.

They sat in silence for a minute or two while Stella did the sums in her head. 'You know I've only been married for one thousand, three hundred and seventy-eight hours?' she said, when she'd finally worked it out. 'I should probably give it another bash. That would be the right thing to do.'

'Ooh, you sound incredibly excited by the prospect. How many hours is one obliged to give a marriage, do you suppose?' Lucy asked sarcastically. 'More than two thousand? Three thousand? Five thousand?'

Just then the curtains parted and Stella and Lucy sat up straight as the doctor returned holding Stella's chart.

'Right,' the doctor said seriously when he reached the side of Stella's bed, 'we've taken a look at your tests and I'm afraid it looks like it's going to have to come off!'

'What, the tattoo?' Stella asked, her bottom lip starting to shake.

'Nope,' the doctor said, 'the whole hip!'

There was a moment's silence and then Lucy burst out laughing.

Stella looked at her, horrified. This was terrible news, how could she laugh so cruelly, and then Stella clicked that the doctor was kidding and she blushed a furious puce.

The doctor smiled, revealing a perfect pair of dimples. Stella eyed him out. He was wearing a pair of jeans with a crisp white shirt and a blue tie. Stella thought he was boyishly good looking.

'Aren't you a bit young to be a doctor?' Lucy asked.

'Lucy!' Stella chided, now even more embarrassed.

'No, don't worry,' the doctor said, full of charm. 'People always ask me that. That's why I wear the tie. Apparently it makes me look more professional. I tried growing a beard, thinking it would make me look older, but it was just too itchy.' Reaching into his back pocket he pulled out a folded piece of paper. He opened it and handed it to Lucy. It was a photostat of his medical certificate. It was faded and worn from living in his back pocket and having been opened and closed so many times. 'I always keep that on hand to show my older patients that I'm actually a real doctor,' he said with a wink in Stella's direction. 'They're normally the ones who worry about how young I look.'

Stella blushed even redder. Lucy had been right, since they'd come into the emergency room she'd had the feeling that he was flirting with her. Unless he just had a particularly friendly bedside manner. But there had been an inordinate amount of eye contact and now all that winking.

'Right,' the doctor said, taking back the certificate, folding it and returning it to his pocket, 'if everyone is satisfied that I'm fit to practise, shall we discuss this little problem you're having, Stella?'

Stella nodded nervously.

'I'm pleased you came in to see me, because this is looking quite bad, and if you'd left it untreated too much longer it might have become a much more serious problem.'

'Told you so!' Lucy said, to Stella. 'I forced her to come in, you know.'

'Well, then she owes you one, because you've done her a huge favour,' the doctor said to Lucy. 'I don't know what you've been up to, young lady,' he continued, turning back to Stella, 'but somehow you've managed to pick up a very nasty infection. One of the worst I've ever seen. So I'm going to give you a shot and then put you on a course of antibiotics. How does that sound?'

'Urgh, I hate needles,' Stella groaned.

'You should have thought about that before you went out and got a tattoo without me!' Lucy said.

Stella stuck her tongue out at her sister.

'All right,' the doctor said, 'how about we change the subject before somebody gets hurt?'

'Yes, please,' Stella said gratefully.

'Okay, so where was I? Oh, yes, and no drinking alcohol while you're on the antibiotics, all right.' The doctor smiled at her warmly. 'And I think you should come back and see me again, same time, same place, next week, okay? Just so I can make sure you're being a good patient.'

Stella nodded.

'Although ...' he said. 'On second thoughts, it might be better if you gave me your cellphone number, just in case you have an emergency.'

It took Stella a second to catch on, but all she could manage in return was an even deeper, even more embarrassed blush.

When he was gone Lucy pinched Stella on the arm. 'What's wrong with you!' she said. 'Why didn't you give him your number, you fool? He's so hot! And a doctor! And he's totally into you; he practically begged you for your number!'

'Lucy, I'm married, remember!' Stella said, wriggling her naked ring finger in front of her face. 'I need to give things with Max another bash. I can't just give up on my marriage.'

'I know, I know,' Lucy said. 'But the least you could have done was give him my number! It's not like you don't owe me one.'

Stella stood in Davenport Road outside the front entrance to Victory Court. Now that she was here she wasn't entirely sure what to do. She didn't know whether to ring the buzzer or call Max to let him know she was downstairs. She chewed her lip nervously. Or she could just let herself in with her key. It was still her home, after all, which made it a weird predicament to be in. People don't normally feel like nervous guests going into their own homes.

Stella considered her options. Letting herself in was a bad idea. She wasn't sure how she would find Max and she didn't want to give him a fright. And what if he wasn't on his own? The possibility briefly raced through her mind that he might also be exploring life as a single person. But then she shook the thought off: she'd known Max a very long time and that wasn't the way he was. She put the key into the front door of the apartment block and let herself into the foyer of the building, noticing immediately that their letter box was stuffed full of mail and flyers. Opening it, she emptied it out, and then she climbed the stairs to the second floor and stood outside their front door feeling nervous. She pulled her cellphone out of her pocket and dialled Max's number tentatively, watching it connect on the screen. She could hear his phone ringing inside the flat. Stella pictured him staring at her name all lit up on his ringing phone, trying to decide whether or not to answer it. It went to voicemail and Stella hung up and rang again. After several rings he answered. 'Yes,' he said, coldly.

'Hi, Max. It's me,' Stella said.

Max didn't respond but she could hear him breathing into the phone.

'I'm standing outside the front door,' Stella said quietly. 'I was hoping you'd agree to talk to me.'

Max didn't respond but she could still hear him breathing.

'Max, are you there?' she asked.

'You're outside?' he asked.

'Yes, I'm standing on the doormat. I have our mail,' she said, looking down at the stack of letters in her arms. It looked like he hadn't cleared the box since she'd left.

She heard his footsteps coming closer on the other side of the door. 'Max, I can hear you're at the door. Please can I come in?' she asked gently.

Stella heard the lock turning tentatively, and then the door opened. Max stood in front of her, staring at her, still holding the phone to his ear.

'Hello, Max,' she said, looking at him, still talking into the phone.

'Hi, Stella,' he said quietly back into his own phone.

Stella laughed shyly and hung up, then waited for him to step aside and let her in. He was wearing a pair of tracksuit bottoms and a grubby old T-shirt. Next to him she felt very silly. She had dressed up in a low-cut black cocktail dress she'd borrowed from Lucy, put on make-up and had even done her hair for the occasion. She wanted to look good for him.

'Can I get you something?' he asked awkwardly, closing the front door behind her and following her into the lounge.

'Um, can I have a glass of water?' Stella asked.

Max disappeared into the kitchen while Stella hovered, unsure of where to sit in her own home. She didn't want to sit in her regular place on the couch, that might feel like she was trying to slip back into what they'd had, and she worried it might come over as a bit presumptuous, so she remained standing, hovering in the middle of the lounge. Max returned seconds later and handed her a glass. She was about to take a sip when she noticed that the glass was dirty and there was something floating in the water, so she just held it awkwardly in her hand.

Max sat down on the one couch, and feeling foolish about towering over him Stella sat down on the other, facing him, about two metres away from him.

'You look different,' Max said.

'Max, I need to apologise for everything that's happened,' Stella said, putting the dirty glass of water on the floor by her feet.

Max nodded, but didn't say anything.

'It's all just become such a big mess and I feel really terrible about everything I've done and all the hurt I've caused,' she continued.

'This hasn't been easy on me, Stella,' Max said.

'I know, Max. It hasn't been easy on me either.'

'Why do you think you did all of this, Stella?'

'I don't know. I think maybe we just got too old too fast, you know?'

'What do you mean?' Max asked.

Stella shrugged. 'Don't you think we used to act a bit like a pair of eighty-year-olds, who'd been married for forty years already?'

'I don't think so,' he said.

'We used to go to bed at ten thirty, Max! It was *CSI* and stir-fry on Wednesdays and *Law and Order* and roast chicken on Thursdays.'

'I kind of liked that,' Max said. 'I work so hard that sometimes it's nice to know what I'm coming home to, and to relax, not have to do or wear or say anything. Isn't that what marriage is all about? Being comfortable and having some kind of routine?'

'I suppose so,' Stella said, chewing on her lip, 'but sometimes it can be too comfortable.'

'I've missed you terribly while you've been gone, Stella. I've been eating pizza every night.'

'I can see that,' she said, looking around and noticing for the first time what a mess the lounge was. Pizza boxes were scattered everywhere and it seemed that he hadn't taken an empty cup or dirty plate to the kitchen since she'd left.

'I've missed our routine. We always had routine at home, growing up. My mom made dinner every single night; Thursdays was always meatloaf. Hey, we should make meatloaf sometime.'

'You mean I should make meatloaf some time!' Stella said pointedly, raising an eyebrow at him. She wanted to add, 'When last did you make anything?' to the end of her statement, but she quickly reminded herself that she was meant to be building bridges here, not blowing them up. 'Max,' she continued, softening her tone. 'I was wondering if you'd let me move back home? I can't stay at my parents any longer, it's killing me, I mean literally. My dad burnt the kitchen down the other night.'

'What?'

'No, don't worry, it was an accident. There's a lot of damage, but everyone's fine.' Stella paused to gather her thoughts. 'So, Max, I wondered if you would maybe consider letting me move back. If you wanted I could move into the spare room at first and we could try to work stuff out, you know, see if we want to carry this thing on, or whether it's in both our best interests to just let it go.'

'Stella,' Max said, standing up and pacing around the room.

Stella held her breath, wondering what was coming. This was the moment she had been dreading. The moment when he told her that he had decided that their marriage was over.

'Stella, I love you. You're my wife,' Max said, stopping his pacing for a second and facing her. 'And I think it's going to take me some time before I can fully trust you again. But I think if you just changed your attitude a tiny, little bit and tried to settle down some, then maybe we can make this thing work. You know, I've been thinking about things a lot while we've been apart, and if we want to have four kids we're going to have to get a move on. Neither of us is getting any younger, and we don't have months and months to spend arguing and making up. I miss you, Stella, and I do love you, and I know you love me.'

'Four children?' Stella sputtered, trying to keep her voice even. 'Max, I always thought you were joking about that!'

'Why would I joke about having children?' he said. 'You know how much I love kids. I'm a primary school teacher, for crying out loud.'

'I know, but four children, that seems a little excessive. Nobody has four children in this day and age.'

'Violet has three,' he countered.

'I know, but have you looked at her lately?' Stella said. 'She hasn't bought a new item of clothing in a year and a half and last time I saw her she had a small jam handprint on the back of her top and she didn't even know it was there. Her life is practically over.'

'I'm confused,' Max said. 'I thought you wanted children, it's what we always discussed.'

'I do,' Stella said, biting the inside of her cheek and wondering whether she still really did. She'd never thought about the specifics of it in any great detail before and there was so much she still wanted to do in her life. But she decided to bite her tongue and hold back, reminding herself again that she was supposed to be making the peace here, not stoking the coals of a new war.

'Phew!' Max said. 'For a second there I thought maybe you'd changed your mind.'

Stella shook her head nervously and crossed her fingers in her lap. Then she thought back over what he'd just said, particularly the bit about him wanting her to change her attitude. She wondered what that meant. She felt like she had already changed her attitude a lot over the last couple of weeks and she quite liked the person she'd found hiding under the conservative, boring exterior she'd always projected in an attempt to please everybody. But she reminded herself yet again that now wasn't the time to go into these kinds of details with Max. She really didn't want to argue any more. She was so over arguing. She just wanted to move back into her flat with her clothes and her things and her life. And she wanted to start rebuilding what she and Max had, just adding in a little spice to make their life together a little more exciting this second time around. They could discuss the children thing down the line, she told herself.

'Look, Max,' Stella said, standing up and running her fingers through her hair. 'I really don't want to argue with you right now. If you'll have me, I was wondering if I could move back in tonight. I've missed you so much; I've hated being away from you. And I thought, maybe, we could try and kiss and make up.'

Stella took a step towards him and put a finger on his chest, running it down to the front of his T-shirt suggestively. She saw his eyes move from her face down to the low cut of her dress, to her chest. He wasn't used to seeing her in anything this revealing and it took him a moment before he got control of himself and quickly looked back up at her face again.

'What do you say, Max?' Stella whispered, putting her hand on one hip and popping the other out in a curve.

Max stepped even closer towards her, breathing heavily. 'Stella, I've really missed you,' he said, reaching for her and kissing her.

She hadn't thought he would want to touch her so soon after the betrayal, but she was pleasantly surprised. His kiss was conventional, polite even, but there was still something nice about the familiarity of him, although he could have done with brushing his teeth, she thought as she held her breath and kissed him back.

'I'll be right back,' Stella said, extracting herself from their clinch and pointing off to the bathroom to indicate where she was going. Then she sashayed out of the lounge, turning back to smile at him, before disappearing down the passage.

In the bathroom Stella looked in the mirror, breathing heavily to try and calm her pounding heart. It was okay. Everything was going to be okay. Max didn't want a divorce and she could move back in. It was all going to work out – even after everything that had happened.

Stella reached over for some toilet paper to wipe her slightly smudged eye liner and her clammy palms. The paper was finished and just the cardboard roll remained, dangling on the holder. Stella shook her head. Some things never changed, she thought. In all the time she'd known Max he'd never once changed a toilet roll. Removing the finished roll she replaced it with a fresh one from under the sink and then flushed the toilet and lowered the seat with another shake of her head.

Turning back to the mirror Stella noticed that the things she'd left behind in the bathroom still stood untouched on her side of the sink. She ran her hand over a basket that contained some of her make-up and a couple of bottles of her perfume. It felt strange to be in her own home again, in amongst all her things. Picking up one of the bottles of perfume she sprayed some of it on, thinking back to her life with Max before their split. It had been comfortable but boring. They went to work, came home, watched TV and went to bed, and the sex had been uninspiring, to put it mildly. Although back then she hadn't known what good sex was. Back then she'd been like a blind person, feeling her way around in the dark. But things were different now. She felt like she understood the kind of intimacy she desperately needed from a life partner, and she hoped she would be able to show Max what it was that she needed to be happy.

Tonight had been only the second time she'd ever tried to initiate sex with him in their entire relationship, and so far it was going better than the booger incident. She liked how it felt to be in control; she got a thrill from the sense of power it gave her. All she'd had to do was show a bit of cleavage and shake a hip at him and he'd been putty in her hands. She looked in the mirror and suddenly felt very positive, she was sure she could make this work. She just needed to have a little patience. She would have to show Max exactly what she wanted and see how he responded. It was her responsibility to get what she wanted and not just lie back like a starfish and hope for the best, the way she always had before. Well, that's the advice she would have given herself if she had written in to Dr Dee. It was about time that she started taking a little bit of her own advice, Stella decided.

A small smile crept onto her face. She lifted up her dress and slipped off her panties, dropping them neatly into her handbag. Then she smiled widely at herself in the mirror, imagining the expression on Max's face when he discovered that she wasn't wearing any underwear.

Stella planned her next couple of moves in her head. First they would have incredible, earth-shattering make-up sex, she decided. Everybody always said that make-up sex was the most powerful kind of sex; it was the main reason most couples argued in the first place. And then, after that, they would begin to rebuild their lives together.

Stella took a couple of deep calming breaths, let herself out of the bathroom and sashayed sexily back into the lounge.

Max was sitting on the couch, playing some kind rugby game on the Xbox. Stella hated the Xbox. When they'd first moved in together she'd packed it away in the cupboard in the spare room. Max would get it out once in a while to play, but it had always gone straight back into the cupboard again when he'd left for work the following morning. But by the looks of things, while she had been away it had taken up permanent residence in the lounge on the floor in front of the television set.

'I'm back, Max,' she said in her sexiest voice.

'Uh-huh,' Max said, not looking up, completely focused on his game.

Frustrated, Stella sat down on the couch next to him and rubbed his arm coyly.

Max looked over at her, paused the game and put the controller down on the coffee table. Taking her head in his hands he kissed her on the forehead, and then on her nose and then on the lips. Then he looked deep into her eyes. 'Stella,' he said.

'Yes, Max,' she replied.

'I'm really happy you're back. I've missed you.'

'I've missed you too,' she said, her heart soaring. This could really work, she thought.

'Listen,' he said, letting go of her head. 'Can you be a love? Won't you just quickly iron my blue shirt for me? I've got this big meeting at school tomorrow and it's really creased.' He paused, patting her knee roughly and then picking up the Xbox controller again. 'I'm just going to finish this game. You can't believe it, I actually reached level eighteen while you were gone! Two more levels and my team make it to the World Cup.' Turning back to the game he unpaused it. 'Hey, have you had dinner?' he asked as he started playing again. 'I'm starving. You don't feel like whipping something up for us, do you? Be a sport. I'm not sure I can face pizza again.'

Stella's heart stopped soaring and took a nose dive into the lounge carpet. Letting go of Max's arm, she stood up. 'I'm so sorry, Max,' she said, bending down to pick up her purse and walking towards the door. 'I've made a terrible mistake. I don't think this is going to work out, after all.'

STELLA AND POPPY

When Lucy opened the front door Stella was standing on her doorstep in her black cocktail dress, surrounded by bags and suitcases.

'Hello?' Lucy said, obviously surprised.

'Do you mind if I stay here for a bit, Luce? I've got nowhere else to go. Please don't make me go back to Mom and Dad's house,' Stella pleaded.

'Come in,' Lucy said, holding the door open and helping her drag all her bags inside. 'What happened with Max?' she asked.

'I thought I could make it work,' Stella said forlornly, 'but I was only fooling myself. That's not the life I want. I just thought it was the life everyone thought I should have. But I realise now that nobody cares what life you have; I'm the only person I need to make happy.' She wiped the tears from the corners of her eyes. 'And I wasn't happy.'

Lucy nodded, not saying anything, there would be plenty of time to autopsy *the situation later.*

'Thank you so much for having me, Luce,' Stella said as they dumped her bags in the spare room. 'I can't stay at Mom and Dad's any longer, they're unbearable. They're all lovey-dovey all the time; she doesn't even shout at him any more. It's bizarre.'

'Yeah, that's just creepy,' Lucy said.

'I'm terrified I'm going to walk in on them shagging, and I really don't think I could handle that.'

'There isn't enough therapy in the world to deal with that!' Lucy said, shaking her head in disgust. 'It will be cool having you here, though.' Lucy smiled sadly. 'It's been kind of quiet around here since Jake left and everything.'

Stella looked at her guiltily. 'Again, I am so sorry about that,' she said, shaking her head.

'Don't stress,' Lucy said. 'I'm over it. He was always too good looking for me anyway. Hey, speaking of good looking, don't we have to go back and see that doctor of yours next week?'

Stella looked at her watch and did the calculations. 'Yes, in just over one hundred and sixty-two hours.'

Lucy went to make popcorn and Stella sat on the edge of the spare bed and stared at the bags lying at her feet. She hoped like hell that she'd made the right decision. But the more she thought about it the more sure she was that there was no way she'd be able to go back to the life she and Max had shared for so long. Stella pictured herself with four children by the time she was forty and shuddered. That wasn't what she wanted. She and Max were two very different people on two totally different paths and Stella was sad it had taken her this long to figure it out. But she also felt relieved that it hadn't taken her any longer. Stella nodded to herself. This route would be more painful for both of them in the short term, but it would be less painful in the long term, at least she hoped it would be.

'Popcorn's ready!' Lucy shouted from the lounge.

Sniffing back her tears and drying her eyes Stella walked through to the lounge and collapsed next to her sister on the couch.

'Stella,' Lucy said, looking at her tear-stained face intently. 'It may not feel like it right now, but everything is going to be okay, you know.'

Stella nodded, grateful to finally be able to talk to Lucy again – it was like being reunited with a part of herself she had lost.

Lucy passed Stella the bowl of popcorn and held up a DVD. 'Desperate Housewives?' she asked.

Stella nodded. 'It seems apt,' she said with a sad smile.

When the door buzzer rang forty minutes later they both sat up with a start. Stella looked at Lucy with wide eyes.

'Expecting anyone?' Lucy asked.

'What if it's Max?' Stella said, biting her lip.

'How would you feel if it was him?' Lucy asked.

'I don't know, surprised, I guess, that he managed to pull himself away from the Xbox long enough to come over here.'

The buzzer rang again, more insistently this time. Lucy got up and went over to the intercom. 'Who is it?' she asked.

'It's me, doofus! It's Poppy!' shouted a voice.

Stella and Lucy looked at each other and shrieked. Lucy pressed the buzzer, releasing the downstairs door, and she and Stella raced out of the front door of the apartment.

'Did you know she was home?' Lucy asked as they ran downstairs to greet their sister.

'Nope. You?' Stella asked.

'No way! I would have told you!' Lucy squealed.

'When did you get home?' Stella yelled in excitement as she caught sight of Poppy pushing her way through the front door of the apartment block, carrying a small, new backpack.

'You never told us you were coming home!' Lucy shouted as they descended on their sister, both of them hugging her tightly at the same time. 'How was your trip, you lucky cow?'

'I only just landed earlier this evening,' Poppy said. 'Mom and Dad fetched me from the airport and dropped me straight off here. What's up with them, by the way, they're acting totally weird.'

'Yeah, they're totally in love again suddenly, it's really gross!' Lucy said.

'Look at your hair!' Stella shrieked, stepping back from her sister to get a better look at her. 'It's so freaking short! You've never had such short hair before.'

'This is nothing,' Poppy replied. 'You should have seen me a month ago.'

'It's amazing to see you, Poppy!' Stella said. 'We've really missed you!'

'Come up, come up!' Lucy shouted, leading the way up the stairs.

They piled into the lounge, all talking loudly and at the same time.

'Listen, Luce,' Poppy said, 'I have an enormously massive favour to ask.'

'What?' Lucy said.

'I know it's a huge imposition, but I was wondering if I could crash here with you for a while? I've kind of got nowhere else to go, and I don't have any money, and I really don't want to have to stay at Mom and Dad's – it's bad enough that they had to pay for me to come home!' Poppy said, sighing. 'I promise I won't get in the way or anything, and I'll start paying my way just as soon as I get a job. I was thinking I might get a waitressing job at the Waterfront, so it won't be long till I'll be able to find my own place. I'm sure it will just be for a couple of months, until I find my feet again.'

'I'm afraid the spare room is taken,' Lucy said, pointing at Stella. 'Stella just moved in. You're about an hour too late.'

'What?' Poppy cried in shock. 'No, Stella! What happened to the happy newlyweds? I thought you and Max were the perfect couple and everything.'

'Urgh! It's such a long story, I'll tell you later,' Stella said, waving her hand.

'Well, I don't mind sleeping on the couch, if you don't mind,' Poppy said to Lucy. 'I've slept in way worse places recently. And I travel light, this is all I've got in the whole wide world.' She kicked her foot against her tiny bag.

'What happened to all your stuff?' Stella asked in horror.

'Paris happened to all my stuff,' Poppy said, with an embarrassed smile. 'Also a long story. So, Luce, what do you say?'

Lucy shrugged her shoulders. 'I don't see why not,' she said. 'Lucy's B. & B. Hey, I should get monogrammed towels. But if you think I'm serving you breakfast every morning, you've got another think coming.'

'It'll just be Lucy's B. & ...' Stella said.

The girls collapsed in fits of giggles. Stella smiled; this was going to be exactly what she needed. She would reinvent herself, decide what she wanted to do with the rest of her life and then do it, without anybody holding her back. Not because she had to, to meet anyone else's expectations, but because whatever she chose would be what she wanted. Hey, she thought, maybe it was her turn to travel and see the world like Poppy. Maybe Lucy would go with her and they would leave Poppy behind to look after the flat.

'Hey, I hear Daisy's gay now!' Poppy said.

'Oh, that's nothing,' Lucy said. 'While you were away Dad burnt the house down.'

'No shit!' Poppy said, her eyes wide.

'Never mind that,' Stella said, settling back into the couch and reaching for the bowl of popcorn. 'Tell us all about your trip.'

'Well,' Poppy said, smiling broadly at her sisters. 'While you two have been sitting around here on your asses watching Desperate Housewives *and eating popcorn, you won't believe all the crazy shit I've been doing.*'

THE THANK-YOU PART

The original germ of an idea for this book came from wanting to write about the incredible bond between siblings, and particularly sisters. Mine mean the world to me.

To the following people, if ever you need a kidney, it's the least I can do. Thank you so much for all your support, advice, friendship and love – Karin, Jen, Chryssa, Amanda, Edyth, Sam, Teresa, Kathi, Tamara, Emma and Ian Waddell (if you need a personal trainer, he's your guy).

And thanks must definitely go to my great friend, Craig, who will know why when he reads this.

My grateful appreciation also goes to Alistair and James at King James for allowing me to follow both of my passions at the same time. And of course to all the guys at Penguin – Alison, Lisa, Reneé, Leanne, Ziel and the rest of the team. You guys rock.

And the biggest thank you and some kind of medal should go to James Woodhouse, my extraordinary, very patient, incredibly talented editor, who painstakingly made sure every single one of these words was in the right order.

Love, appreciation, eternal gratitude and homemade biscuits for all of you.

IF YOU'D LIKE TO GET IN TOUCH, OR READ MORE, I HAVE A BLOG OVER HERE: WWW.AMILLIONMILESFROMNORMAL.COM